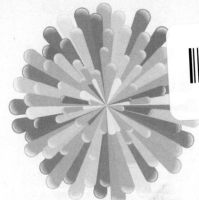

OF HARUHI SUZUMIYA

SURPRISE

N A G A R U   T A N I G A W A

YEN
ON
NEW YORK

The Surprise of Haruhi Suzumiya
Nagaru Tanigawa

Translation by Paul Starr
Cover art by Noizi Ito

Suzumiya Haruhi no Kyōgaku
©Nagaru Tanigawa, Noizi Ito 2011
First published in Japan in 2011 by KADOKAWA CORPORATION, Tokyo.
English translation rights arranged with KADOKAWA CORPORATION, Tokyo,
through TUTTLE-MORI AGENCY, INC., Tokyo.

English translation © 2013 by Yen Press, LLC

Yen On
150 West 30th Street, 19th Floor
New York, NY 10001

Visit us at yenpress.com
facebook.com/yenpress
twitter.com/yenpress
yenpress.tumblr.com
instagram.com/yenpress

First Yen On Edition: May 2021
Previously published in paperback and hardcover by Yen Press in November 2013.

Yen On is an imprint of Yen Press, LLC.
The Yen On name and logo are trademarks of Yen Press, LLC.

The Library of Congress has catalogued the hardcover and previous paperback as follows:
Tanigawa, Nagaru.
  [Suzumiya Haruhi no Kyogaku. English]
  The surprise of Haruhi Suzumiya / Nagaru Tanigawa; illustrations by
Noizi Ito; English translation by Paul Starr.—1st U.S. ed.
      Pages cm.—(Haruhi ; 10)
    ISBN 978-0-316-03898-0 (hardcover)—ISBN 978-0-316-03897-3 (trade pbk.)
    [1. Supernatural—Fiction.   2. Clubs—Fiction.   3. High Schools—
Fiction.   4. Schools—Fiction.   5. Friendship—Fiction.   6. Japan—
Fiction.]   I. Ito, Noizi, illustrator.   II. Starr, Paul Tuttle, translator.
III. Title.
  PZ7.T16139Su 2013
  [Fic]—dc23
                                                                    2013010290

ISBN: 978-1-9753-2420-9

1 3 5 7 9 10 8 6 4 2

LSC-C

Printed in the United States of America

THE
OF HARUHI SUZUMIYA
SURPRISE

NAGARU TANIGAWA

First released in Japan in 2003, *The Melancholy of Haruhi Suzumiya* quickly established itself as a publishing phenomenon, drawing much of its inspiration from Japanese pop culture and Japanese comics in particular. With this foundation, the original publication of each book in the Haruhi series included several black-and-white spot illustrations as well as a four-page color insert—all of which are faithfully reproduced here to preserve the authenticity of the first-ever English edition.

CONTENTS

VOLUME 1

CHAPTER 4

α — 7

It was Monday, the first weekday, and though nothing particularly notable happened, perhaps it was Sunday's lingering lethargy that made the walk home seem longer, and seem to *take* longer, than usual.

Having Haruhi and the others along for the first part of the walk was nice and distracting, but once we parted ways and I was on my own, I started to feel rather lonely—as though being surrounded by the familiar faces of the SOS Brigade had become my natural state. I wasn't sure what to make of myself, having failed to pay close attention and gotten so thoroughly tainted. It was as if I'd poked a sleeping dog with a stick only to realize the stick was me.

"Oh well."

I stopped walking, and looked back without any real intention. The road to the school was brighter than usual in the springtime light. That might've been thanks to the innocence of the new freshmen who had visited the club after school, or maybe it was just an effect of the increased isolation.

"Not that it matters."

My comment itself was also pointless. Sometimes I wonder whether saying something when there's nobody around to hear it has any meaning at all. Words that convey nothing to another person are no more than pronunciation practice, after all. And I don't make it a habit to talk to myself, so the words I'd just spoken were meant as a kind of self-reminder.

The truth was, if Haruhi tainted people, then I'd been thoroughly contaminated for a long time, and even if I could dump paint over myself to cover it up, I had less than a Golgi body's diameter's worth of inclination to do so.

Such were my thoughts as my homing instinct led me back to my house, pushing thoughts of the irregular factors like Sasaki and Kuyoh that had recently forced their way into prominence to the corner of my mind, greeting the evening and bringing the day to a close in my bedroom. It become my natural schedule to do so, and today was no different.

Thus—

Nothing worth any particular mention had happened today.

Theoretically.

β — 7

While it would've been exaggerating to say she had the force of a rock falling from a cliff, Haruhi's speed down the hill would've been a solid challenge for any world-class athlete.

Descending the road from school behind her, as though being dragged by an invisible rope, were Koizumi and I along with Asahina, and by the time we reached the level ground in front of Koyoen Station, I was thoroughly winded. Suffice it to say that even Koizumi, who normally looked like something straight out of a deodorant commercial, was wiping sweat from his brow. Asahina gasped for breath, bent over with her hands on her knees.

But Haruhi, who had to be hiding a radioactive power source

somewhere in her body, seemed perfectly fine. "What're you guys lazing around for? We've come this far, so let's finish with a run!"

She took off at a sprint, heading for Nagato's apartment.

This too was at Olympic speed, and it would've taken an athlete at the top of their career to keep up with her. I sent Koizumi ahead while taking the slower Asahina's bag and following at the best pace I could manage.

"Haaah...hah..."

Minding Asahina with her tangled legs, I arrived late; Haruhi had been waiting for me at the apartment's entrance, but the moment she confirmed everyone's presence, she started pushing buttons on the intercom. 7, 0, 8, call.

The answer came immediately. As though she'd been waiting.

"..."

"Yuki, it's me. Everybody's here to check in on you."

"..."

The intercom clicked off, and the automatic doors slowly slid open.

We entered the elevator that was stopped on the first floor, and Haruhi hit the button marked "7F." I can't say it was particularly roomy, and with all four of us in the elevator it was pretty cramped. The sound of Asahina's breathing was very clear in my ear. Along with the faint sound of machinery.

The box ascended slowly as though under human power, and Haruhi's lips were pursed the whole way. It wasn't as though her mood was particularly poor, though—it was just that whenever she didn't know exactly what expression to make, she defaulted to irritation.

She breezed impatiently through the doors once they finally opened to the seventh floor, pushing the air audibly aside as she marched along, finally hitting the door buzzer for 708 several times.

The door unlocked so quickly it seemed as though the room's occupant must have been waiting just on the other side, and the metal door slowly swung open. Backlit by the warm interior lighting, the shadow of a human silhouette fell across the entryway.

"..."

There in the rectangular space created by the open door was Yuki Nagato, in her pajamas.

"Should you really be up?"

In response to Haruhi's question Nagato only nodded, her eyes deep and unfathomable, then made for her closet to bring out indoor slippers for her guests.

"Aw, forget about that stuff."

Haruhi kicked off her own shoes and stopped Nagato, taking her by the shoulders and marching her back inside to the bedroom. Asahina and I weren't the only ones who'd visited Nagato's place—everyone had been here several times, so even Haruhi had a sense of the room layout. I'd never ventured into Nagato's bedroom, though—the living room and guest room were the extent of my exploration. Not that any of that mattered.

Before bothering to reflect on the strange sensation of entering the uncharted territory of Nagato's bedroom for the first time—a bed was its only furnishing—I took a good look at Nagato, whom Haruhi was busy forcing back into bed.

"..."

Nagato's pale face was unmoved as it contemplated the ceiling, and she didn't look particularly feverish. If I had to identify something that was out of the ordinary, I suppose she had a little bit of bed-head, but that was it. My vision informed me that her eyelids were two millimeters more closed than normal, but she didn't seem to be in any pain. Those unsexy pajamas, though...

Having regained some of my composure, I realized just how much of it I'd lost.

Haruhi put her hand to Nagato's head. "Yuki, did you eat dinner? Does your head hurt?"

Her head still resting on the pillow, Nagato shook it side to side.

"You've gotta eat. I figured you might not have, since you live alone and all. Hmm"—Haruhi put her other hand to her own forehead—"you do have a bit of a fever. Do you have an ice pack anywhere?"

Nagato indicated in the negative.

"Well, whatever. I'll buy you one later. First, dinner. I'm borrowing your kitchen and fridge, Yuki, okay?"

Haruhi didn't wait for Nagato's response, standing while simultaneously grabbing Asahina's arm.

"I'm gonna make you my special rice porridge. Or would my special udon and veggie stew be better? Either one is great for when you have a cold. Mikuru, give me a hand."

"Um…okay—!"

Asahina had been gazing worriedly at Nagato with her arms full of slippers, but perhaps spurred into action, she nodded several times and accompanied Haruhi. But just before they left the room, Haruhi stopped short and spoke to Koizumi and me, who were still standing there like idiots.

"Out of the room, you two. You can't just stare at a girl while she's sleeping."

"In that case," said Koizumi, "let me take care of the shopping. We need an ice pack and some cold medicine, correct?"

"Hang on a sec. I gotta make dinner, and that depends on what's in the fridge. I wonder if she's got any onion. Yeah, I'm gonna make a list. Come with me, Koizumi."

"As you wish."

Koizumi patted my shoulder as he smoothly breezed out of the room, giving me a strange look.

Left behind were me, who stood there with nothing to do, and Nagato, who lay neatly on her back.

I could hear fragments of the orders Haruhi was hurling at Koizumi and Asahina in the kitchen. "There's nothing but canned goods! That's hardly a balanced diet. Her body's all messed up because she's not eating any tasty vegetables. Mikuru, wash some rice and get the rice cooker ready—oh, and that pot too. And Koizumi, some eggs, spinach, scallions, and…"

Haruhi was good at stuff like this. She might claim it's her duty as brigade chief, but it was in things that had nothing to do with the

SOS Brigade where she really shone. And I knew from experience she was a good cook.

But this was no time to let myself get distracted by background chatter.

I had to ask.

"Nagato."

"..."

"Are you all right? Do you feel about the same as you look?"

"..."

"Can you not talk?"

"I can." Nagato had been still vaguely gazing at the ceiling, but then sat slowly up, the comforter still covering her upper body. Even a self-righting doll would have wobbled more than she did. She looked like The Undertaker.

"Is it because of Kuyoh that you're like this?"

"I cannot say that for certain." Nagato regarded me with eyes like polished quartz.

"You don't think she did this? I mean—"

The incident last winter at the mansion where Nagato had collapsed—what had been behind that? We'd wandered in the mountain blizzard for hours, and the source of light we'd found turned out to be an inescapable mountain, wherein Nagato lost her usual lucidity. Could that have been...?

"Under load," murmured Nagato in a near-whisper, her eyes dropping vaguely to the bed.

Had her body always been so small? She'd only been absent a day, and yet she seemed awfully thin and insubstantial now.

Then a sudden revelation struck me.

"When did this start?" I thought back on the events of the previous day. "When did the fever that forced you into bed begin?"

"Saturday evening."

That was the day of our first citywide mysterious phenomenon patrol. There certainly hadn't been anything wrong with Nagato then.

Surely this hadn't started right when I'd gotten that phone call from Sasaki in the bath.

"…" Nagato didn't answer, her vague, unfocused gaze falling on my chest.

Now that I thought about it, it was strange. Yesterday, Sunday. At Sasaki's behest I'd gone out and met Kyoko Tachibana, Kuyoh Suoh, and Fujiwara, but there'd been a surprising intruder.

Emiri Kimidori. She was a year above us, and was another of the Data Overmind's interfaces, along with Nagato and Asakura. The organic humanoid had hidden in either Nagato's or the student council president's shadow thus far. But the idea that she had a part-time job at that café and just happened to be there the same day as the rest of us was absurd. Kimidori was observing Kuyoh, I was positive. But why? Maybe to make sure that Kuyoh didn't pull any crafty alien tricks on me. But usually that was Nagato's job. And Nagato hadn't been there.

A wave of anger hit me, and I wanted to put a cross-counterpunch through my own temple.

How stupid could I be? I should've known—should've noticed.

Kimidori had come because Nagato wasn't able to. Nagato's backup, Ryoko Asakura, was out of the picture. Kimidori, despite being from a different faction, was the only other one nearby. Hence her presence at the café, where she was disguised as a waitress, neither too close to us nor too far away.

Nagato's eyes were duller than they'd ever been. Their shine was like that of an ancient coin dug up from the ground, seeming to lack any liveliness. They had lost their former sharpened-pencil gleam.

Without any air-conditioning, the bedroom stayed at a mild room temperature—yet I felt a chill run across my skin. It wasn't physical, instead emphasizing the cold worry in my mind.

"How can I make you better?"

This was something that neither over-the-counter medicine nor Haruhi's home cooking could cure. It was an alien pathogen. The only one who could come up with a vaccine or a drug to treat it was Nagato, and Yuki Nagato was the one lying here incapacitated.

"…" Her pale lips were closed for ten seconds, after which Nagato finally moved them. "I cannot recover from my current state of my own will. The Data Overmind will determine it."

Her dimwitted boss, eh? He ought to try showing his face in front of me, I said. We'd have a nice, frank chat.

"Impossible. The Data Overmind…" Nagato's eyes drooped another couple of millimeters. "…cannot communicate directly with organic beings…that is why it made me."

Her head fell drowsily back onto the pillow.

"Hey—"

"I am fine."

I checked again. This was no ordinary fever. Whatever it was that was afflicting Nagato, it was something that not even a dream team of the world's greatest doctors could solve.

It was an information attack from the cosmic horror known as the Heavenly Canopy Dominion. They were shutting down her incredible powers by placing this heavy load on her.

"Could we fix this if we talked to Kuyoh?"

I couldn't think of anything else. Just as Nagato was a representative of the Data Overmind, Kuyoh was an agent of the Heavenly Canopy Dominion. While it might not be as easy as it was with Nagato, communication with Kuyoh was possible—I'd learned that much from Sasaki and Kyoko Tachibana. She could speak Japanese, even if it was at a very low level. Which meant she ought to be able to understand the words I would say.

"Words…" Nagato spoke in a thin voice, barely above a sigh. "Words are difficult. I am not currently able to conduct discourse with another organic interface. My verbal communication facility is insufficient."

I'd known that much from the beginning. But her silent nature was an important part of who she was—both for me and for Haruhi, I said.

"I…" she began, her expressionless face transparently biting back the frustration she felt. "If as an individual I had been given social capabilities…"

Her pale expression was infinitesimally close to blank.

"The possibility of my gaining tools like Ryoko Asakura's was not zero. I was not made that way. I cannot change my predefined index. Until I cease functioning, I will be...as...I am."

Nagato's eyes were closed about three millimeters as they gazed up at the featureless ceiling.

I was out of words to offer.

How would things have been if Nagato's and Asakura's positions had been switched? If the silent, unapproachable, book-loving one had been the class representative, while the smiling, sociable busy-body had been the sole literature club member?

It was an obvious mismatch—honestly, I couldn't even imagine it. I hadn't been stabbed by Nagato, then gone on to be saved by Asakura. There was no doubt in my mind that I was glad for the way things were, with Asakura *there* and Nagato *here*. Sorry, Asakura. I hope you never come back from Canada or wherever. Nagato's enough for me. The trio of Nagato, Haruhi, and Asahina is more than enough to fill my cup to overflowing.

"Nagato, please, tell me"—I leaned forward, coming closer to her mussed bangs—"What should I do? How can I get you back to normal?"

"..."

No answer was forthcoming.

Nagato took her time and fixed me in her gaze, and the reply she finally gave me was very short indeed.

"Nothing."

"Nothing? You can't—" I said, leaning forward.

"Hey, Kyon! What're you doing with Yuki?!" Haruhi's eyes were isosceles triangles of rage as she stood there, rice paddle in hand and apron tied on over her school uniform. "Get in here and help me! Koizumi's already gone out shopping, so you could at least try to make yourself useful. Honestly, you're the one who should be working hardest—menial physical labor is your responsibility, after all! Set out the plates, wash the chopsticks, and that's just for starters. Now c'mon!"

I found myself being hauled by my neck and plunked down in the kitchen like a sandbag placed to protect against flooding.

Which was fine. I'd help with anything. If it would help Nagato recover, I'd make any dish. That's right, here and now, if there was any possibility it could help. Whatever revitalizing dish Haruhi made would probably be enough to make even an extraterrestrial life-form turn green and sprint out of the house barefoot. The nastier, the better.

But while I might be driven to tears of gratitude by Haruhi's cooking, my tongue had never rejected it. I will be frank. With all apologies to the mother who raised me, Haruhi's meals were better.

I could hardly imagine her raising children, but there was no danger of Haruhi's immediate descendants developing any taste disorders.

There in the kitchen, Haruhi left Asahina to tend the simmering earthen pot, and after taking a moment to gulp water directly from the tap, spoke.

"Well, that's a bit of a relief. I'd never thought Yuki would miss school, so I was worried this was going to be a worse cold. But she doesn't have too much of a fever, and once she's had a nice, easy meal and gotten some sleep, she should be fine."

"It doesn't seem she'll need to go to the hospital," Koizumi casually interjected. Everybody other than Haruhi knew perfectly well a regular doctor wasn't going to do Nagato any good, but now that he mentioned it, it would've been strange for the possibility not to come up. "I know a fine doctor, so if it comes to that, I'll have him prescribe some excellent medicine."

Haruhi wiped her mouth on her sleeve. "Medicine only makes you think you're getting better. What really cures you is spirit." She'd started lecturing. "The reason medicine tastes bad is to make the viruses or bacteria think, 'Hey, if they're gonna start putting nasty stuff like this in here, I better beat it.'"

"I-is that true?"

"You bet it is."

I wanted her to stop brazenly lying in front of Asahina—what would happen if she believed it?

But I kept my comments to myself, sitting at the powerless kotatsu table in the living room with Koizumi and idly passing time.

Once he'd returned from his shopping, Koizumi had immediately been relieved of duty, and since I'd never been given any particular responsibilities to begin with, I was off the hook once I'd gotten a few utensils out of the cupboard and rinsed them clean, at which point all we could do was watch Haruhi and her assistant Asahina set busily about the cooking proper.

I'd known she was good, but watching her like this, Haruhi put a professional homemaker to shame. From her skill at slicing vegetables to her ability at making the broth, I was impressed with how easily she was pulling it off.

"Anyone can do this kind of thing once they get used to it," said Haruhi, tasting the pot's contents with a small dish. "I've been cooking since I was a grade schooler. I'm better at it than anyone else in my family too. Oh, Mikuru—get some soy sauce."

"Here you are!"

Now that I thought about it, I realized Haruhi hardly ever brought her lunch from home. Did her mother not make lunches for her? I wondered.

"If I asked her to, she would. Sometimes she wants to, but I turn her down. When I need a lunch, I make it myself." Haruhi got a slightly complicated expression on her face. "I probably shouldn't say this, but Mom...I mean, my mother doesn't have the best taste. There's something wrong with her tongue. And worse, she always eyeballs spice amounts, and just guesses at cooking times, so even when she makes the same dish, it always turns out differently. When I was a kid I thought that was normal, and I thought that school lunches were the tastiest thing ever. But when I tried making food myself, it was just so delicious. Ah, Mikuru, get the rice vinegar."

"Here you go!"

"So nowadays I make dinner about half the time. Since my mother

14

works, we just try to help each other out. It's true what they say, that there's no substitute for experience. In cooking or anything else, you've got to apply yourself to it every day. I didn't put any special work in, but the more I did it the more I got the hang of it. Mikuru, taste this. Is it good?"

"Sure...oh, it's delicious!"

"Isn't it? It's my original vegetable soup. It's chock-full of vitamins from A to Z, and great for your stamina. The stuff'll banish fatigue and dizziness to the rings of Saturn!"

Haruhi rattled off her generic ad copy as she poured the soup into bowls, then turned off the flame under the earthenware pot and covered it. My stomach immediately growled. The fragrance definitely got my appetite going.

"This is Yuki's rice porridge. Kyon, stop staring so greedily. You can't have any. Help me bring it to her room. You won't be punished for doing that much."

She didn't have to tell me; at the moment, I was ready to wholly devote myself to public service. In fact, I felt pretty pathetic for this being the only thing I could do.

I set the porridge and vegetable soup that Haruhi had ladled into bowls onto a tray, and carefully prepared to bring it to Nagato's bedside. Asahina followed, carrying the teapot and cup. Koizumi was next, bringing the herbal medicine that Haruhi had specified along with some water, and Haruhi was at the lead. She opened the door to Nagato's room.

"All done, Yuki! Sorry to keep you waiting!"

"..."

Nagato sat slowly up, and she regarded us with silent eyes.

"First, drink this medicine. You're supposed to take it before a meal. In my experience, this stuff works the best. Then, food. There's plenty, so eat as much as you like. You missed lunch, right?"

Haruhi's positive energy was something to behold. It was easy to imagine a cold virus packing up and skipping town when confronted with this power, if it had any sense of self-preservation at all.

"..."

Nagato started to try to get out of bed, but Haruhi stopped her. Koizumi handed over the sachet of medicine and the cup, and after gazing at it as though dubious of its efficacy for a moment, Nagato dutifully drank it.

Haruhi looked as though she would have preferred to feed Nagato, but Nagato refused, taking the soup bowl and spoon in hand. She filled the spoon, sipped, and swallowed.

"..."

Nagato was barely chewing at all as she swallowed the spoonfuls of porridge under Haruhi's intense gaze. It wasn't just Haruhi staring either—Asahina, Koizumi, and I were all watching.

"..."

Nagato looked down at the bowl in her hand as though watching for a color change in a starch that had been touched with an iodine solution, and yet—"Delicious," she said in a small voice.

"Really? Great. Eat more. Eat it all up! Here, have some vegetable soup. I would've liked to simmer it longer, but it should be flavorful enough as it is."

Nagato took the bowl that Haruhi thrust so energetically upon her, and from it she drank.

"Delicious."

"Isn't it?" Haruhi seemed extremely happy as she watched Nagato eat her meal.

Nagato continued to pick steadily away at her food. It wasn't clear whether she was particularly moved by Haruhi's home cooking; she did seem to be savoring more than she did her usual huge servings of pre-made curry, though she might just have been forcibly repressing her lack of appetite. She would eat anything put in front of her, even if she didn't need to.

The whole situation was hard for me to watch.

Maybe because Nagato was still in bed, still wearing her pajamas, or maybe because she was eating Haruhi's food in total silence, or possibly because though she was close enough to touch, something about her aura seemed especially diluted.

"Sorry," I excused myself to no one in particular. "I'm gonna use the bathroom."

I left the bedroom and headed for the bathroom without waiting for a reply. I wasn't letting it show, but if I looked at Nagato any longer I was going to be overcome by a directionless rage.

I sat down on the neat little toilet seat cover and chewed the inside of my lip. And I thought.

My salvation was the fact that I knew exactly who it was I needed to interrogate, and fast. It wasn't clear what I would have to do, but whatever I did, I couldn't let this go.

I had to do something about that Kuyoh girl. The fact that Nagato had collapsed while *she* was totally healthy was completely unfair. Some balance somewhere had been upset. It was unforgivable. First I'd contact Sasaki—

"Wah—!"

My cell phone vibrated in my blazer pocket, and I nearly fell right off the seat.

I looked at my phone's display wondering who could be calling me with such suspiciously good timing, and I saw that it wasn't an incoming call, but rather a text message.

"Huh?"

The sender's address was completely scrambled. Who the heck was this? I opened my inbox.

"Wha?"

My screen suddenly went dark. Surely it wasn't a virus of some kind? Crap. It'd be a real hassle if I lost the data I'd put in my phone.

In the midst of my panic, I saw a white cursor begin to blink at the top left of my phone's screen, and I felt a wave of nostalgia that almost made me dizzy. Somewhere along the line I'd seen a computer monitor look very much like this.

After a few seconds, the cursor began to move smoothly across the screen, leaving characters behind it. I'd seen this kind of smoothly inputted text before too.

yuki.n> There is no need for worry

Nagato ... it was Nagato.

It was just like when I'd been trapped in closed space with Haruhi. Which meant I should be able to respond in kind. I pressed keys frantically. Was she telling me not to worry? That was crazy. I had to reply. I futzed with the tiny keys, painstakingly composing it.

"Your fever is because of those Heavenly Canopy jerks, right?"

Immediately after I sent it, the reply came.

yuki.n> Yes

All I could think of was how careless I'd been, and I wanted to freeze my head in liquid nitrogen and shatter it with a bat. I'd seen the doll-like Kuyoh lined up harmlessly with Kyoko Tachibana and assumed she was harmless. It was my own fault for jumping to conclusions. I'd been so sure they were only interested in me and Haruhi.

I'd figured they wanted to do something about Haruhi's power, and that was all they cared about when they contacted me. I was the emperor of unwarranted, careless assumptions. Just as Koizumi had said, Nagato was the greatest bulwark the SOS Brigade possessed— how could I not have seen that our enemies would strike at her first?

yuki.n> I will not allow them to harm you or Haruhi Suzumiya

I mashed buttons in frustration.

Who cared about me or Haruhi? We could handle ourselves, and were in perfectly good health at the moment. *Nagato* was the one they were harming. And she had to make them stop, I typed.

Send. Then, the immediate response:

yuki.n> this is part of my duti▯▯▯▯data
o▯▯▯▯rmind▯▯▯▯▯▯▯▯▯ttempt communicat▯▯▯▯enly canopy
dom▯▯▯▯

The characters abruptly stopped.
What's wrong? I typed.
The few meters that separated Nagato's bedroom from her cozy bathroom suddenly seemed terribly distant, and the few seconds before her reply felt like an eternity.

yuki.n> my operaä¸è𝑎𝑎å▯ā▯®3å¤§å-¦ã€Œå¯è€³ã▯«æ

I wondered if my phone was broken. I hoped it was.

yuki.n> ▯Œã▯§ã▯▯ã‹ã▯¾ã▯§ã€▯ã▯«å▯„é▯Žç¨ã▯®æ˜ åƒ▯ã€‚

I broke out in a cold sweat. It was totally unprecedented for Nagato to send me genuine nonsense. Was she that bad? What if she couldn't be cured...?

My vision dimmed. It would've been easy for my hand to slip and drop the phone in the toilet, and I could hardly blame it if it did.

But before I could turn my phone into a useless object, another line of characters appeared on the display.

yuki.n> going to sleep for a bit

The short sentence appeared briefly, then faded out as though melting. The message was simplicity itself—very Nagato-like.

I'll say it again: How could she expect me not to worry? How the hell could I do anything else? Sorry, Nagato, I'm not that good of a person. You overestimated me.

I dashed out of the bathroom and ran straight back into the bedroom.

"Nagato!"

Haruhi took one look at my crazed state and was momentarily shocked. "Kyon, be quiet! Yuki just fell asleep." She glared at me with a severe look. "She fell over as soon as she was done eating, and went to sleep on the spot."

Just as Haruhi said, Nagato was still, her eyes closed. She was like a frozen princess; you couldn't even tell she was breathing.

"I'm sure she feels better. It's times like this when living alone's no good. You've gotta have other people around. Even if you sleep alone, having the feeling of other people moving around in the house is really important. It's just pleasant, y'know? No matter who it is, just having someone nearby is—"

I turned my back on Haruhi's entirely reasonable explanation. I wanted to listen, but at the moment I just didn't feel like it. My body moved on its own, without my head's input.

"Kyon, where are you—"

I dashed out of the bedroom and picked up speed as I headed for the front door. I didn't feel like waiting for the elevator to take me to the ground floor, so I took the stairs. Passing through the entrance, I left the apartment building at a flat run.

I had no idea where Kuyoh would be at this hour. But she'd been wearing a Koyoen Academy uniform. If she was anything like Nagato, she'd be very careful about attending school every day, so she'd have to be there. I didn't care what the security guards tried to do to stop me; I'd get past them by hook or by crook. Even if I managed to get into the staff room, there was no telling whether her address would be on the student roster. I'd just have to cross that bridge when I got to it.

The one thing my body wouldn't let me do was sit still and do nothing.

Eventually my stride started to feel unsteady, as though I were wearing winged shoes bestowed upon me by a goddess—this had to be thanks to my good-for-nothing cardiopulmonary system, which resulted in my running out of breath right in front of a rail crossing.

It had been close to a year ago. Right around here, I'd listened to Haruhi deliver a long monologue.

I focused on breathing in an effort to recover, and happened to look across the rails—at which point both my gaze and my feet froze in place.

Kuyoh Suoh.

Nagato's enemy and mine stood directly opposite me across the tracks. As though she'd been there all along.

"—"

The black uniform, the wide fall of hair. And the transcendently blank expression.

The crossing gate's warning lights started to flash. Simultaneously, the bell that announced an approaching train began to ring, and the crossing gate started its reluctant arc down.

Why was she here? It was like…it was like she was waiting for me…

Kuyoh did not move. She maintained her distance from me, so rooted to the spot that a cardboard robot cutout would've had more visible humanity.

Ding, ding, ding—

The gate had completely lowered, and the rumbling tracks and rushing air heralded a train's approach. I stared at Kuyoh, with no idea what it was she was looking at. This timing was impossible. This was not a coincidence. She…

She *had* to be waiting for me.

With a gust of wind the train rushed past, hiding Kuyoh behind it. Though the train did not have so very many cars, it seemed as though time had come to a stop. I had the terrible illusion that I could look at the peering faces of every one of the train's passengers, which then led to a powerful premonition.

I was as sure as though I'd already seen it that once the train had passed, Kuyoh would be gone. And she would be standing behind me, her ghostly white hands reaching out…

A terrible hallucination.

When the train passed and the red warning lights stopped flashing, their duty complete, Kuyoh's dark form was still across the tracks. Was she being strangely cooperative, or was this some sort of performance? Or were such notions too human for her to even conceive?

As I waited for the yellow and black bars to squeakily rise, Kuyoh started to move, as though walking through water. She was coming toward me. I wanted to know how she managed to walk without disturbing either her hair or her skirt.

Like some insubstantial hologram, her form stopped a few meters away from me.

My hands hung at my sides; I balled them into fists. "What did you do to Nagato?"

Kuyoh's huge, marble-like eyes stared through me. My instincts warned me not to meet her gaze. She'd suck my soul out with those eyes. That's what it felt like.

"I wanted to learn about humans...No"—though we were still separated, her voice sounded like a whisper next to my ear—"no, that is wrong. What I wanted to learn about..."

She cocked her head. The strangely human gesture tripped me up.

"...Was you..."

What?

"Will you...come with me...?"

What was she saying?

"I don't mind..." She reached her hand out to me.

The alien.

Ding, ding, ding—

The crossing signals started to ring again. The red lights started their alternating flashing. These were the indications of an approaching train, but for me it felt like a warning of something far more terrible than being struck by a runaway locomotive. It felt like an emergency. What was this? What was going on? There wasn't enough coherence to this story. What was this sudden transformation, as though a witch had magically brought a lead figure to life?

Kuyoh's hand continued to approach. It came closer, closer, this thing that looked like a human but was not.

This being with which mutual comprehension was impossible, which had come from a place beyond the galaxy and beyond human knowledge, whose visible form was inconceivable. This girl with hair like fluttering wings...

Her eyes black as a new moon. No, don't look. The world would go dark.

Stop—I wanted to say, but my mouth wouldn't move. It was pathetic. To come all this way, and...

"Stop right there."

The voice that stopped Kuyoh's hand was not mine.

And again I found myself stunned.

I heard the voice directly behind me, and it brimmed with imposing confidence and an obvious cheer. It was a girl's voice, one I hadn't heard in quite some time, and I can't say I'd ever hoped to hear it again.

"I won't allow you to approach any closer. After all"—the voice laughed sparklingly, right at the nape of my neck—"this human is my prey. If your kind means to have me turn him over, I'd rather do this."

An arm reached out over my shoulder. It was clad in a long-sleeved North High uniform, and its hand grasped an object I was rather familiar with—a razor-sharp knife, its blade flashing wickedly.

The combat knife was held in a reverse grip, its tip pointed directly at my throat.

"Either way, it doesn't much matter to me," she said with a pleasant laugh, which made the hair on the back of my head stand up. A sweet, narcotic scent reached me as it wafted faintly through the air.

"You're..." I finally forced the words out. "Asakura."

"I certainly am. Who else would I be?"

From behind me echoed the unmistakable voice of my former Class 5 classmate, Ryoko Asakura.

"Nagato is resting at the moment, isn't she? Hence my appearance. Does that bother you for some reason?"

I couldn't turn around. I couldn't help feeling that if I turned and witnessed Ryoko Asakura's form behind me, something terrible would happen. As Nagato's former backup and member of the Data Overmind's radical faction, she'd tried to kill me twice, and the second time I'd very nearly died. Both times it had been Nagato who'd saved me, but Nagato was not here. Instead, Kuyoh was here. Ridiculous. The tiger or the wolf—it was hard to imagine either of them was on my side. What kind of absurd dilemma was this?

"We detected an emergency. That's why I've appeared. Is it really so mysterious?" she said sweetly. "I mean, I *am* Nagato's backup, after all. She can't act, so I'm up next. That's how things work, you know."

Nagato couldn't act—.

This was an extraordinary situation. So much so that the once-deleted Ryoko Asakura had been revived. So much so that I had no choice but to seek aid from a killer.

"How rude. I'm not a killer, you know. I mean, look—I haven't killed anyone at all yet, have I?"

Well, then, maybe she could point that knife somewhere else. I couldn't even swallow.

"Now that I can't do. So long as she's over there, I must carry out my duties." Her index finger uncurled from around the knife's handle and pointed to the stock-still Kuyoh. "So you're a humanoid terminal for what we're calling the Heavenly Canopy Dominion, are you? How interesting. If you die here, I wonder how she would react."

Asakura said the most chilling things as though she were chatting about the weather. She hadn't changed at all from when she'd been the class rep. Was there anyone else in the world like Ryoko Asakura?

I was as still as a dried fish left in the middle of a desert. I couldn't even tell whether it was hot or cold. All I knew was the dull, chilling glint of the knife's blade, and Kuyoh's eyes, quiet as a fourth sub-basement room.

It was *too* quiet.

The realization hit me. What had happened to the crossing signal's flashing lights? Where had the raucous clang of the warning bell gone? Why hadn't the train come?

I looked up. The red signal light was frozen on. The guard bar jutted out diagonally, stopped halfway through its downward arc. There was absolutely no wind. Not a single person walked the path along the road, and there were no cars.

The world had come to a halt.

The clouds in the sky were completely still, and shockingly, when I spotted a crow frozen in mid-flight, I finally realized what had happened.

Space had been frozen.

"What is going on here...?"

Asakura giggled. "I didn't want anyone interfering. This way no one can observe us, can they? Manipulation of spatial information is my specialty. No one can escape."

A trap, then. But for whom?

"Now, then, Miss Kuyoh," continued Asakura happily. "Shall we talk? Or shall we fight? I would love to see just what your kind is capable of. That's part of my job too."

Kuyoh remained motionless and expressionless, but she spoke. "...Release that human. The danger is significant...your intent to kill is genuine..."

After she blinked slowly, I saw light in her eyes for the first time.

"It is not you. I have no interest in you. You are not important," said Kuyoh with the faintest trace of emotion.

"Well, that's not a very nice thing to say. But, fine, if that's how you feel—"

The hand holding the knife moved, leaving behind only an afterimage. The movement was instantaneous; it was hardly surprising that my eye couldn't track the motion. I already knew this from my previous experience with Asakura's extra-dimensional battle against Nagato in the Class 5 classroom. From what I could see,

Asakura threw the knife with but a flick of her wrist, sending the weapon flying at Kuyoh at nearly the speed of light, but it took several seconds for my brain to process what I'd seen.

"...Threat level increased two levels," murmured Kuyoh, stopping the knife by grabbing its hilt. The blade very nearly touched her nose, but she showed no sign of fear whatsoever, and though from my perspective it looked as though she were about to stab herself in the face, it was just the opposite. "...And still rising."

Both the knife and the slender arm that restrained it were trembling slightly. My god—despite being intercepted by Kuyoh, the projectile Asakura had thrown was still trying to pierce her. Kuyoh's monstrous ability to stop the ultra-high-speed attack was bad enough, but Asakura was even more horrifying. Just how much kinetic energy had she imbued the knife with? I didn't want to think about it.

"Not bad," said Asakura, impressed. "That was just a probe, but it did exceed your estimated capacity. This will be interesting."

The air behind me began to stir. I was sure that if I looked back I would see the locks of Asakura's hair begin to float up like so many snakes, but I didn't dare check to be sure. I couldn't cover my ears, though.

"Expanding range of data control. Commencing deployment of offensive data. Shifting to termination mode. Requesting authorization of limited-space combat simulation for analysis of target."

Just as I was putting together the contents of Asakura's rapid-fire speech, the surrounding scenery shattered and collapsed. It was like a jigsaw puzzle landscape coming to pieces, falling away and revealing what lay behind them. And for a second time I witnessed the mad geometry of Asakura's data jurisdiction space.

"...Threat level stabilized." Kuyoh's pale face was starting to become flushed. Her voice was changing too. "Move away from that human." Despite the knife still directly in front of her face, her voice betrayed no concern. "You are irrelevant."

Her statements were now far more comprehensible. Very slowly, as though calming a wild horse, Kuyoh moved the knife aside. As soon as she reached a distance such that the blade would not pass through her hair, she cocked her head and let it go.

The knife Asakura had thrown immediately accelerated to its impossible speed, flying off like a missile, when—

"—!"

I was stunned for a third time. It was starting to get a little tiresome.

A third figure was visible behind Kuyoh—and just as my brain managed to process that fact, Asakura's knife sped for the figure at hypersonic velocity, and in a carbon copy of what Kuyoh had just done a moment before, the figure caught it right in front of her face. And who should the owner of such acrobatic knife-catching skill be but—

"Miss Kimidori," said Asakura. "What brings you to a place like this?"

The school uniform–clad Kimidori floated strangely through the geometry of our surroundings. She wore the same calm smile she'd had when she stood beside the student council president. It was such an ordinary expression that it seemed all the stranger given the incomprehensible circumstances. Sorry—I just can't put this stuff into proper words anymore.

Kimidori turned the hand with which she'd caught the knife, pointing the blade at Asakura. "I've come to stop your deviant activities. Your actions are not founded on the consensus of the Data Overmind."

"Oh? Is that so?"

"Yes. I cannot authorize them."

"Oh really? That's fine," replied Asakura with unnerving agreeableness. "Would you give that back?"

Kimidori opened her hand, and the knife flew back through the air, this time at a speed even my eyes could track—but no sooner had I noticed this than Asakura murmured a brief phrase.

The knife suddenly accelerated, heading straight for the back of Kuyoh's head, and not at a speed that could be dodged. It was like a laser beam.

28

"?"

I doubted what my eyes saw.

Kuyoh's figure seemed to turn two-dimensional, and in the next instant had disappeared.

It was as though she'd suddenly become a flat plane, then disappeared by turning sideways. The sight distracted me such that I only reacquired the position of the knife because it was again in Asakura's hand, this time held in an overhand grip, its point again at my neck as though she were again readying to slit my throat.

As soon as I comprehended this, a cold sweat broke out on my head.

If Asakura hadn't stopped it, the blade would've gone right through my windpipe. I could barely stand from the terror.

"Did she escape," said Asakura, uncertainty in her voice.

What, no comment on what had nearly just happened to me?

"No," said Kimidori, shaking her head, then tilting her head up. "She is here."

Kuyoh descended directly before my eyes.

Her form came down as though lowered onto a stage from above, and she grabbed Asakura's knife-holding hand at the wrist, readying her other hand for an open-palmed strike, then unleashing it in a blur of non-motion. At what?

At my face.

"?!"

The situation was fluctuating so rapidly I was completely exhausted. Yet there was not a single thing I could do about it. I was only understanding things well after they'd happened—and this was happening *now*.

A wind that felt like a solid object hit my hair, and I flinched my eyes closed in spite of myself. I hastily reopened them, and was met by the following scene.

Kuyoh's hand was stopped just a few millimeters from my forehead, only because Asakura had reached out and grabbed its black-school-uniformed wrist. The hand that wielded the deadly blade had been stopped, just as the hand that *was* a deadly blade had been stopped. And between the two girls who looked human but were monsters within stood my idiotic self. I'll say it again: Pathetic.

Was this now twice that Asakura had saved my life? Now wait just a minute—how much sense did that make?

"Miss Kuyoh," said Asakura teasingly. "What do you want to do with this human? Kill him? Or let him live?"

Kuyoh's gaze stabbed through me as though I were nothing more than a sandbag, but it then shifted to somewhere past the side of my head, presumably where Asakura's face was.

"—Query meaning unclear. Define 'human.' Define 'kill.' Define 'live.'" Her voice seemed to come from some sort of speaker rather than human vocal cords.

"—Define 'Data Overmind.' Provide information."

She spoke as though talking to herself, her expression shifting—well, let's say it shifted dramatically.

She smiled.

It was a terrifyingly cold, beautiful smile.

While it seemed more like a perfectly executed high-level simulation of a smile than an actual expression of affection, even the most stoic man would find himself stricken with affection upon encountering it. I was about the only one who could withstand it. Someone like Taniguchi who didn't understand the circumstances would've fallen for her in an instant. I was at a total loss for words as Asakura started to speak with bold nonchalance.

"What lovely features you have, Miss Kuyoh. But let's end this now, shall we? I will not yield a single thing to the Heavenly Canopy Dominion, including the life of this human."

Their hands bound in mutual deadlock, Kuyoh and Asakura conversed.

—Just what the hell are they talking about?!

I was getting more and more angry.

Incidentally, let me just say this: I am fundamentally a nice person. How nice, you ask? There was the time my sister thought it would be funny to wrap Shamisen up in my favorite muffler, to which he instinctively reacted by converting it to mere wool with his teeth and claws. I let them each off the hook with no more than a poke in the forehead; that's how nice I am.

And yet this whole situation was starting to really piss me off.

Yeah, yeah, I know.

Anyone who'd stand in the middle of this ridiculous situation was screwy. If you need proof, remember that the three other people there were all extraterrestrials.

I was the only normal one. Hence my abject terror. Got a problem with that?

"—Define 'Heavenly Canopy Dominion.'"

Completely ignoring the chat-bot-like query that came from Kuyoh's exquisite smile, Asakura spoke. "Commencing offensive data strike."

The ground at my feet started to bubble. The burbling, boiling sound made it feel as if we were in some poisoned swamp. Next, Asakura's knife sublimated into nothingness, like so much crystal sand. Kuyoh's wrist where Asakura gripped it was wrapped in a blue-white mosaic. The pattern of hexagons traveled up her arm with startling speed, but no sooner had I witnessed this than Kuyoh's form seemed to again turn two-dimensional, and in an instant she was no more than a line.

Gooonnngg!

"Hngh—?!"

A loud metallic clang echoed through my ears, as though some kind of colossal tuning fork had been struck. But the sound did not linger, and a sudden silence descended, as though some giant's hand had simply wiped all sound from the air.

"..."

Ever so hesitantly, I opened my eyes, and saw that Kuyoh was nowhere to be found. The only person in front of me was Kimidori. Behind me still lingered the presence of the other, more terrifying girl.

The harsh-looking geometric background was swept away, and the scenery returned to its previous setting beside the rail crossing, bringing my surroundings closer to normal, though at this point I was no longer surprised by such changes.

"Did she actually escape this time?" From behind me Asakura put the question to Kimidori.

"The data protection field you erected was penetrated by an unknown form of focused data. I am currently tracking the target and repairing local space."

"A shift in the physical dimensionality of her corporeal data… clearly she's a very different sort of terminal than we are. She has no need for authorization."

"She does not seem to have been created to communicate with humans. In fact, I would surmise she was constructed as an interpretation platform for discourse with *us*. We could even deduce that her interest in Haruhi Suzumiya comes from conclusions derived from observing the Data Overmind."

"It's hard to imagine she's a mere terminal. She broke my data offensive without needing to decode it."

"Given that their logical foundation is so different, inflicting fatal damage will require analysis of the algorithms of the domain to which she is connected."

"I'll leave that to you, Miss Kimidori. You managed to collect a little data in all of this, didn't you? Wouldn't it be a good idea to pick up all the fragments and analyze the greater structure of the platform?"

"Independent action is not authorized."

"You sound like Miss Nagato. But I think at the moment she would be inclined to agree with me."

"I will suspend you. The Data Overmind has not authorized this."

"Goodness," said Asakura, affecting surprise. "And just when did you become the Data Overmind's representative?"

"The interface designated Yuki Nagato transferred a subset of her autonomous judgment heuristics to me. She proposed the transfer, which was approved by the central consciousness of the Data Overmind. My actions are consistent with the general consensus of the Overmind."

"Did you say 'consensus'? You mean those lazy conservatives desperate to maintain the status quo? Or are you just trying to call me the minority?"

"Both."

Asakura laughed in her perfect-student voice. "My behavior patterns are unchanged from their previous alignment, and have still not been overwritten."

"You are a backup resource to be deployed only in emergencies. Yuki Nagato and I have acknowledged only that your abilities are necessary in a limited capacity. Your utility is only slightly greater than the risks you pose."

"I suppose I should thank you, then. I was revived because of you."

"I have been given the authority to cancel your data integration."

"So I can't beat you, then. Fine. All I plan to do is take action according to my own will. I learned that from Miss Nagato—where the potential for self-evolution lies. Don't you know, Miss Kimidori? She's no longer a mere terminal. Given that, don't you think we can do the same thing?"

No, I didn't. One Nagato was more than enough for me. I had to thank Asakura for stopping Kuyoh's attack. But I had to say it again:

Nagato was enough for me. As for you, Asakura? I don't need you.

"How cruel you are!" said Asakura, obviously amused.

I wanted to say another thing, I told them. Why were they having a philosophical debate with me right here between them? Would it kill them to put themselves in my shoes a little and think about how this absurd conversation sounded to me?

"You heard the boy, Miss Kimidori."

And another thing—if Asakura had time to be pointing a knife at my throat, she could damned well go and make Nagato some food or something, I said. That was the kind of person she used to be, anyway.

"Is that the way you talk to the person who saved you from the evil alien?" said Asakura happily, her feelings seemingly not hurt in the slightest. "Unfortunately, I can't maintain this form for long periods of time. If you've got complaints on that count, talk to our illustrious upperclassman and the majority faction of the Data Overmind. Or try asking Nagato? If she agrees, I might even be able to come back from Canada."

No thanks. I couldn't see any way Haruhi would accept such a development. Asakura could just stay an exchange student for as long as she liked, I said.

"Oh? That's too bad." Asakura laughed like a little ripple. "Well, it looks like my limited activities are about to end. Call me again sometime. I'll always come out. So long as the scary girl over there doesn't stop me, that is."

Given that I had no memory of summoning her in the first place, I kept my mouth shut, at which Asakura's voice came still closer.

"Miss Nagato and I are like opposite sides of a mirror. Do you understand that, I wonder? I'm much closer to Nagato than Miss Kimidori is. The interface in front of you won't help you one bit. Her job is only to observe."

I could feel her breath on my ear.

"Why won't you turn around? Won't you look at me even to say good-bye?"

Not if I had any say in the matter. One look at her class-rep smile and my terror might vanish, I said. I could be totally taken in by that smile. But as far as I was concerned she was as bad as Kuyoh.

"Rude to the very end, I see. Well, that's fine. Good-bye, then. See you again."

Her voice faded away and her presence behind me vanished, but I still didn't move. At this point it was a waiting game.

Kimidori regarded me wordlessly. As soon as I noticed her skirt and sleeves start to flutter in the wind, the rail crossing bell started back up, which made me jump five millimeters off the ground. The red warning light flashed and the bar descended. The distant clouds above us began to move, and the crow resumed its flight through the sky.

The ambient sounds had returned to normal, somewhere along the line. Time was moving.

Kimidori started to slowly walk, stopping at exactly the right distance from me. I was certain she was going to explain everything to me, but no matter how I waited, her lips never changed from that little student council secretary smile of hers.

I gave up waiting.

"Kimidori."

"Yes?"

"That...Kuyoh. What *is* she? I just can't figure her out at all. Her actions make no sense at all—is it because she's not human?"

"The behavioral principles of the Heavenly Canopy Dominion defy comprehension. We have yet to determine whether it even possesses an independent consciousness. It is not even clear whether or not it can be properly classified as life."

...Uh, okay. That was a problem, then. Well, I had my own problems. But anyway, there was something else that bore mentioning here.

"Can't you do something about Nagato's fever?"

"Nagato has been given a special duty—establishing high-level communication with the Heavenly Canopy Dominion itself."

"Nagato is in bed, unable to move. What part of that is her 'duty'?"

Kimidori smiled at me, but her eyes were distant. "I am referring to such a high level of communication that it does not involve words. Hers is a mission that would be fundamentally impossible for a human. We have established physical contact with them for the first time. While indirect, it is a huge leap forward from our previous mutual incomprehension. Miss Nagato serves as a relay between us and them. She does so even now. Please watch over her."

"But that's no reason to force all of this off on her alone." It was all I could do not to end the sentence with an exclamation point. I glared at Kimidori's serene face, calm as a dandelion swaying in a spring breeze. "Why can't you or Asakura do it?"

"Miss Nagato was the one with whom they first established contact. She is also the interface closest to Miss Suzumiya. I would consider her the obvious choice."

Her calm, rational answer was starting to seriously make my head hurt.

So she was really telling me to just leave Nagato alone? These Data Overmind people were a bunch of assholes. It was something like a miracle that Nagato had been the one dispatched here, and thus been the first to meet Haruhi. If Asakura and Nagato's positions were switched, or if it had been Kimidori in the literature club, this present moment would never have come. This was all thanks to Nagato. I'd be perfectly happy to leave the word "interface" somewhere in the orbit of Neptune. It was enough to make me think that what Haruhi had wished for was not just any alien, but Yuki Nagato specifically. The majority faction, the radical faction—let's just see them show themselves to Haruhi. Let them weigh themselves against Nagato. I was sure Haruhi would pick Nagato every time, I said.

"Please forgive me." Kimidori bowed with ridiculous politeness. "There is not very much I can do. My directives prevent any deviation. If there is anything else you need, please let me know."

The pleasant older girl walked past me and headed for the train station, giving me another small bow as she did so. I knew there was no point in following her. I understood that these aliens were involved in things my brain couldn't hope to comprehend, but there was still one thing I wanted to say.

"Look, this is Earth. It's not some playground for aliens."

My voice mingled with a gust of wind and was gone, by which time Kimidori had disappeared.

Yet—

—*An amusing joke . . . indeed.*

I couldn't tell who it was that said it. I wasn't even sure if it was Kuyoh, Asakura, Kimidori, or someone else.

But I'm quite sure that my brain didn't just create words out of the sound of the wind blowing across my ears.

Cell phones seem to ring when you least expect them. This time was no different.

I was trudging heavily back to Nagato's apartment when a call from Haruhi stopped me short.

"Geez! Where'd you go, anyway? Did some evil god summon you away? You really freaked Mikuru out, disappearing like that!"

"Uh...sorry. I'm not far, so I'll be back soon."

"Explain yourself!"

"...Uh, I realized I hadn't brought Nagato a get-well present. I was thinking I'd get her some canned peaches or something."

"What year do you think this is? Get her a fruit basket. Or, well, I guess we don't need to make a big production out of it; it's not like she's in the hospital or something. Just get some orange juice. The one-hundred-twenty-percent-pure-fruit-juice kind."

I told her to tell me exactly where to find that kind of juice.

"Fine, make it one hundred percent. And get back here within three minutes, got it? Okay, bye!"

I wasn't irritated at her unilateral hanging up. She did that all the time. Her straightforward, one-way method of doing things was improving my spirits a little bit. Never change, Haruhi Suzumiya. If she weren't the way she was, she'd never be able to lead a ridiculous group like the SOS Brigade.

I went into a supermarket near the station and sleepwalked through the aisles, and once I'd purchased the one-hundred-percent-pure California orange juice Haruhi had directed me to buy, I walked rather sullenly back to Nagato's apartment. I got to the front entrance's automatic doors and dialed Nagato's apartment, whereupon Haruhi answered and let me in.

By the time I got back to Nagato's room I'd exceeded Haruhi's stated time limit by a couple of minutes, but our fearless brigade chief said nothing, and taking the juice bottle I offered her, she passed it straight to Asahina, who was sitting right next to her.

"Put this in the fridge, will you, Mikuru?"

"Sure!" Asahina, by now completely used to taking orders, trotted off to the kitchen. She certainly was cute. Definitely in the top three people that I wanted to protect no matter what.

"How's Nagato?"

"She opened her eyes a little bit a while ago, but then went back to sleep. So don't go in her bedroom. It's creepy to stare at other people when they're sleeping."

Haruhi pursed her lips, but seemed hesitant, and it was only after a four-minute pause that she spoke.

"Something like this happened before, didn't it? Yuki had a fever, and we were taking care of her. I know it was a hallucination, but it seems so real now."

That was because it *was* real. That nonsense about group hypnosis or whatever was a pack of lies from Koizumi. Of course, I couldn't very well say that to Haruhi, so I held my tongue.

Haruhi continued, murmuring almost reverently. "This is the same as then, isn't it? We were at Tsuruya's villa, and Yuki got better right away. She'd just caught a chill on the ski slopes. We're on the verge of spring right now, and people often get sick when the seasons change. This could be no more than seasonal allergies," she said, as though trying to convince herself. "That's right, this is no big deal. She'll be better within three days."

I wanted to get snarky and ask just who'd said that, but unfortunately the answer would be "me." I was envious of Koizumi's way with words. No matter how crazy the situation, he could always come up with some kind of absurd explanation for it. I was sure he'd wind up serving the Prince of Lies in hell one day.

It almost felt as though there were KEEP OUT tape strung across the door to Nagato's room, so I passed obediently by it and went into the living room.

Koizumi had his long legs nestled under the kotatsu table there, and he gave me a look as I entered the room.

"Where'd you go?"

"A place just as boxed-up as one of your closed spaces."

"So it seems." Koizumi rested his elbows on the table. "There were reports that both Kuyoh Suoh and Miss Kimidori were sighted." He indicated his cell phone, which he'd left on the floor beside him.

"They were seen only for a moment, but looking at the expression on your face I'm guessing it was no mere chance encounter."

"Yeah."

It had gotten so that I didn't know who was an enemy and who was on my side. Whatever those aliens' goals were was a mystery to me. Kuyoh, Asakura, Kimidori, all of them—they might have looked like humans, but they were monsters. Humans might do unbelievable stuff from time to time, but you could at least guess at what they were thinking. But who knew what went on in a monster's mind? Their behavior patterns were too erratic, like crappy NPCs in an RPG—made worse by the fact that their stats were totally game-breaking.

"Do you really have no plan at all?"

"I'll do everything that I can. Prodding Kyoko Tachibana might produce some kind of reaction, but from what I can deduce the chances are slim. There is essentially no connection between her faction and Nagato's current condition. They have chosen the wrong allies. Kuyoh Suoh is not someone who can be communicated with. The idea that humans could understand an entity that even the Data Overmind cannot comprehend is absurd."

So what about the time travelers? That jerk Fujiwara or whatever his name was didn't seem scared of Kuyoh at all. Ugh, I couldn't stand the thought of owing him for something. Plus his goals were totally opaque, I pointed out.

"It's certainly true that his aim is not merely observation of Suzumiya. That's true of both time traveler factions. Though our Asahina may not have been told as much."

Koizumi's eyes moved horizontally to take in the sight of Asahina doing dishes in the kitchen. Haruhi was there too, moving busily around—pouring the soup from its pot into smaller bowls and packing up excess ingredients into plastic containers.

"I've decided. I'm going to keep making dinners for Yuki until she gets better. I'm doing it, and that's that. I don't care if she says no; I'm still coming over."

It was a strangely loud statement given that she was just talking to herself, and that she asked for nobody's approval.

She was probably the most selfish girl in the galaxy. I hoped she never changed.

Haruhi produced a spare door key from who-knew-where, locked the door to Nagato's apartment, then slipped the key into her skirt pocket as though it were a grain of gold dust. We put unit 708, in which Nagato slept, behind us, and split up in front of her apartment building.

"I'm suspending SOS Brigade activities for a while." Haruhi looked up at the apartment, anger in her eyes at the twilight-dyed sky. "Until Yuki starts coming to school again, nobody should bother coming to the clubroom. We'll come here instead. I'm counting on you tomorrow, Mikuru."

"Yes, of course!"

I nearly shed a tear at Asahina's earnestness. Damn.

It looked like Haruhi and Asahina were prepared to take charge of Nagato's bedside care. It seemed somehow Haruhi-like that she didn't add any excuses about how this was only her duty as brigade chief.

There was something I could do as well. No—something *only* I could do.

I had to get home as fast as I could. There was someone I had to contact.

The only person among my new acquaintances whose phone number I knew.

"Sorry it took me so long to reply, Kyon. I was in the middle of cram school, so my phone was turned off. I got your message. Tomorrow afternoon after school, right? I don't have cram school tomorrow, so yeah, I can probably be at the station's north entrance by 4:30 or so. I'll call the other three too, of course. I'm willing to bet they'll come. I daresay they've been waiting for you to contact me. I can tell you're

pretty mad about something, Kyon, but I'm thinking it would be best if you tried to calm down a little—your anger is probably part of whatever they're planning. I mean, I have no idea. But it's what I'd do if I were in their position. Okay, well, see you tomorrow. Good night, my friend."

CHAPTER 5

α — 8

The next day, Tuesday.

Thanks to the rare fact of my awakening before my alarm clock's ring, I got to take my time climbing Heartbreak Hill up to school. There was nothing particularly novel about the unchanging scenery of the climb, but at the sight of all the new freshmen so seriously making the climb I couldn't help being reminded of myself from a year earlier. I might as well enjoy the climb while I could; in another month I'd be totally sick of it.

I yawned hugely and stopped walking, for no particular reason.

It was strange. The day was starting out totally ordinarily, and yet something felt odd.

I hadn't had any contact with Sasaki since our suspicious encounter—but it had only been the previous Saturday, so there wasn't any rush, and yet that was the source of my worry. Knowing for certain that they would eventually set some kind of trap for me, but not knowing *when*—it was an uncomfortable feeling. Kuyoh Suoh and that nameless time-traveler guy seemed especially likely to try something, even more than Kyoko Tachibana, the friendly kidnapper. When I'd first met them all, the time-traveling jerk seemed particularly reluctant to show his face, which was another thing to worry about. From the way Sasaki was talking, it was clear enough that he was back in this time period. But was he really content not to take action for a while? Who could fathom the minds of time travelers, Asahina the Elder included? Last time he'd looked on as Kyoko Tachibana attempted a kidnapping, so would he have Kuyoh do his dirty work next time?

"Hmph."

I did my best impression of the student council president. Thinking about it wasn't going to get me anywhere. First I had to get to the classroom. Then maybe I'd pay my respects to the brigade chief. School didn't really start until I'd done so, after all. When had this become my lot in life?

Just as I was about to resume my trudge up the hill, someone patted my shoulder.

"Good morning."

It was Koizumi.

Was this the first time I'd run into him on the way to school?

"Hey."

As I returned the greeting, Koizumi pulled alongside me. He had a serene smile on his face, as though he were a crew member on a starship who'd just awoken from cryogenic sleep to find his destination planet right in front of him. "You seem like someone who has something on his mind. Did something happen?"

I always looked like this when I had to face a climb like this first thing in the morning, I said. A better question was why he looked so overwhelmingly pleased. Wasn't he usually the biggest victim of Haruhi's emotional volatility?

"Yes, about that," said the picture-perfect handsome boy, brushing a lock of hair from his face. "Closed space incidents were once frequent, but they've suddenly stopped. This comes as quite a relief to me. It seems Suzumiya is so occupied with the many issues surrounding the recruitment of new freshmen that she's temporarily forgotten to manifest her subconscious stress."

I shook my head helplessly. Haruhi really was a simple girl, I said.

"She may seem simple, but she's quite complex. We can't control her, after all. Suzumiya herself can't control things, and she's the one at the helm—so it's certainly impossible for mere passengers like us. I never would have anticipated so many applicants to join the SOS Brigade."

I felt bad for the eleven new students. After all, it wasn't as if they'd gotten into the school just to become Haruhi's playthings, but they were the perfect diversion for her.

"It would be nice if she remained thusly diverted, but it will last a week at the outside. It will be very interesting to see how many of the students that visited yesterday knock on our door again today."

Did he want to bet? I said. I guessed that maybe six of them would come back. At that rate, they'd all have stopped coming by the end of the week.

"A perfectly valid figure. I'll bet on five or fewer, then."

Sounded good to me. Loser buys the winner a drink.

As we passed through the school's gate and the entrance came into sight, the stuff I'd been thinking about came back to the front of my mind.

"By the way, Koizumi—is it really a good idea to just leave that crowd alone? I mean Kuyoh, Kyoko Tachibana, and that nameless time-traveler guy."

"And Sasaki as well, yes?" Koizumi's smile was as pleasant as a clear day in May. "I'm not sure. From what I am aware of, they have not taken action yet. We haven't witnessed them having a functional coalition, so at the moment careful observation is all we can do."

As we prepared to go our separate ways in front of the shoe lockers, Koizumi pointed in the direction I was heading.

"It's likely the key figure is the time traveler. The Agency will deal with Kyoko Tachibana, and there's nothing wrong with their alien doing some sightseeing on Earth. But if our opponent is from the future, we cannot afford to be careless. Their goals are neither so clear as Kyoko Tachibana's, nor as unfathomable as the alien's—their half-formed nature makes them hard to read. You can probably find them out more quickly than I could."

Standing around talking wasn't my favorite thing to do, so I told Koizumi I'd see him after class, and he hurried to put on his school slippers, ready to preserve his perfect punctuality and attendance record.

I arrived at my own shoe locker and, sweeping aside the hesitation I felt, opened it.

All it contained were my dingy school slippers; there was nothing in the way of letters from the future.

For once I would've been happy to have someone telling me what to do, but Asahina the Elder apparently wasn't feeling generous. I wondered if the first thing she said the next time I saw her would again be "It's been quite a while."

During class that day, Haruhi was so restless that it seemed as though she would float away if she hadn't been tied down. And she wasn't the only one who was so distracted; I was right there with her. I had my bet with Koizumi, after all. So how many of the freshmen that had come by yesterday were crazy enough to return after hearing Haruhi's speechifying?

The one that worried me was the girl in an overlarge uniform, which both drooped from her shoulders and looked as though it had just gotten back from the cleaners. Given her reaction the previous day, she was the only one I figured would come back. There was nothing particularly special about her, save for her smiley-face barrette. Despite her youthful, childish demeanor (which seemed somehow different than Asahina's) she'd stayed totally calm in the den of thieves that was the clubroom. That might have been the only reason I remembered her. What other freshmen had come? I couldn't remember any of their faces, but that only proved that there hadn't been anything particularly notable about any of them.

Our school wasn't especially strict, but there weren't usually many freshmen who broke the uniform code. Occasionally someone would wear garish red socks or make some kind of prohibited alteration to their uniform, but that didn't last long once the student council's conduct enforcement squads got moving. Haruhi wouldn't give the time of day to students who went that far, considering them beneath her contempt, and turning up her nose at anyone who decided to even halfheartedly imitate them.

What Haruhi was on the lookout for wasn't students who were participating in some kind of Batesian mimicry, but rather those whose innate qualities shone through. It was an internal attribute. Asahina seemed like an exception, but even she was no mere mortal, and proved that Haruhi's ability to see a person's true nature bordered on the godlike. I was sure she'd had a look over the entering freshmen once the new school year started, and having failed to find a single one who piqued her interest, that meant there would be no Haruhi abductees this term, which gave me a comfortable, pleasant feeling.

Even if there was someone who could pass the entrance examinations Haruhi was administering, it was clear that they would be 100 percent normal in every way. So essentially they'd be just like me, and a freshman to boot, which meant there'd be a new member on whom I could foist all the menial labor that Haruhi made me do.

And yet the truth was I still wasn't really looking forward to it.

Incidentally, as far as the math quiz went, I nailed it—thanks, I should say, to Haruhi. While it was frustrating to have to ascribe the first time I'd felt confident on a test in quite a while to knowledge received directly from the brigade chief, it was too late to quibble. I just hoped Haruhi took care to avoid suffering the fate of Prometheus's latter years after he taught humans the secrets of fire.

Of course, I'd like to see any god try to chain Haruhi up.

I don't know what strange wind it was that was blowing, but when the chime that ended class hours sounded, Haruhi didn't immediately dash off to the clubroom, instead remaining seated in the classroom. She then headed up to the teacher's lectern to avoid getting in the way of the other students on cleaning duty, and called me over.

What's up? I asked. There wasn't supposed to be a test tomorrow, but did she have information about a pop quiz or something?

"I'm waiting for the new students to assemble in the clubroom," said Haruhi with a grin. "A good performer always shows up late. Or doesn't show up at all. There's something wrong with the idea of me sitting there as freshmen trickle in. So I'll burst in at the last moment, making the kind of grand entrance a brigade chief should make. And in the process, I can fail anyone who shows up later than me."

Had this been her plan all along? Just how late did she plan on showing up, I wanted to know. Was she going to use Pink Floyd's "One of These Days" as her entrance music?

"I don't normally care about that kind of stuff, but that's actually a pretty good idea. Too bad; I should've brought a cassette player from the clubroom."

Good thing I hadn't shot my mouth off earlier during lunch. Just the thought of having to follow Haruhi around lugging a boom box with me was enough to make me cry. I wasn't a pro wrestler's evil manager, and I definitely wasn't going to take orders like an obedient luchador.

I tried to look as tired as I felt, and Haruhi looked up at the clock. "I think being thirty minutes late is about right. Having to wait is part of the test. Although making the brigade chief wait definitely deserves a severe punishment. Are you listening, Kyon? I'm talking about you, you know."

Yeah, I knew—that was why I was constantly getting fined, I told her. Fully half of my allowance went straight into her and Asahina's stomachs.

"That's what you get. Time is money. All it takes is five minutes to look back and speculate over hundreds of years of history, so you're getting off cheap!"

Seemingly having reminded herself of something, Haruhi reached into her bag and produced her world history textbook.

"What are you choosing for your humanities elective? I decided to do world history, so you should do the same. It's better to decide these things early. World history's great, you know. You learn way better words there than in Japanese history. I mean, doesn't 'Treaty of Westphalia' sound way better than 'Laws for the Military Houses?'" she said, continuing on in a manner unbefitting a Japanese citizen. "While we're killing time, I'll go over the stuff we learned last year. Oh c'mon, don't make that face. Since you're a brigade member, I'll even waive my tutoring fee."

Given how crazy she was for thinking someone would want to be subjected to a course they hadn't even asked for, I thought my expression was pretty reasonable. The phrase "with extreme reluctance" comes to mind—and it was indeed with extreme reluctance that I pulled out my history textbook, opened it to the page Haruhi rattled off, and set my mental clock to the Mesopotamian era.

"It's easy; all you have to do is memorize it. And you don't really have to remember the exact years. You'll be doing great if you just get the basic time line in your head so you know what certain historical figures were thinking and doing and when. Take the pyramids, for example—they were either built because ancient people had way too much time on their hands, or because they wanted to leave their descendants with something to attract tourists."

I supposed that no matter what era you were in there were charismatic people who were just going to say and do whatever they wanted without asking the people around them, I said. From the perspective of modern history, there was such a person in front of me at that very moment.

"I'd never build anything that got in the way that much. But now that you mention it, I would like to leave some sign of the SOS Brigade's existence somewhere on the school grounds. I better start thinking about the design. Maybe some kind of stone somewhere. Marble, do you think? Or granite?"

It seemed as if she wanted the SOS Brigade's name to endure through history. Maybe that's what the pyramids were for too. Were the ancient Egyptians so desperate to leave some trace of their existence behind that they went to such efforts to carry and place those great stones? I wondered.

"That's it, Kyon!" Haruhi's eyes sparkled as though facing a particularly bright student. "That kind of thinking is why history's important. It's way better for your brain than just cramming for tests. That's also part of how you remember stuff. You get it, don't you? Thanks to me, of course."

Fine, fine. I admitted she was a good teacher. She'd really helped me out during last year's finals. That little glasses-wearing kid was going to be pretty smart indeed. Smart enough to invent a time machine.

I had no doubt as to whether he was taking good care of that turtle, and that he wouldn't say anything about it to Haruhi. I kind of wanted to know what name he'd given it, but I couldn't really ask Haruhi. Maybe I'd have a chance to ask him directly.

Whether or not it was her pride as brigade chief and concern for her subordinates that motivated Haruhi to help me, the least studious of the SOS Brigade members, in any case she seemed more insistent than Mr. Okabe that I not stray from the path of academic study. This was why an academics-obsessed PE instructor wasn't much use as a homeroom teacher.

Still, doing overtime history study in the classroom as it was being cleaned up—even going to the length of standing and facing the lectern—it was certainly an odd study style. I endured Haruhi's unilateral lecturing, circling proper nouns in the textbook with a red pen, meekly and powerlessly accepting everything I was told as pure fact.

In the face of such a potent opponent's active assault, the poor victim could only let itself be swallowed into the whale's belly along with all that water. Eventually I would be digested in Haruhi's stomach.

At the moment I didn't particularly want to pass through her digestive tract and become part of her body, so I would need to step up and pack some world history knowledge into myself, for my own sake.

"The people and places that show up on the tests are basically fixed, so just memorize these. If you just get so you're able to remember and write down names you have a vague recollection of, you'll do all right on tests. The best thing is to really get so you love history, but I don't expect you to do that. You're pretty much terrible at memorizing anything connected to studying, after all. Maybe you should ask Yuki for help next time. I bet she can recommend some good historical novels."

Did she even have any historical fiction on her shelves? I seemed to remember she at least had some mythology, I told Haruhi.

"That's a good enough place to start. It's natural to want to know more about something you're interested in. Doesn't matter what, having the wisdom to stick your chest out and say proudly 'This is my obsession!' is the important thing. Got that? This is the most important time in your life, because whatever your passions lead you to learn now will be with you for the rest of your life. Somebody said that, long ago. And it'll determine your path in life. Your brain cells are most active in your mid-teens, you know. If you don't explore a bunch of different interests while you can, you'll regret it later."

Haruhi spoke as though she were an adult ten years older, looking back on her past experiences, then launched into her world history lecturing. The facts she was interested in were more trivial than anything covered in class, but they were far more interesting than the conveyor-belt lectures the teachers delivered, and the fact that the contents were so readily carved into my brain was a testament to Haruhi's ability to deliver wisdom to total ignorants.

She had the authority of a commanding officer. The title of brigade chief was no mere show. Her mental acuity was better than that of any prime minister in history. Although I'll admit she wasn't very democratic.

I spent half an hour there at the lectern listening to Haruhi's lecture, and our fearless brigade chief only put down her red pen once she felt that the appointed hour had drawn nigh. Classroom cleanup was long over, and the only people left in the classroom were Haruhi and me.

"That should be enough," Haruhi said, putting the textbook back in her bag. "The freshmen should be in the clubroom now. C'mon, Kyon—time to go make a grand entrance and get a look at the faces of whoever's got enough pluck and guts to show up. My intuition tells me maybe six people will be left. I made yesterday's test pretty easy, so losing five people sounds about right."

If that was true, then Koizumi was going to lose the bet, and I wondered if things would go so well. If half the original lot showing back up was a success, then anything less than that would suggest that there weren't very many eccentrics in this year's freshman class. And from what I saw, the number of freshmen who would come back out with a straight face out of nothing more than a sense of curiosity was close to zero. And if it *was* zero, I could stop worrying about all this stuff and return to my normal, everyday life.

Haruhi shooed me out of the classroom and dragged me to the clubroom, where I saw Nagato listlessly absorbed in a book, Asahina in her school uniform rather than her maid outfit, pouring tea into paper cups, and Koizumi amusing himself with a game of solitaire—

—Along with the out-of-place figures of exactly six students.

Three boys, and three girls.

It was no time to rejoice over having won my bet with Koizumi. Was this for real? If there were really so many students intrepid enough to want to join the SOS Brigade, this was going to be complicated.

In any case, the brigade chief puffed her chest out in satisfaction, then spoke in a voice as strident as any trombone in the brass band club.

"Very well! I underestimated you. I was sure only one in ten would come back, but it seems that's not the case. This year's freshmen are promising indeed! Now, then—" Haruhi tossed her bag at me, heading directly for the brigade chief's desk. "I now proclaim the second phase of the SOS Brigade entrance examination open!" she declared, producing a "Chief Examiner" armband from within her desk.

"It's a written test. No, don't worry about it too much. It's more of a personality test or survey. It won't directly affect your acceptance, but it will be used for reference. I'll be responsible for handling all personal information, so don't worry—it will never be shared with the faculty or student council. Not even the other brigade members."

Haruhi's eyes were like a boiling undersea volcano. She really did act just like a geyser.

"So, Kyon, Koizumi, and Mikuru, you should all leave the room for a bit. Oh, Yuki can stay. Hurry, get to it! Freshmen, sit evenly around the table. Oh, I guess we're short on chairs. Kyon, go get some more."

I had to do as I was told. Dictators are dictators because their orders are always followed without dissent. Haruhi had treated the literature club room as her own private property for nearly a year now. I hoped the student council would push back a little to stop her from putting a sign up proclaiming it hers even after she graduated.

Then Koizumi, Asahina, and I headed into the hallway and stared at the closed door to the clubroom with a variety of expressions. If Nagato was allowed to remain in the room, Haruhi must've decided she wasn't going to get in the way. Did Haruhi just think of Nagato as SOS Brigade furniture?

"I'll go get some water," said Asahina, holding the kettle as though it were a precious thing and trotting off, the pitter-patter of her school shoes fading away down the staircase. I watched her go off on her errand, then to buy a little bit of time I tossed my bag back into the clubroom before heading off to do exactly what I'd done the previous day—namely, asking other clubs to lend us folding chairs. If I'd known I was going to have to do it again, I wouldn't have returned them.

Anyway, I figured I'd hit up the computer club first, but Koizumi raised a light hand. "If you're looking for chairs, I've already collected some. There was quite a bit of time before you and Suzumiya arrived, after all. I made the rounds and collected what I could. They're over there; you didn't seem to notice."

I ignored his teasing tone and calmly looked, and indeed, leaning up against the wall of the old school building were five folded chairs.

"You should've said something about them before we got kicked out of the room, Koizumi. We almost wasted a bunch of time."

Koizumi's face came close alongside mine. "We waited for a full half hour before you showed up. Just what did you and Suzumiya use that time for? I have to admit I'm rather interested."

His face made it seem as though he thought it was an incredibly rare event, like the orbits of Mars and Earth were overlapping for the first time in tens of thousands of years. We didn't do anything. Haruhi never did anything for such superficial reasons.

I coughed. "She seems to think that being able to make other people wait is a form of status. She was purposely waiting for the freshmen to arrive. All I did was go along with her."

"And yet the fraction of times she's been late to our train station rendezvous point is exceedingly low. It's as though she's pouring out her heart just to be able to wait for you. One can't help but imagine that while she might make other people wait, she'll never make *you* wait."

He was sure being stubborn. The one time I'd managed to get there first, the three of them didn't show up. That was the only time. And even then I'd wound up paying the check. I was pretty sure she never planned on spending any money on me.

"I'm not sure you can confidently state that. When it's just the two of you, even Suzumiya won't just make you pay for everything. Worst case, you'll just split the check. I don't know what she was like before, but as far as the current Suzumiya goes, that's the truth. Why don't you just give it a try?"

What did he mean by "try," I wanted to know.

"It's quite simple. Pick a day and give Suzumiya a call. All you'll have to do is ask if she's free on Sunday and if so, if she wants to go out with you. You're welcome to ignore Asahina, Nagato, and myself. Why don't you go somewhere, just the two of you?"

I thought about it for a moment.

"Are you trying to get me to ask Haruhi out on a date? Are you crazy in the head?"

"Goodness, I don't seem to recall saying anything like the word 'date.' But if that's how you feel about it, I'm certainly fine with that. And why not? Why not take the brigade chief to a movie and get to know her better? No, even better—distance yourself from the SOS Brigade entirely and just do something fun as two normal high school students? You might discover something new."

Annoyingly, Koizumi looked at me like a mother bird watching her fledgling about to leave the nest, so naturally I had to put him in his place.

"If I actually did anything like that, it would be a major symptom. Honestly, I'd want you to tell me. Even if the Earth stopped spinning on its axis, I would never do such a thing. If I did, it would mean there was something wrong with me and I just hadn't noticed it yet. If that ever happens, I'm counting on you. You'll have to get me back to normal. I'd want you to do whatever you had to."

"As you wish. Although I must say that would be the exact opposite of what I would wish for..."

Just when Koizumi was getting a nasty smile on his face as though he were going to add something to that—

"Kyon! Do you have the chairs yet or what?!"

Haruhi's raucous voice echoed from inside the clubroom, at which Koizumi and I both slumped like identical twin mimes, then headed for the folding chairs that had been left in the hall.

Just as I was leaving the clubroom entrance, I heard the sound of the printer whirring and spitting out sheets of paper. What was she printing?

*   *   *

I soon found out.

1. Explain the reasoning behind your ambition to join the SOS Brigade.
2. If you are admitted, in what way can you contribute?
3. Of aliens, time travelers, sliders, and espers, which do you think is best?
4. Why?
5. Explain any mysterious phenomena you have experienced.
6. What's your favorite pithy phrase?
7. If you could do anything, what would you do?
8. Final question: Express your enthusiasm.
9. If you can bring along anything really interesting, you get extra credit. Please try to find something.

The printer was nearly out of ink, so it labored mightily to print the above letters onto its copier paper, but that's definitely what they spelled out. Written test, indeed.

Koizumi and I finished setting up the folding chairs, and once the freshmen were all settled and ready, Haruhi passed out the brigade entrance examination.

"The time limit is thirty minutes. There's no limit on length. You can write on the back if you like. If you're caught looking at anybody else's test, you're instantly disqualified, so make sure to use your own head."

She then made a flourish with her pointer.

"Begin!"

Haruhi and Nagato were the only ones allowed to watch the freshmen hastily follow her directions, so once again Koizumi and I were exiled into the hallway. I grabbed an extra copy of the written text that had been printed.

"Put this on the door," said Haruhi, her tone indicating that she would brook no argument, and left me with a piece of paper with KEEP

OUT scribbled on it before slamming the door closed. Helplessly, I tacked the warning up and stood still there in the hallway.

I gave the test I'd picked up to Koizumi. "What kind of exam questions are these, anyway?"

"Indeed." Koizumi gave the paper the once-over and stroked his chin. "This isn't all that different from a real examination. The questions themselves aren't terribly difficult, so answering them should be easy. It won't require much thought to get a good score." He flicked the printout, amused. "This is a cognition test. Suzumiya wants to know how the examinees think and answer questions. Given those answers, she can determine the examinee's capacity for speculation. It's a kind of psychological evaluation. Of course, she probably intends to use this as an entirely serious examination."

It ought to be serious, given how much time she'd spent coming up with the questions.

I took the paper back from Koizumi. "But if you want to kiss up to Haruhi, how would you answer? I'd have no idea. What does a person's favorite proverb tell you about them?"

"I'm rather more interested in question three. Which would be your pick?"

—Of aliens, time travelers, sliders, and espers, which do you think is best?

"That's way too abstract." I turned my face away from Koizumi's pleasant inquiry. "What does 'best' mean? They're all totally different. Now, if you want to know which one is the most useful, that I can answer."

"Oh, and which would that be? I'm fascinated to hear."

Since that depended on the circumstances, I couldn't really be definitive. My usual answer would obviously be Nagato, but Nagato aside, there was no telling what aliens as a group were thinking. Being able to freely manipulate time would let you amass vast wealth, but having access to easily understandable forecasts and insights along with teleportation like Koizumi had seemed as though it would be pretty interesting too. They all had their advantages and drawbacks. The only one I could easily rule out was sliders, who didn't seem particularly convenient in any way.

As I was staring at the Haruhi-made entrance exam to kill time, Asahina returned, carrying the heavy-looking kettle like some kind of spring-water fairy.

"Oh, can we not go back in?"

"Looks that way."

I took the kettle from Asahina's hands, and since standing there holding the heavy thing made me feel like some dope who was being punished, I set it down on the floor by the wall.

"I thought I'd make tea for everyone, but I wonder if there's going to be time to boil water…" Asahina gazed at the clubroom door as she worried about the freshmen. How charming she was! I would've liked to have kept gazing at the beautiful senior who always wanted to make sure there was fresh tea for her friends, but standing guard out there for half an hour was going to be boring, so I tried to figure out what to do.

"Perhaps we should go to the cafeteria. The food line is probably closed, but I can at least treat you to some coffee from the vending machines."

Since Koizumi had primed the pump, both Asahina and I nodded our agreement. That was an awfully reasonable suggestion. The last half of his proposal was particularly attractive.

Koizumi gave me a light wink. "I did lose that bet, after all."

Which was true, now that he mentioned it.

The three of us first headed to the vending machines installed along the outside wall of the cafeteria, and once we'd all obtained drinks in paper cups, we sat at the round tables out on the terrace.

The cherry blossoms that were spring's main event were fading in favor of the deepening green of the season. It occurred to me that a year earlier, I would never have imagined I'd be sitting here with these particular people.

I savored the sweet *au lait* as I drank it.

"Kyon, what kind of entrance examination is she using?" Asahina asked, her hands wrapped around her cup of black tea as though to keep them warm. I gave her the exam sheet I'd folded up and slipped into my pocket.

"It was this thing. Honestly, I have no idea what kind of person she's actually looking for."

"Hmm." Asahina looked intently at the paper, like a grade schooler trying to memorize the sevens column of her multiplication tables. It was adorably heartwarming.

"Still, this is a rare event," said Koizumi, his cup seeming like Meissen porcelain as he inclined it to his lips. "This combination of the three of us, I mean. We should appreciate these thirty uninterrupted minutes we have." He smiled still more charmingly. "Don't you agree?"

The thought had occurred to me. With all the time-travel craziness, I'd spent a lot of time together with Asahina and Nagato, which for various reasons meant Koizumi was relegated to a mere supporting character. There wasn't a lot of opportunity for an esper to play the hero, save the occasional cave cricket–type incident. Although I did have the Agency to thank for their handling of our kidnapping problem.

Just when I thought I'd try to get some kind of consensus from Asahina the time traveler on what kind of things might be happening with Haruhi next, I instead wound up making small talk with Koizumi. Asahina made small sounds of agreement as she took tiny sips of her black tea.

The topics of Haruhi's strange powers, what they might mean for the world, and our enemies' capabilities were not spoken of at all as we chatted about things happening at school—our amusing classmates, jokes our teachers had made, what board games to buy next. This must be what they mean by "small talk."

Asahina smiled happily or nodded her head in interest, and from the outside it would have looked as though she were an ordinary senior enjoying a pleasant chat with some younger students. And given that we were just trying to pass the time, maybe this was the best way to do it.

With a time traveler, or an esper—

No, none of that mattered. We were just fellow club members occupied in some unofficial activities, that was all.

The moment was all the more precious for its ordinariness, I suppose. In that one moment I was free of all obstacles. There was no new time traveler or alien causing me trouble, and while leaving Haruhi alone was always risky, it was only for half an hour.

I thought about it, and I really couldn't imagine the SOS Brigade gaining a sixth member. My mind just couldn't picture another member in addition to Nagato, Koizumi, and Asahina, never mind the idea of losing one of them.

Who was it that had said change was the only constant? I felt as if I wanted to argue the point with them. There were things in the world that never changed. My memories of the past, for example. Even if it wasn't in any photo album, the memory of me, then, with Haruhi and everyone else—that would always remain.

My mind busied itself filing away the image of Asahina's happy smile, and I couldn't help feeling rather sad. In only a year, the seniors would be graduating.

But here and now, this single page of memory would live on within me and Asahina and Koizumi.

That was the way it should be, I mused to myself, sipping my hot *au lait*. It wasn't especially tasty, and so I didn't feel particularly thankful to Koizumi for having treated me.

But it was its own pleasure, in a way.

In that moment, I could still take the time to enjoy the small things in life.

Ten minutes after the prescribed half-hour exam time, we returned to the clubroom to see that the only two people there were a satisfied brigade chief flipping through the completed tests, and a silent Nagato more invisible than any Invisible Man.

"Where'd the freshmen go?" I asked, and Haruhi told me.

"They went home. This is it for the written exam, and regardless of whether they passed or failed I told them all to come back here tomorrow, so I bet the really motivated ones will stay."

"How are you deciding whether they passed or not?"

Haruhi tapped the stack of tests against the desk to even them up. "I have no intention of making a hasty decision just based on this test. I mean, there weren't any 'correct' answers to the questions, but if they came up with interesting things to say, I'll take that into account."

It seemed as though she just wanted to make them take a test. I could accept that going along with the brigade chief's crazy ideas was part of our responsibility as brigade members, but it seemed unfair to make the poor freshmen do it too.

"That's stupid—obviously I'm thinking about this. Taking the test is itself part of the test. I'm testing their endurance. The unmotivated ones just won't come back tomorrow, don't you get it?"

So she was separating the wheat from the chaff. Well, it was a pretty coarse screen, if you asked me.

"I was thinking it would be nice to make tea for everybody," said Asahina, sympathizing with the freshmen. "Have they all left already? That's too bad."

I couldn't help feeling bad for them, having not gotten a second chance to drink Asahina's tea.

I watched Asahina as she set about boiling some water.

"You should be thankful, Kyon—you got into the brigade without having to take any tests." Haruhi sat in her seat and folded her arms. "If you're not careful, you might get passed by an up-and-coming member. If anybody manages to pass the final stage of the exam, they're going to be a person to be reckoned with. Although I'm planning an interview for the last stage."

Haruhi busied herself marking up the tests she'd received with a red pencil.

"Hey, do you want to give the interview a try? Depending on your answers, I'll consider giving you a promotion. It's good practice for job interviews too."

That didn't sound as though it was going to have any practical relevance to any industry I could think of. If Haruhi were the company president and were directly conducting interviews, it wasn't as if normal answers would get you the job. The idea of anyone learning interviewing habits from her crazy brigade interviews, thereby wrecking their own future prospects, was too terrible to consider.

"I'll pass."

"Fine." Haruhi didn't seem the least bit concerned as she happily returned to the tests. Honestly, even I was sort of interested in seeing them.

"Hey, Haruhi, let me see those. I want to see what kind of answers those little freshmen came up with."

"Absolutely not," said Haruhi flatly. "That would be a betrayal of confidence. They contain personal information, so I can't just go flashing them around. I'm the one making the decision, anyway, so there's no point in showing them to you." She glared at me with large, shining eyes. "Curiosity's an especially bad reason. Choosing brigade members is the brigade chief's job."

I slumped. Good grief. If the chief was the sole arbiter of new member selection, then it looked as if she was just going to ignore anything we happened to say. Aside from Nagato and me, who'd essentially been drafted on her whim, Asahina and Koizumi were both Haruhi-designated appointees.

But still, I wondered how many of today's six applicants would reach Haruhi's final stage.

"Hm?" I was watching Asahina from behind as she poured water into the teapot when something occurred to me. Had all six of today's freshmen been in yesterday's group of eleven? One of them might have come for the first time today. There wasn't any guarantee that all of the interested freshmen would come on the same day, so it was possible that the dropout rate was more than fifty percent.

I tried to connect the memories.

Wait—had that girl been here today? The one from yesterday who'd caught my eye—she'd seemed so familiar. If I hadn't been shoved out of the clubroom so quickly, I could've taken the opportunity of the exam process to get a better look at the six faces.

Something bothered me.

Koizumi produced a set of Uno cards and started shuffling them. I didn't have to look twice to know that watching his face as he dealt the cards wasn't going to give me any answers. Even after Asahina finished setting cups of richly fragrant tea in front of each member and the three of us (having nothing better to do) started playing a game, unease weighed heavily on my mind. It felt as if I had thirty seconds left to finish a test, and couldn't figure out a question that should've been obvious—but why?

I gave Nagato a casual glance.

The still-reading literature club member had no reaction, and had not moved a single millimeter from her chair. I had no trouble imagining her exactly this way during the test, still as a bronze statue, but the fact that Nagato was neither moving nor talking meant that nothing was happening. At the very least, none of the new freshmen were from the Heavenly Canopy Dominion, like the embarrassingly named Kuyoh.

"..."

In the space of an eighth-note rest, Nagato turned the page, her finger stopping as though she'd spotted a misprint, then looked up mere millimeters.

With eyes like a stone tablet just wiped clean she gazed at me, then, as though nothing had happened, returned to her book.

That was all it took to set me at ease. So long as Nagato was in the clubroom absorbed in a book, the world wouldn't be thrown into a poisonous mandrake soup of a crisis. Haruhi was absorbed in grading the tests, and Koizumi, Asahina, and I were passing the time by playing a card game.

I had to feel sorry for the poor freshmen who'd come by the SOS Brigade out of random curiosity, but it was nice of them to amuse Haruhi for a while.

If it were possible, it would be nice if three of them returned tomorrow. We'd probably lose a fair number of them given the dropout rate, but it wouldn't be any fun for Haruhi if they all left at once. I hoped they lasted until the weekend.

β — 8

The next day, Tuesday.

You've got to admire the construction of the human brain. Despite finding it terribly difficult to fall asleep, my body was too anxious to let me enjoy a few more minutes of sleep, so thanks to my eyes snapping open before my alarm clock went off, I was able to take my time trudging up the brutal hill to school. But I didn't feel remotely good about any of it, and as I melted into the utterly clichéd scene of freshmen walking to school, my feet took me through the school gates a bit earlier than normal.

At this rate I was only going to feel more depressed. The best course of action would be to unload my sorrows, and the first step in that would be articulating to Haruhi just how un-merry I felt.

When I got to the classroom, Haruhi's seat was empty, and I realized I must have arrived before she did. There were all sorts of things I wanted to say, and the fact that the number of things I could actually tell her was so small had nothing to do with my vocabulary. I knew all too well how Asahina must have felt. How are you supposed to communicate things you can't say with words? Body language? Should I draw a picture?

No to both, I think. Let's just leave it that some things shouldn't be explained. So long as Nagato returns to being a part of our daily lives, everything will be fine. And the sooner that day came, the better, because the longer Nagato was afflicted by her fever, the more suspicious Haruhi would be. Who knows what lengths Haruhi would go to in order to cure Nagato?

For example, it wouldn't surprise me if she reset everything back to the day of our freshman entrance ceremony. I really didn't want to go back to the beginning now that I'd spent so much effort to get this far. I wasn't confident I'd be able to play my cards very well, and considering everything I was rather attached to our current situation. We'd come this far—like hell I was gonna let the whole year go to waste. I'd make sure we would break the tape at the finish line together.

"Oh, so that's it."

I sat down on the hard desk chair and my brain immediately arrived at the answer. I'd realized just why I was so anxious, and felt rather proud of myself for achieving this feat of self-analysis. In short, I was afraid that someone close to me was going to disappear. When I thought back on it, it was obvious. Even if I left out the incident with Haruhi disappearing and the world changing around her, when I'd seen Asahina kidnapped before my very eyes, or when Nagato had missed school, my heart had immediately started hammering. Even if it were just circumstantial evidence, it was seriously convincing.

The same reasoning applied. Just turn time back a year and see what happened. If I had to listen to Haruhi's crazy self-introduction again, I'd say the odds were no better than fifty-fifty that youthful capriciousness would lead me to talk to her, so that encounter leading to actual events was no more than a coincidence, and I could just as easily have wound up without spending any of my time in classroom 1-5 with Haruhi Suzumiya or her old acquaintance Taniguchi, never getting dragged to the literature club room, never meeting Nagato and seeing the glasses disappear from her face, never seeing Asahina kidnapped and returned. Koizumi would never have transferred into North High, and we never would've had a fake island murder mystery or shot that stupid movie, and swept along by ceaseless time, nothing would have happened. There was a possibility I would have sought tranquility and idleness, and moved normally into my second year of high school.

And yet that was only a possibility, and here in the present with the results already in, it was a meaningless eventuality, with a 0 percent chance of happening. Reality was that which did not change no matter how you looked at it.

Don't ask me which I would have preferred. I didn't have time to hesitate over answers that should have been obvious.

So I had to take responsibility. I wasn't going to rely on anyone else to do something that only I could do, and I'd let others do what I couldn't. That's what I'd done so far, and I was going to keep doing it. Even without Koizumi's eloquent explanations, I could reason that much.

When Nagato had fainted last year at Tsuruya's ski villa, Koizumi's capable mind had come into play. This time, though, he had his hands full with other things. If it had been in his power to do something about the irregular extraterrestrial life form Kuyoh, he would've long since done it.

And thanks to the directives the Data Overmind had given Nagato, Haruhi and I were both in a situation that made neither of us very happy. And when it came to people who could do anything about it, once you left Haruhi out there was just me.

I owed Nagato quite a bit so far. If I didn't pay her back now, it would reflect badly on all of humanity. No, I would not help either the knife-wielding maniac Asakura or the mysteriously disappearing and reappearing Kimidori. And neither would my old middle school friend Sasaki, who while eccentric was still the most normal-seeming of all the involved parties. It didn't matter what sweet words they whispered in her ear; I knew Sasaki wouldn't do anything. I'd spent enough time with her to know she was trustworthy. She was odd enough for even Haruhi to say so, and I felt roughly the same way about my old middle school friend. The fact that we were boy and girl had nothing to do with it at all. I had absolutely no biologically derived feelings for her, and I was certain she felt the same about me.

I was glad I'd remembered to mail her a New Year's card. I'm sure we were both looking forward to having a good time at this year's reunion. Sasaki had enough acting ability that she'd be able to make all these problems go away and take us back to our middle school days. On that count I could trust her more than anyone.

Only now did I realize how true it was—Sasaki, you really are a good friend. Good enough that even a decade from now she'd be able to come up to me and say, "Hey, Kyon," which was a rare thing. She was smart enough not to let Kyoko Tachibana or Fujiwara trick her into doing anything; she'd keep her feet firmly planted on the ground.

Kyoko Tachibana was Koizumi's enemy. Fujiwara was Asahina's enemy. Kuyoh was Nagato's enemy. But Sasaki was not my enemy. She was my old friend, my middle school classmate, and nothing else. Kyoko Tachibana, Fujiwara, Kuyoh—you picked the wrong target. The Sasaki I know isn't some meek Earthling easily swayed by sweet words. She's harder to deal with than me, but has more common sense than Haruhi.

Settling that much was enough to restore some measure of calm to my mind, so all that was left to do was wait for Haruhi.

When the first bell rang, she still hadn't arrived. I fixed my eyes on the blackboard, feeling her lack of presence behind me; she was on the verge of being late for class, which was very rare.

The day did not begin when my eyes opened; it began now. My usual routine was to consider the day begun when I turned around to face Haruhi in the seat behind me, and it had been so for quite a while.

And by that schedule, today was shaping up to be the longest day ever.

Hold on, Nagato. We'll do something about your sickness. The one opponent we absolutely have to strike at is definitely Kuyoh Suoh, the supposed platform of the supposed Heavenly Canopy Dominion. We could deal with the time traveler after that.

Just as I was feeling uncharacteristically resolved, the bell indicating the beginning of homeroom period rang, and Haruhi finally appeared in the classroom, cutting it very close—she entered almost exactly the same time that Okabe did. Unlike the teacher, she entered quietly through the classroom's rear door, and also unlike the teacher, her expression was not very lively.

Just as Haruhi was about to reach her seat, she noticed my gaze on her and returned it. Producing a key from the pocket of her uniform, she jingled it around and then quickly put it away. That was enough explanation, but she went ahead and said it aloud anyway.

"I went to go check on Yuki," Haruhi explained in the short break between homeroom and first period. "I thought I'd make her breakfast, so I let myself in."

"How was she?"

"Yuki? She was sleeping. When I peeked into her room, she opened her eyes and looked at me for a second. I guess she felt better after that, because she closed them again and went back to sleep. I didn't want to wake her again, so I made breakfast and headed back out. Her fever didn't seem too bad. I guess getting plenty of rest is still the best thing to do."

"Yeah, I guess."

Haruhi sighed softly. "When I look at Yuki sleeping, I just wanna, like..." She hesitated for a moment, then lowered her voice. "I mean, don't take this the wrong way, but I just want to gather her up and hug her. It feels like if I don't, she'll just disappear. I know that's not true, but still..."

Haruhi propped her head up with her hand. She didn't look uneasy so much as vaguely irritated, and I felt as though I could see what she was feeling so clearly that I felt it a little bit myself. It was almost certainly in my imagination, though. And even if it wasn't, it went without saying that there was no way I was going to give Haruhi a hug.

But whatever the root cause, it was clear that Haruhi and I were of one mind. Koizumi and Asahina too.

A healthy Nagato...something about the phrase is strange, but I didn't want to see her bedridden and weak for any longer. She belonged in the literature club room. She could sleep in there if she wanted, honestly. The place was well enough equipped for it, after

all. The literature club room without Nagato was like a Last Supper scene without Christ.

In any case, there was something I absolutely had to tell Haruhi. It was something that might well have made her eyes bug out of her head, but just as I was about to say it, the biology teacher arrived and interrupted me.

The next ten-minute break between classes seemed as if it would bring a likely opportunity. The single line weighed heavily on my mind in direct proportion to its importance.

Immediately after the class (which I cared nothing for and of which nothing stuck in my head) ended, I turned around to inquire of the views of the brigade chief.

"We need to talk."

"What?" Haruhi's eyebrows shot up, but the eyes that regarded my expression widened only slightly. "Can you ask here? If it's a secret we can go to the roof or the emergency exit stairs."

"Nothing like that. Look, are you going to Nagato's place again tonight?"

"Of course."

"About that—it doesn't look like I can make it. Something else came up. I'm worried about Nagato, but…"

I was inwardly chilled as I wondered what sort of reaction awaited me, but Haruhi's eyebrows and eyes merely resumed their previous levels. "Huh, oh yeah?" She rubbed her chin as she seemed to think something over. "So what is it? Is Shamisen going bald again?"

I gulped. "No, nothing like that. Just a thing I have to take care of. It's kinda…" I stumbled over my words, lacking any sort of ability to make stuff up on the spot.

"Sure, whatever. It's pretty much the same whether you're there or not, and it's no fun for Yuki if everybody keeps making a big deal about it. Mikuru and I can take care of dinner—or just me, if it comes to that." She considered the matter a bit more deeply. "Hmm, yes. I guess that's something to consider too…yeah, definitely."

It seemed I'd pushed a button that had set her on a different track entirely.

"We can't really neglect either one, can we?" murmured Haruhi, having evidently come to some kind of internal conclusion. She nodded firmly and leaned close. "You shouldn't come today. Koizumi either. Mikuru and I will go to Yuki's place—I bet she hasn't been bathing, and having boys around while we're cleaning her up would just be a hassle. Don't worry about it. It's just a little cold, so lots of rest is the best thing for her, anyway."

Haruhi sat back down in her chair, then thought better of it and stood back up. "We'll have to tell Koizumi about this. I feel a little bad leaving responsibility to the lieutenant brigade chief, but this is the right thing to do. I really can't just ignore the situation," said Haruhi cryptically.

She got that smile she gets whenever she thinks of something, and sprinted out of the room. The speed she went from thought to action was right in line with the velocity of a subatomic particle.

I watched her speed away like a bottlenose dolphin cutting through a school of sardines, and sighed, and when my gaze returned to the classroom it fell directly on Taniguchi, who was grinning at me.

"Heya, Kyon. What're you whispering about so seriously with Haruhi, there? Finally gonna start filing jointly, eh? You traitor!"

I had no idea what he was talking about. The only tax I paid was sales tax.

There was no way he could've failed to see my dismissive hand wave as I shooed him off, but he just sniggered like some strange bird.

"You're about the only guy in the world who could go out with Suzumiya for an entire year. You're constantly breaking the world record, easy! Who knows how you could last, eh? Kyon, you've got a real talent with weirdos. I know these things."

His notions were constantly off the mark, I pointed out. Any quiz sheet from any class told the story perfectly well.

"Hey, you're no better! Anyway, academics aren't the only place to show talent."

That was the kind of line that a person with actual talent should have been delivering, I said. You had to have results. When people like us who hadn't accomplished anything yet said stuff like that, it just sounded as if we were detached from reality.

"Maybe." Taniguchi draped his arm over my shoulder, as overfamiliar as ever. "But there are things that're obvious even to me. And you're perfect for Suzumiya. Nothing like with Asahina. Shall we leave it at that? Hmm?"

"Hmm," my foot.

I picked up Taniguchi's hand from my shoulder. "So what about you, huh? Are there any new girls you're gonna make a pass at?"

"All in due time, my friend. There's plenty of time until summer. First comes golden week. I'm gonna pick up a part-time job and see if I can make something happen that way. Nothing ventured, nothing gained!" Taniguchi stretched his other arm idiotically toward the sky.

"Moron." My comeback was entirely appropriate. There wasn't any other word for it. Hadn't he said the same thing last year? And how'd that gone? If my memory was correct, it was a long line of perfect zeros.

But whatever. I was glad to be in the same class with him again, and he hadn't added to my feeling of being a frontline commander surrounded by mechanized infantry, with only a shovel to dig entrenchments. It was hard to explain just how important having a friend like Taniguchi I could have idiotic conversations like this with was for my peace of mind. Words didn't do it justice. He was a friend on my own level. Even if we each regarded the other as the biggest idiot ever to live, that was fine—we were each the only ones who knew just how ridiculous we had been in the past.

And if there was someone who didn't know that, they were either a genius of unprecedented ability, or an organism whose vanity formed such incredible armor they were like unto some giant tortoise.

I found out what Haruhi had said to Koizumi at lunch.

I finished my box lunch and headed for the washroom, when who did I find leaning against the wall waiting for me but the SOS Brigade's lieutenant brigade chief. No sooner did our eyes meet than he started to speak.

"I have two things to report," he said, arms crossed. He stuck two fingers out, eyes as clear as those of a meteorologist reporting a 0 percent chance of precipitation. "The first is good news, and the second is neither good news nor bad."

I told him to start with the second one.

"Suzumiya's ordered me to remain on alert in the clubroom."

I couldn't see the reason Haruhi would have for giving him a sentence like that, I said. Unless he'd gotten involved in a bloody sword fight in some castle somewhere.

Koizumi let the joke slide. "To put it simply, I'm room-sitting. She just wants me to spend a certain amount of time in the clubroom after school. Apparently she doesn't want to leave it unoccupied."

Why not? Neither the original resident, Nagato, nor Haruhi the brigade chief, nor Asahina the maid would be there. The utility value of the room wasn't even worth a single cicada shell.

"Oh my, have you forgotten? The posting that says we're recruiting new members is still up and has yet to be removed."

...I had in fact forgotten that.

"We can't be sure that sharp-eyed students with strange tastes won't consider the SOS Brigade. In fact, Suzumiya is hoping for exactly that. 'If you're not interested, don't come; you'd only drag us down'—something like that. But at the moment, she's not even thinking about that; it seems to be lower on her priority list."

With Nagato the way she was, Haruhi was concerned enough to let herself into the apartment this morning to check on her, so she really wasn't thinking about new brigade members.

"Indeed she was not. Yet she hasn't entirely abandoned the idea that we might yet recruit some freshmen. She's showing excellent leadership qualities as a brigade chief. She's much calmer than you are."

If he was being sarcastic, he needed to be more obvious about it, I said.

"I'm merely stating my impressions, but yes, you're right in your own way. In fact, you might be *too* right—might you be considered self-righteous? Unfortunately, anyone who opposes your beliefs is labeled an enemy or a tool of one. And this is because you feel you're right."

Given that these words were coming from Koizumi's bland smile, I got the sense that I wasn't being complimented.

I glared at Koizumi like a hungry spectacled caiman, which he ignored. He spoke in a smooth, cello-like tone. "I'll move on to the good news. Regarding the closed space and <Celestials> that Haruhi has been creating every night—they have stopped appearing entirely. From our statistical analysis, we feel we can state that they will remain dormant for some time. This is a significant load off my shoulders. Despite the continuing hazard pay, I was constantly sleep-deprived, so this should be treated as welcome progress. At least in my opinion."

Haruhi had started creating closed space again after the day she'd met Sasaki. The fact that they'd stopped was probably because Haruhi had found something she was more worried about than Sasaki.

"Naturally," said Koizumi officiously. "The problem with Nagato. The abnormality of Nagato missing school has focused all of Haruhi's attention."

Maybe it wasn't so bad if <Celestials> rampaged a little more. I couldn't imagine that Haruhi would care more about Sasaki than she did about Nagato.

Koizumi seized the opportunity to agree. "Individually speaking, Haruhi is concerned about Nagato, but she's not irritated. So long as you don't involve yourself with Sasaki any more than is necessary, Haruhi will simply think of her as an old acquaintance of yours. While Nagato has been and will continue to be an important member of the SOS Brigade. Their relative importance is barely worth comparing."

I knew that already. Haruhi was quite fond of Nagato. That had been made perfectly clear last winter on the ski slopes.

I went back through my memories, thinking of the strange western house that had appeared in the blizzard. Haruhi had been more concerned than anyone else at Nagato's collapse. Was that because she considered it her duty as brigade chief? Absurd. That was just the kind of person Haruhi was. She couldn't just leave someone by the wayside, especially not a good friend she'd spent so much time with.

What pulled me out of my retrospection was Koizumi's voice, speaking as though sentimentality was something for other people.

"I didn't plan on this, but there's another thing I personally think I should say. To be perfectly honest, you are being too considerate of Nagato. It's been especially noticeable since winter vacation."

Yeah, and did he have some kinda problem with that? I asked.

"Not at all. Nagato is clearly worthy of that level of trust. I'm sure it's difficult for you to accept that she's fallen into a state of malfunction. But if you worry about her to the exclusion of your surroundings, you're misplacing your priorities."

He better not be implying that Nagato was a minor detail.

"Indeed I am not. Please, think about this. An unknown interaction with another extraterrestrial life form is what's causing Nagato's present condition. Neither the time traveler's nor the esper's groups are involved, and indeed they couldn't do anything even if they wanted to. But this kind of conflict can be manipulated by a third party."

This didn't seem like the kind of conversation we should be having outside the bathroom, but Koizumi smoothly continued.

"Logically, people from the future should have knowledge of the past. So Asahina is not an ordinary time traveler. And that's what makes her unique. It's not clear what her position of ignorance implies, but it's also not impossible to guess. From the perspective of people further in the future than Asahina, she's the perfect decoy for us in the past."

He'd said something like that before.

"Consider this: Given that there must be people who knew in advance that Nagato would be forcibly deactivated, they would be able to move with that timing. She's the SOS Brigade's most powerful asset, and she's won your trust above all others. And you've gained hers. And since you now surely regard Asahina's enemies as your own, that means Nagato does too. What a time traveler least wants to see intervening is a humanoid interface from the Data Overmind, especially Nagato, who happens to be our beloved comrade."

So now that Nagato was out of commission, that time-traveling bastard Fujiwara or whatever his name was…this was his best chance.

But what was he planning? I asked.

"That I do not know." Koizumi gave a hopeful smile. "I was vaguely hoping you would be able to shed some light on that."

Fine, then. It looked as if his hopes rested on my efforts. Fine, then, Koizumi—you just stay in the clubroom and wait. Haruhi and Asahina's job was to nurse Nagato back to health.

And I'd go do my job.

"Finally, this isn't a report so much as it is a low-probability conjecture on my part, but…" Koizumi seemed to hesitate, not sure whether he should continue or not. Noticing his serious face, I jerked my chin up, motioning for him to continue.

"As I said before, <Celestials> have stopped appearing, which is curious. One possible interpretation is that Suzumiya's attention has been diverted—but we may have seriously misunderstood the situation."

So what was that supposed to mean? Those jolly blue giants are just trying to trick us into thinking they've disappeared, when they've actually gone off to train?

"Something like that, yes. I can't rid myself of the suspicion that the <Celestials> have gone off to build up their energy reserves in anticipation of something else they expect to face. This may be no more than ungrounded worry on my part, but it *is* something I'm worried about."

So they were saving up their power? Surely not, I said. I couldn't imagine those glowing blue monsters were capable of that kind of forethought. They weren't in the training montage of some shonen manga, after all.

"Indeed, I may be overthinking the situation. In any case, should the <Celestials> reappear we will also be summoned, so we'll know about it immediately." Koizumi smiled, and brushed his hair aside as though it was his signature pose.

Not wanting to chat in front of the boys' washroom any more than I had to, I took my leave of Koizumi and headed merrily back to my classroom.

And then I realized I'd forgotten my original reason for heading for the washroom, so I turned around and went back. What of it? Go ahead and call me an airhead; I don't mind.

Even someone like me has enough time to go to the bathroom during lunch.

When I didn't have time was after school, when I met up with Sasaki and the rest of her crowd.

The chime rang out over the school PA system, signaling the end of the day's classes—roughly simultaneously with that, Haruhi took her bag and flew out of the classroom. I imagined she was heading for the senior classroom where Asahina was stationed.

I could've walked with Haruhi all the way to Nagato's apartment before I split up with her, but there wasn't any reason for me to. The only thing on Haruhi's mind was the image of a sick, bedridden Nagato.

One could hardly doubt Haruhi's skill at cooking, and I'd personally experienced her fixation on nursing, and she and Asahina made a fetching pair, so I had no qualms leaving Nagato's daily care to the brigade chief. At the very least, Nagato wouldn't go hungry. And the fact that the cause of the problem wasn't within Nagato at all meant the burden of actually solving it fell to me.

So who was I going to have to lean on? Both the Data Overmind and the Heavenly Canopy Dominion were well out of my grasp. I had to rely on Pascal's law. If I applied pressure to one area, that pressure would be transmitted elsewhere.

Now, then—where to poke?

As I walked down the hill from school alone for the first time in quite a while, I tried hard to stay cool and focus my resolve. I couldn't communicate with the alien. Trying to have an honest conversation with the time traveler seemed impossible. That left Kyoko Tachibana, if I could get to her through Sasaki.

I drifted through the groups of students heading home, but my thoughts were on the clubroom. Right about then, Koizumi was probably killing time there, playing his role as doorman. Or maybe he was chatting with a freshman who'd popped in after having seen one of Haruhi's flyers...

That was the place where the brigade members would all eventually meet back up, even if they'd gone their separate ways. Our lieutenant brigade chief had better watch over it. If any new member hopefuls came by, I hoped he'd send them politely on their way. We had to avoid wrecking the lives of the youth, after all.

The path I silently trod seemed long. Subjectively, it felt as if it took twice as long as usual to reach my beloved bicycle, which I mounted, pedaling myself toward the station. I had plenty of time until my meeting with Sasaki, but I just couldn't relax, and hurried myself along for no good reason. Why couldn't I save up time to use later? I couldn't help thinking that if I'd been able to move this block back to this morning, the whole day would've been more meaningful.

Of course, I didn't hold my time as precious as Haruhi did. She was eccentric enough to want to fill every single day with fun memories that would last forever, but unlike her I wasn't so abnormal, and thus killed time by riding aimlessly around the predetermined spot, stopping in front of the station at the scheduled meeting time of four thirty PM. Sorry, city officials—I had to leave my bike there for a little while. But at that hour I doubted any would be coming to check.

I waited for a while, and eventually in the flow of people leaving the station I spotted my former classmate wearing a school uniform that was relatively uncommon in this area, along with a pleasant smile. Something about her smooth stride made me feel better. Something about her appearance gave off the sense of being a pleasant person, and I knew from experience that it was true. Sasaki was about a million times better of a person than I was.

It almost made me feel bad that she considered me a good friend.

"Heya, Kyon. Did you wait?"

Not too long, I said. The minute hand had several minutes to go before it pointed straight down. And one girl who'd levy a fine for early arrival was more than enough.

Sasaki chuckled, her eyes and mouth curving beautifully. "I made you wait, didn't I? Well, the time you spent is equivalent to my subjective time, so let's just call it even."

What was that supposed to mean?

"It's simple. I was actually on a train that arrived here about half an hour ago. School just happened to get out a little early, you see. And while it's nice to arrive a bit early, half an hour would just make me look bad—but it's still not much time. But there's no fun in just waiting for that long, I was thinking, and just then I saw you ride by on your bike. You had this look on your face like you were thinking really hard about something, so instead of calling out I just watched you. I was impressed how long you rode around without getting bored. Do you really enjoy cycling so much?"

How could I hate it? This bike was my beloved partner of many years. And my brain worked better when I was moving around than when I was standing still. The reason my test scores were so bad was probably because I had to crouch over a desk the whole time, I said.

"How practical of you. Although you may be suited to scholarship too. You're quite right. The reason we think of things so easily while bathing or walking is because our brains find mechanical action boring, which gives them the capacity to consider other topics. Bathing, exercising—these are things we're accustomed to. There's no particular need for conscious thought, so they get done without it. That might be a better way to think, as opposed to just racking our brains. It's true that routine work is never fun, but by getting on a train with a set destination, we're free to appreciate the scenery along the way. Depending on the person, there are some who would consider that a waste of time, but I don't think there's much potential for happiness in that kind of time-is-money attitude."

I wasn't going to check her references, but the argument seemed sound.

"Similarly, Kyon, I always make sure to leave an escape route for myself. That way, regardless of how difficult the situation might be, I always know there's something I can do. And that, in turn, lets me be a little adventurous. It's like a horror movie or a roller coaster. They always end. Regardless of their form, nothing in this world lasts forever."

At the moment, I wasn't particularly hoping anything *would* last forever, so I was only half-listening to what Sasaki said. If this conversation went on like this much longer, I was going to lose track of the reason I'd skipped Nagato's apartment to come here.

I looked around and confirmed that there was no sign of Sasaki's minions—with all due respect, I couldn't think of a better term for them. "So where are they?"

"They've already arrived. Half an hour ago I contacted them and told them to wait in the café," she said as though she were saying hi to the neighbor lady, then picked up her light-seeming bag and slung it over her shoulder. She gave me a furtive, upturned glance, and then in a voice like she was heading out to cheer on her school's baseball team from the bleachers during a championship game, said, "Shall we go?"

But of course. That was why I was there.

I was facing a battle on whose outcome rested my own right to exist. This was for world stability. This was to ease Haruhi's subconscious stress level, to reduce the amount of the Agency's covert activity (and also let Koizumi catch up on his sleep), to lower Asahina's internal anguish, and to restore Nagato to health.

It all depended on my ability to smooth-talk—the organization that opposed the Agency and mistakenly revered Sasaki as a god. The Heavenly Blah Blah Dominion, those super-stupid aliens who despite their lack of any clear goal had put Nagato out of commission. That time-traveling clown who'd come all the way back from the future just to snicker at us behind his mask, his face a conceited sneer as though he really was a descendant of the noble Fujiwara lineage.

I was fully aware that this was the decisive battle—my Tennozan, my Red Cliffs, my Sekigahara. It was as though I were in currents of history. If I could've split into two, I could've divided my forces like the Sanada clan did, but unfortunately I possessed but one physical body. I would have to be ready.

I could ask no one for help. Koizumi was keeping watch in the clubroom, Haruhi had returned to Nagato's apartment, and this was no place for Asahina. I hadn't gotten any secret messages from her older self recently, which meant this was a historical event that not even the goddess Asahina the Elder could change. Should Kimidori happen to wander by, or Asakura be revived yet again, I was fully ready to tell them "no need." And I'd repeated it as much as necessary.

This was Earth, and Earth belonged to the Earthlings.

That authority did not rest with any single person. Not with the secretary general of the United Nations, much less with Haruhi.

Haruhi had but one title, and that was brigade chief of the SOS Brigade, an unauthorized student organization at North Prefectural High School—no more and no less.

That was the greatest evidence in a database that hadn't changed since the beginning of her first year of high school. Like Haruhi had once said…

—In times like this, whoever strikes first wins!

The thought struck me afresh. Haruhi, you're amazing. You said you were going to form a brigade before you had any idea what shape it would take. And to think it came together exactly the way you'd envisioned it would—no wonder Koizumi's passively stated thesis that "Suzumiya = God" had managed to transfix me so.

Of course, whether or not I actually believed it was a different matter.

If we were just talking about faith, I'd never given confession or been baptized, but even so I sometimes wanted to cling to the idea of God. Or to the dingy shrine whose offering box I sometimes tossed coins into. Or even the priests who'd come during the Bon festival to chant sutras, even though I had no idea what sect they were from.

If a little worship was all it took to make things work out, that would be the easiest thing in the world, and in the entirety of my experience, doing so had not resulted in even the smallest lessening of my difficulties, so I recommended just saying a prayer in front of a little roadside *kasajizo* Buddha and leaving it at that. On top of the fact that relying on a higher power to realize your hopes was pointless, it wouldn't do you any good either. Better to just pick away at a problem yourself, just like the guy in *Onshu no Kanata ni*. If he can dig through a mountain by hand, then so can I.

Now for the first step. With Nagato sick, it wasn't just Kuyoh I had to worry about; Asakura and Kimidori had shown themselves as well. They were all using the Earth as a stage for some kind of martial arts skit, minus the audience. The only person watching the performance was me, and having seen it I couldn't just stay silent.

It fell to me to resolve all of this peacefully before Haruhi couldn't take it anymore—and this was doubly true given Nagato's illness.

Kyoko Tachibana had claimed that Sasaki was the one who should hold true power.

Fujiwara had said that it didn't matter who had the power.

Kuyoh Suoh had said that what she was interested in was neither me nor Haruhi, but the Data Overmind's interface.

What a mess.

If only I had a little more time. Maybe that fake SOS Brigade had enough time on their hands that they could wander the land as if they thought they were the Crepe Seller of Echigo. Unfortunately, this wasn't the Edo era, it was the Information Age, and the Tokugawa crest didn't carry any authority here.

On top of that, no matter where I looked, it was hard to imagine that any of the non-normal human players were on my side. Asakura and her knife had been revived. Regardless of what Kimidori's leanings were, her only job was to report back to her boss. Kuyoh was a mechanical doll who didn't seem to care much whether I lived or died, and whatever it was that Fujiwara knew about this time period, he couldn't keep that derisive sneer off his face. The only one who seemed to feel any urgency at all was Kyoko Tachibana, and from what I could tell she was the least powerful. About all she seemed capable of doing was getting manipulated by Koizumi's Agency.

So she was the one I'd have to deal with.

To Koizumi: a mysterious being. To Asahina the Elder: a temporal junction. To Nagato: the key to the possibility of self-evolution.

In other words: me. And I myself had no idea what I was. I could admit that I was living a somewhat unusual life for a high schooler, but that didn't mean there was anything particularly special about me. Up until the day Haruhi grabbed me by the collar and slammed the back of my head down onto the desk behind me, I'd been a totally normal, unremarkable, generic student at a prefectural high school.

What did I have to do to get things to turn out the way I wanted them to? In what direction did I need to go? Should I continue along with Haruhi, or would I need to try to foment a change in doctrine?

I wondered if those questions would be settled at the familiar café to which Sasaki and I were headed.

So here are some questions for you. If you've already forged a path for yourself and decided to pursue it, but then discovered an easier parallel path, which do you choose?

Do you stick to your original intentions despite the difficulties, or take the less burdensome path?

It was exactly that choice that I was being confronted with.

There in the same old café, against the wall sat three figures, with three different expressions on their faces.

Though it might have been an act, only Kyoko Tachibana seemed pleasant; Fujiwara was as cynical and derisive as ever, and Kuyoh didn't so much as twitch an eyebrow. I don't know whether the fact that she could sit there as still as a stop-motion puppet despite yesterday's big dust-up with Asakura and Kimidori was because she was just that gutsy, or rather because her psychology simply didn't account for such context.

"Hmph," I sniffed, looking carefully around before I sat down, trying to make sure there were no apron-clad classmates of mine in the area. At the very least, she didn't seem to be within my field of view. If she hadn't turned invisible, maybe she'd been taken off the shift. No, that couldn't be. She had to be there. I was in the middle of yet another unbalanced meeting. There was no way she wouldn't be observing.

Which was fine with me. Give me Kimidori's irrepressible smile over Asakura any day of the week. It was like the difference between a flashbang grenade and a wire-guided antitank missile. To the extent that she never came at me with a deadly weapon, the pleasant senior was far more prudent than my former classmate. I really didn't want to get sucked into another alien battlefield.

"Over here!" said Kyoko Tachibana, waving casually and pointing to the seats across the table from them. "You can sit there. Thank you so much for coming. I appreciate it." And then, to Sasaki, "Thank you, Sasaki, for bringing him along. You have my gratitude."

"Don't need it," said Sasaki as she sat down in the far seat. "Perhaps it's better to say 'we refuse' instead of 'we'll pass.' Even if I hadn't called him, we would have held several meetings with Kyon eventually anyway. Otherwise, our lives would have continued on perfectly parallel tracks. Am I wrong?"

The last question seemed to be aimed at Fujiwara. But that errand boy from the future sniffed, as though mocking me. "That may be. Still, both of you"—he said, sweeping his gaze across my face—"would do well not to think too much of yourselves. This isn't advice—hah. It's a warning. These meetings are a waste of time from my perspective. There's too great a difference in knowledge and understanding between you and me."

I felt curiosity before anger caught up with it. Why was he constantly trying to rile me up so much? What was the point of that? If he wanted to get me on his side, wouldn't a different method be better? Fujiwara's manner was too blunt, too honest. The lack of difference between his thoughts and speech was almost Asahina-like. Were all time travelers like this?

As the question rose up in my mind—

"Now, then, what are you going to do next? What does it feel like to lose your most powerful shield? The alien terminal who'd do whatever you told her is out of commission. So how will you protect yourselves? That's what I want to know. What will happen to the harbor without its seawall now that the typhoon has arrived?"

I was furious at Fujiwara's irritating questions. Did that bastard really want to pick a fight? Because I'd be happy to take him at face value, if he did. Just as I was reflexively loosening my nonexistent gloves in preparation to challenge him to a duel—

"Now, Kyon. Let's sit, first. That sense of justice is very like you, but I can't just sit by and let you get violent. That goes for everyone else here too, by the way. I'm fairly mild-tempered myself—I only get angry about once every two years—but when I do, I scare even myself. The last time I lost my temper was just about two years ago, and I'm getting close to breaking my own record, so I'd like to avoid resetting all my progress."

She had the same mild tone she always did, but I did as Sasaki said.

I had never seen an angry Sasaki—nor a crying or frustrated Sasaki—and I didn't want to. Haruhi and Asahina weren't the only ones who looked their best when they were smiling. Koizumi, on the other hand, could have stood to restrain his smiling a little bit, while Nagato by contrast needed to relax her frozen features. And it was true that getting into a fight with Fujiwara here and now wouldn't do anything to improve her condition, so if I just had to throw down, my target needed to be not the time traveler, but the alien.

Such thoughts occupied my mind as I glared at her.

"—" Kuyoh only stared five meters past me, her gaze totally empty of anything like a challenge. I couldn't help doubting my optic nerve. Kuyoh Suoh was far from harmless to the SOS Brigade. I tried to get hold of myself.

This was her fault.

I stared at Kuyoh as though she were the *Flying Dutchman*. She stood out here in the café—a high school girl in her school uniform with far too much hair. Hell, she would've stood out anywhere.

And yet she seemed insubstantial, like a hologram, like a late-night local TV commercial frozen, as irritating as any mosquito. Nagato was bedridden, and yet Kuyoh was fine and dandy. As far as I was concerned it was a failure of justice. If they were both afflicted, that would've been one thing, but this alien didn't understand the meaning of restraint. I still didn't fully understand what sort of beings the Data Overmind's humanoid interfaces were, but at least Nagato, Asakura, and Kimidori each had things about them that seemed—human.

As far as Nagato goes, I don't think I need to explain more than I already have. Asakura was every bit the normal high school girl, perfectly suited to being class rep, aside from her habit of waving knives around all the time. And while I didn't know very much about Kimidori, she was at least capable of conducting a normal high school life. The two of them did manage to put some effort into pretending to be human.

Kuyoh had none of that. There was no sense whatsoever that she understood what *Homo sapiens* really was. She had less presence than the Invisible Man. It made me wonder if the high school girl form she wore was completely empty inside. It felt less as if she was wearing clothes and more as if her head and limbs were simply growing out of the holes. I was probably the only person that thought so. Not that I cared.

The point is she made me feel uneasy. If her reactions had ever fallen within the domain of the human I could've dealt with that, but she was a human-shaped puppet controlled by an entity that even Nagato couldn't communicate with, and nothing was harder to manage than a person whose motivations you didn't understand. Now that it had come to this, the fact of the matter was that her actions were even harder to predict than Haruhi's.

Whether or not she sensed the hostility I was radiating, Kuyoh slowly fixed her gaze on me like some prehistoric fossil, a Naumann's elephant about to be put into deep freeze. Her fossil-like lips parted slightly.

"—Yesterday...—Thank you—" she said in a voice like a beetle pupa. "—These...—words of gratitude...—" she added.

Totally unprepared to be thanked, I was stunned into silence. Fujiwara was resolutely uninterested, Kyoko Tachibana seemed surprised, and Sasaki had an amused smile, though none of the three said a word. Our awkwardly silent little corner of the café remained so. All I could hear was the classical music playing over the café's speakers, and the coughing murmur of the other customers.

What to do?

Before I had much time to worry about it, Kyoko Tachibana seemed to decide that nothing would come of just sitting there. "So," she said, taking on the role of facilitator. "Kuyoh, did something happen yesterday? Ah well, it doesn't matter. I'll hear about it later."

Kyoko Tachibana sat up straight and regarded me confidently like a well-bred young lady. "Thank you for coming today. I'm sorry to impose, but this meeting is quite necessary, and isn't something that can be put off."

I was the one that had called the meeting, I said. She didn't need to tell me how necessary it was.

"That's true," said Kyoko Tachibana, not hiding the seriousness of her tone. "This would have happened sooner or later. Indeed, from our perspective this is later than we would've liked. We would have liked to move sooner, but we lacked the power necessary to oppose Koizumi and his group," she said, looking to Kuyoh and Fujiwara with a satisfied nod.

"I've finally assembled the power—the power to move the world. You may not regard me as a comrade, but you can cooperate with me and fight by my side nonetheless...can't you?...Right?"

Fujiwara did not answer, and Kuyoh may as well have been submerged in a sea of silence. Kyoko Tachibana sighed and closed her mouth as our waitress appeared, bringing ice water for Sasaki and me.

"Two coffees. Hot," said Sasaki quickly without bothering to consult me. I took a look at the waitress, who looked like a high school student working a part-time job, just to make sure she wasn't Kimidori. She probably thought I was being weird, and her stride on her way back to the counter was notably quickened. Something occurred to me, and I checked the space in front of the three people across the table from me. Kyoko Tachibana and Kuyoh had both ordered parfaits, of all things. It was a completely unremarkable scene, and it made me feel as if I was trying to find the last detail in a "spot the differences" game. Kyoko Tachibana had eaten roughly half of hers, which was now mostly melted, while Kuyoh's was not only untouched, it hadn't melted at all. If it was because of some strange alien trick, I had no idea how that was accomplished. Fujiwara was fingering an empty cup that had contained some kind of liquid at some point, which I likewise didn't want to know about.

Kyoko Tachibana restarted the discussion. "So, then. To put things in order—the reason we've assembled today," she began, smiling at me, "is that through Sasaki, we've heard your proposal.

You have something to say to us, don't you? Let's begin, then. Please, go ahead."

She gestured to me as though passing me a mic, though her hands contained nothing. I didn't play along with the motion.

"This is about Nagato," I said, looking at Kuyoh. "I don't know what it is that you're doing. And you don't have to tell me. What I want is for you to stop it immediately. Stop this ridiculous attack on Nagato. I'm not going to repeat it forever. If you aliens want to fight, go do it on the fringes of the galaxy."

"—Fringes." Kuyoh moved her lips as though she were an ancient insect trapped in amber. "—Of...—galaxy. —Is here. Stars...—in this area...are—sparse..."

She spoke in a voice that was like the fog that rolls out of an opened freezer. Was she making fun of me? If she hated this season that was warm enough to make Shamisen shed his winter coat so much, she should just dive right into the center of the sun, I told her.

"—May do so...—when business concluded."

Well, then let's conclude it. Right here, right now.

"—"

Kuyoh cocked her head slightly and blinked.

It seemed like a signal, somehow.

"Heh." Fujiwara let a snicker escape, and he regarded me disparagingly. "Yes, let us. That is your proposal, after all. Or going by how you spoke to Kuyoh, it's more like an order. You've got enough nerve to pick a fight with an extraterrestrial intelligence, so I feel like I have to praise you for that, even if your bravery is born of ignorance. I'd love to research just what part of your brain makes you support that organic probe—what was her name, Yuki Nagato?—but I'll restrain my curiosity."

Taking advantage of Sasaki's and my quiet, he continued.

"In any case, I see you won't allow that doll of yours to malfunction. If so, that makes things simple. Listen to me now: I can stop the Heavenly Canopy Dominion from interfering with the Data Overmind's terminal."

If a mirror had been placed in front of me, I would've been able to see the expression someone makes when they suspect someone else of fraud.

"You don't believe me? Well, it's the truth, and has been all along. The Heavenly Canopy Dominion is far easier to control than the Data Overmind. They accepted our proposal quite readily. Oh, and by the way—Kyoko Tachibana agreed to this as well. So what I'm about to say is the consensus of the three of us here. To keep things short, let me just explain what we're ordering you to do."

He looked at Kuyoh for a split second, then spoke the following line past crooked and sneering lips.

"Transfer all of Haruhi Suzumiya's power to Sasaki. Agree to this. Your only choice is to say 'yes.'"

Only Kyoko Tachibana nodded her head up and down in agreement. Kuyoh remained still, eyes fixed on the wafer still stuck in her green tea parfait. Fujiwara watched us with his infuriating derision. Then, after a moment—

"Hmm," said Sasaki, touching her index finger to her cheek. "That's what Kyoko proposed the other day, isn't it, Fujiwara? At the time didn't you say you didn't care who had the power? I'd like to know what changed your mind."

"I still don't care who has the power." Fujiwara turned his narrowed eyes aside. "The situation is the same now as it was in the past. But depending upon the values of the person observing the situation, the path to its conclusion differs. Even if the goal is the same, if the path to it is different, the ensuing developments also change. One times one is the same as one divided by one, even though the operations are completely opposite."

"That's just sophistry," shot back Sasaki. "That just sounds like an excuse to me. Or if it's not, this is no more than an act. Isn't it true that it would be inconvenient for you if Suzumiya retains her power? It is. Yes...claiming that you don't care is a lie."

She stroked her chin with her slender fingers and put her thoughts into words.

"I see...it doesn't have to be me. And it could be anyone—but not Suzumiya. Fujiwara, isn't it true that you want to take Suzumiya's mysterious power from her? There must be some reason she can't be allowed to have it. It's just a coincidence that I'm here..." Sasaki's eyes glittered. "...But some things can't be mere coincidence. Like the fact that I was Kyon's friend in the past. So, Mister Time Traveler, how much of this is a fixed event?"

I was speechless at the speed of her thought. Sasaki was about the only person I knew who could face down a time traveler like that. And she wasn't even in some kind of crazy organization the way Koizumi was.

Fujiwara's face was an expressionless mask in that instant, but he soon regained his chilly smile. "Am I supposed to feel chastised? I don't care how quick your wit is, it's still pointless. I'm not lying. I'm simply trying to help things progress smoothly. Isn't that right, Kyoko Tachibana?"

"Er, yes," said the named girl hastily. "That's right, this is at my request. I thought it would be best to cooperate. I begged him."

The silent alien and evil time traveler were apparently manipulating the esper, and it was hard to look at her serious face. I turned back to Fujiwara.

"Now wait a just a second. Kuyoh there is the one responsible for Nagato's condition, right? Are you saying you're the one that put her up to it?"

Fujiwara's eyes made him look like the villain in some old stage play. "That doesn't matter. Whether it was at my behest or she simply took advantage of an opportunity, the result is the same. Whether or not I had anything to do with that opportunity, I knew about it. If it was going to happen, I would have let it, and if it wasn't, I would have brought it about. Fixed past events, when viewed from the future, have nothing more than archaeological value."

What the hell was this guy talking about? Just who was the real mastermind? Was it the time traveler faction that opposed Asahina, the Heavenly Canopy Dominion, or was it Kyoko Tachibana that was pulling the strings?

I was starting to feel as though none of them could be trusted. I wanted at least a few seconds to think it all over, but Fujiwara wasn't going to allow that.

"Just how dense are you? You said it yourself—you want Yuki Nagato to recover. I told you I can do that. I can order Kuyoh here to cease her interference with your precious little puppet."

He certainly did cut to the chase. Fine, then, as the SOS Brigade's representative, I'd take him on. I was sure my question was one Koizumi would want to ask too.

"Why do you have that power, exactly? I thought they were some kind of extra-whatever life-form that communication was impossible with."

Fujiwara dismissed my question. "Let's just say that's classified information."

"You gotta be freaking kidding me."

"If you want to take it that way, sure. I'm doing you a favor to even tell you that much."

Like I was going to believe that.

Just then, Kuyoh's crystalline lips quivered.

"—I will execute order."

She spoke with a suddenness, like a piece of taxidermy come to life.

"—Will cancel interference and seek alternate method...that is also a possible branch." Kuyoh's eyes, like some kind of dark matter, focused on my brow. "—Direct contact impossible. Indirect vocal contact with terminals was noise. Mutual concept transmission overloaded. Waste of energy. Failing to instantly stop equivalent to eternity."

Okay, somebody needed to translate that.

"What she means," Sasaki said, resting her finger beside her eye, "is that Nagato's condition is her fault, but she's determined that the action she's taking is ineffective. If Fujiwara says the word, she'll stop immediately. But that's conditional on transferring Suzumiya's powers to me. And Tachibana, you feel the same way?"

"Yes," said Kyoko Tachibana, narrowing her shoulders. "Though the nuances of my position are a bit different than Fujiwara's. But in the final calculation those differences are—"

"You shut your mouth." Fujiwara's cold words stopped Kyoko Tachibana in her tracks, and her mouth froze, half open. "So that's how it is," he took the opportunity to say. "We want to see the situation change in a way that benefits everyone here. Tachibana wants to worship Sasaki as a god, apparently."

"No, er, that's not exactly—"

Fujiwara ignored Kyoko Tachibana's protest entirely. "Kuyoh's faction wishes to study Haruhi Suzumiya, but that's impossible with the Data Overmind present. She's protected by two or three layers of defense. But there is a way to break through. The important thing is that unknown power. We need only transfer it to a third party."

And who in this world is capable of doing that? I asked.

"Kuyoh will do it," said Fujiwara casually. He then continued with mocking pity, "Hey, c'mon, don't tell me you've forgotten. Her powers have been used by a third party before. Are you telling me you don't remember when her abilities were used to transform the world? It was a short-lived past, but you of all people should remember it."

Nagato—.

What I remembered was Haruhi disappearing from classroom 1-5, and Koizumi along with the rest of Class 9 being gone as well. Tsuruya twisting my arm around, and the pain on my face when Asahina slapped me. And alone in the clubroom, a pale-faced, bespectacled Yuki Nagato, tugging on my sleeve with her fingertips.

It was just about jingle bell season last year when I'd run into a serious problem. I'd discovered some things I never wanted to lose again, as well as others I hoped never to lose in the first place.

These bastards—.

I glared at Fujiwara and Kuyoh by turns.

They were right. Nagato had done it. A mundane human like me could hardly say what these information life-forms were and were not capable of. Both the Data Overmind and the Heavenly Canopy Dominion were far more advanced than mere humans, with abilities to match. My intuition told me that while it might be for a different reason, Kuyoh was no better at lying than Nagato.

"So you're going to hold Nagato hostage, then?" I demanded, my voice resonating with 120 percent pure rage. "If I want to save Nagato, I have to hand over Haruhi's power?"

Did they actually think that such blatant coercion was going to work? Never mind that it was a total cheap shot. They actually thought that if they used Nagato as a shield we'd just obediently follow along with whatever they told us. Naturally I wanted Nagato's mind and body immediately restored to all-green status, but that was a separate matter.

And anyway, Sasaki was my good friend.

"I dunno," said Sasaki, shaking her head twice. "I don't really want that power. I wish you guys would consider my opinion, given that I'm the interested party here."

I should've welcomed this cover-up, but I was so furious that it only served to kindle a bit of doubt in the corner of my mind. Well, no—"doubt" is going too far. It was just a simple question.

I turned to look at her profile—she was no more than moderately troubled. "This is a world-changing superpower we're talking about. Doesn't that move you at all, even for just a moment?"

Sasaki faced me with glittering eyes. A faint smile played about her lips as she spoke. "Kyon, I don't particularly want to change the world. If I do it wrong, I could easily wind up changing myself in the process of changing the world. And I myself wouldn't even realize I'd been changed. Don't you see? I'm of this world; I'm one of the components that makes it up. If I change the world, then whether I like it or not I'm changing myself. In such a case, even though I was the one whose will changed the world, I would never realize that the world I lived in was the result of changes I'd personally made. I'd lose those memories, because I'd change myself along with the world. Which brings me to a dilemma—I would have amazing powers, but I would never be conscious of the effects of those powers."

It was a little hard to understand, I said.

"People have two reactions when they encounter something they don't understand. They deny it, or they try to understand it. Neither is particularly correct. Everyone has their own individual system of values, and they have no obligation to twist them around in the name of understanding—and yet it's impossible for that system to remain unchanged their whole life. People need to ask themselves why it is they can't understand something, and come up with a satisfying answer to that question. If you could simply control the whole world, you'd never encounter anything odd, or have to interpret anything."

Sasaki faced the three people sitting across from us.

"I do not understand you. I don't particularly want to explain why. The answer is within me, and I have no intention of releasing it. If I did, it would be improper, because it's rather embarrassing, you see."

"I don't give a damn what you're thinking," said Fujiwara bitterly. "All you need to do is shut up and nod your head."

"Ah, in the end," said Sasaki, not shutting up, "people can't create anything that lets them exceed their abilities, not even if they're pretending they can. It's just so much smoke and mirrors."

It was like the second stage of a three-stage rocket had been ignited. I felt the load on my back lessen by an order of magnitude.

"Even Sasaki is saying so. And I'm sure as hell not going to accept such an unfair proposal."

I nearly added *you should've come two days ago*, but then I remembered he'd done just that. It wasn't a line you could really use on a time traveler.

"Anyway, even if I did have the power to change the world or whatever, I doubt I'd have many opportunities to use it," said Sasaki, patting my shoulder. "And if I did, it would probably be for stuff like finding change left behind in vending machines. Stuff like that, more or less. I just don't have many complaints with this world. To be frank, I've given up on it. The world with all its contradictions is the result of events that have been accumulating ever since the emergence of humanity. No insignificant amount of individualism can change that. And even if I did have that power, I couldn't begin to guarantee that I'd be able to change the world for the better—I don't have even two bytes' worth of that kind of confidence. I'm not being humble. I don't think anyone else could do it either. Humanity hasn't advanced far enough for that. We're just passengers on spaceship Earth on its voyage through space. But if this spaceship somehow became aware of itself, it might conclude that things would go better if it just ejected this mysterious species of primate into space. So long as humans live as humans, we can't become gods—because gods are an idea created by humans. And in all of recorded history, no gods have ever appeared. They were never there to begin with. I have not the slightest desire to become the manifestation of an abstract concept. Before God died, He was never born. Maybe 'zero' is the very essence of God."

Just as Sasaki finished her speech, Kuyoh started suddenly laughing, as though she'd been scheduled somehow. Her voice was both high and low, and the sound made me think there was something wrong with my ears.

"—Ha—ha ha—ha ha ha—hah...how absurd—hah..."

What the hell was her problem? She could laugh at me, but laughing at Sasaki made my blood boil.

"I'll explain it for you," said Fujiwara in place of the still-laughing Kuyoh. "What is it that makes you so certain you even have the right to choose? We're not listening to your opinion because we think it's useful. Don't get the wrong idea."

The tiny amount of hope that had bloomed within me disappeared.

"I'm not Kuyoh, but it still makes me want to laugh. You think a bit too highly of yourself, I'd say. Do you believe you have the right to decide all this? That you have the right to choose the world's fate?

Hah—who do you think you are? Do you fancy yourself a player in some foolish game? Heh. That's not even good comedy. I feel so sorry for you I can't laugh. Listen to me: No choice has been given to you. You're merely a puppet. I'll admit you move well, but that just makes you a very well-made, easy-to-control puppet. Your actions have nothing to do with your own volition."

Struck by comprehension of the meaning of his words, I felt a chill run up my spine.

Kuyoh was still laughing.

The thought occurred to me once again. Just as I'd realized when Haruhi had disappeared—Nagato was full of humanity.

But these things—.

They didn't care about us—about humans.

Kuyoh didn't, and I was sure Asakura and Kimidori didn't either. That was why they all wanted to hear my opinions. No matter what I said, they could smash it with ease. That's all I was to them. Kuyoh's smile made her look like a girl who'd been given a new toy. But they all shared the resplendent innocence of a child who crushes an ant with her foot just because it's there.

And as for my good and faithful friend Sasaki—her brow darkened.

"Hearing that, do you really expect me to cooperate? Such things will only have the opposite effect. I've been friends with Kyon far longer than I've known any of you."

"Your preference is unimportant to me. How many times are you going to make me say it?" Fujiwara snickered again.

"Ah." Kyoko Tachibana shrank even more. "Everything is spoiled now. This is terrible." She sighed, and I suppose the fact that she avoided appearing obviously depressed was commendable. Unsurprisingly, she looked at me like a missionary about to deliver her message.

"Please, just think about it. I know you care about Suzumiya and the SOS Brigade a lot, but try to think about it this way—so long as Suzumiya has her powers, Nagato's condition will continue to be poor, and you'll still be getting constantly sucked into strange events."

What was she trying to say?

"Even if Suzumiya loses her power, it's not as though she'll become an ordinary person and break up the SOS Brigade, right? Nothing will change. Koizumi will still be a representative of the Agency, Nagato will still be an alien, and Asahina will still be from the future. But you won't have to worry about Suzumiya's actions. Everyone will still get along as they always have, and you'll be able to have fun with your brigade chief just like usual."

We'd barely qualify as even an interest group anymore, I said.

"Exactly. That's what I wanted to say. Don't you think that would be nice? And if you still wanted to experience the kinds of mysterious events you've endured thus far, you have usefulness. Kuyoh is an alien, and Fujiwara is a time traveler. And although I don't really want to admit to being an esper, I suppose it's true. All you have to do is think of them as extracurricular activities with Sasaki. I'm sure all sorts of things could happen."

I was dumbstruck. She was inviting us to organize a second SOS Brigade—to remove Haruhi from her place as the spirit of the SOS Brigade, and install Sasaki as the leader of the newly reborn brigade...

"Also," said Kyoko Tachibana, "I'd like to lighten the heavy burden poor Koizumi's had to shoulder for so long."

"Huh?" What did she care about Koizumi's burden?

"I'm sure he'd be quite grateful. I mean," said Kyoko Tachibana as though it were the most obvious thing in the world, "didn't you know? Koizumi created the Agency from the ground up. He's been the leader from the very beginning. He's the number-one guy. He may not see eye-to-eye with me, but I can't help but respect him."

"—"

Her words placed a considerable load on my mental faculties, but I remained mutely expressionless. For that reason, I didn't want to say anything. I didn't know how much of what she was saying was true, and she might have simply believed it to be true. I didn't know how much truth might have been hiding in the many long-winded explanations I'd heard from Koizumi so far, and the same was now true for Kyoko Tachibana. Trying to decide which I trusted was just laughable. Still, there was no reason for her to just make something like this up—but wait, maybe there was. If she was just trying to get me confused, this was certainly an obvious way to do it. And yet her face was tinged with what looked like simple, honest respect.

...

I give up. It was time to hit the emergency shutdown on this line of thinking. At the moment, it didn't matter what the organizational structure of Koizumi's Agency was.

Fujiwara snickered his nasty snicker again. "Let me tell you something else you may find interesting. Special treatment, let's say. This is information you could only get here and now, in this precise location. Whatever could that be, you ask? I'll tell you. An explanation of something you've been totally ignorant of until now—the TPDD."

Anyone who launches into bizarre backstory explanations without having been asked can't be a very worthwhile person. Fujiwara was a perfect example, I was sure.

"There's a bit of a problem with the way Asahina and I travel through time. Because of the method we use, it's impossible to avoid penetrating the time plane. In other words, we travel by poking holes in time. Don't worry; a single one is too small to cause any real changes. It's easy to fix. Of course, the lengthier the time jump becomes, the more numerous the damages to the time plane are. Also, the more a particular point in time is used as a destination, the more holes there are. Do you understand so far?"

I wanted to plug my ears. I didn't care if he wanted to tell me, but he didn't have to tell Sasaki all these secrets. If someone was going to find themselves drawn and quartered by this stuff, I wanted it to be me.

"The point is that use of the TPDD is accompanied by the risk of destroying existing time. The holes must be filled. It's like how a neglected leak in a roof can lead to the house's frame rotting. The consequences can echo into the future. The main duty of temporal field agents is to repair those distortions. Mikuru Asahina is an exception. She doesn't know it herself, but she's been given a special mission. Heh, poor girl. It's such a carefully guarded secret that even she wasn't told of it."

Fujiwara's words came to a stop. But just as I was sure he was done with his speech—

"For example, what if all of what I just told you was actually information that you were never supposed to have? It would mean I'd just changed your personal history. Shall we make this even more interesting?"

If it got any more interesting, there was a real chance I would die laughing.

"Now that you've heard me, you can't help being influenced by what I've said. That is my advantage over you poor people in the past." Fujiwara's tone finally improved. "You just think about that. I'll decide what to do once I see whether your primitive brain comes up with any answers. If you manage to change what's already been established, I might actually have some fun."

Just when I thought he was finally done, he kept going.

"I'll be waiting. I'll say that you should remember well what you've heard at this meeting today. Although it doesn't much matter if you forget. I'll fulfill my mission either way. Whether Haruhi Suzumiya continues along the path to her destruction, or is rendered harmless—that much you're free to choose."

I wanted to ask him whether he knew the day and time when I'd give him my answer. He should, since he was a time traveler. This guy wasn't like Asahina. I wondered how long Fujiwara would stick to the script. Was there any room to escape it? I saw Asahina's face in my mind. The maid version and the young teacher version flashed in my head like a pedestrian crossing signal.

"Why are you giving me that time?" It was a pretty reasonable question, coming from me.

"Would you believe me if I told you it was a fixed event? You don't have to. Anyway, happy hour's over. No more freebies." Fujiwara adroitly uncrossed his legs and stood. "It's the height of idiocy to be constrained by time, but if the flow has already been set, there is nothing to be done about it. But swimming against the flow is possible—just ask any ancient deep-sea fish left behind by the march of evolution."

After leaving us with that final afterthought, he turned around and left the table.

I watched his tall form head for the door; he hadn't left behind any money at all. As his miasma lingered in my nostrils, Kyoko Tachibana casually picked up the receipt.

"And if you'll excuse me, I must get going too. You need time to think, don't you? Though I don't recommend you think too much…"

Kyoko Tachibana's slim frame seemed tired, perhaps thanks to the toxic miasma Fujiwara had given off. I couldn't help feeling some sympathy for her plight—having to deal with him would take a toll on anyone.

"I'll want to confer with Sasaki. Sasaki, I'll call you. Regardless of how this turns out, I'd like us to remain friends."

"That would be nice," said Sasaki. The corner of her mouth quirked up. "I'd very much like for us to simply be friends."

Kyoko Tachibana did not answer, only sighing as her gaze went worriedly to Kuyoh (who sat there like a very polite doll) before heading for the register. Once she settled up the bill, she gave us a wave and left the café, while Kuyoh remained motionless.

It was only after I finished drinking my entire glass of water that I realized the two hot coffees that Sasaki had ordered for us had never arrived.

Despite all this, progress did not seem very likely.

Once the waitress (who, thankfully, was not Kimidori) brought our coffee, I added quite a bit of cream and sugar to it, which didn't seem to lessen the bitterness at all. Right about when I finished my cup, something occurred to me as I stared at the creepily motionless

Kuyoh, who was eerier than an abandoned doll found in some countryside attic.

Why wasn't she moving? Fujiwara had disappeared, Kyoko Tachibana had left; so was the fact that she was still sitting there staring at us some kind of alien signal that she had something yet to say?

Trying to interpret alien nonverbal communication was totally beyond me.

As I watched Kuyoh, Sasaki set down her empty cup, a smile appearing on her face. "Kyon, we should get going. I'm not Fujiwara, but what we need now is time to deliberate. It was rushed and unpleasant as meetings go, but I'm not ready to call it pointless. Going by how he was talking, there's still a bit of room left."

I hoped so, I said, but my problem was that I didn't know what to deliberate.

"Good point. It seems we don't have the ability to choose, so I have no idea how to make them give up. But there should be something we can do."

This was not a fun situation. Give Haruhi's god powers to Sasaki? It was a question of choosing between a difficult, stubborn god with no self-awareness, or a reasonable god with full knowledge of her own powers. If someone asked me which I thought was better, I'd have to admit it seemed as if Sasaki would be.

And yet.

It just didn't sit right with me.

How can I explain it? I didn't want Sasaki to have these bizarre godlike powers. I wanted my normal friend to stay normal. Haruhi was already Haruhi, so what did it matter? The gods of mythology were always being selfish and unreasonable. Compared with them, ours wasn't so bad—at least we could talk to her. You didn't see shrines changing which deity they were dedicated to—but wait, what was I thinking? Haruhi already had one defense attorney, Koizumi, so she didn't need me. I must've been more disturbed by all of this than I'd realized.

But of course I was. Asakura back, Kimidori observing, and now that time traveler had managed to join up with Kuyoh just to bully us—this stuff had been going on since last night and on into today, and I wasn't born with enough of the Buddha essence to keep a cool head with all of that. I still had a ways to go until reaching enlightenment.

"Also, Kyon. Don't you have someone besides me you can talk to? To be honest, I have no idea what I should do. If we can get someone to tell us what's going to happen, that would be very welcome."

The first person I thought of was Itsuki Koizumi and his above-average face. There was nobody else. The bedridden, horizontal Nagato was out of the question. Asahina the Elder seemed fairly reliable, but so far she had not shown her face. Was this event outside the purview of her fixed events? If so, things weren't going to work out the way they had on that Tanabata. In which case, game over.

"Kuyoh, do you want to leave with us? Or do you want to finish your parfait? Tachibana paid the bill already, so you can take your time."

The dark form of the enemy alien did not answer or even move a muscle, her eyes affixed on empty air.

"Are you awake, Kuyoh?" Sasaki waved her hand in front of Kuyoh's nose.

"—I am not asleep," she said as though fighting off intense sleepiness.

I couldn't help letting irritation slip into my tone. "The last part. Were you listening?"

"—Comprehension complete. Execution concluded."

What did that mean? It would be nice if she meant she had immediately canceled her assault on Nagato.

At Sasaki's urging I left the table. I was a little worried about leaving that strange nonhuman behind by herself, but my worries were unfounded. Surprisingly, Kuyoh also stood up, and for some reason followed us out. I assumed she would quickly vanish, but she held her position behind me, following a short distance back.

Once Sasaki and I left the café, she kept following us, which was enough to make me rather nervous. On top of that, the sky was mostly dark.

"Is there something you want to say?" Sasaki looked back and saved me the trouble of saying it. But the alien, apparently ignorant of manners, did not answer, her eyes seeming to stare off into the future. I got the sense that she had no interest in humanity, or that our wavelengths were just incompatible. I'd say her personality was unreadable, but I honestly wasn't sure whether or not she even *had* a personality. There didn't seem to be any connection between the version of her that had smiled during yesterday's battle with Asakura, and this version. Did she have multiple personalities?

I was so focused on what was going on behind me that I didn't notice what was up ahead. My own fault.

"Hey, Kyon."

When the familiar voice from up ahead hit my eardrums, I nearly tripped on the perfectly flat asphalt.

Sasaki stopped and I followed suit. Kuyoh did likewise.

"Man, it's weird running into you here." It was none other than my classmate Kunikida, wearing his uniform and carrying his bag, obviously on his way home from school.

Kunikida was not looking at me. He was looking at the person next to me, my old middle school pal.

"It's been quite a while, Sasaki," he said.

"Has it?" Sasaki chuckled throatily, looking Kunikida over as she spoke. "I feel like I saw you at the national mock exams, but maybe that was just a lookalike?"

Kunikida smiled softly. I think it was the first time I'd ever seen him smile like that. "So you did notice me. I was sure you'd notice the fact that I noticed you."

"That's true. I'm hypersensitive to the gazes of others," said Sasaki in a businesslike tone. "Normally I don't get very much attention, so when I do the pain receptors on my face go crazy."

"You never change, do you?" Kunikida nodded as though relieved, when from the side a hand reached out and patted him on the shoulder, accompanied by a grinning face that would've made anyone think *Why did I have to run into you, of all people.*

"Kyon, you cunning son of a—! I just can't turn my back on you. So this is the girl, eh? Kyon's mysterious former you-know-what."

... Taniguchi. I really had no desire to know why he was wandering around with Kunikida in front of the station like this, but all of that aside, I was begging him—please, just go home. With three rocket boosters strapped to his back, if possible. Lift off! Heck, if he'd be willing to go into orbit, I'd get the astronomy club to help with the calculations, I said.

"Aw, don't be like that, Kyon. Why not make the most of this coincidental meeting?" Taniguchi grinned lazily, his gaze flicking back and forth between me and Sasaki. "Seriously, look at this guy. He's already surrounded by so many babes, and yet it's not enough? C'mon!"

I knew perfectly well what he was trying to say, which made me hate myself a little bit. Just as I was getting ready to assume a crouch in preparation for a high-speed sprint escape, Taniguchi finally calmed down.

"So are you gonna introduce me? I'm your pal, aren't I? Just say what's on your mind."

"This is Sasaki. We went to the same middle school."

Although it wasn't as if he couldn't stand to watch it any longer, Kunikida took the baton from me anyway. "Sasaki, this is Taniguchi. We've been Kyon's classmates since our freshman year."

It was a textbook introduction.

"Nice to meet you," said Sasaki, bowing smoothly. "You seem like fine friends. Though it doesn't look like Kyon causes you too much trouble."

Ignoring her candid observation entirely, Taniguchi flashed his white teeth at me and pressed his attack. "Still, man, I gotta give you credit—you've got an eye for looks. Must be nice. Can't imagine you have any complaints about your life. Kinda pisses me off, really... Kyon...K-Kyo—?!"

What was his problem? Was that his impression of the call of some tropical bird? Was this kind of teasing popular now?

Half–fed up with Taniguchi, I was considering staring him to death with my patented thousand-yard stare, but—what was this? Taniguchi wasn't looking at me. Nor was he looking at Sasaki.

"...Wha?!"

Taniguchi jumped back, and froze in place awkwardly as though halfway through a stick-up. His eyes were wide in surprise, his expression stiff with something like terror. I didn't have to guess what it was that was inspiring Taniguchi's face to look even stupider than it usually did. My beloved classmate's gaze was taking in the sleepy catlike face of the person standing behind us—Kuyoh Suoh.

So far normal people had completely ignored her, and even I forgot about her existence occasionally. So why could Taniguchi see her?

"—"

Now this was even more surprising. Kuyoh had reacted to Taniguchi. The school uniform–clad girl raised her left arm, turning her hand to reveal her pale wrist. I realized for the first time that around it was fastened a strangely stylish watch. Even more shockingly, it was cute, and analog.

"—I thank you. I—...will not return it."

Huh?

"Aw, it's fine. It wasn't expensive, so if you don't like it you can just pawn it or throw it away. I mean, please do."

Taniguchi and Kuyoh were having an actual conversation. Although Taniguchi was sweating way out of proportion to the season, his arms and legs fidgeting weirdly in a suspicious way that would catch the attention of any officer who happened to be on patrol. And yet—this was some kind of miracle.

"He said he sent her a Christmas present."

Hearing Kunikida's explanation did nothing to dispel my astonishment. On the contrary, it doubled. A watch? Kuyoh thanking him? Christmas? What the hell was going on here? Was I dreaming?

After casually tossing me and my surprise-dislocated jaw into a lake of question marks, Kunikida turned his attention to Sasaki.

"Can I ask you one thing? What're you doing with Kyon, after all this time?"

After all this time? That was full of strange implications...but no, this was hardly the time for that. Taniguchi and Kuyoh were far stranger than Sasaki and I.

But Sasaki seemed to ascribe significant weight to Kunikida's question. "It's a long story, and I don't have any intention of shortening it. When you've got time, ask Kyon about it."

"I don't think I care quite *that* much, so I'll pass. Still, it's a small world indeed, meeting both you and Kuyoh at the same time."

"You know her too, Kunikida? I would never have guessed. I'm sure I'm more surprised than you are. How did you meet Kuyoh?"

I was rather interested in knowing that myself.

"Kuyoh...you mean, Suoh? It was over winter vacation. This guy here—wait, where'd he go...?"

Taniguchi, eh? He seemed to have done his best impression of the failed hit-and-run strategy of General Takeda during the Battles of Kawanakajima. He'd run off. I had to admit, the speed of his escape was impressive.

"Anyway, Taniguchi, who was here up until a moment ago, introduced me to her. He said she was his girlfriend. Isn't that right, Suoh?"

"—Yes," answered Kuyoh, though it was hard to distinguish from a breath or a sigh. "—My memory supports your accuracy."

"And you broke up about a month ago?"

"—Confirmed."

Ugh. What the hell.

So the girlfriend Taniguchi had mentioned last December was Kuyoh? The one he'd split up with just before Valentine's Day? That had been Kuyoh all along? Now wait just a second.

Stunned, I spoke. "Which means, before Naga—...I mean, before that thing happened to her, you were already here on Ear—I mean, you were already here?"

"—I was. I cannot find any problems with that sequence of events."

I didn't know whether I was angry or just flabbergasted.

"...Why were you dating Taniguchi?"

"—It was a mistake," she answered readily.

"What?"

"That's what Taniguchi said she said. That's what she told him when they broke up," said Kunikida simply. "When did you meet Suoh, Kyon? Did you already know her?"

Nope, I'd just met her.

At a loss for words, I looked sideways, and saw Sasaki chuckling.

"I met Kuyoh just recently. As luck would have it, Kyon met her through me."

"And she's Taniguchi's ex on top of all that. What an amazing coincidence. I wonder what the percentage would be?" said Kunikida, cocking his neck curiously.

"Are you talking about probability theory? If we assume that synchronicity happens constantly, then any improbable event, no matter how hard to believe it might be, can be described in terms of its probability. But in this case..." Sasaki smiled mischievously, tilting her head slightly. "...Perhaps we should ascribe it to an omnipotent, omniscient deity in the sky."

"That doesn't really sound like the kind of thing you'd say, Sasaki."

I had to agree. Wasn't God on vacation somewhere?

Kunikida shrugged, at a loss. "Kyon, Sasaki is saying that all of us meeting here at this moment is a coincidence—she's just being really roundabout, is all. It's nothing to get worked up about."

What part of that *wasn't* worth getting worked up about? One or two events like this could be written off as coincidence, but three or four made me suspect that someone had a rope around my neck and was pulling me around. It was a pain unique to me, given how much stuff I'd been dragged through. Even though I knew that seriously agonizing over it was a waste of time.

Somehow Kunikida seemed to notice that I was whirling helplessly in a vortex of silence. "There's a book I've ordered from the bookstore in front of the station. I came to pick it up after school. Taniguchi was free, so he came along. And since we were already here, we thought we'd come by the café." He looked back in the direction of the escaped Taniguchi, then shook his head. "But he's gone now, so…"

Maybe this whole thing should be called Taniguchi the Coward's Magnificent Retreat.

"Anyway, I'd feel bad if I messed up your plans, so I'll be heading home."

Just as Kunikida turned his back to go, Sasaki spoke up. "Kunikida, should we meet again somewhere; please don't hesitate to speak up. Reminiscing about the shared experiences of the past is one of life's great pleasures, after all."

"How like you to say that."

I couldn't begin to keep up when clever people talked, each one of them planning three moves ahead.

"Yup. So long," said Kunikida by way of parting words, evidently satisfied with his discourse with Sasaki, and without asking anything further about Kuyoh—he didn't seem to think much of her one way or another.

I watched his form shrink as he receded into the distance, then decided to stop worrying about the Kunikida/Taniguchi combo. I doubted either of them would say anything about the encounter to Haruhi. Kuyoh had apparently traumatized Taniguchi, and Kunikida was the kind of guy who understood the nuances of these situations.

"Kuyoh." I turned to face the mop-topped girl who stood there motionless, like a chick that had fallen from its next. "You had already come to Earth last December, right? And then you got close to Taniguchi." I had a mountain of questions I wanted to ask, but this was the first thing I wanted to get straight. "Did you approach Taniguchi because you wanted to get close to Haruhi and me?"

"It was a mistake—" She sounded like a talking scrub brush as she delivered the short reply.

"*What* was a mistake?"

"—Mistook him for you."

"You..."

So Kuyoh had mistaken Taniguchi for me, and started dating him? Hey, hey, c'mon, why did I have to be confused with Taniguchi, of all people? That was a hell of a way to destroy a guy's confidence in himself.

"It seems that data was confused somewhere. The possibility of jamming by some party also..." said Kuyoh softly, "...exists."

At the very least, it didn't seem as if Nagato would've had a chance to do that.

"When Nagato screwed up the world, what happened to you?"

"I was not changed." Kuyoh lifted her head up. There was a bit more color in her lips, which spoke, whose movement made it seem as though I were looking at a frame-by-frame playback. "You all were in illusory space. It made us feel a novel surprise. Overlapping worlds. A world that had formerly existed, but currently did not. Exclusive action. Localized alterations. Fascinating."

What the hell was she talking about? And why had her tone changed again? It was as though she really *did* have multiple personalities. I remembered her smile from the previous day.

"—Today has no tomorrow—yesterday has no today—tomorrow has no yesterday—it was there."

Uh, what?

Sasaki raised an eyebrow. "She sounds more like a fanatic than a lunatic. I would've liked to hear more about such things back in the café, not just standing here. And maybe with a notebook handy." Sasaki glanced at Kuyoh's wrist and continued, teasingly. "In any case, if you're still wearing the watch he gave you, you must still have a bit of lingering affection for that interesting fellow."

Kuyoh's gaze fell to the analog watch (surely bought on discount) like drops of india ink.

"—I said...I wanted it."

I was getting tired of being stunned.

"—Time is not a unidirectional, irreversible phenomenon. To engage in biological activities on this planet's surface it is necessary to stabilize pseudo-objective time flow."

Hence the watch? But it was just made of tiny springs and gears. A watch doesn't dictate the flow of time. It's just a convenient way of numbering the progression of people's activity in the day, I said.

"—Time is randomly generated. It is not continuous."

I rubbed my eyes. Just what was this alien talking about?

Sasaki's innate curiosity had evidently been aroused. "So how do you interpret past and future, then, Kuyoh? Or are you saying that Akashic Records exist?"

"—Time is finite."

"So what does that mean? Show me proof by infinite descent. How much time is there between one second and the next?"

"None. However, there is no danger in thinking otherwise."

This seemed to be a debate Sasaki could really get her teeth into.

"Hmm, so what about this—if there are parallel worlds, can't they be infinite in number? As Hugh Everett would have said."

"—Nothing unobservable can exist."

"Really?" Sasaki had the look of a budding young scientist who'd just witnessed a new phenomenon.

"—Already recorded—questions...pointless."

"I see." Sasaki stroked her chin, seemingly understanding all of this. I couldn't stop myself from shooting my mouth off.

"'You see'?! Why don't you finish digesting what you 'see' so you can explain it to me, huh? Make sure a complete idiot could understand."

"Yeah, hmm. Listen, Kyon, that's impossible. All I've understood is that Kuyoh and whoever made her are fundamentally different from us humans, that they possess a totally different way of thinking. So I believe that true understanding is impossible, no matter what."

So no matter what happens, things would be the same? I asked.

"Not necessarily. Discovering that language is a poor method of communication of our intentions is a big step forward. Here and now, her words are basically noise. But what if a more effective translation device could be invented? Human ingenuity may make such a device possible someday. Humans have already accomplished many feats that pessimists would have called impossible."

Someday—. Someday far in the future. Maybe in Fujiwara's time. In a time when boats float using something other than simple buoyancy.

"Hey, Kuyoh—" My voice never reached its target, and merely scattered into empty space.

Kuyoh's abnormally dark form had disappeared as though she'd vanished into thin air. As though she'd fallen into some invisible crack in the ground.

I wasn't particularly impressed, since I was well aware that Nagato, Asakura, and Kimidori were capable of similar feats. But somehow Sasaki wasn't much moved either, and she regarded the space Kuyoh had once occupied with a pleasant smile.

"That's an alien for you, I guess," she said, as though she were looking at nothing more remarkable than an airplane's contrail.

C'mon, was that really her only reaction? I asked.

"Another word, then," said Sasaki, shifting her glance. "I'm fascinated to see what she'll do next," she said.

My graceful former classmate's face was not the least bit perturbed. I'd never seen anything like it. It brought to me a calm I couldn't explain.

"Kyon, you needn't overestimate her. Just as we can't understand Kuyoh, it's hard to imagine that she can accurately understand us. We may be sad, limited creatures, bound by gravity, but we still have enough value to draw her to Earth. And it's difficult to be certain that we won't evolve further, physically and psychologically. As for me...I suppose I'm counting on the blind watchmaker."

I didn't really understand what she was talking about, but she seemed to be trying to offer some encouragement.

"See you later," Sasaki said to me, her eyes reflecting the streetlights' radiance there amid the hustle and bustle of the station. "I'll think things over. The answers to all of this might have fallen by the wayside somewhere. I wouldn't be too optimistic, but if we don't at least do what we can, we won't be able to avoid accusations of irresponsibility. Fear is often greater than the danger, after all. Farewell for now, Kyon."

I gazed at Sasaki as she gave a casual, cool wave, some strange feeling welling up within me.

Compared with being stuck in the cave-in of my own thoughts, getting dragged around all of creation by the melancholic Miss Haruhi was a pleasure like unto a beam of light streaking through the center of the galaxy.

I was certain that Haruhi would return. Her homing instinct was one of her virtues.

Of course, it wasn't exclusive to her. Everyone in the SOS Brigade, from the lieutenant brigade chief on down to the menial chore boy, had a place to return to, as fixed as the Earth's tectonic plate would be if the moon disappeared—the first headquarters of the SOS Brigade, where Nagato waited, where Haruhi had broken in, and where Asahina and Koizumi had been forcibly dragged.

My cerebral cortex lit up with impulses that signified my desire to get everybody in the clubroom and play stupid games to pass the time.

That's right, Sasaki. I was on their side, and I couldn't ever leave it. A new SOS Brigade? The nerve of them. It wasn't something you could just run off copies of. It was a brigade made of *us*. We would soldier on, our membership changing, not leaving a single one behind. That had been Haruhi's very first wish. But I realized that it hadn't taken long for that to be a wish that Asahina, Nagato, Koizumi, and I all held as well. We were like the accretion disc held in place by the tidal forces of the small black hole of the brigade chief. We could neither fall in nor escape the orbit; we could but remain. That is, until the mysterious gravity that held us disappeared.

Afterward, I headed home, totally absentminded. I was surprised I managed to remember to bring my bike home. When was the last time I was so fatigued that I heard every rattle and squeak of my bike? It was all I could do stay conscious.

Somehow I managed to finish eating dinner, despite feeling as if I couldn't move the chopsticks. I collapsed onto my bed without even turning the light off, lacking so much as the energy to play with Shamisen and my sister. Mentally, I was a tattered rag.

Just before I blacked out, I remember thinking that I'd feel bad when I woke up if I went to sleep like that. To the best of my knowledge, I did not dream. Of course, in that state, anything short of the most beautiful dream imaginable would've been forgotten the instant I woke up.

CHAPTER 6

α — 9

The next day, Wednesday.

I didn't know whether it was temporary or would continue to increase, but the day's sunshine was leaps and bounds beyond what you'd expect from spring, and felt more like early summer. I seemed to recall the previous year was like this too. Evidently the Earth really was warming up, and if it really was humanity's fault, we'd better do something quick; otherwise the mailboxes of power plants the world over were going to start filling with letters of protest from polar bears and penguins.

Thus it was that my shirt was quickly made sticky with sweat as I contented myself with the hike up the hill to school. The verdant green of a neighbor's grass caught my eye, but did nothing to assuage the deep resentment I felt for schools with air conditioning. I was going to have some words for the student council president the next time I saw him. Whether or not it was practical given the budget, I was sure that Kimidori's alien powers would make the instantaneous installation of twenty or thirty air conditioning units no problem at all.

Incidentally, I expected that Koizumi would have informed

the student council president of Kimidori's true nature by now. Although given the president, he probably wouldn't care whether his secretary girl was an extraterrestrial or not.

I hugged my light schoolbag over my shoulder, gazing at the backs of the many North High students climbing the hill. I felt refreshed, and was making unusually good time as I went—wait, what?

I stopped, cocking my head. It was a meaningless performance, and I had no idea why I felt the way I did.

The spring was at its beautiful height, and with the monsoon season still far off and the humidity nothing to complain about; it was some of the most pleasant weather there was, a time that came only twice a year, in fall and spring, and you didn't have to be Haruhi to just relax, free of doubt—and yet something bothered me.

I groped around in the darkness of my mind, and by the time I'd climbed the hill I'd arrived at something like an answer.

"It's too peaceful."

I honestly don't know why I felt the need to murmur those words aloud.

Haruhi was in benignly high spirits as she continued with her recruitment, Asahina was devoting herself to practicing the art of tea service after school, Nagato had thrown her duties as literature club president into the garbage and was absorbed in reading, and Koizumi just smiled the days away.

I'd prepared myself for the appearance of Sasaki, Kuyoh, and Kyoko Tachibana to be a harbinger of a series of abnormal events, but since their appearance, there'd been nothing. Not even from that nameless time-traveler guy, although that might well just have been foreshadowing for his being revealed later. I felt as if sooner would be better, though I would be grateful if it were put off for later, and whoever could put him on indefinite hold would get a letter of appreciation from me—but the question was, who could I expect to do that? Nagato, or my dear not-quite-good friend, Sasaki?

I thought back on the words and actions of my middle school classmate. It had mostly been about entrance exams or stuff that wasn't any help at all when it came to living my life. And yet that was probably why she was able to run rings around aliens and time travelers. It would probably be a good idea to give her a call and check in on the situation. The time traveler was especially worrisome.

Absentmindedly heading for the freshman classrooms was something that only happened the first few days of the new semester. Mechanically I changed into my school slippers and wandered over to classroom 2-5 to take my seat. There was nothing to do besides wait for the days when I could stop fanning myself with my pencil board, which wouldn't happen until fall came.

As I was sitting there, Haruhi entered the classroom just before the bell, like a racehorse vying with Mr. Okabe for the early lead. She wound up beating the PE teacher by two lengths.

"You certainly took your time. Still have more preparation to do on the brigade entrance exams?" In the few minutes before homeroom ended and first period began, I took the opportunity to talk to her.

"Mm…" A noncommittal reply issued from Haruhi's lips. "I made myself lunch. For some reason I woke up early today, so I thought it might be nice, for once."

Huh. What strange wind was blowing today? Haruhi was behaving like a normal high school girl.

"Must've taken a while. Did you pack it in a cute box or something?"

"I got so into trying to make sure it was nutritionally balanced that I was late leaving the house. But it's really tasty. I'm excited to eat it at lunch." Haruhi pouted, not quite like a duck, but more than an owl. "Hmm. It was weird, though. I just got this feeling like I needed to do some cooking. Maybe I had a dream about it or something. I don't really remember, but it was like I had to cook for somebody else. Oh, and just so you know, I didn't make extra. I'm going to eat it all myself."

She didn't have to point that out. If she gave me some of her handmade lunch, just where on the campus was I supposed to be able to eat it? I sure as hell wouldn't be able to eat it in the classroom.

"Anyway, you hardly ever bring your lunch. Is there some kind of reason for that? Like your mom's a terrible cook or something?"

Haruhi was silent for a moment. "How did you know? Yeah...it's hard to say, but I don't really want to admit it, but...you're right. Mom—er, my mother's sense of taste is a little different than normal people's."

So in other words, she was a terrible cook.

"When I was little I thought it was like that at everybody's house. A normal family goes to a restaurant every once in a while, right? It was so delicious I almost cried, and I thought it was like that because it was a restaurant. But when I started elementary school, I started thinking it was a little strange. Depending on the menu, sometimes there was stuff the other kids didn't like, but I shoveled it all in, no matter what. I'd eat all the stuff my friends left on their plates."

She looked out the window, her eyes distant as she reminisced.

"So then I tried my hand at it. I just tried to copy what I'd seen—I think it was beef and potato stew. The first dish I ever made myself. And how do you think it tasted? Just like something from a restaurant. It was like a fish scale fell out of my eye and everything was suddenly clear. It hit the ground with a *pop* and rolled away."

That was one big fish scale, I said.

"It was like something from an arowana or arapaima. But ever since then, I tried not to eat at my house too much."

"Huh."

I had a strange feeling. Something in what Haruhi had said nagged at me.

Was it her lunch...? No. Did restaurant menus have beef and potato stew? Was it her mention of a scale from Amazonian freshwater fish?

Just as I was silent, having gotten the very last word in the crossword puzzle as far as my throat but no further—

"By the way, Kyon," said Haruhi, suddenly changing the subject as she looked at me from slightly downturned eyes. "About the first annual brigade membership exam."

Hm? Oh yes. That certainly was the most obviously pending issue.

Haruhi switched suddenly away from her family's dining habits— or rather, seemed eager to sweep that topic of conversation away. "It's a pain to have them over several days, so I was thinking of collecting 'em all together and just finishing them up. What do you think?"

I was stunned that she would solicit the opinion of a lowly brigade member on the matter. I had assumed that arbitration would lie solely with the highest-ranking member. Looks like my judgment had been rather hasty.

"Hmm...I guess that depends on the contents of the exam," I said, fishing for the first idea that came to mind. "I assume you're not going to do a race to catch a hundred and one hamsters or anything like that."

Haruhi froze as though she'd caught a face-on glimpse of Medusa, looking at me as though she were a criminal who'd blurted out an important piece of evidence. "...How'd you know? Right down to the number, even."

I felt as if her thought processes were slowly poisoning me. To think I'd guess perfectly the very first time. Horrified at my own notion, I had to ask. "Just where do you think you're going to get that many hamsters?"

"Okay, we'll change it to a contest of catching Shamisen's fleas."

He'd been a house cat for some time now, and my sister regularly bathed him. He didn't have any fleas, I pointed out.

"Then a cooking contest using only grass found on school grounds!"

Sure, so long as she was willing to be the judge.

"How about a contest to see who can wave a plastic bag full of flour in front of the police station and get arrested first?"

I'd feel bad for the beat cop on duty. And they might not get the joke either.

Haruhi made the special patented combination of crocodile eyes and duck mouth that she made whenever she was irritated. "Okay, so what kind of contest should it be, then?"

That wasn't something I should have to answer. Anyway, why was she so fixated on contests, I wanted to know. This was an entrance examination. It didn't have to be a big event. Although speaking of events, I'd be happy with a takoyaki contest. If we went to a utensil store we could probably get the stuff cheap.

Haruhi let my banter flow away like a babbling brook. "Kyon, this is not the only year we're going to have an entrance exam. Obviously we'll have to do one next year too. Since it's going to be an annual tradition, of course it's got to be a big event. That's what an event is!"

But this wasn't some ancient religious ceremony, nor was it some long-held festival tradition. Think about the Olympics, or the World Cup. They'd get boring if we did them every year.

"Think about this, Haruhi," I said, trying to make my case. "Did Nagato or Asahina take a test? I mean, Koizumi got in just because he was a transfer student. There wasn't anything like a test last year."

Come to that, the biggest mystery of all was my own inclusion in the SOS Brigade, but I let that pass unmentioned.

Haruhi scrunched her lips up in a clever impression. "Geez. Do you want new members, or don't you?"

If she was asking how I really felt, the truth was: Not really. If there was a slider from another world among the freshmen, in Haruhi's eyes they wouldn't be new members so much as intruders. The fact that there had been no such indications meant that there was nobody like that among the new students. The tragedy of a normal person made to abandon their normalcy was already in the process of being performed by me, and definitely didn't need to become a trend. There was no sense in repeating a tragedy. Well over two millennia had passed since the beginning of recorded history, and one hopes humanity would have learned a few lessons. And that depended on one tiny corner of humanity (me) having carved said lessons on his heart.

Haruhi continued to mutter away, evidently still thinking about what to fill the blank of "————competition" with. I decided to pray to the god of rodents or something that she didn't settle on a hundred and one hamsters.

Maybe Daikokuten, god of wealth and friend of mice, would be okay?

And soon enough classes were over, and I continued what had become my habit over the past several days, which was receiving study assistance from grandmaster Suzumiya. It goes without saying that I did not enjoy this. Although if you were to ask why I said something that supposedly goes without saying, I wouldn't have a good reply.

"Tests are so stupid. I mean, no matter how great my answer is, the best score I can get is one hundred. I hate anything that has restrictions like that on it. If I'm going to be stuck within bounds I can't escape, forget about it. I mean, just think about it, Kyon. If the test-taker's ability exceeds the test-maker's and they think of an answer that requires a greater mental leap than the question required, but then makes a careless mistake on another question, they won't get a perfect score. Don't you think that's weird? If it were me, I'd give two hundred points, or even one thousand, for a truly great or elegant answer. That's what I don't like."

Haruhi flipped sloppily through the textbook as she spoke.

"Also, tests just make you memorize what's written in the textbooks. Totally boring! There's nothing like mechanical repetition to make you lose your humanity. It's corrupt! Corrupt!"

Whether or not she was being helpful, at the very least her words weren't going to help me get a better grade on my English test. Unless she became a politician and reformed the Japanese educational system, that is.

"Comprehension is more important than rote memorization!" Just when I thought she was going to denounce the entire examination system, she continued. "You've got to memorize it as a story. If you remember what someone was thinking, then what they did will come up like pulling up a whole row of potatoes. Kyon, listen—once you understand the basic concepts, the next step is seeing what the test-maker was thinking. There's no way of telling what people in ancient times thought, but it's not hard at all to guess what modern humans are thinking. You're not trying to guess what's going to be written on the test—you're understanding what the person who wrote it was thinking about. Once you do that, there are all sorts of hidden possibilities."

From the perspective of the test-taker, isn't it easier to just fill in the correct answer, instead of trying to figure out the hidden angles? Why did she always have to exceed expectations?

"Because it gives you moral superiority. We're mere students, but that's only a matter of age. Enlightening the complacent teaching class is our great privilege as students. We've got to use our youth as a weapon. I guess it's obvious, but this is the only time we're going to have that weapon. We don't have much time left to use it on the greatest battlefield of all—high school."

I sort of understood, and sort of didn't care, but at the moment I was exhausted just trying to lead my normal high school life, and I couldn't hear any more of these words heavy with implications. You could say that a sparrow couldn't understand the philosophy of a falcon—the level of their DNA was too different. Sitting on top of power lines trilling birdsong seemed as though it fit me pretty well. I'd leave the rest to people with burning ambition, like Haruhi or good old Julien from *The Red and the Black*. My biggest ambitions of late seemed to be a desire for sleep, so what else could I do?

"That's a pathetic declaration of intent." Haruhi shook her head sadly, looking at me as though I were a cowardly samurai who always wore a sword but never had the courage to draw it. Her lips curled up. "Anyway, I'm not here to critique your life philosophy. Still," she said, her voice strengthening. "In school, class, and tests, that might be good enough for you, but it's not good enough for the SOS Brigade. In there, what I say goes. I have extraterritoriality. Whether it's Japanese law, common sense, traditions, social rules, presidential orders, or the decisions of the Supreme Court, none of that matters in the brigade. Got it? Any problems with that?"

Yes, ma'am. No, ma'am. There was no need for her to restate what I already knew perfectly well. I knew better than anyone else why she'd caught the attention of intelligence from beyond the galaxy. So it's all up to you, Haruhi. Any decision to be made within the SOS Brigade is all yours.

But Nagato and Koizumi, as well as Asahina the Elder, all felt the same way I did. You'll forgive me that much, won't you, Haruhi?

However Haruhi might have interpreted my sighs, she closed the textbook, seemingly satisfied, and began to put her notebook back in her bag. It was the signal that the day's after-school tutoring plus deliberate ploy to arrive late for the brigade meeting was concluded.

It was only ten minutes, but the time was a precious break for me, like halftime at a game—and yet what was the psychological source of that sense of relief? It introduced only a bit of lag into the process of assembling in the clubroom, and even delayed the time until I could sample Asahina's tea, and yet for some reason these days I was aware that I was trying to avoid the clubroom.

Why was that? Maybe I just couldn't face all those bright-eyed freshman applicants, and perhaps I'd fallen victim to an irrational disquiet, a baseless dread, but whatever it was, a halo of light still awaited me in the clubroom, thanks to Nagato (whose sense of self had been nice and strong after Haruhi's disappearance), Koizumi (who still took delight in solving any problem), and Asahina (who was as lovely as ever).

So long as all of us were together, we were effectively invincible within the school, and yet I felt a strange unease, like trace amounts of helium seeping into the corners of my lungs.

What was it about?

Although the random encounter with Sasaki, Kyoko Tachibana, and Kuyoh definitely worried me, I didn't get the sense that they were planning anything. Given that Sasaki was on their side, and would thus befuddle them more than Haruhi could, I figured she'd give them a fair amount of trouble—that much wasn't hard to imagine with even my paltry deductive abilities. I knew Sasaki well. Just like Haruhi, she was a hard person to influence—although the vectors were different, of course. Haruhi wouldn't listen to anyone, ever. Sasaki would listen, then deliver an eloquent rebuttal. Her identity was extremely solid, and not even an edict from Zeus or Cronos could make her betray it. Although she might listen to Prometheus or Cassandra.

Anyway, even if that crowd were to appear before me as home tutors, I doubted they would be able to make things as easily understandable as Haruhi did. Objective analysis based on hindsight suggested that historical understanding was the most profitable source of information. Although this would never happen, if my name went down in history, I would have no reason to complain about their analyses. I'd be a ghost by then, and the dead do not speak, and only the people of the future have any right to cite people who are dead and buried.

And if someone near me happened to die, I had about a cat's flea's egg's worth of desire to write a eulogy for them. So nobody better die on me. Disappearing without a trace was also right out. So long as Haruhi and I were here, nobody involved with the SOS Brigade was allowed to leave. The membership could grow, sure. But shrink? No. The status quo was maintained, and would continue to be. It was one of the SOS Brigade's most important rules, and while it may not have been written anywhere, it was still common knowledge.

As I turned all this over in my head, Haruhi's special tutoring session ended, Haruhi turning her back to the vague smiles of the students who'd pulled cleaning duty and striding purposefully out into the hallway like a young member of the Nazi party off to attend a national convention of the Hitler Youth.

With the remainder of Haruhi's Special Review Course put off until the next day, I enjoyed a few moments of peace, but as we walked side by side and reached the dim hallway that led to our final destination, the clubroom, I couldn't very well forget the lingering doubts I felt. While I found them deeply befuddling, Haruhi seemed not to notice in the least.

I wondered which was more important to her—improving my test scores or examining new members. As we walked down the hallway, her footsteps nearly sounded like tap dancing, and I realized she enjoyed all sorts of things. I wondered if the new freshman candidates looked like so many hamsters to her.

I hoped the applicants had the animalistic nonchalance of the feline order, rather than the quick reflexes of the rodents. It would be a lot better for their long-term prospects to relax and curl up into a ball than it would be to become the animal subjects of Haruhi's psychological experiments. There was only one person with enough doglike, tail-wagging loyalty for Haruhi, and that was Koizumi. The kind of person most likely to blend into the clubroom would have the inscrutable empty-headedness of an iguana, but from what I'd seen the odds were slim that any of the new applicants were like that.

It was likely that Haruhi was thinking the same thing—that instead of dragging out the examination process, quickly and decisively sorting things out would be better for both the SOS Brigade and the fresh-faced new students.

And just as I'd expected, the number of provisional new members—or hamsters, from Haruhi's point of view—was indeed slightly reduced. There was a full house in the clubroom: three boys and two girls. That was one down from the previous day, but it still seemed like quite a few remaining. I really wanted to ask them all individually just what it was about the SOS Brigade that they found intriguing, but unfortunately that was Haruhi's job, and when the highest-ranking brigade member, in whom resided all rights of supervision and control, entered the room, she made a loud-voiced proclamation.

"The SOS Brigade admission examination has begun!"

Asahina was already in the room, and her hand froze in the middle of pouring tea as she blinked, while Koizumi, who'd been ruminating alone over a children's shogi board, spread his hands helplessly. Nagato sat in the corner, turning the pages of a used book, giving no reaction whatsoever. After ten seconds of silence, I finally spoke up.

"So this is the end, already?"

"Yup," said Haruhi haughtily. "It'll just make everybody's lives difficult if we take too much time. Plus I've already gathered more than enough data. All I need to see now is guts! Friendship, effort, and success aren't necessary at all. I mean, you haven't been around us long enough to foster feelings of friendships, and 'effort' is just an excuse people who can't deliver results use. And as for success, what's important is triumphing over some*thing*, not some*one*. In this case, if you can't beat me, you haven't achieved anything at all."

Haruhi looked over the assembled five freshmen with a weather eye, then nodded.

"Well done, everybody. You all listened to what I said and brought your gym clothes. All right, change into them."

The group of freshmen sitting in folding chairs looked each other over. Well, of course they did. They'd been told to change, but where exactly were they supposed to do it? Still, while I had no idea when they'd been informed of the required equipment, I was impressed that they'd each brought bags containing their gym clothes. It was the time of year—everything was new to them. They had to be wondering why this club, which was about as far away from a sports team as it was possible to get, required gym clothes, but this year's freshmen still dutifully complied with the orders of our tyrannical brigade chief.

"Ah, yes." "Yes, ma'am."

Such things they murmured, standing and taking their uniforms in hand.

But standing was all they did. Evidently here in this mixed-sex room, their feelings of embarrassment were strong enough that coed clothes-changing was a bit too much for them.

Koizumi, Asahina, and Nagato made no move to leave the room, seemingly implying "Don't mind us, go right ahead." Koizumi grinned (he was being awfully quiet), while Asahina went with the flow of things, looking for enough teacups to serve everyone. There in the corner, Nagato kept her head down, as though she were reading the minutes of a student council meeting.

It seemed the only person remaining to lend a hand to the dubious-faced freshmen was me. Just when I took a deep breath and braced myself for impact—

"Right, current members all have to leave the room. You too, Yuki! You can read your book in the hallway." Haruhi was showing surprising initiative. "Girls change first. Boys wait in the hallway, and change once the girls are done. I believe in gender equality, but in my view you've got to account for physical differences. Hurry, now—out, out!"

You would never have guessed that she was once a girl who would start changing clothes in the middle of classroom 1-5, paying no mind to the boys' gazes. But maybe that was just my imagination; maybe Haruhi's smile had slowed down my thinking a certain amount.

But there was one thing I did have to ask her.

"Just what are you going to make them do?" I assumed it would be something athletic.

"Didn't I tell you? A marathon!" said Haruhi, folding her arms and looking as though what she'd just said was totally reasonable. "A long, boring series of tests just isn't my style. But deciding quickly, like this, will give a nice decisive result. Anyway, the trial club membership period is ending soon, and I have to be considerate to the students who don't make it, because they might have other clubs they want to try. So I started thinking. To be really decisive in times like this, it's gotta be a test of strength! Of energy! And what's better for that than an endurance run?"

As I wondered whether the SOS Brigade had ever done anything that tested our endurance, I spoke. "Hey, c'mon now." I thought about not saying anything, but there didn't appear to be anyone else in this small room that would protest Haruhi's rampancy. "What about the stuff you've done so far? You're just gonna toss all that out and decide things with a marathon? You should've done that from the beginning!"

"Tsk tsk tsk!" Haruhi clicked her tongue disapprovingly, like an examiner who's just received a question she'd expected all along. She continued, her attitude like an elder monk enlightening a young apprentice who was repeating secondhand information. "You're not thinking this through, Kyon. Listen, the other tests and interviews were certainly not wasted effort. I have a good eye for people. I've got as much perception and concentration as an eagle on the wing, hunting for mice hiding between the crags below."

Yeah, and pretty soon one of those poor little mice was going to be caught and served up on a plate back at your nest.

"The reason I've been constantly talking about tests all the time is, um, like...the MacGuffin in a suspense movie!"

"Wouldn't that be more like a red herring, then?" Koizumi calmly stepped in, but I kept silent, not knowing what herring and pound cake had to do with each other. Haruhi seemed not to know either.

"Whatever, who cares. The point is, any measure of aptitude worth being called a 'test' is...umm...well, it's based on human observation, which I've been doing. I've been testing them. The nature of the tests wasn't important. It was all just to filter out the new recruits who didn't make it this far, that's all. And so..." Haruhi extended her index finger and gestured across the noses of the assembled five students. "You've all successfully crossed the hurdle. Congratulations. You've gained the right to undertake the final challenge. Rejoice! While you still can. But the real test is just beginning. I'll just say now that it's going to be a lot tougher than what you've done so far. You'll need strength, guts, courage, and the most important skill humans possess—the persistence never to give up! Beyond this challenge awaits the ultimate victory!"

It felt as though she was just trying to say sort of generically inspiring things, but I couldn't claim that they didn't fit the occasion. Haruhi Suzumiya played things by ear, every time. If she couldn't manage that this time, then who in the world could have?

I couldn't help letting slip a pained smile. It was because Haruhi was like this that I sometimes...

With effort, I stamped the thought out. Dangerous—too dangerous. Even if the words had only existed in my mind, never to be vocalized, only ever heard by me, the very fact of them being so meant I couldn't pretend not to have heard them.

Language was cognition. And if I became conscious of *that*, there was a real possibility that I could become aware of a notion that would pose mortal danger to a life I hoped would be a long one. It might have been cheeky of me, but at the moment I was determined to remain free of all ideologies or policies.

Consequently, I immediately canceled my train of thought, and decided to think about happier things—like the flower viewing party at Tsuruya's villa, or my anticipation of a sequel to a video game I'd beaten.

"..."

Perhaps having caught me trying to hide something away in my mind, Nagato lifted her face smoothly up, then dropped her eyes back to the book.

"Aw..."

It was fine. It didn't matter who knew—so long as it wasn't Haruhi, the world would remain at peace. Still, maybe it wouldn't hurt to let her know a little bit...or at least the thought occurred to me for a moment—sorry, I took leave of my senses for a second there. No, seriously. Seriously.

Sigh. Needing to make yourself listen to your own excuses would only result in years of agonizing experiences. The human brain is an ill-made thing, letting you remember with perfect clarity only those things you most want to forget. I hoped someone was nearing completion of the human felinization project—cats didn't seem to worry much about the future at all.

*   *   *

Haruhi must have concluded that going to the locker room was a waste.

She oversaw the alternate clothes-changing of the boys and girls in the clubroom, and as a matter of course Koizumi, Asahina, and I all withdrew to cool our heels in the hallway. But even when it was the boys' turn to go and change and Haruhi ordered Nagato matter-of-factly out of the room, Nagato remained nose-in-book, not moving a muscle. And yes, I did think about asking Nagato to give a little consideration to these poor little freshmen who would have to change in front of an older girl, but honestly the three boys didn't seem too worried about what she might see at this point, plus this might have been part of Haruhi's exam. It then occurred to me that if that was so, I should've been allowed to stay in the room when the girls changed, at which point the freshmen had all finished changing and we were heading for the field.

I wasn't too upset about it, if I'm honest. It wasn't something that was in either my nature or my ethics to do, plus what would Asahina have thought?

Thus, after much ado, Haruhi finally introduced her long-awaited SOS Brigade Final Entrance Examination, which was all well and good, but for some strange reason she had also changed into her gym clothes, which worried me. Also worrying was the inner state of the girl who strode unhesitatingly along, taking great bouncing strides like some sort of street hip-hop performer about to improvise a lyric. But the biggest outstanding issue was the fact that we were currently heading to the school's sports field.

No exposition is required to explain that the grounds were the site of fierce competition among the sports clubs, and here at a prefectural school where no special facilities were apportioned to any of the sports teams, such competition was a daily occurrence. At the moment, major players like track and field, soccer, and baseball, along with more minor sports, were constantly pushing for more territory, like tiny nation-states making shows of strength along their borders, always trying to expand.

The track and field team had a legitimate claim to the four-hundred-meter track, but Haruhi strode spiritedly toward them, her five freshmen in tow. Her lack of restraint made her seem like the leader of a school of baitfish leading a charge.

Though I'd come along this far owing to circumstances, I decided to hold position at the top of the stairs that led down onto the field, given that I participated in no athletic activities save PE class and the daily uphill trudge to school. Koizumi and Asahina did like-wise. They both had been hanging around Haruhi long enough to have a good idea of what she was planning to do next. Nagato had been disinclined to observe the proceedings all along, and at that very moment was probably enjoying a book in the clubroom. It goes without saying that she had excellent judgment.

Essentially, the three existing SOS Brigade members—us minus Nagato—had chosen to act as mere rubberneckers. I would brook no clumsy attempts to get us to participate further.

As I watched, Haruhi started by taking issue with somebody on the track and field team, and taking no notice of the increasingly irritated aura of the team as a whole, lined up the brigade candidates at the starting line.

"C'mon, we're at least allowed to run! The track and field team's not good at anything else, anyway, and we're running in service of a higher goal. It'll only be for today, and we're not even really in the way, and as North High students we have as much right as anyone to use the field. Any objections?"

About a tenth of a second after she finished her rapid-fire questioning—

"No? Good. Well, then—"

The assembled track team didn't even have time to reply before Haruhi gave the signal to her would-be minions. It was very simple.

"Ready, go!" she said as she went flying off, leaving behind the stunned freshmen, who hadn't even been told what they had to do.

"What are you doing? Hurry up and follow me!" Haruhi's strident voice jolted them from their petrification, and they started chasing down her gym-uniform-clad form as she headed down the track. Going by Haruhi's pace, this wasn't going to be a sprint—oh right, it was a marathon.

But just how many thousands of meters was she going to make them run? She hadn't even brought a stopwatch.

That said, it was a good thing the final test was a simple marathon.

"I'm just glad I didn't have to find a hundred and one hamsters," I murmured, sitting down at the top of the steps and looking down at the field. Haruhi shouted to encourage the flagging freshmen, winging her way ahead like some kind of sheepdog.

Koizumi narrowed his eyes and watched, gracing me with a response. "It wouldn't be impossible, but I doubt they're a particularly significant object in Suzumiya's mind."

"What would you have done if Haruhi really had wanted that to happen?"

Koizumi held his palms facing upward, as though feeling the weight of some object. "Of course I would have done everything in my power to collect them. I'd call up all the shops in the chain of pet stores my associate runs. They're charming little creatures, hamsters are."

Yeah, as long as you didn't pack a hundred and one of them into a box. We weren't practicing kodoku magic, here.

"By the way, Koizumi."

"Yes?"

"About the students in that ridiculous marathon—are they all, you know, clean?"

"But of course. So far as our investigations can tell, there is nothing to worry about. Not one of them is an alien, time traveler, or any other category of person that would differ from standard modern humans." Koizumi then put a finger to his chin. "However..."

"However?"

"If you're asking if there's a student among them that worries me,

there is. That they're a normal human is clear enough, so this is nothing more than my intuition. Or perhaps you could call it a premonition. It would hardly be surprising for Suzumiya to decide that having everyone fail the test would be boring, so one student will pass. So who will remain? I feel as though I know already, though it's only a very slight feeling, with nothing whatsoever to back it up."

I got the feeling it was the same person—the same girl—I'd noticed.

"Her background's normal, right?"

"Yes. We checked. Although she was a slightly special case..."

Special? Special how? Tell me. Now, I told him.

Koizumi chuckled, an amused smile on his face. "I'll have to leave that a secret for now. It's a trivial thing, really. We've concluded it's nothing that could possibly harm us. Indeed, she may even help us."

His implication-heavy answer bothered me, but if Koizumi said so, I believed him. When it came to Haruhi-related matters, Koizumi was even more nervous than I was.

"Still..."

There was more? I asked.

"Yes. It's just, lately I've been feeling an extremely difficult-to-explain sense of unease—shallow though that may be. It doesn't have anything to do with the new candidates. It's solely regarding myself."

I told Koizumi I was happy to listen to his problems, so long as they weren't romantic in nature.

"I don't have the sense it's the sort of problem that's helped by talking about it," Koizumi said, gazing at the daisies that were in bloom alongside the stairway. "The truth is, I've started to feel like I'm getting fainter. How can I explain this..."

From what I could see, his face was the same half-smiling iron mask it always was, I said.

"I don't mean externally. It's more like wondering whether what I'm experiencing right now is really my own volition, or whether it's some unreal dream world another version of myself is dreaming. I've been thinking about it a little bit, that's all."

So the grave robber of Haruhi's subconscious had finally run into a mummy, eh? I suggested he go visit a mental clinic. If it was a serotonin problem they could probably write him a prescription.

"I'll seriously consider it. I hope this is just a personal problem of mine. I'm sure it is. Suzumiya is having lots of fun, and I doubt the Agency will need to take action for a while."

I looked down at the grounds as I took in Koizumi's words.

"I wonder if they'll be thirsty after they run. I'll go make some tea."

Asahina was still in her maid outfit; her considerate words echoed in my ears.

Surprisingly, the pace Haruhi set was abnormally fast for a distance race, and she seemed content to just keep circling the track. She wasn't even bothering to measure time, so it wasn't a time-limited event, and there didn't seem to be a set number of laps after which the race would end either.

Having figured out that much, I finally understood Haruhi's intentions, and felt a deep sympathy for the poor freshmen.

Haruhi actually intended to run until every last one of them had collapsed. The ones who couldn't keep up would be left to fail by the side of the track, and she'd probably just say some vaguely nice words to the last one to fall before wrapping things up.

It seemed as though she hadn't been able to think of a selection criterion more interesting than the hamster-catching contest. So instead, she was just going to finish things up with a marathon. It made me want to ask why she'd bothered with that written exam, but honestly this was all you could expect from someone who got bored as easily as Haruhi did. Or maybe she'd actually cared quite a bit about the freshmen who'd played along with her for so long.

But the most likely possibility is that she hadn't actually wanted any new members at all.

The final test—an endurance run of indeterminate length.

By the time Haruhi stopped running, there wouldn't be a single freshman remaining behind her, I was sure. Haruhi was a high-speed comet of a girl who couldn't abide anyone being able to keep up with her.

As though to validate my thinking, after a few laps the freshmen began to lag. Anyone could've predicted the outcome, given that not even in the entirety of the assembled track and field club was there a single person would could keep up with Haruhi's fleet feet—and yet there were still a few in what could be called the chase group who were devoting their entire beings to keeping up with the lead group—composed solely of Haruhi.

Normally an endurance race had either a set distance or time, but Haruhi had thought of neither. She was just running. And she would run until she was satisfied. The finish line had no existence in either time or space, so for the freshmen behind her, this was no more than physical and psychological torture.

What was worse, the source of Haruhi's mysterious energy would let her run happily on and on till the break of dawn. Were the mitochondria in her body really of this Earth? Even if her cells did have some unexplained way of generating ATP, I couldn't even stay surprised at every little thing she did, having gone past shock straight into frank admiration at her full-throttle performance.

I'm not sure how much time passed as I watched the freshmen be worked over like new naval recruits.

Ready to acknowledge their service regardless of whether they passed or not, Asahina had returned to the clubroom to prepare tea, leaving Koizumi and me as the sole observers. Well, no—there were others. Most of the other clubs that used the field to practice had started watching this strange race. That's how good Haruhi's running form was, like an antelope on the plain.

Well, that was Haruhi for you. She was always like that.

But.

Not long after that, the scene on the grounds could only be described as a field of carnage.

Here and there on the track lay freshmen felled by Haruhi's endless marathon, an exercise of such psychological intensity that it had no place at North High, which wasn't particularly sporty to begin with. I sympathized deeply with them. If Haruhi had held an exam like this a year ago, there was no way Asahina or I would have passed. Whether or not that would have been a good thing didn't bear thinking about, but I won't hesitate in saying that I was thankful for Haruhi's caprice in that particular regard.

Naturally, I didn't hold any illusions that a single freshman would pass this endurance test, but eventually the compulsory exhaustion would reach its end—and that would be when even Haruhi's breath ran ragged enough to blow up a dust storm, and she stopped.

The scene before me was shocking enough to make me lose confidence in what little life experience I'd accumulated thus far.

The prospective brigade members had collapsed around the track, and had been dragged off of it by track and field members, who seemed to regard them as mere obstacles. The half-zombified freshmen surely wanted nothing more than oxygen and some freshly brewed tea.

However—

Just one freshman remained, having stuck with Haruhi for the entire race and crossing the finish line only moments after Haruhi did herself and declared the ordeal over.

She was gasping for breath and soaked with sweat, but she'd done it. And yes, by "her" I mean that same freshman girl from before.

Her baggy uniform did not fit her petite frame well, and as she tried to fix her sweat-matted hair, her childish efforts only made it look more like a bird's nest. The thing that stuck out the most was that same smiley-face barrette.

"You..." said Haruhi, subtle surprise coloring her voice, "...did very well. Managing to keep up with me...were you on the track team before?" Haruhi's own breath was fairly ragged.

"Nope," said the girl immediately. "I've stayed a free agent in all my club activities. What I've been aiming for—*whew*—is the SOS

Brigade. I worked really hard! I knew I'd do whatever I had to do to get in, so I've been preparing for this day!"

Regardless of the who-knew-how-many kilometers she'd just run, her voice was full of energy. She had more than enough left over to keep a smile on her sweat-soaked face.

That answer seemed to satisfy Haruhi, who, even as she continued to catch her own breath, replied, "You're the only one to pass. Still, this was only the first aptitude test, so the testing might continue. Are you ready?"

"I'll do anything you tell me I have to do! Even if you tell me to catch the moon's reflection in the water, I'll do it!"

Koizumi and I watched the exchange from safe ground, our mouths agape with shock.

There was someone whose strength and lung capacity matched Haruhi's, and she was a freshman. The track club wasn't going to let this opportunity slip away. After they regarded these proceedings with irritated disgust, the eyes of the track club members were already turning aggressive. They were the eyes possessed of utter determination to catch that promising-looking freshman.

Haruhi was a lost cause, but a brand-new student might well be persuaded to convert—they were like Portuguese missionaries who had found a warlord eager to distance himself from the influence of Buddhism. It was an entirely understandable avarice, give the aptitude for distance running she'd shown. I felt the same way, honestly.

The girl wiped sweat off of her satisfied face as she looked up and met my gaze. As she narrowed her eyes and curved her lips in a smile, I was struck by an intense, inexplicable feeling of déjà vu.

Did she *know*? Was she a powerful being that had somehow slipped past both Nagato and Koizumi, part of the mysterious other group, the fourth power...the thought crossed my mind, but Sasaki aside, she didn't have the scent of Kuyoh, Kyoko Tachibana, or that time-traveler guy.

Surely she wasn't a *fifth* power—?

C'mon, that couldn't be. Just how many people did I have to deal with here? Despite being assaulted by the irritation of the idea, I didn't feel any instinctive danger from her at all. She was just an eccentric freshman. It wasn't hard to imagine Haruhi wanting just one new member candidate. This probably didn't mean anything more than that. It had been a long time since Haruhi had declared her desire to associate with aliens, time travelers, and espers—a year, by now. And during that time, all of her crazy wishes had come true, albeit without the knowledge of the wisher.

Her latest wish was for a promising new member, and since it probably didn't matter if they were some kind of special being or just an ordinary *homo sapiens*, Haruhi had desired a second conveniently normal person—a second version of me. If so, the girl who'd passed Haruhi's crazy test would probably become an NPC-like errand girl, or possibly the new mascot who would take over once Asahina graduated.

If she happened not to be a standard human, presumably she would approach me soon. I could afford to wait to worry about it until that actually happened. I was used to dealing with weirdos.

The girl was bent over, hands on knees, as she recovered her breath. There was absolutely nothing superhuman about her, nor anachronistic, nor alien.

She was a human. I didn't need advice or warnings from anyone. I'd come to this certainty on my own. Just as humanity had evolved from some indeterminate protozoa through unfathomable stages, so truly had I arrived at this undeniable truth.

Even I came to correct conclusions once in a while.

Thus, at the incontrovertible decision of the brigade chief, the final decisive SOS Brigade entrance exam came to an end.

Of course, I still had a few misgivings. I felt as though I'd seen the freshman girl who passed somewhere before, and there was the fact that she'd caught my eye even the first time I'd met her. Koizumi had determined there was nothing particularly special about her, but the fact that she'd passed Haruhi's entrance exam and attracted her attention alone meant that she was no ordinary person.

But in what way was she out of the ordinary? Someone like Tsuruya was still a human resident of this Earth, but if she were in the alien/time traveler/esper category, then it would be as if I'd been given a problem from an entirely new problem set.

"Mmm."

I didn't realize I was groaning until Koizumi patted my back.

"There's nothing to worry about. There won't be any problems with her. If we're talking about high school students with stamina roughly the same as Haruhi's, I'm sure there are many of them if you bother to look. I would've thought you'd welcome the arrival of a cute junior member. She seems like she'll be quite adept at errand-running."

Evidently that was how he really felt. Koizumi's face never lost its soft, unconcerned smile.

But I just couldn't rid myself of that strange sense of déjà vu, like I'd met her somewhere before.

I had no memory of her, and yet it still bothered me, though it was quite clear we had just recently met—indeed, we obviously had no connection at all, so why did I feel as though I knew her? The questions rose up within me like puffs of smoke from a fire, and there was nothing I could do about it.

"Wait."

Maybe this wasn't a problem with her—maybe it was a problem with my own mind. Despite my tendency to worry about things, I found this hard to believe. She was just one freshman girl, and at a glance she was cute in an ordinary way, without health problems, the sort of petite girl who was loved by all, so why would I find her so disturbing?

By then Haruhi and the sole freshman to become a new brigade member should have made it back to the clubroom and finished changing. The door opened from the inside, and the girl leapt out, nearly dealing me a glancing body blow, but twirling aside like a butterfly on a spring wind.

"I'll be going home for today, then! See you tomorrow!"

Her smile was like a summer flower in full bloom. Her ill-fitting uniform clearly hadn't been made to measure, she had that strange hairpin, and yet she radiated health like one half of a binary star system—along with a youthful smile.

Koizumi was standing next to me, posing like a male model, but the girl didn't even glance at him, instead looking dead at me for a moment, before giggling.

"Seeya!" she said like a robin who'd just remembered where it was going, and heading for the stairs, she disappeared.

We were speechless for a moment.

"She seems to like you," said Koizumi, perhaps thinking his grinning tone was appropriate. He continued, quietly. "My, but she's charming. Just as a freshman, but all the more so as a junior member of our club. She seems quite a cheerful girl. What do you make of her?"

I didn't make anything of her. I hadn't actually thought Haruhi would bring in a new member, so mostly I was just astonished. She'd obviously be aiming to fail everybody with that marathon race of hers, so I was busy being impressed with the girl's determination at being able to break through that challenge, and doubting my own athletic ability.

"Although distance running isn't particularly related to athletic ability. It's understood to have more to do with heredity. But no matter. Let's just leave it at that."

Koizumi was being strangely easygoing. Did he know something I didn't?

Koizumi just shrugged me off with a smile. Just then, there was a shout from inside the clubroom, which brought an end to my investigation.

"You can come in! I'm done changing!" Haruhi's voice, in high spirits.

Haruhi sat in her usual spot at the brigade chief's desk, sipping hot tea from her personal cup. Asahina was busily picking up and folding the gym clothes that had been scattered on the floor. She really did seem like the head maid of the Suzumiya family staff. And the family's selfish daughter insisted on bringing her personal maid to school with her—was this not a reasonable way to describe the scene?

"Is this really a good idea, Haruhi?"

"Is what a good idea?"

"Bringing in a new member."

"Yes, well," said Haruhi, finishing her tea and placing it loudly on her desk. "To be honest, I wasn't expecting any of them to make it. That's why I made the final test a marathon. But for one of the freshmen to actually be able to keep up with me, that's like an exclamation mark and a question mark right next to each other. Like this." Haruhi air-scrawled an exclamation point and a question mark.

So she really hadn't intended on letting anybody in. All of this business about an entrance exam had just been Haruhi playing around.

"But I was really surprised to find out that there was a freshman with enough stamina to keep up with me. That's really not an everyday occurrence. It's quite a phenomenon, really. If she joined the track club she could definitely be their strongest middle-long distance runner, and go all the way to nationals."

If that were so, maybe we should tie a ribbon on her and give her to the track team, I pointed out.

"That'd be such a waste! Of course the track team would be happy; they haven't won anything at any of their meets lately. The other clubs would do anything to get their hands on her, but I'm not just going to let her slip through my fingers. She knocked on the SOS Brigade's door. What would it say for the health of our educational system if we just ignored her wishes like that? It's not worthy of a democracy."

Despite having no interest whatsoever in ideologies like "the health of our educational system," Haruhi was happy to espouse them when it was convenient.

I could only assume that being the object of the other clubs' envy was something she found highly pleasurable. But this wasn't the era of the Three Kingdoms in China—there were no rival warlords vying for territory—so she didn't have to go around assembling personnel like she was Cao Cao.

"And that's not all." Haruhi rummaged around in one of the drawers of the brigade chief's desk, pulling out a sheet of copier paper she must have stowed in there earlier. "Take a look at this."

I took it and looked, and saw that it was the written portion of the brigade entrance exam—more like a survey—that Haruhi had had the assembled applicants take.

"I incinerated everybody else's, so hers is the only one left. It's got the spirit of a new brigade member on it. I figured you had a right to see it too."

I was certainly interested. This was crucial data left behind by the new member who'd managed to ace Haruhi's capriciously created test. I looked over it immediately. Her neat pencil handwriting filled the spaces underneath the questions, which I'd seen before.

Here is what they said.

1. Explain the reasoning behind your ambition to join the SOS Brigade.
   Resolve creates luck. I'm already in love with it.
2. If you are admitted, in what way can you contribute?
   Anything I'm allowed to do, I will try.
3. Of aliens, time travelers, sliders, and espers, which do you think is best?
   I'd want to talk to an alien the most. I'd most want to be friends with a time traveler. An esper seems like they'd be the most profitable. A slider seems like they would open up the most possibilities.
4. Why?

I wrote my reasoning as part of my previous answer. Sorry.

5. Explain any mysterious phenomena you have experienced.
   I haven't experienced any. Sorry.

6. What's your favorite pithy phrase?
   "Unprecedented and unbeatable"

7. If you could do anything, what would you do?
   Build a city on Mars and name it after myself. Like "Washington, D.C." Heh.

8. Final question: Express your enthusiasm.
   If I absolutely had to, I'd purposely mess up my vision and wear glasses.

9. If you can bring along anything really interesting, you get extra credit. Please try to find something.
   Understood. I'll bring something soon.

...I was pretty sure President Washington hadn't built Washington, D.C., himself, or given it his name. And what did the "D.C." stand for, anyway? I said.

"I don't know, 'Direct Control'? Something like that, anyway," said Haruhi irresponsibly.

" ... "

I wasn't sure if she had been listening, but Nagato's bangs only twitched slightly, and she did not offer a correction.

She probably thought correcting us would be a waste of information. Something about her silence said "just look it up yourself."

"Mm," I muttered, noncommittally.

Suddenly I realized that I hadn't yet heard the name of this girl who'd gotten herself unofficially admitted to the brigade. I casually turned the test sheet over, and looked for her name. For some reason her class and seat number weren't written, but—

Yasumi Watahashi

Her full name was written there in neat ink letters. But...

"How is that pronounced? Taimizu Wataribashi? No, that can't be it…Yasumizu…maybe?"

"Yasumi Watahashi, she said," said Haruhi in response to my question. As though it were nothing. As nonchalantly as though it were just a regular name.

"…"

Yet something about it tripped me up. I felt somehow like a tiny fish who'd been swept away in the current, then scooped up alone in a net. But who was it who'd been scooped up, really? Was it me, or this Watahashi girl?

"Huh…?"

Again with the déjà vu. I knew this name. My faint memory insisted it was so. Yes, I'd definitely heard it somewhere.

Watahashi. *Watahashi.* I didn't remember the name, and I didn't remember the letters, but the *sound* of it was familiar.

Watahashi—

"…!"

The rusty gears of my brain snapped suddenly into place. I had a vision of un-lubricated, seized clockwork springing into motion as the memory came back sharply, as though viewed through clear water.

"It's me. M-E, me." Atashi wa, watashi.

I'd answered the phone in the echo-prone bathroom, but what I'd heard was definitely a girl's voice. A girl my sister said she didn't know.

Atashi wa, watashi. It's me.

She hadn't been posing some kind of riddle. The girl on the phone had just been saying her name.

So—

"Atashi wa, watahashi." It's me, Watahashi.

I was only able to enjoy the feeling of a mystery solved for a brief moment before doubt anew swirled within me.

Yasumi Watahashi…

...What *was* she? Even if I was allowing for that call to have been a random prank, her trying out for the SOS Brigade and actually passing Haruhi's absurd test such that she'd be a full brigade member tomorrow wasn't something an ordinary freshman would do. There was no way.

And while her motivation was unknown, it was troublesome that she had enough chutzpah to call me up personally ahead of time. She was a complete and perfect question mark, and she'd waltzed right into the SOS Brigade.

What was her true nature? Did she work for the other secret organization, was she an agent of the Heavenly Canopy Dominion, or was she part of the anti-Asahina faction of time travelers?

And yet in spite of all that, while Asahina, Nagato, and Koizumi had all been surprised at the fact that Watahashi had remained, none of them were particularly concerned about her. If she'd been an esper, Koizumi should have said something—same for Nagato, if she were something like Kuyoh, and Asahina, if she were a time traveler. But they all merely looked a bit surprised, and Asahina even seemed happy. There was always the possibility that Asahina (as usual) simply didn't know anything, but it would've been nice to find a letter from Asahina the Elder in my shoe locker.

What did this resolution mean? Was it just a coincidence? Did the only girl with enough physical stamina to match Haruhi just happen to be compatible with the unauthorized student organization known as the SOS Brigade—was that all there was to it?

I was not so naive as to think that this was simply happenstance.

I mean, what had that phone call been about?

My sister had brought the receiver to me in the bathroom, where I'd heard that short comment and been curtly hung up on. What did that mean?

"Ugh."

I'd thought things were going to be peaceful for a while, but if I wanted to protect that peace, I was going to have to learn more about about the freshman Yasumi Watahashi.

Still, "Yasumi Watahashi," huh?

Haruhi flipped the survey paper over, and read the writing in the "notes" section.

"'Please call me "Yasumi," if you would, and try to pronounce it using katakana,' it says."

The pronunciation would be the same in katakana or kanji, I pointed out.

"I can't agree with that view, Kyon. Hiragana, katakana, and kanji all have their own meanings and intonations. They're all different. I mean, just say my name in hiragana and see how it sounds."

It might have felt a little softer. Haruhi (はるひ) as opposed to Haruhi (春日) or Haruhi (ハルヒ). But that aside—

Yasumi (ヤスミ) instead of Yasumi (泰水), eh?

I thought about it. After about thirty seconds of quiet contemplation, I came to the unambiguous conclusion that her name was nowhere in my recollection. Even taking into consideration the fact that she was in the academic class under mine, the snowy plain of my memory remained unsullied by the footsteps of her name. I was certain of it.

I did not know this girl.

And yet my brain stewed in the contradictory sense of unease I felt, that somewhere, somehow I had met her, or known of her.

Haruhi seemed completely unworried.

"I wonder what we should make the new recruit do? We hunted for mysterious phenomena last year, and it's probably too soon to make her the lead in our next movie…I should've asked if she plays an instrument!"

Evidently the only things Haruhi was worried about were the morale activities she was going to put our promising new member through.

Was I the only one who felt something amiss in this strange disharmony? This strange unease, like a petite bomb had fallen to disrupt our peaceful days?

Yasumi Watahashi's secret.

What was it? Was it something that merited investigation?

I looked to Koizumi.

But the SOS Brigade's lieutenant brigade chief only sipped at the buckwheat tea Asahina had prepared, and didn't so much as blink at the eye contact I so generously spared him.

Hmph.

…Well, fine. If he wasn't going to worry about it, then I didn't need to worry about it either. Isn't that right, Koizumi?

β — 9

The next day, Wednesday.

A day containing hardly anything, leaving me free to ruminate.

After being forcibly awakened by my sister, who came to roll around on the bed with Shamisen, my first conscious thought was only, *Ah, now I have more time to spend agonizing over everything.* I had too much to think about, and no idea how or with what to start.

Naturally, waking up this way wasn't very pleasant, and as soon as I awoke I was plunged into melancholy. Sometimes you have occasion to remember just how pleasant being unconscious is. Sleep can be the perfect getaway. But it's also a perfect way to procrastinate, and a perfect waste of time.

The fact that I watched my sister carrying Shamisen innocently around by the scruff of his neck and felt not indulgent happiness but frank envy probably pointed to a character flaw on my part as her older brother. I should've been just as innocent and childish a few years ago as she was now, but I had no memory of it at all. On the contrary, all I had were memories I wanted to forget. Despite that we shared the same DNA, my path and my sister's were totally divergent. Was it because of our differing sexes, or birth years? Or was it because our blood types were different? I didn't believe in either blood type personality analysis or horoscopes; such superstitions were absurd, but perhaps it was true that one's personality could easily be shaped by the surrounding people, particularly friends.

I'd grown up as a cynic; my sister was straightforward and honest, and there'd been little change in this pattern for several years. As her older brother, I couldn't help hoping that she wouldn't turn totally rebellious upon the change of environment that would come with middle school and its pressures. I wanted her to be able to stay carefree, like Tsuruya had. Maybe just sending her to the Tsuruya household to stay as an adopted daughter would be a good idea. Tsuruya would certainly enjoy educating a little girl, and would probably snicker all the while as she accomplished the task of mingling their assembled interests. Although the notion of a Tsuruya number 2 appearing did give me pause.

Incidentally, Tsuruya was the most trustworthy normal person I knew. Sometimes I wondered if she would end up being the one who took decisive action to solve the SOS Brigade's problems, especially the ones related to Haruhi and Asahina. One way or another, she just didn't seem like a completely unconcerned party. Isn't that right, Tsuruya?

There was, after all, the out-of-place artifact she'd been entrusted with—that object and message we'd excavated from the mountain, left behind by the Tsuruya ancestor ages ago. I was sure we'd need it eventually. There was no way it was just some cultural relic. It was another trump card in my hand. Whether it was an item that could be used against time travelers somehow, or a weapon capable of finishing off an alien, while its purpose was unknown I was certain the day would come when I would need it. Although of course I was also prepared for the possibility that it was a useless piece of scrap from the Genroku era.

But you could never have too many jokers. Even if they were like red fives, ura dora, or open riichi in mah-jongg.

Like always, the routine work of having to climb the hill to school was no more than a bullet point on the day's outline.

My gait was at about its usual pace, although I sped up a little bit to avoid that heartless gate closing on me just as I approached it. As usual, the reason I couldn't give myself a little leeway in going to school was because the time I left my house was basically fixed, and if I think back, the truth is because there hadn't been much change in the time I awoke between last year and this one. Having managed to get to school on time once, I would assume I could wake up at the same time the next day and do the same thing—this was the result of accumulated human experience. Students who made it a point to get to school early despite no need to do so must've just had an unhealthy fetish for our dingy campus buildings.

On this day in particular, as I gasped my way up the hill during the depressing commute to school that I'd nonetheless been making for over a year, an unexpected voice called out to me from behind.

"Kyon!"

It was Kunikida. He must've hurried to catch me, because his breath was ragged, and he was looking bewildered in a way I'd never seen.

"You're every bit the person I've always known. You haven't changed a bit," he said suddenly, going completely off the script of morning greetings.

What was this? And moreover, why did he feel the need to inform me of his feelings about me at this exact moment?

Kunikida came alongside me, and I slowed my stride a bit. Once his breathing became calmer, he continued, ignoring my confused expression.

"Sasaki's the same. She's just like she was in middle school. My impression of her hasn't changed at all."

What of it? Why was Sasaki's name coming out of his mouth, with this particular timing? I asked.

"I'm saying, you, me, and Sasaki have all become high school students. But when I first met Kuyoh, she felt different somehow. I feel bad for Taniguchi, saying this, but I got the sense that I didn't want to get too close to her. I still feel that way."

You couldn't exactly call that perceptive. I can't imagine any reasonable person who wouldn't look at Kuyoh and feel something suspicious. Kunikida's impression was completely normal and understandable.

"She's just not a normal, regular, average human. I can't tell if that's a good thing or a bad thing. But I definitely wouldn't go out with her. I guess Taniguchi would. Oh, also—" Kunikida lowered his voice and brought his head closer to mine. "I feel bad saying it, but I get the same feeling about Asahina and Nagato. I think it might be my imagination, but there's something different about them. But since Tsuruya hangs out with you guys pretty regularly, I figure there's nothing to worry about. Sorry, Kyon—don't worry about it, okay? I just wanted to say something. If the SOS Brigade ever needs my assistance, I want you to let me know."

We talked about trivialities after that, until reaching our classroom and concluding our conversation. It was as though having gotten it off his chest, he was no longer worried about anything at all, so we chattered about our worries about the upcoming midterms, complained about the two-thousand-meter run in gym class, and other such magnificently normal topics of small talk.

Did he just want to provide me with a little bit of advice? I couldn't help noting that while it was a little vague, his mention of Tsuruya was quite insightful.

So it seemed that I had a friend that was a little worried about us, despite the fact that he didn't know much. Although he was about the only classmate of mine who knew about Sasaki. It wouldn't be surprising if he'd sensed something of the strange relationship that existed between me and her. I supposed I was happy to have a friend who was so perceptive on my behalf. He'd helped me out before tests, and we'd known each other since middle school, and it was quite possible that soon he'd be elevated above "random classmate A" status in Haruhi's mind. I hoped Taniguchi, on the other hand, would be left out. He was more suited to remaining an eternal one-man comedy act.

I was sure Kunikida felt the same way, which was probably why he'd chosen the time he did, when it was just the two of us, to approach me.

Somehow my instincts seemed to be getting sharper than those of the normal people around me. Whose doing was this?

Morning and afternoon classes passed without incident, and I dozed my way through about half of my classes before I realized the chime signaling the end of school was ringing.

After school, as she'd said she would, Haruhi went straight to Nagato's place to take care of her, taking Asahina with her, leaving Koizumi and me alone in the clubroom. Without the three regular female members, the clubroom was a desolate place indeed. And of course not a single freshman member had appeared. I didn't particularly mind that—honestly, I was grateful. If anybody did come with things as they were, it would be as if they'd shown up for a part-time job interview while the manager was on vacation.

"Hm?"

Suddenly I realized something. The simple fact was that without Haruhi there *was* no SOS Brigade. Nothing would be accomplished without her presence; we couldn't even do an informational presentation. It was like a passenger train without an engine; it had no locomotive ability, and could only sit motionless on the tracks.

As I sat there, glumly silent, Koizumi spoke up.

"What shall we do? We've played all the board games out, so shall we get some exercise?" he said. The artificiality of his suggestion was totally obvious.

"Sure, why not." I figured some physical activity would help my mood.

Koizumi got a cardboard box down from up on the shelf, and showed me its contents.

Inside was the dented aluminum bat and battered baseball glove that had previously shown up when we'd played in the city baseball tournament. Haruhi had swiped them from the school's baseball team and never bothered to give them back, obstinately keeping them here. She really was a hamster that just hoarded things in her nest. I hoped she wasn't planning on entering another baseball tournament this year. Entering was one thing, but using a magical bat that hit only home runs two years in a row would certainly be frowned on—and for my part, I didn't want to stand on the pitcher's mound a second time. Give me backyard soccer any day.

I peered in the cardboard box, but found no baseballs of any kind. Instead was a tennis ball that Haruhi had picked up somewhere. If we were playing in a courtyard, that'd definitely be safer.

Thus Koizumi and I took the worn-out glove and shaggy fluorescent yellow tennis ball, and left the room, which seemed unlikely to host a visitor any time soon.

The courtyard was completely free of occupants. Those students who went home after school had done so, and the art and culture clubs were in their various rooms conducting their various activities. The only thing I could hear was the clumsy trumpeting of the brass band club, almost drowning out the faint sounds of shouting that came from the athletic clubs on the field.

None of the students who came to the courtyard to eat their lunches were around, so the only things stopping us from playing catch were the cherry trees that were planted here and there. Hardly any petals remained; green was spreading such that I was sure the basket worms would be overjoyed.

"I'll start, then," said Koizumi pleasantly, then lobbed the ball to me.

There was hardly any sound as the ball landed in my glove. It was obvious he was taking it easy. I grabbed the tennis ball and chucked it back to him, sidearm.

"Nice throw," said Koizumi, giving his standard hollow compliment. He tossed it back to me like an infielder catching a grounder and throwing it to first for an easy out.

After Koizumi and I had killed some time silently tossing the ball back and forth for a while, I couldn't help remembering the words

Tachibana had said—words that I thought I'd forgotten, indeed, had wanted to forget.

—*I can't help but respect him.*

There weren't many people who revered the ceremonial lieutenant brigade chief of the SOS Brigade. Especially leaving out his popularity among the girls in his class owing to his looks and affability.

"Koizumi."

"Yes?"

"Uh…" I stumbled over my words, and hated myself for it. Koizumi himself was the leader of an organization of espers, and Mori, Arakawa, and the Tamaru brothers were all his subordinates? I wasn't so naive as to just buy that. "Never mind."

Koizumi didn't show a hint of suspicion at my sudden silence, and instead replied as though he was already aware of what I was going to say. "Can I ask you a question, then?" he asked back at me. "Have you ever heard the term 'Gnosticism'?"

"Never. I don't know a thing about politics. I don't even understand the difference between communism and socialism."

"It's something I think you should understand. For your future reference, let's say," said Koizumi with a rueful grin, adding that he meant Gnosticism. "You can think of it as a philosophy, or perhaps a religion. It would be difficult for a polytheistic nation like ours to simply embrace it. Simply put, it's considered heretical even among those who believe in a single omnipotent God. To find its origins you must go back quite a ways—while it's thought of as heresy now, it was well established by the time Christianity was created."

Unfortunately I tended to sleep through social studies, so I had no idea what he was talking about, I said.

"In that case, maybe I should give you a brief overview of Gnosticism. If you'll allow me to summarize it, that is."

I had no objections, so long as he could summarize it such that a grade school kid could understand it.

"Ancient people felt that the world was filled with wickedness.

If the world had been created by an omnipotent, infallible creator, then that creator surely wouldn't have made something so full of pointless suffering. Surely He would have created a more perfect utopia. But societal conflicts spread injustice far and wide, and the wicked rose to power and tormented the weak. Why would God create such a terrible place, and then leave it alone?"

He probably realized his game was on the path to the bad ending, so he got bored and left, I said.

"Quite possibly," said Koizumi, tossing the ball straight up in the air, then catching it. "However, couldn't we think about it this way? The world was not created by a benevolent creator, but rather by a malicious one."

It amounted to the same thing, didn't it? Whether or not the carpenter was malicious, if he followed bad building plans, the building was going to be flawed. Let the courts settle the question.

"And if God is malicious, it makes sense for Him to overlook evil acts, because He Himself is evil. But humanity is not entirely wicked. We also possess a sense of righteousness. The fact that we can recognize evil for what it is is proof that we can resist it with good. If the world were entirely evil without any good anywhere, we wouldn't even be able to have the concept of goodness."

Koizumi rotated the ball around in his fingertips.

"And so the ancients believed that the world was created by a false god, and believed that their ability to recognize that fact was the single ray of light that shone in from none other than the true God, who still existed somewhere. In other words, God doesn't exist within the world, but watches over it from outside."

Well, they'd have to think so. Otherwise what would the point be?

"Indeed. And because this tradition holds the creator of the world to be a demon, the adherents of other religions quite understandably tried to suppress it. Have you learned about the Albigensian Crusade in world history class yet?"

I wasn't sure, but I said I'd ask Haruhi later.

"Incidentally, it's reasonable to say that gnostic beliefs are broadly in accord with modern thinking. That said, human psychology has not changed appreciably since ancient times. What we can conceive of now, earlier people could as well. No matter how much our technology and precision of observation improve, the biological limits on our intelligence will not change dramatically. We've reached a dead end in our evolution, and not just recently either. It's been a condition throughout human history."

I felt as if he was making some logical leaps, but I wasn't particularly adept at academic witticisms, so I stayed strategically silent. Making dumb remarks that prolonged the conversation was against my principles.

"So, now, to put our current situation in context—"

So all this lengthy explanation was just a preamble? How very like Koizumi.

"Tachibana's faction regards Suzumiya as a false god. She may well be the creator of this world. But she lack self-awareness, and they feel that lack of awareness proves their thesis, that she is not the true God. In which case, there must be a true God somewhere in which they can put their confidence. And they've found her. Although it's also possible that they only think they've found her."

And that was Sasaki. My strange middle school classmate and self-proclaimed "good friend."

"There is also the matter of closed space," said Koizumi as though making small talk. "Suzumiya's closed space is filled with the will to destroy. For a creator, she's not very interesting in creating. It's not as though her space is going to attract any public enterprise," he said, tossing out a bad joke before continuing. "On the other hand there's Sasaki, whose closed spaces are, I've heard, very stable, almost like the steady-state theory of the universe. Apparently they're eternally peaceful. It's likely that more people would prefer such a world. There are no <Celestials>. Only quiet and tranquility."

I thought back. I remembered the deserted street, suffused in light. For being totally unpopulated, it gave off a soft, gentle feeling.

It was a place that gave you a glimpse of peacefulness. Stressed-out students trying to find a quiet place to study for exams would probably seek permission to visit there in droves.

"To go even further," continued Koizumi, "if closed space like Sasaki's kept being created, there would probably be fewer problems. That said, Suzumiya does possess a reasonable mind, and she doesn't immediately explode just because she didn't get her way; she's capable of calming down. The situation is like a lit fuse. If it's put out along the way, nothing will happen, but if we let things accumulate, the fire will reach the powder stores."

So she's the Balkan Peninsula in the twentieth century, then?

"Boom," said Koizumi, spreading his arms. "This is how closed space is created; <Celestials> accelerate the process."

Koizumi stroked his chin, as though he were a famous detective about to present the results of his trademark deduction.

"On the other hand, Sasaki constantly creates a fixed amount of closed space, and doesn't allow them to run rampant. Maybe that's their reasoning."

So which was the right way? Irregular releases of pent-up pressure, or a steady dribble—which was better for the most people?

"As far as that goes, I don't know," said Koizumi, evading an answer while flicking the ball with his thumb. "Since I'm on Suzumiya's side, my decision can hardly be said to be unbiased. Even if an objective decision is possible, I certainly can't make it. I can only play out my part. I'm confident that I won't overstep my own role. While she is technically my specialty, my vision when it comes to Suzumiya is rather clouded. I would rather leave the decision up to someone who knows both Suzumiya and Sasaki equally well."

Whoever could he have meant.

"There's one more thing I'd like to say," said Koizumi, his words as pleasant as a spring skylark. "At this moment, the SOS Brigade enjoys the greatest unity it's ever had. Whether it's our alien, our time traveler from a future Earth, or a limited esper who sympathizes with Suzumiya, there are essentially no barriers between us.

Our desires and goals are all the same. And at the center, there's Suzumiya. And—"

Koizumi paused like some stage director had told him to. With an exaggerated gesture, he finished his statement.

"—there's you."

There was no point in trying to feign ignorance, so I pointlessly punched my mitt. C'mon, lemme have it.

"This is the problem facing everyone in the SOS Brigade. We're all involved. Nagato and Kuyoh, Asahina and Fujiwara, my Agency and Tachibana's faction. You and Sasaki. We're all connected by a thread, all heading toward a single point at which, no matter how the action there resolves, there will be a conclusion. This may no longer be just your problem."

"So what am I supposed to do? Crack jokes? Watch from the side? Try to record events as best I can for the sake of future historians?"

"You can do whatever you like." Koizumi rotated the ball in his hand like a pitcher trying to decide between a two-seam and a four-seam fastball. "I expect you'll know what to do when the time comes. You may not be able to help it, honestly. You need only act according to your own will. You probably don't have to think about it. Humans are generally capable of taking the best available action, so long as their judgment hasn't been affected. And so far your actions have all been right. I'm half convinced the next time will turn out the same way, and half looking forward to seeing it."

He said all that, and seemed to be finished talking. Koizumi threw the ball again. It was a straight throw with a lot of heat on it. As I felt my glove close around it, I decided I didn't have anything else to ask.

It was true—.

It wouldn't be Koizumi, or Asahina, or Nagato. And it certainly wouldn't be Haruhi.

The duty of finishing this had been passed to me. It had always been that way. Usually I'd mutter it off saying something like "Oh brother," but now probably wasn't the time to unseal that particular line.

I'd felt that way all along. I'd always known. Naturally I didn't know what I was supposed to do, but I knew that I would do it. The image of a prone Nagato, along with Haruhi and Asahina's worried faces, flickered in my brain. And here I was playing catch with Koizumi?

This was not what I was supposed to be doing. The SOS Brigade's operations didn't include anything this stupid. Not so far, and not starting now.

"Hmph."

I raised my arms in a proper windup, and threw the ball at Koizumi's glove with all my strength.

"Nice curveball," he complimented me, though I'd been meaning to throw a fastball.

"Ah, whatever." However reluctantly, I could admit that it was a result that was very like me. So long as the batter was confused, right?

Time for another pitch. Though I wasn't sure exactly who the batter was.

I threw my best breaking ball.

The ball hit Koizumi's glove with a pleasantly dry *thwack*.

"If I could transform into Superman, or someone else out of American superhero comics..." I knew it was an impossible absurdity, and yet I still said it out loud. "If I just had the power to set the whole world straight in one go—if that happened, I wouldn't be a good guy. I'd just beat up everybody I didn't like."

Koizumi was about to toss the ball back to me, but froze his motion, and looked at me like a biologist in the deep jungle who's discovered a rare organism of some kind. He chuckled with that faint smile of his. "That's not impossible. All that needs to happen is for Suzumiya to wish for it. If she believed you had powers you were keeping hidden, and were constantly battling your enemies in secret—if you could get her to truly believe in that setting, then you really could become a superhero. I won't withhold my assistance, but…do you really prefer that kind of battle? To defeat the alien with a punch, to scatter the plans of the time traveler with a shout? I'll say it again, but depending on Suzumiya, that's not impossible."

I didn't even need time to think about it. That was not my role. Suddenly becoming a superhero and beating the crap out of my enemies? I mean, really—solving my problems with force?

What was this, some kind of kid's show from who-knew-what era? Hadn't this kind of thing died out like thirty years ago? For something like that to happen these days, it would be conclusive proof that human culture was mired in nostalgia, and wasn't moving forward at all. I preferred to be connected to modern narratives, thank you very much.

After all, I was kind of a cynic, sorry to say. Old-school stereotypes like that were worth about as much to me as toilet paper.

I caught what was either a low lob or a slow curve from Koizumi, and gave thought to the manner of just what devilish spin I would put on this tennis ball to trick the batter, before remembering the saying that a bad idea was worse than no idea at all.

Having bored of playing catch, Koizumi and I returned to the clubroom. Unsurprisingly, no one was there. There was neither hide nor hair of anything resembling a new applicant, which I found a bit surprising. Out of so many new freshmen, you'd think at least one of them would have a gear loose upstairs, but maybe my thinking so was proof that my brain had been contaminated by Haruhi.

There was no news from Haruhi or Asahina, who were probably living it up over at Nagato's place. No news was good news. Haruhi doubtless still thought Nagato was simply suffering from a cold, and planned to cure her with a combination of folk remedies and sheer will. Asahina was probably helping out quite a bit, despite her wariness of Nagato—no doubt her concern for a fallen comrade would take precedence over whatever ideology she held. Future Asahina aside, *this* Asahina was a good person through and through. Just so long as Nurse Asahina wasn't actually wearing a nurse outfit...

Though we returned to the clubroom, we had about as much to do as a rookie starting pitcher who wound up getting pulled after the first inning.

So after we finished playing catch, we put the equipment away, made sure nobody had turned the PC on, locked the room up, and put the school behind us. It was a good opportunity to go home and meditate again to summon my resolve for the task to come.

I stopped my beloved bike at the front door, and opened the unlocked door, only to be met by the sight of my sister's colorful shoes scattered about the entryway, along with a pair of black loafers with which I was unfamiliar. Given the size, they probably belonged to a girl. I went inside, thinking little of it other than assuming that Miyokichi was probably visiting again, and when I headed upstairs to my room and walked in, I nearly backflipped, so freaked-out was I by the sight that greeted me.

I no longer found the sight of my smiling sister trespassing in my room particularly surprising, but seeing her playmate gave me a shock like being smacked in the forehead by a giant dragonfly out on a countryside road.

The girl had Shamisen on her lap and was stroking him indulgently. She looked up and narrowed her eyes at me in a friendly smile.

"What a nice cat. I read it in an essay somewhere, but cat personalities are hit-or-miss completely irrespective of breed or lineage. Apparently it has more to do with the owner's qualities. So far as I can tell, you really nailed it with Shamisen here. You're not just lucky for owning a male calico. How do I put this: It's like he's got a certain cleverness about him, but also retained a certain wildness, such that it makes you wonder if he doesn't understand humans better than even a human child would."

"I get the feeling he doesn't even think of himself as a cat. Sometimes he definitely acts superior to humans."

"Kyon, you've got it backward. Cats think of humans as being like them—in other words, cats. They think of humans as just being slightly larger cats. That's why they don't show us any deference, since from their perspective, we're less agile and we can't even catch our own food. We're just clumsy animals who are only good at sitting. That's where they're different from dogs. Dogs have had to fit themselves into human society for ages. And because humans and dogs are both creatures that have to live in groups, it's easy for them to get along. Dogs probably think of themselves as being the same species as humans. That's how they can be so loyal to their owner or leader."

"Sasaki," I said in a hoarse voice, forgetting to even put my bag down. I then finally faced my sister. "Where's Mom?"

"She went to get groceries for dinner!" said my sister, totally oblivious.

"I see. Well, no matter. Anyway, get out."

"Whaa?" She puffed her cheeks out. "I've been having fun with Sasaki! Kyon, you meanie!"

She did her best to tilt her head and look cute, but I was having none of it. "No way. I have important stuff to talk about with Sasaki. Also, were you the one who let her in? I thought you knew better than to let strangers into the house when you're alone."

"She's not a stranger! Sasaki used to come over with you all the time. I mean, at least to the front door. I used to see you together on your bikes all the time. Right?"

My sister turned her pleading face to Sasaki for backup, and Sasaki nodded with a chagrined smile. "I'm happy you remember. Kids sure do grow up quickly, though. I barely recognized her. I guess it's a little rude to say 'kid.' You're a lovely girl."

Really? From where I was standing, her appearance and personality had hardly changed since then, I said.

"That's how siblings always are. You've always been together, so she's just a part of your everyday scenery. You're watching her maturation in real time, so you can't see its precise result; it's like an

analog clock to you. On the other hand, I have a digital snapshot of her, so the change for me is really significant."

I supposed that made sense, but Sasaki hadn't come to my house to talk about my sister growing up, I pointed out.

"True enough. I'm not controlled by my emotions to the extent that I take such random actions."

I picked the purring Shamisen up off of Sasaki's lap, and passed him to my sister, whom I then pushed out of the room.

"Meow!"

I ignored Shamisen's cry of protest. "Just go play downstairs. We have something just the two of us need to discuss. It wouldn't even be interesting to you, and we're not playing. Go put some of the catnip spray on the scratching post in the living room. And he'd be thrilled if you clean the litter box and brush his fur."

"Whaa? But I want to talk with Sasaki too! I wanna know what you're gonna say!" Holding Shamisen, my sister made a full-body protest, but I forced her out. For a while I could hear the grade schooler and the cat grumbling on the other side of the door, whining and meowing respectively, but eventually I heard them go downstairs, and finally calm returned to me from its place high above the clouds.

It's also possible that Sasaki's chuckling had something to do with returning me to my normal state.

"She's very, very cute. You don't have to talk with her much to know she's your sister. You're her closest relative, and she thinks of you as being almost magical. Just when she was thinking she wanted a cat, you happened to bring that calico home. She really respects you quite a bit."

Funny, I never detected a bit of respect from her. Up until two or three years ago she was a helpless crybaby. How many times did I fantasize about shoving a gag in her mouth? But I knew from experience that there were people whose families didn't include a little sister, and so the word calls to mind a certain image, so I suppose I could see how it would look that way from the outside. But none of that mattered.

Or so I thought, but Sasaki pressed her attack.

"By the way, this is totally unrelated, but why do you think cats prefer drinking used bathwater instead of fresh water?"

What was she talking about?

Sasaki chuckled. "Like I said, it's totally unrelated."

"And?" My bag was still hanging over my shoulder; I finally set it down on the bed, then sat myself down cross-legged in front of Sasaki, regarding my old classmate's pleasantly smiling face. "So what is it you came to talk to me about? I very much hope it's not 'unrelated.'"

"All sorts of things." Sasaki's gaze was as pleasant as a cherry blossom tree in full bloom. "I was thinking you must be getting pretty close to your limit. Our last meeting had too many interruptions, in more than one sense of the word. For my part, I've been hoping to get to talk to you alone. I was so sure you would have some kind of plan that I stayed up all night waiting for your call. I actually thought it was a bit of a joke that there was no ringing at all."

Surely it wasn't that big of a deal. I was totally at a loss myself. How was I supposed to deal with that alien, for example? It wasn't as if I could just look up the dispatcher for the galactic cops in the yellow pages.

Sasaki gave me a mischievous look as though she knew where all of my traps were hidden. "How cruel! Ah well, no matter. I'm used to you. I've no compunctions about engaging the spirit of forgiveness. So, moving on to the topic at hand."

I was still a little vague on what the topic at hand was supposed to be, but I went ahead and nodded anyway. If she was going to tell me, the least I could do was hear Sasaki out. She'd gone to the trouble of making a house call, after all. Whatever she was going to say would be worth hearing.

"First, I'll tell what I've learned about Kuyoh Suoh after much trial and error."

That was definitely one of the things I wanted more information about. I'd turn my ear to her until it was at about the level of a dachshund, if I had to.

Sasaki picked off some fur Shamisen had left behind on her legs, and gazing at it, continued. "Ever since I was a kid, I've imagined what extraterrestrial life would look like, if it existed. In manga and novels, we're often able to observe them optically, and being able to communicate with them is something of a prerequisite. For example, establishing if they understand things like prime numbers. Items like universal translation devices were also not uncommon."

The number of space novels that began with such premises were too numerous to count. Thanks to Nagato's influence, even I'd started reading tricky foreign SF novels. You can learn a lot from fiction, I said.

"Well, leaving that aside," said Sasaki, twirling Shamisen's fur about in her fingers, "Nagato's Data Overmind and Kuyoh's Heavenly Canopy Dominion are fundamentally different from the easily understood aliens humans have created in their stories."

I wanted the old SF authors who wrote about humanoid aliens on Mars or Mercury to hear that sentence. It might have motivated them to write more interesting stories at the time.

"Good point. And that's not just limited to SF either. If John Dickson Carr had lived in this era, he could've used modern technology to create even more amazing locked-room mysteries, which I would have been totally addicted to. I wonder if we could bring Carr back into the current era. Would you ask Asahina about that for me? I'm being serious."

Unfortunately, even I had found traveling into the past to be traumatizing enough, and I'd never been to the future. Thanks to all that classified information stuff, I guessed taking someone ahead into the future was probably against the rules.

"That's just a digression, though."

The bit of calico fluff fell from Sasaki's slender fingers.

Her clear gaze took in my face. It was the sign that the small talk was over.

"What I think is that Nagato and Kuyoh are unable to understand human reasoning and values. They've forced themselves down from a higher dimension of existence to be among humans, so even if they understand what we're saying, they don't understand why we're saying it. Or maybe they don't understand why we would need to say such things. If out of the five W's and one H, you only understand 'who' and 'where,' and find the other four completely incomprehensible, do you think you'd be able to have a conversation with a being like that?"

I did not. I could barely understand what Nagato said, so when it came to Kuyoh it was hard to know even what role she played in this particular whodunit.

But Sasaki continued. "This issue of incomplete communication is not actually a very complicated problem. For example, can you understand the values of a water flea or a paramecium? Do you imagine having a conversation with the whooping cough bacteria, or a mycoplasma?"

I allowed as how that would be difficult, at my intelligence level.

"Even if single-celled organisms or bacteria had human-level intelligence, I'm sure they'd feel the same way. They'd wonder what those bipedal mammals were thinking when they did what they did. What do humans want out of life, they'd wonder. They'd probably be totally shocked after they asked what humans wanted to do with this planet, this universe."

I wasn't even sure myself what my purpose in life was, or what I wanted to do. And in that regard, I was pretty sure I was in the huge majority of humans.

"For example, Kyon—what's the most precious thing in the world to you?"

How was I supposed to answer a question like that on the spot? I asked.

"I couldn't do it either. In this society of complex, rapid information, no one ever quantifies their value systems." There was no change in Sasaki's tone or expression. "For example, for one person it might be money, for others it might be knowledge. For still others it would be relationships. Each person's values are so different that it's impossible to use only your own to try to judge everything in the world—as you and I are well aware. Which is why we can't answer that question quickly."

I supposed that was true.

"But I don't think people in the past would've had to think so much about that question."

I supposed that was true.

Right now, people could access almost any information they wanted to. But just a hundred years ago, or even a few dozen years ago, the information you could access was much more limited. If you went back to the Sengoku era or the Heian era, would they hesitate over what to choose in life more than people did today? Their choices were surely more limited.

Even if you say that freedom of choice has greatly increased, if you consider it to be instead an increase in the worry over what to choose, an increasing number of options would actually be a bad thing. When you have to choose without any information, people choose according to the majority. But that's putting the cart before the horse. Far from diversification, that led to concentration and homogenization.

"Seems like the aliens have privileged the evolution of homogeneity," said Sasaki calmly. "But they're showing signs of having realized there's another side, and my guess is that meeting Suzumiya and you was the trigger for that."

Sure, Haruhi, definitely. I could see her getting a bunch of Martians to elect her president. But me? I didn't have that kind of vitality.

"No, no, the truth is you're quite impressive. You managed to pull off a tense negotiation with an extraterrestrial you could barely communicate with. That's not something just anybody could imitate. No one would even think of it. It's thanks to your experience, I'd say. I envy you, Kyon. From what I've heard, Nagato is a charming being. I really do want to talk with her about her favorite books someday. Kuyoh hardly ever talks in front of me."

She was joking around, but I could tell that Sasaki was at least half-serious.

"So what should I do?" I asked.

"Well, let's think about that. Fortunately, Fujiwara and Kyoko, and even Kuyoh, can all understand our language. This is our biggest weapon. Kyon, think about it; we just need to pin them with our words. I won't claim it'll be easy, but I'm sure you can do it. So can I. After all, thinking and explaining your thoughts to others are abilities every human is born with."

I would love to know just what I could do with a high school–junior level of education and reasoning. Wasn't this a problem better suited to a Nobel prize–winning physicist? I didn't even know if Ganymede was bigger than Triton or not. The only person I knew who was assuredly less academically inclined than me was Taniguchi.

"If that's the extent of your problems, then those aren't problems at all. Because, you see, these matters revolve around Haruhi Suzumiya. Her consciousness is the basis of everything. All the factions have her actions and cognition as their fundamental underpinnings. And that's the weakness we can use."

Sasaki gave a smile that seemed as if she'd grown up ten years in an instant.

"On the other hand, I think adults would only get in our way. They'd want to analyze, break down, figure out a plan of attack… it would all be a waste of time. All of it. Listen, Kyon—this story belongs to you and me. And I think the plot should be about you and me doing something about it."

I couldn't help feeling sorry I'd gotten her mixed up in all of this, I said.

"There's no need to apologize. I've never had so much fun.

Honestly, I feel like I haven't thanked you enough, so my plan is to listen to whatever requests you might make," Sasaki said in a tone that I couldn't tell whether it was joking or not. "Also, I think we have a good chance of winning. We're one planet of a backwater star, but we're the stage for this grand galactic-scale conflict, and so long as the aliens with their magic-like powers are here, they have no choice but to move on an Earth-scale level. I'm sure the Data Overmind and the Heavenly Canopy Dominion have either restrictions or unwritten agreements like that between them. Otherwise, there'd be no reason for them to battle covertly the way they are. The same is true of the time travelers. I don't really understand them, but they seem to be operating under certain restrictions. And I'm thinking that's our opening to returning the situation to normal."

But if Sasaki was right and taking action was the right thing to do, how could we know that for sure? I asked.

Sasaki chuckled her distinctive chuckle, like a young girl who was quite sure that Santa would be coming down the chimney to leave her the present she wanted.

"We'll be able to do something soon. I'm sure of it. You can't possibly want the current situation. I doubt Suzumiya does either. And naturally neither do I. With everyone in agreement like this, I can't imagine the situation will develop in the wrong direction."

Seeing Sasaki in her school uniform and looking somehow very pleased gave me a strange feeling of déjà vu, and I realized it reminded me of Haruhi's smile the day she'd formed the SOS Brigade. If Haruhi at the time was like a sunflower, Sasaki now was like a morning glory.

"So—"

So, what had she actually come here to tell me?

"I just wanted to have a face-to-face talk. That's all. Just the two of us, nobody else. Telephone conversations and text messages are no good. The walls have ears, you know?"

In that moment I imagined my sister with her ear pressed up

against the door, and something occurred to me. Was Sasaki really worried about eavesdropping? I was sure that wiretapping a phone was a trivial task for even a moderately sized organization. Certainly Koizumi. Mori and Arakawa...or Kyoko Tachibana's and Fujiwara's respective organizations. If she'd wanted to subtly convey that to me, that would explain this surprise visit.

"Another thing. Fujiwara wants to settle things quickly, is my feeling. Tachibana is easygoing and who knows what Kuyoh is up to, but our time traveler has been very clear about his willingness to pursue his goals. I get the feeling that if it doesn't matter whether a thing is done sooner or later, he'd rather do it sooner. So I think it's very likely he'll take action as soon as tomorrow."

If I could travel back in time to the Yamataikoku era, I'd want to go and find out how much of Chen Shou's writing was accurate. Fujiwara, too, could afford to take his time and do some sightseeing, but he just had to speed things along. Or was he saying there was nothing of even archaeological value in this era?

"But you'd prefer that yourself, wouldn't you?"

What I wanted was to resolve this vague situation and bring Nagato's fever down, I said.

"This is a total guess on my part," prefaced Sasaki, "but the problem that we're facing may be just showing our reason for existence. It's possible that everyone is working so hard just because they're trying to make their raison d'etre into a reality. This isn't a matter of being an alien, time traveler, or esper. Each of them must exist, and try to get another being to acknowledge their existence—and they're all taking action with that single goal in mind. I mean, Kyon, have you acknowledged that Kuyoh, Tachibana, and Fujiwara all exist here and now? I mean just to the extent that you wouldn't forget them, even if they all just disappeared. They were here, in this place, in this time. Perhaps their wish is but a single plaintive sentiment—'Don't forget us.'"

I didn't get it. If that was it, they didn't have to do it in this particular era, right in front of me. I mean, I didn't doubt that I would remember their forms and actions until I died, but so what? I wasn't the clerk responsible for keeping court records, nor the editor of a historical textbook. They should've just gone back to the time of Tacitus and Herodotus and caused trouble there. Or at least found some people with similar interests in this era.

As I thought Sasaki's words over, my former middle school and cram school classmate started rubbing her cheeks with her fists for some reason, her eyes narrowing as she did so. What was this? Facial calisthenics? I asked.

"Nope," said Sasaki, putting her hands down. "It's just that when I talk with you I always wind up with my face stuck in a smile, so my facial muscles were getting tight. We're talking about serious stuff, though, so I wanted to see if I could change my expression. What do you think?"

I looked with concentration fit to tell the difference between a seven-spotted ladybug and a twenty-eight-spotted one, but all I could say was that I didn't see much change. She was sort of grinning, or smiling...come to think of it, I wasn't sure I'd seen an expression other than some kind of smile on Sasaki's face since middle school.

As I gazed at her face, something occurred to me.

"So what's your reason for existing?"

She answered immediately, as though she'd predicted this question in advance. "Speaking as a single human, it's to pass on my genes, of course. To have children and send the elements of your composition down into the future. This is the nature of all living things. Or at least of all living things on this earth."

I wasn't asking about her views on evolutionary theory. I mean from our perspective, even if we knew how we were going to pass our genes on, what then? And anyway, for the moment such questions were not exactly relevant to us.

"Good grief. Questions like why are we born, why do we live... these are no more than Zen riddles. You might think they contain some intellectual value, but in reality they're meaningless. But given that, if I were to answer again, I would say that my first reason for existence is 'to think,' and my second is 'to think some more.' I'll only stop thinking when I'm dead, and likewise, not thinking seems equal to death to me. The individual called 'I' would disappear, leaving only an animalistic being."

Sasaki chuckled her low chuckle.

"I want to keep thinking. About the whole of the universe. Until I die."

And what remained at the end of all that thinking? I wanted to know. Other than childbearing.

"That's an excellent question, Kyon. An extremely human question. If you're going to leave behind something that will endure in this world other than your genes, then there's no need to be too concerned about twin helices made of amino acids. Since the beginning of history, we humans have left behind all kinds of things—from huge, possibly futile monuments to small but epoch-defining tools, technological innovations, nationally sponsored works of cultural art, or completely new theories that take us into the future..."

From Sasaki's expression, I could tell that in her mind she was crossing through the eras of history as she considered the issue.

"All the great figures we've learned about in world history have left their mark by doing something worthy of the term 'greatness.' My mind and body can only be considered small and weak. But if I use my ability to think as the first step, I might well come up with some new idea that endures into the future. To be honest, that's what I want—to create something, raise it up, and leave it to endure. Something besides my own DNA."

That was a grandiose ambition, I said.

"I'm fine just leaving behind a word or an idea. If we're talking about ambition, that's my only one. But I want to do it on my own power. I don't want any help from aliens, time travelers, or espers. My thoughts are mine and mine alone, and I don't want any interference. My reason for existing, as I've defined it, is arriving at conclusions on my own. I want to create my own original ideas or words. So they're an obstacle—Kuyoh and Fujiwara are. As for Tachibana...I feel like we could become good, close friends. She's that group's sole redeeming member."

I was pretty sure I'd never heard Sasaki speak so passionately about something. Or so honestly. Okay, fine, I'd match her candor with some of my own.

"Sasaki. If you had power like Haruhi has, you could make all of this come true."

"You think so, Kyon? I'm still a regular person, you know. I have all sorts of conflicting desires and emotions. Sometimes I just wish so-and-so would die. But if my wishing for it made that person actually die, I'd be deeply affected and would never forgive myself. I'd have to prohibit myself from ever thinking certain things, even a little bit. I could never be like Suzumiya. If she really does have god-like omnipotent power, then it's a miracle she's able to live a normal life in the world. I mean, her very being is essentially equivalent to a miracle."

Sasaki curled her lips into their usual sardonic smirk, and looked straight at me.

"Of course, I was on the side of those who rejected the notion of a godlike being. Even if such a being existed, they were not in this world, much less unaware of their own powers. Think about it. Would you jump into a goldfish bowl of your own free will? Would you smash the glass at an aquarium or jump the fence into a zoo, to join the fish or the caged animals?"

I felt as if she was dodging the question. This was why I avoided having intense one-on-one conversations with smart people. It would've been nice to get some backup from Koizumi.

"What I mean is, a higher being would fall into a lower plane of existence. There's no difference between gods and humans in that sense. That's what I think." Sasaki waved her hand exaggeratedly, and half-jokingly continued. "Suzumiya is supposed to be something like a god. And somehow, people think that's true of me too.

If she and I, both demigods, are directing affection to you, then it's hardly the case that you can't do anything. If something happens, you'll be the one to do it. You're the one who's going to lower the curtain and raise it on the next scene. Wake up, Kyon! You are the fulcrum—you hold the master key in your hand."

I was the key figure when Haruhi disappeared, but this time I wasn't so confident.

"You will end up resolving this matter. That's a little prophecy I can make in this moment." Sasaki laughed, and it sounded like the cry of a dove in the morning. "I've put the whole of my trust in you, Kyon. You're my dearest, dearest friend."

No matter how much she massaged her face, all I could see in it was that soft smile.

"I know you can do it. In fact, I think you're the only one who can. So you should. If it's impossible for Suzumiya the god, Nagato the extraterrestrial, Koizumi the esper, then it falls to you, the representative of the normal. It's your nature, and it's also your great advantage. Kyon, you didn't meet them and us for no reason. You have a role you're meant to play. I'd bet the beloved stuffed cat I've kept since childhood on it."

As though that were some kind of ending signal, Sasaki glanced around my room, then stood. "I should be going," she said, smiling at me. And then almost as an afterthought, added, "No need to see me out. You've already improved my mood. Give my best to your lovely little sister and that magnificent cat. I hope to play with them more the next time I come by."

There was a strange pause.

Standing, Sasaki fixed me in her gaze. Not knowing what to do, I didn't react at all, and eventually Sasaki spoke, this time with a hesitation in her voice I'd not heard before. "Actually, Kyon, I had another reason I came today. It's nothing particularly deep. It doesn't have anything to do with Fujiwara, Tachibana, or Kuyoh. It's just about my school life. I just thought I'd talk to you about it a little bit..."

I didn't think I was a good enough student to give Sasaki any kind of advice about her own life—I wasn't going to be able to figure out anything that had already stumped her. But maybe Sasaki agreed, because she continued.

"No, forget it. I'm glad I got to talk with you like this. I feel a lot better. I get it now. In the end, you have to solve your own problems. I shouldn't have said anything. It's my own weakness, I guess. I shouldn't have talked about something that wouldn't have been helped by talking about it, much less started to ask your advice. I presumed too much. My apologies."

Saying you wanted somebody's advice on something, then suddenly going back on it, was like handing someone a blank test sheet, then immediately snatching it back. Since I would have been unable to give any useful advice to whatever problem Sasaki had considered bringing to me, maybe I should have been grateful that my pride was spared.

"Still," Sasaki said, quirking one corner of her mouth up in that distinctive smirk of hers, "I'm glad I could come see you and chat. I feel like my mind's made up now."

I saw her off as far as the front door, accompanied by my sister holding Shamisen. She had what looked like a sleeper hold on him, and Shamisen looked rather put out by the position.

"Come again!" called my sister, her face full of joy.

Sasaki smiled and waved to the two humans and one animal, then walked energetically off, not turning around.

From the front door I watched her go until she rounded the corner and was out of sight. She really didn't look back once. I didn't know what it was that she'd wanted to ask me about, but—.

It was a very clean, very Sasaki-like exit.

It wasn't until evening, when I was in the bath, that I started to really wonder what it was she'd come to do.

I was staring at a plastic Takkong figure that bobbed in the bathwater; my sister had left it here. I'd been in the bath for a good while, so my circulation was good, but the answer simply wasn't jumping out of the depths of my mind. In the end all I knew for sure was that the final matter that she'd brought up but refused to ask me about wasn't the main issue, but her just shelving the question left a bad taste in my mouth.

Also, I had the feeling that there was a word during my conversation with Sasaki that I'd somehow skipped over and forgotten, but what had it been? It was as if I'd mistyped a computer command and erased that sector of the hard drive. Seemed like a hint that my mental storage was getting overloaded. Maybe it was time to buy a heat sink to cool things down if I wanted to be able to think properly. That said, taking a bath and getting my blood moving wasn't going to chill anything, but it was my habit never to skip a bath or a tooth-brushing, and there wasn't a thing wrong with that. I wasn't some kind of neat freak, but I felt gross if I missed a day, and I know I'm not the only person in the world like that. Right?

Anyway, thanks to Sasaki coming by today I have to confess that I felt relieved. Having talked with her, I understood—she really was trustworthy. Her way of talking and thinking was a little eccentric, but she really was a normal high school girl, and hadn't changed a bit from when I'd known her in middle school. If Sasaki hadn't gone to that prep school, and instead come to North High, I wonder what would've happened? Maybe Koizumi and Tachibana would've transferred in at the same time, making my first year of high school even crazier. But there was no point in dwelling on what-ifs. I had other things to think about.

"Still—" I said to myself with a sigh. "All that said..."

My voice echoed off the walls of the bathroom. To be honest, it was pathetic that I couldn't think of anything.

"At this rate, I might as well go to sleep and ask for some divine inspiration in my dreams."

I murmured what amounted to wishful thinking, then climbed

out of the bathtub. I slid the folding door open, whereupon Shamisen, who'd been waiting impatiently on the bathmat, bolted into the bathroom and began drinking from the sink basin, his tongue lapping noisily for a while. Eventually he looked up at me.

"Myar!"

He said, more or less. It was as if he was speaking cat-ese to point out the error of my thinking. Before I had the chance to interrogate him, his cat claws scratched against the floor as he hurried away and up the stairs. Not that it mattered—I knew he was heading for my bed.

Maybe I'd bring him along the next time I met Kuyoh. Maybe the whatever-they-were life-forms in his head could be of some use with her. It was a faint hope, but one never knew—

And yet.

"Better not."

I'd abandoned the doctrine of depending on others for aid. I'd have to get this done on my own. I needed to think less about whether or not I could do something, and instead just give it a try. That's what Sasaki had suggested, and anyway, putting my hopes in a life-form stupid enough to blunder into Earth and wind up stuck to a dog by accident would itself be pretty stupid. Why not prove that the natives of this solar system had the home-court advantage over any *Andromeda Strain* virus?

That's right, it was time to prove to Kuyoh and Fujiwara that they couldn't just walk all over modern-day humanity. I probably should've entrusted this task to someone whose position, name, and IQ all exceeded my own by several ranks, but I could hardly expect some random stranger to handle all the crazy things that happened around Haruhi Suzumiya. I didn't think anybody would want that job, and honestly, I didn't want to give it to them. This pop quiz had fallen to the SOS Brigade to solve, so we had to be the ones to do it.

And somehow I'd been assigned the central role in all of this, and was the one who would have to do the most running around. I was the only one who'd heard the sickened Nagato's true wishes.

Whether or not she herself was aware of it, Nagato was depending on me. If I couldn't save the few members of a tiny organization like the SOS Brigade, then just what could I save? All I'd be good for was helping my sister with her homework and stopping my mom from shaving Shamisen's fur. If I was stuck in the flow of events like this, I might as well try to swim upstream like a salmon heading home.

My ultimate goal was very simple: to get Nagato back to normal.

I felt energized.

My willpower spiraled into the heavens. If I could have directed that kind of energy to my studies, my mother would've wept with joy. But that had nothing to do with this—sorry, Mom. Anyway, there were no intelligent life-forms on or off the Earth that could stop my determination. That's right—had the quality of a heroic protagonist begun to bloom within me? If I hadn't just gotten out of the bath and been stark naked, I would've raised my right fist into the air in a display of how pointlessly energized I was.

There was no inaccuracy in saying that there was no one who could dampen my spirits. I was sure that Sasaki had come by to give me a smack on the head, given that even a glum snail being rained on in the height of the monsoon season would've laughed at me. In the process of talking about all that unrelated stuff, she guided the listener's mind to a new place—she was actually quite the psychologist. It was a little scary.

"Might as well go for it. I've got an alien, time traveler, and esper to smack out of my line of sight."

It went without saying that Asahina the Younger, Nagato, and also Koizumi weren't part of this. And what about Mori and Kimidori…?

I felt like I was drunk on optimism, but as I talked a big game, in the corner of my mind there lurked my coolly sarcastic other self, cynically deriding me. If I'm honest, that other self was more like the real me. Even I can't deny that superego, who always threw cold water on me at the most crucial moments.

And that other me said this:

Wasn't there someone besides me who could take up the role of the transcendent hero?

It was none other than—had to be—her.

It had to be her.

Or something.

VOLUME 2

CHAPTER 7

α — 10

The next day, Thursday.

The day with its routine of regular classes crawled along, until the end of homeroom freed Haruhi and me from Class 5's room.

Evidently my personalized instruction with Haruhi was only meant to run until the previous day, which brought an end to the strange tutoring that the students on cleaning duty had been able to watch, and so we just left the classroom. And let me just say that our honorable brigade chief was dragging me by the arm, so this was more or less compulsory. I'd like that much to be clear. Although I'll admit I was overjoyed not to be subjected to any further after-school academics.

And just as the route that we took side by side to the literature club room was the same as it always was, so too was the spring atmosphere of the school totally normal. By mid-April, we were entirely used to the season. Not for nothing was it that the faithful, unasked-for reappearance of the seasons controlled life on Earth, I suppose.

But one couldn't resist the constant march of time. Since spring of the previous year, even the SOS Brigade had undergone changes that were impossible to ignore.

Waiting for us was someone who could act as a perfect Exhibit A for that should we need to present evidence at court.

She stood up from her folding chair as though having waited for the precise timing when Haruhi and I would open the door.

"Ready and waiting, ma'am!" shouted the sole freshman to pass Haruhi's absurdly difficult entrance examinations, her voice high like a swallow chick greeting its mother upon the latter's return to the nest. Her hair was a wild tangle, like a failed perm, and to it was affixed that same smiley-face barrette. Her eyes shone like Christmas lights as she looked to us expectantly. "As of today, I'm a member of the SOS Brigade! It's very nice to meet you!"

She bowed deeply.

Yasumi Watahashi. Despite her slight lisp, she had such volume that I wondered if maybe she wouldn't have been better off joining the choir, and her face shone like Venus just before the dawn. At the very least, I could conclude that she had energy levels to match Haruhi's.

"Well…nice to meet you too, I guess."

My halfhearted reply didn't seem to bother Yasumi in the slightest. Her head popped up from her bow. "Yes! You guess right! I'm gonna give it my all!" Her honest, open gaze was like a particle cannon, and it felt as though if I kept looking directly at her energetic smile, it would overload my retinas, so I casually averted my eyes, looking elsewhere in the room for help.

The usual suspects were all there. Asahina had already changed into her maid outfit and was putting the kettle on the burner, and Koizumi was sitting at the table, setting out playing pieces on a game board that was neither shogi nor go. As for Nagato, she was at her usual spot, absorbed in the pages of some hardcover book, ignoring the rest of the universe.

Haruhi seemed pointlessly satisfied, and plopped herself down at the brigade chief's seat. "Now, then!" she began, her voice full of grandiosity as though she were Pope Gregory VII meeting Emperor Henry IV at Canossa, "I'm sure you all know, but I'll introduce her again. Having passed a series of fair and public examinations, this is our new member, Yasumi Watahashi. It's our duty to thoroughly educate her in the lessons that we of the SOS Brigade have learned in the past year—sometimes harshly, sometimes indulgently, like giving cotton candy to a child. She needs to be drilled good and hard in order to become the cornerstone of the next generation of the SOS Brigade!"

"Drilled...?" Asahina looked to Yasumi, then surveyed her own jurisdiction, where the tea implements were, her face like Sen Rikyu wondering how to teach the true meaning of tea ceremony to a general from the provinces. This wasn't the tea ceremony club, so it didn't seem as though such careful tea preparation was called for, but compared with the perfunctory stuff Haruhi brewed, Asahina's fine product was like sweet honeydew melon, so it was worth teaching the Mikuru Asahina school of tea to the new member in order to pass it on to the next generation.

In fact, maybe she could teach Haruhi too. Haruhi's tea was mostly tasteless, being nothing more than hot leaf juice.

"Yes! Tea, tea, I'll brew it, I'll serve it! Please, Asahina, despite my limited ability I hope you'll see fit to instruct me in your ways!" Yasumi seemed to acknowledge Asahina as her master on the spot, immediately advancing into her territory. Asahina seemed flustered for a moment, but seemed to take Yasumi at her word.

"Er, well, this is Suzumiya's cup, and this is Kyon's. Oh, and remember everybody has different temperatures they like. The tea leaves are up here on the shelf. I choose them based on the day's temperature and humidity. What I'm researching right now is this tea here—"

Yasumi watched and nodded, her eyes shining as she followed Asahina's every move like telephoto lenses, not missing a single second.

"Also, I want to wear a maid uniform! And a nurse one! Oh, please let me! Please, please!"

What was the source of Yasumi's energy, that she seemed so like

a 100,000-horsepower robot? Was it nuclear fusion, or solar power? Surely not photosynthesis. And the first thing we teach her is how to make tea? What was she, a new employee at a firm somewhere?

But speaking up would be pointless. To be perfectly honest, there was nothing else to learn in this brigade. I put my bag down on the floor and sat across from Koizumi.

"How about a game?" Koizumi was watching Yasumi with interest, but he suddenly turned away from her and pushed the game board toward me.

"What's this?"

Strange, round pieces were on the board. They gave no hint as to how they were to be moved, with Chinese characters carved on them that said things like *general*, *elephant*, and *cannon*. That Koizumi— had he finally gotten tired of losing at Othello, go, and shogi, and brought in a game he thought he could win?

"It's Chinese chess. It's called *xiàngqí*. Once you understand the rules, anyone can play. It's really not difficult. At the very least, games are shorter than in shogi."

Those "rules" were the problem. Until I memorized them, wasn't it obvious that I would be the one racking up the losses? Couldn't we play with hanafuda cards instead? I asked. I had a decent amount of experience with oichokabu or koi koi thanks to playing with my mom's family in the countryside.

"I didn't consider card games. I'm sure I'll bring some eventually. As for *xiàngqí*, once you understand that it's a zero-sum game like go and shogi, that's quite sufficient. I'm sure you'll get the rules down in short order. If you can glance at a go board and immediately see who's winning, then you'll have no trouble at all. As a board game, it has no real elements of chance, so I think you'll enjoy it quite a bit." He flashed an easygoing smile. "Let's play a practice game, shall we? It won't count toward your win-loss tally. So, about this 'soldier' piece—it moves like so..."

He launched into a casual explanation. Didn't he have any thoughts about Yasumi? She was a girl of such exceptional talent that she'd passed Haruhi's gauntlet with comparatively little difficulty. She might well become the next brigade chief! Assuming Haruhi didn't have some kind of blind spot, how about it, Koizumi? What do you think? I was assuming the two blue gems stuck in his face weren't made of lapis lazuli.

Koizumi grinned as he lined the pieces up. It kind of freaked me out—it was the smile of the rank-and-file operative whose shadowy boss often called upon him, and you couldn't tell how comfortable he was with that.

He made as though to start lining the pieces up on my side, leaning toward me. Koizumi whispered, "I am not worried. Far from it, I'm actually quite relieved. No matter what happens now, it won't be bad for us. Given that, I would suggest you relax, hmm?"

I had no such confidence, thanks to my rebellious nature. Thus far, were there any examples of new characters appearing only to retreat without doing anything? And even if so, there was the suggestive appearance of that weird new group with Sasaki, Tachibana, Kuyoh, and the nameless time traveler. They didn't seem to be doing anything at the moment, but that in and of itself was strange, and it raised the question of why they'd appeared in the first place. If it was a foreshadowing device, it was a damned clumsy one. All they'd done was show up and say "hi," I said.

If I were reading a mystery novel with a setup like that, I wouldn't just put it down, I'd throw it at the wall as soon as the detective started making deductions.

"That's not very serene of you. Books should be read with a generous heart. Even the trashiest of stories can later become food for the mind. You know how the saying goes—the best teacher is a contrarian one."

That was the first I'd heard of it.

"I'll bet. I just now invented that saying, after all. But I don't think it's terribly incorrect."

"…Hegel was a genius," I muttered, at which Koizumi favored me with a smirk.

"Exactly. For people living their lives in society, he was the philosopher who left behind the best advice. Anybody can put his ideas into practice."

I didn't really think the Hegelian dialectic had anything to do with winning or losing this game of Chinese shogi.

I set out the pieces as instructed by Koizumi, and listened to the explanations of how each one moved. It was similar to shogi, but the details were quite a bit different. Still, I was getting bored with chess and Othello, so throwing a new board game into the mix wasn't a bad idea.

As Koizumi and I were concentrating on the *xiàngqí* board, I stole glances at the other brigade members in the room.

Nagato was reading her book. Quietly. Whether or not it had occurred to her that adding a new brigade member might also give the literature club new clout, her demeanor in this room over the past year had been as unchanging as the permafrost in Iceland. The pages of the book in her lap were slightly brown, and I wondered if it were a rare volume she'd dug up out of a used-book store. Had she expanded her operations beyond the city library? As I imagined Nagato's trotting footsteps on the way to some used-book store, I found myself calming down.

Just when my battle with Koizumi on the game board was heating up—

"Sorry to keep you waiting!" came Yasumi's voice, as clear and high as a piccolo, and she popped into my field of view from the side holding a tea tray with cups on it. Behind her was Asahina the maid, who was unable to hide her nervous fussiness as she watched us carefully.

"This is rooibos tea! It's caffeine-free, good for your digestion, and very healthy! Please, try some!"

I guess we didn't have a spare maid uniform. Yasumi was still in her slightly overlarge uniform as she set the steaming cups down on the table in front of Koizumi and me.

The cups had "Kyon" and "Koizumi" written on them in Haruhi's bold brushstroke handwriting. Given that the writing was magic marker on mass-produced cups, they had no sense of wabi or sabi about them, but given that I didn't really care about the aesthetics of tea ceremony, it didn't much matter to me.

I did my best not to meet Yasumi's glittering eyes as I brought the red-brown liquid to my lips, and a few seconds later I looked to Koizumi, who was doing the same thing.

"...What a curious flavor." Koizumi offered his opinion with a faint, wry smile; my opinion, incidentally, was identical. It was certainly not bad. Yet neither was it particularly tasty. Rather it was an odd sort of flavor. Which meant that I should've been more than happy to gulp down some green or barley tea instead, but to be honest I was too much of a coward to do so.

"It's, um...well...I've never had tea quite like it. I can, uh, definitely tell that it's good for me. It certainly feels healthy."

"Wow!" cried Yasumi happily as she floated over to place the designated cup in front of Nagato.

"..."

Nagato gave the cup on which Haruhi decided to write "Yuki" a brief glance.

"..."

She returned her attention to her book as though having looked at dried seaweed that had yet to be rehydrated.

This was nothing unusual, so none of us took much notice of it, but when I looked to Yasumi to check her reaction, she seemed totally unconcerned, skipping back over to Asahina.

"Hey, wait." It was the absolute ruler of this space who raised her voice. "Where's *my* tea?" Haruhi's irritated face looked out from behind the computer's display. "Shouldn't you serve the brigade chief first, in times like these? What's the idea, serving me last? Mikuru, you've gotta keep educating her, okay?"

"Oh...I'm so sorry!" Asahina said frantically. Beside her, Yasumi giggled.

"Sorry! I forgot. I was probably just nervous. I'll make you a special cup now, so please wait just a moment."

She didn't seem the least bit concerned with Haruhi's crocodile eyes. Yasumi flitted around like some kind of winged fairy, efficiently bringing Haruhi a steaming-hot cup of tea. As usual, Haruhi gulped down the near-boiling drink in a single swig. Her eyes rolled and she panted like a dog for a moment before speaking.

"Make sure you remember next time! It's a pretty important rule. Mikuru, you're the teacher, so you've got to educate our new recruit properly."

When had Asahina become responsible for Yasumi's education?

"Anyway, I guess this tea is good enough for now." Haruhi's mood sure changed quickly. I doubted she'd even had time to taste the tea. "Yasumi Watahashi, was it? Hey, are you good with computers?"

"Only a little, but yes! Yup, definitely!"

"Really? Well, then…"

The monitor that sat on the the brigade chief's desk had been procured from the computer club, and on it was currently displayed the SOS Brigade's web page, in exactly the same state it had been in when I'd first made it. It had the same cheap layout and half-assed content it always had, with the only meaningful text being an e-mail address. In the world of the ever-advancing network, our home page could only be described as hopelessly out-of-date. It was the embodiment of the digital divide. Blog? What's that?

Haruhi had always had designs on updating it, but the responsibility of doing so fell entirely to me, and I had no interest whatsoever in actually doing it, and had thus constantly come up with reasons to procrastinate. The truth was that putting the SOS Brigade's name on the Net did not seem likely to have any particular benefits whatsoever, given what had happened the previous year with the computer club president. I was hoping Haruhi would just forget about the whole thing, but it seemed she hadn't yet abandoned her desire for more page views and Internet fame. Of course, she didn't know Nagato had doctored the logo she designed.

"I want to make our site more eye-catching. Think you can do it?" Haruhi pointed at the monitor, which had been left turned on.

"Kyon made the SOS Brigade's main site, but it's totally bare-bones and we've never done anything with it. It's not pretty to look at either. The world is full of sites that are stylishly designed and full of useful information, but ours just makes the Internet cry."

Geez, sorry.

"So, Yasumi, can you just get on that computer and whip up something better for us? Oh, this is part of our training regimen for new members. If you think your trials were over with the entrance tests, you better think again! The road to full brigade membership is a harsh one!"

"Yes! I'll do it, I'll do it! Please, let me!" Yasumi answered immediately, whether or not she understood the import of Haruhi's words. "I want to try. I'll give it a shot. Just let me take a crack at it!" she said, and as the echo of her cries reverberated, I found myself surprised at her overtly positive reaction. And I couldn't help asking—

"Hey, have you ever even made a website before?"

"I have not!" she said, smiling like my sister did upon receiving an animal-themed chess set. "But, but! I'm confident I can, because I really want to be useful to you all! So if it's just one computer, I'll train it up right!"

Computers were just boxes that did calculations; it didn't matter how much you "trained it up," they weren't all-purpose tools that would do whatever you said, like a hunting dog or something.

But before I could stop her, Yasumi brushed the sitting Haruhi aside, pulled the keyboard out, grabbed the wireless mouse, and immediately started typing and clicking away like some veteran career woman at an office somewhere.

After surveying the contents of the hard drive, she spoke.

"There's a pretty comprehensive set of tools here. But, if you have apps like these, I'd think you would've been able to make a flashier site. This one's filled with useless tags—who made it? Wow, it's pretty much text-only. Totally retro. The table layout is awful too... let's see, view source. Oh man. What do these font tags even mean?

Augh, you didn't even use style sheets! Any slightly geeky middle school student could've done better than this."

Haruhi had just then made it clear that I was the one who'd done the site. This Yasumi Watahashi certainly didn't seem to mind being rude when offering opinions. I wasn't going to forget her name.

"Okay, I'm gonna make some tweaks here!" she announced brightly, then began manipulating the computer. Yasumi was cheery enough to be humming a tune, and when I listened more closely, I realized it was the tune Haruhi had sung during last year's school festival when she'd acted as a substitute vocalist. Obviously Yasumi would've been in middle school then, so she must have happened to wander by at that moment.

Even I couldn't deny that Haruhi had really shone, then. Of course, having awakened to the idea of band-related activities, she then dragged the club into a bunch of superfluous, miscalculated effort, but still.

Haruhi stood behind Yasumi, a second cup of tea in her hand as she radiated a sense of satisfaction. She seemed every bit the mid-level manager pleased to finally have found a competent subordinate. The determination to assign all random tasks and irritating chores to Yasumi from now on practically wafted off of her like so many fungal spores.

While I indulged in the beautiful dream that I would be finally released from handling such tasks myself, this was Haruhi we were talking about—a more contrary, unreasonable, impetuous person you would never find. Winding up even lower than Yasumi was all I could expect. Getting passed by an underclassman in a single day made my tenuous reason for existence even more tenuous. Not that I was particularly worried about it.

As Koizumi's and my *xiàngqí* face-off was reaching its climax, the cup Yasumi had brought over was just about empty. Naturally I won the game, but since it didn't feel like much of a victory and it was a game I wasn't used to yet, I was a bit tired.

"Another game?"

I ignored Koizumi's attempt at getting revenge and stretched, when for no particular reason my eyes happened upon a cardboard box. It sat on the shelf, and contained the SOS Brigade's war spoils thus far—I suppose you could call it our arsenal.

Sticking out of it was the aluminum baseball bat and gloves we'd used in our baseball game the previous year.

I felt a little awkward, given that this was the club's first new member. I was a little wary of this Yasumi Watahashi—there was that strange phone call to consider—so maybe that explains why before I knew it, I spoke up.

"Hey, Koizumi. Wanna play some catch?" It was a bizarre suggestion, I admit.

"Oh?" Koizumi met my eyes for a second, then grinned hugely. "Certainly. Without activity, our bodies will deteriorate, and moderate exercise is good for both mental and physical acuity."

Having thus decided, Koizumi moved quickly, and without needing to stretch he pulled the cardboard box down and took out two battered gloves and a tennis ball. Good old Koizumi—he'd read my mind.

The SOS Brigade had gotten along for a year with five members. As we'd moved up, this new freshman had slid in to become our first junior member, and while there didn't seem to be a place to include her, I could do enough self-analysis to realize that maybe thanks to all the various occult and scientific happenings we'd endured as a five-person club, the idea of changing our pentagram to a hexagram inspired a strange sense of unease in me.

To put it simply, I felt—not thought, but *felt*—that Yasumi was a foreign body in our previously stable club. I just found it hard to imagine the duties that Yasumi would perform within the club, and that Haruhi would accept that.

The phone call I'd received from her in the bath also nagged at me. Even if I could chalk that up to her overeagerness to join the club, why would she call *me*? Although I supposed there wouldn't have been any point in calling Nagato, Asahina, or Koizumi. Those three had special responsibilities behind the scenes. But still, there wasn't any real reason to call me either. And at the time, Yasumi hadn't even bothered to introduce herself properly before hanging up. Honestly, she was just as opaque as Haruhi was.

The point was, Yasumi was now in this room, which was why I wanted to escape. To that end, my excuse for leaving was a game of catch. That was one game that definitely wasn't possible in the clubroom.

"So, anyway," I said, addressing Haruhi as she watched over Yasumi's computer work, along with Asahina, who'd started researching new tea, and Nagato, who was still absorbed in her book. "We're going out for a bit. Koizumi and I can't really teach her anything, so we'd just be in the way. We'll leave the education of the new member to you."

Koizumi was already carrying the two gloves, the pleasant smile on his face directed at no one in particular. "Indeed. Things will proceed more smoothly if we simply let the girls of the club act unhindered. We boys would only be in the way, so we'll take our leave for the moment."

The lieutenant brigade chief was second to none at backing people up.

Haruhi shot me a sharp glance. "Sure, why not? I want to teach Yasumi about the club duties Kyon's had so far. Listen up, Yasumi, and I'll tell you why this guy's the only one in the club without an official rank. Honestly, he's just useless. You should do the opposite of whatever he does. Our brigade practices absolute participation, so I'm sure you'll leave Kyon in the dust."

Oh yeah? Well, so long as she thought so, I was relieved. I hoped to graduate without achieving any of her bizarre ranks.

I gave Koizumi a look. Koizumi seemed to understand what I was trying to communicate with my eyes, and tossed me a glove. "In that case, we'll take our leave. We'll come back when we're done." He gave me a wink that was so broad I was surprised it didn't come with a *ting!* sound, and patted me on the back. "It'll be nice to have some guy time for once."

Before leaving the room I looked back and saw that Nagato was continuing to practice the art of book absorption, while Asahina was pondering the art of tea—"I wonder if I should blend this with something else?" she was saying to herself. Haruhi stood behind Yasumi as Yasumi adroitly used the computer. She had a look on her face as if she understood what Yasumi was doing, but the truth was she didn't.

With the addition of just a single new member, the mood in the room had changed quite a bit.

Having left the clubroom's building, Koizumi and I made for the courtyard and started playing catch.

To anyone else, we wouldn't have looked like anything more than two students killing time.

The courtyard between the clubroom building and the classroom building had a lawn, and was easily visible from the open window of the literature club's room on the third floor. From where we were, it was easy to look up and see if anyone in the room was watching us.

"Having another girl in the club certainly brightens things up," said Koizumi, lobbing the ball to me in an easy arc.

"What, you would've preferred a guy?"

Koizumi caught my slow overhand toss. "It's all about balance. Don't you think we're at a bit of a disadvantage with only two boys, but four girls? Our right to speech was already bad enough."

It was sad, but true. To be honest, our problem was that Haruhi's speech was like a powerful subwoofer that drowned out everybody else.

"I don't think that girl's going to be easy to handle either." Koizumi threw the ball with more force.

"Are you saying Yasumi's got some kind of strange background?" I caught the yellow ball in my glove with a *smack* sound.

"No," said Koizumi with a strange smile. "You can relax on that count. There's no strange organization behind her. She's totally innocent. Not attached to anything, not directed by anyone. She has her own will, nothing more or less. That's why she's so interesting."

I grabbed the ball, staring at it as if it were a fresh-picked lemon.

"Quit being so roundabout, Koizumi. If you know something, spit it out. Why did Yasumi Watahashi worm her way into the SOS Brigade?"

"I don't know her reason," said Koizumi with his hands raised in surrender. "I know—or rather, can guess at—only one thing." He easily caught the ball I'd thrown at him with a wind-up motion. "It's because Suzumiya wished it so."

That reason, again.

"It was inevitable that Yasumi Watahashi would be a member of the SOS Brigade. That's because Suzumiya chose it, wished for it. She was accepted because of Suzumiya's firm belief that she's a necessary person. She probably manipulated reality without being conscious of it."

Koizumi gave me a meaningful look, as though he was changing the subject.

"Why did you decide to come out and play catch? An invitation from you is a rare thing indeed."

I didn't know myself. Why had I gotten the feeling that I had to use these baseball implements? Maybe I didn't want to leave them to sit there so long they developed self-awareness, I said.

"Is that so?" Koizumi seemed to immediately accept my explanation. "If the items in the clubroom gained awareness, it would certainly complete the transformation of the clubroom into an alternate reality. However, I can understand how you feel. I also wanted to play catch, for some reason. No—I felt compelled by a strange compulsion to do so."

Koizumi intercepted my throw, then dropped the ball. He scooped it back up.

"What the hell does that mean?"

"I don't know. But the possibility exists that it was inevitable—

perhaps we *had* to come out here and play catch. A predetermined event, as the time travelers would say."

I didn't get it. If that were the case, I should've gotten some kind of roundabout message from Asahina or Asahina the Elder. But I hadn't. And anyway, what would this fake game of baseball have to do with the future? I asked.

"I would suggest putting that question to Asahina, but..." He looked up at the room on the third floor, and sighed softly. "I doubt she is aware of anything, and moreover we did this voluntarily. It's more likely that we're simply being suspicious. If we start doubting things like this, we'll just play more and more into the time travelers' hands. As a past-dweller, I don't want to lose to the time travelers. This doesn't have anything to do with being an esper or in the Agency. It's just a matter of pride as an inhabitant of the present."

That sounded awfully sincere, for Koizumi. He seemed to sense my skepticism.

"There's nothing wrong with being looked down on. Our opponents have a greater organization than us, and with more power. But personally, I loathe the idea of resigning myself to such disdain. The stronger the opponent, the more one desires to rebel against them—wouldn't you say that's a classic pattern, no matter the era?"

He sounded like a hero from some weekly comic magazine. But if there were such a thing as instant training or hidden powers that would conveniently awaken such that Kuyoh and the others could be dealt with in one fell swoop, then there'd be no need for me to do anything.

"That particular role," said Koizumi, throwing me a change-up, "is well suited to you. With Suzumiya backing you up, and you backing her up, there's nothing in the universe the two of you couldn't accomplish."

He grinned, and continued.

"I've said it before, but you could start over as Adam and Eve. Or perhaps since we're Japanese, Izanagi and Izanami. So long as you are fruitful and multiply, the world will come to be filled with people like you and Suzumiya. A pleasant scene, if surreal, don't you think?"

That was well inside the range of a ridiculous joke. Well, in this absurd proposition, I had no intention of leaving any descendants. And if they were all of Haruhi's descent, I doubted history would even get as far as Noah's ark. If the captain had any sense at all, he'd have to be prepared to refuse to get on the boat.

Even for the sake of scholarship, I rejected that proposal—rejected it, I say! But go ahead and dig up the frozen soil of Mount Ararat. You might find a wooden spaceship.

"More's the pity." Koizumi held the ball in his hand and swung his arm about like a windmill. "And yet I'm relieved. I'd like to be able to see you all for a while longer. Nagato and Asahina, as well. As a human, the only species on Earth born with both imagination and intellectual curiosity, it's my desire to see all this through to the end."

Koizumi then changed the subject abruptly.

"So is your after-school study with Suzumiya progressing well?"

So he knew about that, eh? I managed to keep my cool. "Not bad, which is nice. Although it's not so much me being taught as it is her enjoying teaching."

"That's good. I'm sure you and Suzumiya are both bound for college. If you could possibly manage to attend the same university, it would certainly make my life easier. Please put forth your best effort during the entrance examinations."

Enough already. It was bad enough having my mom constantly worrying about my academic future. Fortunately I still had almost two years to go, so I didn't have to panic and start carrying around practice quizzes with me all the time yet. I had more important things to do at the moment, I said.

"Oh? Such as?"

...For example a new video game I hadn't gotten around to buying yet, or the games I'd heard were good that were starting to pile up.

Koizumi only smiled faintly. He was in the same year as me, so why did his easy, slightly exasperated smile rattle my nerves so much? Son of a—. Sometimes I wanted to be able to smile like that and mystify the people around me too.

"So then, what should I throw next? I've got a cutter, knuckleball, slider, and a few others I know."

I asked for something I could catch. Unfortunately I had no experience as a catcher. Just call me the eternal second player.

Koizumi's next throw was a fastball straight down the middle. It was probably some kind of declaration of intent. It had enough heat on it that I never would've imagined such a throw could come from his arm. If he was that good at baseball, he should've been standing on the mound as a reliever last year during the baseball tournament. If he had any other hidden talents, I hoped he'd reveal them soon.

I continued to play catch with Koizumi for a while, silently. I don't have any special interest in baseball, so I was starting to get bored, when—

"Hmm?" said Koizumi, looking up, which prompted me to do likewise, following his gaze to its end.

It was a paper airplane.

The simple glider looked as if it had been hastily, perfunctorily folded as it banked around the courtyard. There was no wind to speak of, so it gently descended, tracing a path like a high-jumper making a bad landing, eventually falling at my feet. I looked and saw that it appeared to me made out of the same copier paper we had in the clubroom.

I picked it up.

On the wings was a single word hurriedly written in black marker. "OPEN!"

Quickly, before Koizumi could come over and see, I unfolded the glider into a simple piece of paper, and for a moment, I froze. In the same marker was scribbled a short message that despite its brevity was deeply shocking.

"I found the MIKURU folder!"

I looked reflexively up—at the clubroom window, naturally.

Depending on who was standing there, I was preparing myself for the impeachment proceedings that would surely follow, and my heart pounded, but—

There looking down from the open third-floor window was none other than the petite form of Yasumi Watahashi. After making sure I'd received her primitive airmail, she put her index finger to her lips, then disappeared from the window like an actress exiting stage left.

It seemed Yasumi's IT skills were not to be underestimated. I'd let my guard down, having gotten used to Asahina, who was useless with computers, and Haruhi, who used such precision instruments in only the most haphazard of fashions. Nagato probably already knew, but her mouth was shut and locked with hands of iron, so that wasn't a problem.

Still, I was impressed she'd found and opened the hidden, password-protected folder. It seemed I was going to need to tighten security. Maybe I'd talk to the computer club president.

"Is something the matter? Is something written on there—?" Koizumi turned his greedy gaze toward the former paper airplane in my hands.

"Don't worry about it. It's just Asahina's and my little secret. Pointless information that will have no influence on your life, I guarantee it."

Koizumi did not reply, only grinning and shrugging. I ignored his pointed look.

Then I looked back up to the clubroom. Drawn in from the side, the curtain fluttered in the breeze, which prevented me from seeing what was going on in the room.

I'd felt this way for a little while, but I couldn't help expressing my opinion of Yasumi again.

"Weird girl," I murmured.

A little while later we returned to the clubroom. In front of the computer, Haruhi seemed ecstatic.

"Kyon, look! Behold this beautiful, gorgeous page!"

I let Koizumi handle the baseball stuff, and went over to Haruhi, who was moving the mouse around like a kitten playing with a piece of string.

"Whoa," I said, letting a sort of exclamation mark escape my lips at the sight that greeted me. "This is the SOS Brigade's site?"

"Can't you tell by looking? It's written in huge letters!"

It was true that the logo was there, but nothing else remained of the perfunctory site I'd set up before. Everything from the background to the fonts to the index had been redone, and all the letters sparkled and danced, while the page colors themselves were totally gaudy. If the site I'd made before was an Adamski UFO, this one was more like a chandelier type. But wasn't it going a little overboard, I wondered?

"This is is more eye-catching and attention-grabbing," said Haruhi enthusiastically, as though she'd made it herself. "Plus, time on the Internet moves in dog years. If we don't put these technologies to use, what's the point? I had Yasumi use all the resources available. See, if you click here—"

Some obviously free music started playing. To be honest, it was irritating.

I regarded the site skeptically; it was a textbook example of what not to do.

"What do you have for content?"

"An e-mail form."

That was all?

"That was all I could think of!" Haruhi said, her lip twisting. "We had a bunch of pictures of our club activities, but you stopped me from using them!"

Ah, right, the pictures of Asahina. Haruhi had a good memory.

"But I do have this." Haruhi moved the mouse cursor, stopping on a section labeled "games." She clicked on it, and the display changed. The background was now a starry sky, and it seemed to be the menu screen of some kind of video game. I read the title, which was written in a pointlessly heavy font.

"'The Day of Sagittarius...5'?"

"I got it from the computer club!"

She said it as if it was no big deal.

"I guess they made an improved, online version of the game we played before. Apparently now you can battle with anyone anywhere in the world. I don't really get it, but it's better for us to have it on our site, right? Obviously you can play for free."

Who'd want to pay for this? Although if they'd gotten all the way to version five, it probably had its appeal for the people that cared about this kind of thing. That's how much of an effect their loss to us had had. Well, they'd gotten what they deserved.

"By the way, I've asked the computer club to do some more game development for us. This one isn't very SOS Brigade–like. I want something more, like, arcade-y!"

I wondered if she'd confused "asked" with "ordered." I contemplated the computer club's likely bewilderment at being told to create an SOS Brigade–like game, then realized something.

"Hey, where'd Yasumi go?"

She was nowhere to be seen in the room. The only people there were Nagato, who was still reading in the corner, Koizumi, who, having finished putting the gloves and ball away, had returned to his seat, and Asahina, who was serving tea. As she set out the cups, Asahina answered me.

"She went home, just a moment ago."

"Huh?" She'd left early on her first real day as a club member?

"She said there was something she absolutely had to attend to, and apologized over and over again before running off."

Asahina served me tea, a larger than usual smile blooming on her face. I asked her why she was so happy.

"She's just so cute!" she replied, sounding totally charmed. "Her voice, her attitude, the way she does things, her expressions, the way she bows...it's all just so cute I can't take it!"

Asahina clutched the tea tray to herself and squirmed, looking rather cute herself. To think that such a charming older student

could herself be so stricken—Yasumi Watahashi was a force to be reckoned with, indeed.

"I don't really see it, but whatever," said Haruhi, looking slightly exasperated with Asahina's antics. "She's like a baby chick, scampering all over the place. But she certainly seems to have hit the bull's-eye with Mikuru. She seems to be interested in all sorts of things, so I guess she won't get bored easily. It's only the first day, but I think that's enough time to get a sense of her capabilities."

Asahina was still wiggling around in adoration. "She even glommed on to Nagato. She must be good at making friends!"

Seemingly coming back to her senses, or possibly having noticed the conspicuously silent Koizumi as he gazed at the table, she returned to the kettle and began filling the lieutenant brigade chief's cup. I looked at Nagato, trying to imagine what technique Yasumi could've employed to foster instant trust.

Nagato seemed to have guessed my thoughts correctly; she slowly emerged from her sea of words.

"I lent her a book," she murmured in a too-controlled voice. Then, evidently feeling that further detail was necessary, added, "She asked me to."

This seemed to satisfy her. She looked back down.

"The book had a name like some kind of satellite, or maybe a Greek myth," said Haruhi casually. I choked down my anxiousness like a piece of dry ice. But Nagato did not respond to Haruhi, so I had to maintain my poker face.

Thankfully, Haruhi seemed not to care much about the matter. She made no further references to Nagato's library, instead clicking the browser closed and turning off the computer. It was a clear indication that the day's club activities would soon be over.

"Having a new member join us bodes well for the new school year. The SOS Brigade must not neglect the education of the next generation. We have to show such spirit that even if the entire school were destroyed, the SOS Brigade would remain. And we are the very foundation of that spirit—or rather, we must become it!"

Still standing, I sipped my tea. "If you say so, I guess that's how it'll be."

Yasumi's face floated up in my mind as I delivered my halfhearted reply. I owed her a large debt of gratitude for keeping quiet about my special Asahina folder, but it still bothered me. I glanced at Nagato and saw that, as usual, she hadn't looked up from the hardback she was reading. As she served tea to Koizumi, Asahina's affect was the same as before. But there was just no way the new brigade member Haruhi had picked was a regular person. It might not be obvious, but there had to be something about her.

The phone call I'd gotten in the bath, the strange unease that had plagued me for the past few days—these things made everything feel fuzzy. Even if you chalked that up to the unresolved problem of Sasaki, Kuyoh, the nameless time traveler, and Kyoko Tachibana, then why was this feeling of tension in my chest directed so specifically at Yasumi? And why did it feel almost optimistic, of all things?

Yasumi wasn't obviously an enemy or an ally. That would've been too easy. The feeling I got from her was nothing like the way I felt about Asahina and Nagato, or about Kuyoh and Kyoko Tachibana. If anything, she seemed more like—

I glanced at Haruhi, who hummed merrily away as she packed up to head home.

She wasn't an alien, time traveler, or esper. The feeling I got from Yasumi Watahashi was like what I felt from Haruhi and Sasaki.

But I had no idea why.

The uncertainty was like the moment after having mistaken chiku-wabu for chikuwa and having popped a piece in my mouth, and I held on to this bright unease all the way home, until I opened the door to my room and was stunned.

"Welcome home, Kyon!"

The fact that my sister beamed at me like a friendly cat while Shamisen glared at me like an irritated human as the two of them rolled around on my bed was not particularly surprising—it was pretty much normal, really.

What froze me in my tracks with my mouth hanging open was the fact that in addition to them, there was a face I'd seen not long before; the person sat opposite my sister, but immediately jumped to their feet like a pencil rocket.

"Hi, Kyon! Sorry to bother you at home!" she cried out in a clear, high voice, then bowed deeply. She had very good manners.

"Wha…"

I couldn't begin to comprehend what was happening.

Yasumi Watahashi was in my room. There was no way I could convince myself that this was a hallucination. It was impossible.

She'd left the clubroom because of some kind of urgent business, so what was it, and why was she here?

No, wait. Let's be rational. Given all the absurd events I'd been wrapped up in up to this point, I should have been used to this kind of thing, however unwillingly. Compared with Haruhi's disappearance or the many time jumps I'd done, having a new brigade member waiting for me in my room was a perfectly ordinary occurrence. It was like a mystery novel where the culprit's motives went unexplained until the end. All right. I was calm. I'd try to get an explanation from the people at hand.

Yasumi clasped her hands in front of her chest, looking at me with eyes aglitter. "I really wanted to come yesterday, but things took longer than I expected. I shouldn't have hesitated."

I did not understand what she was saying. Expected? Hesitated? What the hell? Whatever. I'd figure that stuff out later. I grabbed my smiling, carefree sister by the collar. "Did you bring her in?"

"But, 'cause—" She squirmed ticklishly. "She said she was your friend!"

There was such a thing as being too nice. It was one thing when they were people you recognized, but I was going to have to teach her not to just trust the word of complete strangers. It was my duty as her older brother.

But Yasumi came to her rescue before I could draft a proper lecture.

"When I met her at the front door I knew right away that she was your little sister. Heehee, she's such a good girl! I wish I had a sister like her. I just want to pick her up and take a nap with her. Also, that kitty! What a wonderful calico. He seems super smart— I'm really impressed." After rattling all this off at a quick tempo, Yasumi seemed slightly gloomy. "But I can't have any pets. It's too bad... still! I love playing with other people's pets when I visit their homes!"

Feeling physically overwhelmed by her voice, I flinched slightly away. "I thought... I thought you said you had to leave early, that you had something to do. Don't tell me..."

"Yes. I wanted to come over at least once—you know, to your place. Heh," said Yasumi casually, without a trace of anything suspicious in her voice or manner. Her trademark barrette moved slightly as she bowed.

"Hey, hey." My sister tugged at Yasumi's sleeve. "So, um, I was just saying, I really want that barrette. You can't buy 'em anymore, right? Can I have it?"

"Sorry." Yasumi bent down so she was at my sister's level and looked straight into her big, round eyes. "This is a treasure I've had since I was little. So I can't give it to you now. But I might come around to it eventually. We're both little boats floating on the river of the world. So I might wind up floating back here, sometime. Or maybe even just this barrette. Eventually, someday."

I got the feeling that the smiley-faced hair ornament didn't just keep her wild hair in order, it served as proof of her identity—but such speculation was trivial. What was far more important was that as I was pondering such things, Yasumi had walked over to my bed, peered under it, and pulled Shamisen out from under it by his ear. "This cat is great! Super great, really."

After offering said comment, she leapt over to my sister and hugged her, then resumed her still posture right in front of me, speaking her intentions in a clear tone.

"I'm going home."

I see, was all I could manage in reply, which felt pathetic. I should've had better vocabulary installed, but frustratingly, I just couldn't put what I wanted to say into words.

Yasumi looked up at me penetratingly, but then her expression suddenly turned almost nostalgic.

"I always dreamed that when I went to a new school, there'd be some interesting club, and some kind of coincidence would suck me into it, and I'd wind up joining. That I'd keep quiet and they'd approach me. Isn't that how it is? The narrators of every good story always have something like that happen. And the club is full of fascinating older students, and I'd wind up getting close to one of them—that's the kind of protagonist I wanted to be."

I felt as if I had heard someone say something like this before. But before I could search my memory for the reference, Yasumi lowered her head quickly, then bent her body as if it was spring-loaded.

"Just kidding! Actually I just wanted to see your room. Sorry for intruding! But I'm totally satisfied now. I won't come again."

The smile that Yasumi directed at me made me understand why Asahina had found herself so helplessly charmed by the girl; it was like that of a baby animal looking up at its caretaker with total trust, enveloped in some kind of soft light. Surely no pet shop customer could ever walk away empty-handed after being gazed at in such a fashion.

"Now, may we meet again! Kyon, please don't hate me!" No sooner had she spoken than Yasumi patted my both my sister's and Shamisen's head affectionately, then dashed away with all the energy of spring's first storm. There wasn't even enough time to tell her to wait up. Before I knew it, the brigade's newest member had disappeared from my house.

My sister forcibly picked up the yawning Shamisen. "Who was she?"

No one wanted the answer to that question more than I did.

"Ah—" Suddenly I remembered something I'd forgotten to ask. I was positive that Yasumi was the one who'd called while I was in the middle of taking a bath.

But why me? She'd only given me her name. Had she already been confident that she would be the only one to pass Haruhi's gauntlet of tests? It was as though she was precognitive, but according to Koizumi there was no reason to think that. Which meant she was just a regular student who just happened to come to North High, and just happened to get tangled up with the SOS Brigade—but that was just too many perfect coincidences.

—Nothing in this world is coincidence. Everything is predetermined. Humans merely refer to predetermined events that they don't understand as "coincidence."

Someone had told me this—or wait, maybe it had been in a novel someone had lent me.

I mulled it over vaguely as I took Shamisen away from my sister and brought his nose up to mine. As usual, he turned away, looking annoyed.

"What do you think of Yasumi?" I was well aware that it was no more than me talking to myself, but somehow it felt as if I was pouring out my soul to someone.

"Her name's Yasumi? Is she friends with Haru-nyan and Tsuru-nyan?" asked my sister with eyes even rounder than the calico cat, whose face showed his patience was at an end, so I put the irritated Shamisen down. He ran out the room, and fortunately my sister chased after him, so I was finally left in peace.

No matter how much I thought about it, I couldn't put the pieces together. It felt as if I'd been told to solve the "four fours" puzzle up through infinity without using the *log* operator.

She was Yasumi Watahashi, a freshman at North High and the first new member to be admitted by Haruhi into the SOS Brigade.

But who *was* she?

β — 10

Thursday.

I had so much to think about that I had no idea where to start.

If you were going to count up the number of things I could actually do, you would only get as far as the index finger on your right hand. In the end, all I could do was go to school like usual, and absentmindedly attend class, like usual.

Somehow, Haruhi seemed to be in the same state as I was. Even before classes started, her attention was elsewhere, her mind seemingly back in Nagato's room.

"Hey, Kyon." No sooner had first period ended and the short break begun than Haruhi poked me in the middle of my back with her mechanical pencil. "About Yuki—do you think maybe it would be good to force her to go to the hospital?"

Her expression was very serious, like that of a small dog who'd lived with a family for a long time but had just been denied a walk.

"It's just a spring cold, right? That's going too far for something like that."

It hurt me to shut her down like that, but I was well aware that her condition wasn't something that antibiotics or dietary adjustments were going to improve.

"But still. I'm just worried," said Haruhi, clicking the end of her pencil. It was probably an unconscious tic. I gazed at the gradually extending lead at its tip and replied.

"Have you told Koizumi? If it comes down to it, you can probably forcibly get her admitted." I took a deep breath and prepared myself for what I was about to say. "But Nagato herself said she was fine. Has she ever been wrong about anything in the past?"

"That's . . . true, but still . . ." The clouds of doubt did not clear from Haruhi's face; it was like a dawn so misty that Venus couldn't be seen. "It really bothers me. It's not just Yuki either, it's like . . . I don't know how to say it, but it's like there's something strange going on on a bigger scale, or something."

Something like a mysterious space-borne illness spreading throughout the Earth, like something out of an old SF movie? I asked. I remembered there being a lot of movies like that on TV when I was a kid.

"Nothing so crazy as that. That kind of old-fashioned worldview doesn't work in the modern world. Nowadays scenarios like Mars attacking or some biological weapon threatening humanity only make people think you're so dissatisfied with your life that you've got a death wish and enjoy fantasizing about catastrophes. But people like that don't even have the courage to commit suicide, so they just enjoy imagining all of humanity dying. They're naive! Naive!"

Haruhi's comment would surely have made the masters of science fiction grimace. She sniffed.

"I shouldn't have bothered asking you. I knew you'd just make some tasteless joke; I must be going senile or something. Listen, Kyon: just forget it. No, I *order* you to forget it. My ideas are my own, and it was obviously a mistake to share them with anybody. I guess I have to acknowledge that much."

I see. Well, I was fully aware that I lacked the ability to construct a creative fake story, so having that pointed out by Haruhi now didn't exactly pain me. Calling someone an idiot when they already know they're an idiot will only earn you a derisive laugh. And idiot described me in that moment.

After that conversation, Haruhi remained preoccupied, and she continued to space out until afternoon classes were over, her body seeming like a cast-off skin, her mind having flown off somewhere far away, as unresponsive as a Buddhist priest in meditation, until at the final chime she came suddenly awake, as though it were her alarm clock.

She hurriedly put her bag over her shoulder. "I'm going to Yuki's with Mikuru. You don't have to come. Just stay in the clubroom."

I pointed out that without Nagato or Asahina in the room, there wasn't any reason to be there.

Haruhi's eyes angled slightly up at me. "New. Club. Members!"

Her mouth made her look just like an irritated waterfowl.

"They might come, so I need you to follow up with them. Plus, Koizumi aside, you're totally useless when it comes to taking care of Yuki." Haruhi seemed to hesitate for a moment, then seemed to decide to plunge ahead regardless. "My guess is you'd even make her worse. You're like a god of pestilence, Kyon. Plus it's cowardly for a guy to bust into a girl's room, especially when she's sick. So you and Koizumi don't need to come. Just watch over the room. It's your job as a brigade member."

Thus I was given a direct order by the Brigade Chief to watch over the room. Was there anything else I could do?

I tried to think about it. The person I needed to face down next was Kuyoh. She and her boss were the cause of Nagato's illness, and if we didn't do something about the problem, the situation wasn't going to change.

The other thing to keep in mind was Fujiwara. So far all I'd heard from him was obfuscating cynicism, but I couldn't afford to doubt that the self-proclaimed time traveler and Kuyoh had some kind of connection, or possibly even an alliance. From what I could tell, they were just using Kyoko Tachibana. She couldn't really go toe-to-toe with our Koizumi either. Kyoko Tachibana didn't really have what it took to deal with aliens and time travelers. I'd gotten that sense ever since she'd run out of resolve at the end of Asahina's kidnapping ordeal. I felt bad for her, but she was no match for Koizumi. She was a minor character at best. But our roles are assigned to us without concern for our feelings. Disrespect was forbidden, but let's just say Kyoko Tachibana wasn't overly impressed with whoever it was that handed out those roles.

"...so it's gotta be Sasaki," I murmured to myself, quietly.

"Did you say something?" Haruhi's sharp ears caught my muttering.

I decided her apparent irritation was due to her worry over Nagato, so I lightly raised both hands. "Like you said, I'll stay in the room today. If any freshmen show up, I'll do what I can for them, so don't worry about that. I figure it'll probably be more inviting without you around, anyway."

Haruhi sniffed. "Well, thanks. Call me if anything happens. I'll call you too. If I feel like it. Bye!"

Then Haruhi, whose motto was "do everything swiftly," nearly flew out of the room, like a piece of cat fur swept up by a broom.

She really was deeply worried about Nagato, in her own way. And so was I.

But the method and objective of our worry were very different. We were both doing our very best by Nagato—Haruhi in her way, and me in mine. Neither of us was right. The correct solution didn't exist.

But both of us were trying to find some kind of answer. And at the moment, one of us was closer to the heart of the matter—and that was me.

I'd wanted to start running to Nagato a long time ago. But at the moment I left that duty to Haruhi. So what was it that I would do?

I would wait. It would come to me eventually. And not in the distant future either. Kuyoh's attack, Asakura's revival, Kimidori's interruption...

These were all hints. For three aliens who didn't understand the idea of time very well, it was impossible that they'd all appeared in the same moment by coincidence. It was an omen. A strange message that only I could understand.

Very soon, things would start to move. Even if they didn't, I would. And then I'd *make* them move.

I was sure that Sasaki was thinking the same thing. These premonitions had moved on from being vague notions into being palpable feelings within me.

Nagato probably couldn't do anything.

But I had Haruhi, and Sasaki.

While their nature was unknown and unconfirmed, there existed two people that all involved parties insisted were on a godlike level. So long as those two bastions of humanity existed, no alien terminal, no miscreant time traveler, no worthless esper could lay a hand on us. Of course, there was the possibility that any one of them had prepared a trap for us. And no matter how high that possibility, Haruhi would laugh it off as though it were nothing, while no matter how low, Sasaki would discuss the notion thoroughly.

My own sudden thought terrified me. The idea seeped into my chest like methane hydrate. Haruhi and Sasaki—if those two joined forces, they really could control the universe. But now, such a situation would never come to pass. Haruhi would never wish for that. And Sasaki would laugh and start lecturing. I could picture both girls' expressions with perfect clarity.

"Welp—" Just as I hefted my minimally packed schoolbag over my shoulder and started to make for the clubroom, I caught sight of Taniguchi, the eternal slacker, getting ready to head straight home.

Though he wasn't someone who was any use to me in my current predicament, I raised my voice and asked him the question that came to mind anyway.

"Hey, Taniguchi."

"Yeah?" He turned around, looking put-upon. He was giving off a distinct sense of wanting-to-be-left-alone-ness, and I would've liked to do just that, but he was an important data point, though he himself didn't know it—he didn't know that he'd spent more time with a certain extraterrestrial humanoid interface than anyone else.

"I've got something I want to ask you about Kuyoh."

The instant I said it, all expression disappeared from Taniguchi's face, the life draining from him, a weary aura surrounding him so thoroughly that it seemed as if even the living dead would've had a little more vitality.

"Kyon, buddy. I just want you to forget about her, and I don't want to remember her myself. Something was wrong with me back then. When I think back on it, it makes me want to die—but I don't even remember very much, probably because my own memory can't handle how stupid I was. So please, don't bring her name up in front of me. Just consider that if I throw myself out of the classroom window tomorrow, it'll be your fault."

I had plenty of sympathy for Taniguchi, whose dark face was a mix of foolish heroism and wasted effort, and yet I couldn't help pressing him. Sometimes you had to harden your heart for the sake of information. And anyway, Koizumi was in the dumps at the moment, but I didn't have to consult the Akashic Records to be quite certain that before long he'd be back to his usual bad-influence self soon.

"What kinds of things did you do with Kuyoh after Christmas? You at least went on dates, right?"

"I guess." I couldn't meet Taniguchi's gaze—it swam as he wandered through his memories. "I told you she was the one that approached me. It was just before Christmas. Like I said, she was really quiet and blank, and I never really understood what kind of girl she was, but man—she was hot."

I thought back, and that sounded right, although her eerie aura was so off-putting that I hadn't really noticed her looks.

"So then," Taniguchi continued, "the old year turned into the new year, and we went all over the place. Mostly to places a healthy high school couple would go. Mostly it was me inviting her, but sometimes she would suggest places to go too."

I wondered what sort of destinations an artificial extraterrestrial life-form would want to visit. In Nagato's case, I'd accidentally discovered that she loved the library, but would a different alien have different tastes?

Taniguchi had no idea of the academic questions that occupied me. "You know, the usual spots. We went to movies, or out to eat. Suoh…well, she was a little weird. She always wanted to go to fast-food places. I'm pretty broke, so that suited me just fine, but I thought it was a little weird."

There was about two months' worth of time between Christmas and Valentine's Day, so I asked what kind of conversation they'd filled the time with. I doubted Kuyoh would ever initiate conversation, though.

"That's not true," said Taniguchi, surprisingly. "She was quiet, sure, but sometimes she'd talk like someone had flipped a switch. I mean, like, she'd be the one to speak up and everything."

Kuyoh volunteered conversation? I asked.

"Yeah. The truth is I don't really remember it very well. She said something about wanting to have a cat. She insisted that cats were more advanced life-forms than humans, and went on for two hours about the ways cats were superior to humans. I damn near fell asleep halfway through. She just seemed to like the most annoying topics. I mean, what would you say if you were asked what you thought about human progress? And I mean on the scale of hundreds of millions of years."

I tried imagining Kuyoh chatting away. It was impossible. Maybe it was the capriciousness of the Heavenly Canopy Dominion, or maybe her interior had been swapped out before I'd met her.

"But you just kept going out with her, in spite of all that?"

"You bet I did. That was the first time a girl had tried hitting on *me*. And…I mean…she was pretty hot…"

So that's what it came down to. I guess there were both men and women who only cared about looks. I suppose there was room to forgive his airheadedness. Just as I was despairing over seeing just what youth valued most in romance—

"And then our relationship was over in a flash." Taniguchi looked skyward, as plaintively as any tragic hero on the stage. "I rushed to meet her at the promised time, and she was waiting there to tell me 'I was mistaken.' I didn't even have time to ask what the hell she meant. By the time I realized what had happened, she was gone. Just like that. She's ignored every message from me, and there's been precisely zero contact from her side. I agonized about it for a while, like an idiot. But I've been dumped. Even I know that much."

And right before Valentine's Day too. This last February. That whole winter incident, when Koizumi and I had dug holes all over that mountain, and there was all that fuss about (Michiru) Asahina, and my first encounter with Kyoko Tachibana and Fujiwara.

To think that whole time, Taniguchi had been making conversation with Kuyoh.

But in listening to Taniguchi talk about her, I realized that Kuyoh Suoh was actually quite foolish.

If Kuyoh had made contact with me before Haruhi's Christmas party, it was quite possible that the incident with Haruhi's disappearance and all the crazy stuff around Nagato would've been much more of a pain to deal with. It was a lucky thing that Kuyoh had mistaken Taniguchi for me. I'd more or less used up all my resolve traveling four years into the past toward disaster. I would have to thank Taniguchi for keeping Kuyoh occupied for so long.

"So, you're done talking?"

I'd sunk into a thoughtful silence, so Taniguchi slung his bag over his shoulder and positioned himself for an immediate retreat. "Yeah."

I replied with a sunny expression. "Taniguchi."

"What's with the creepy face?"

"You might not realize it, but you're actually a pretty amazing guy. I guarantee it."

"Wha?" He might have been worried about my mental state. His voice had a note of pity in it. "Coming from you, that doesn't really make me happy. Have you taken one too many roundhouse kicks from Haruhi or something? Or—did you finally do it, huh?"

Taniguchi turned his face aside in irritation, but his expression soon returned to normal, and he grinned like his good old bad-influence self.

"Anyway, same goes for you, pal. You're serious business, Kyon. You lasted a whole year in that crazy club. I'm counting on you to keep babysitting Suzumiya until graduation. I mean, you're the only one for her."

Just as I was thinking that Taniguchi didn't usually say stuff like that, he dashed out of the room, as though needing to get away before he looked embarrassed or awkward.

Assuming we progressed through school together, we'd probably be singing "Aogeba Totoshi" or some similar graduation song together. Hopefully by that time we'd each have settled on our post–high school plans.

I didn't really think I wanted to go to the same college as him, though. It didn't seem as though dragging your old acquaintances with you into higher education would do anything other than get in the way of making new friends. In a new environment, you had to have new relationships. I wasn't sure whether it would be good in later life, but in any case it was what I thought. And it didn't seem as though there was much to be gained from hanging around in the same group all the time.

But I wondered if Haruhi felt the same way.

Haruhi, our brigade leader, who was like unto a god.

Having finished a peaceful, yet odd conversation with Taniguchi, I proceeded as usual to the clubroom.

My motivation for doing so was low, knowing as I did that only Koizumi would be there to greet me, but the brigade chief's orders could not be disobeyed. And on the off chance that a potential new member actually showed up, it would be a big deal. I obviously didn't want any to come, since it seemed like a new brigade member would be an enormous hassle, but the day when Haruhi found out I'd let her prey escape would far surpass the term "hassle" and go right on into pure violence, which would pointlessly increase the number of wounds I took from the neck up.

There was something I'd heard from someone—your chances of winning the lottery were lower than your chances of being in a plane crash. And I was sure that the odds of a new applicant to the SOS Brigade appearing were even lower. This high school was neither a casino nor an airport.

Holding on to that certainty, I opened the door to the clubroom, and when I saw the form of the person who occupied it, I momentarily lost my footing.

"Huh?"

The interrogative utterance did not come from my mouth. Someone had spoken up before I could, and arrived at the room before I did.

A petite girl stood by the window and turned quickly to face me. She was a freshman I'd never seen before, wearing a baggy, ill-fitting uniform, and a smiley-face barrette clipped to her wavy, permed-looking hair. I could tell her class year from the color of her school slippers. Rather, for some reason I was absolutely sure that she was younger than me—somehow that impression wedged itself into my mind. It was an incredibly vivid sensation, even stronger than when I'd first met Asahina, though why I should feel that way upon encountering her for the first time, I had no idea.

"Huh?" was my idiotic reaction. Hopefully I'd be allowed such a three-letter vocalization, given that there was a girl I'd never seen before here in a room that normally contained only the usual suspects.

Just as I was thinking the silence was getting awkward, the girl reacted and broke it.

"Oh, it's you!" she said with a cheerful smile. I had no clue why she seemed to recognize me.

But then the girl straightened herself and bowed politely, and when she looked back up, she stuck her tongue out cutely and beamed. "It looks like I got mixed up."

Mixed up? Mixed up how? Mixed up the rooms for the club you want to join? If she was looking for the literature club, she wasn't mixed up at all—she'd hit the bull's-eye, I told her. Unfortunately, Nagato wasn't here.

"No, that's not what I mean. This is the SOS Brigade, right? That much is correct." Before I could respond, she continued, rapid-fire. "I'd planned to come here, but I got off track. I guess this is my first time meeting *this* you, isn't it? Heehee, that's okay. This isn't that big of a mistake. You can remember meeting me or forget me, either way's fine. They amount to the same thing. Gosh, I really was careless! This whole thing is such a hassle. I hope you'll forgive me—these things happen, you know? You'll understand soon enough. I mean, there's no way you won't, after all! But if something weird tries to stop you, you have to promise not to freak out or be swayed by emotion, okay? You gotta promise me that much. It's a deal, right? Good!"

It didn't matter how "good" she said "it" was, I couldn't do anything besides stand there, dumbstruck.

The possibility that she was actually a cross-dressing Koizumi seemed remote. It wasn't Haruhi, nor Asahina, and certainly not Nagato. So what reason would any of the freshman girls have to be in the literature club room? On top of that, she was advancing on me with her incomprehensible assertions like Edward the Black Prince and his longbow army invading France, and all I could do was try to defend myself. And yet the strength of her advance reminded me of a certain someone—.

As I mulled it over, the girl with the baggy sleeves whirled around and flew toward the still-open door.

I would've liked the chance to tell her to wait up, but she was one step ahead of me.

"Well, then—" she said, turning and bowing a crisp, naval bow. "Until we meet again! Good-bye!"

Leaving behind only a pleasant smile, she breezed through the door. Strangely I don't remember hearing any footsteps. It was as though the moment she entered the hall, she vanished like morning dew.

"..."

For how many seconds did I stand there, stunned? Or was it minutes?

When I finally came to my senses, I noticed there was a small, narrow-mouthed flower vase on the windowsill. There was a single flower placed in the ceramic piece, which hadn't been there yesterday.

It was a pretty flower, of a kind I'd never seen before. There was no doubt that the mystery girl from a moment ago had brought it.

Asahina wouldn't have done it. I wanted to know what was up with the flower, but more importantly—who was that girl?

She's acted awfully familiar to me, peppering me with rapid-fire chatter before suddenly retreating like the first storm of spring—all of which suggested she'd been confident that neither Haruhi, nor Asahina, nor Nagato would come to the room.

So did she have some kind of business with me? I seriously doubted she'd infiltrated the clubroom just to put that flower vase on the windowsill.

No, wait a minute—could she seriously have been a prospective new member? She *did* look like a freshman...

Even so, she was an affable girl, not at all shy. I wished I could've kept her here until Koizumi showed up.

"Wait..."

Maybe she'd disappeared so quickly because she was trying to avoid seeing Koizumi.

If so, she must've had business with me, specifically.

—Until we meet again! Good-bye!

But what business? Where and when might I meet that girl again?

"Beats me."

I already had my hands full with Nagato and the Heavenly Canopy Dominion, Kuyoh and Sasaki, that good-for-nothing time traveler Fujiwara and Ryoko Asakura, and their anti–SOS Brigade association. I didn't have time for another mysterious person to show up.

I wished for another self. I could leave trivial stuff to him while I dealt with the challenge that had been given me. Even considering that if things got really bad I could ask Koizumi for help, not even his Agency backup was going to help him when it came to aliens and time travelers. The same reasoning ruled out Tsuruya. Kuyoh was just too awful. The only ones who could oppose her now were Kimidori and Asakura, but they weren't worth placing any trust in, since unlike Nagato they were from other factions within the Data

Overmind. If we were to fail horribly, they might well either just quietly watch, or smirk and say "Told you so." I can't be the only one who would find that annoying, right?

Tossing my schoolbag lazily onto the table, I sat down in a folding chair.

On the table there was neatly arranged shogi-like game board along with its playing pieces, which Koizumi had presumably put there.

As I was gazing at the game, of whose rules I had not the faintest notion, twilight began to fall, and the "Silk Road" theme signaling the end of extracurricular activities rang out over the school PA system.

I was the only one who engaged in SOS Brigade activities that day. It was hard to believe even Koizumi had been absent. That didn't bode well, but obviously a student's true duty was to academics, and not some sketchy club. Koizumi was probably going to start seriously thinking about his academic future soon. Given that it was him, he'd probably keep following Haruhi around even after graduation. So where was Haruhi going to go for college?

But even before that happened, what was going to become of Asahina, who would graduate a year ahead of us? Would we get a younger student to replace our charming upperclassman maid, and would she also be a time traveler?

"This is no good. Thinking about the people getting left behind next year is nothing to laugh about."

Forlorn, I shouldered my bag and quietly put the clubroom behind me.

Being alone there made it feel like a room in an abandoned countryside hospital somewhere, or something.

This was probably the first time since entering high school I'd felt so sentimental. It wasn't like me. Maybe it was normal for a regular high school guy, but I'd gotten used to being an SOS Brigade member, which meant constant buzzing activity, like the cicadas whose cries rang out every summer.

"Crap," I uttered, as a matter of course. It felt as though someone had taken over my soul, somehow.

That night I got a call from Sasaki.

"We'll meet in front of the station again tomorrow. Fujiwara said to."

So it had come to this, eh?

Sasaki's voice was different; it sounded decisive. If it was obvious enough for even me to notice, she had to have been long-since aware of it.

This was a good time for the decisive battle to happen. No—honestly, it was overdue. I knew all too well that more long-winded talk at the café wouldn't improve anything. Not even when our opponent was an alien or a time traveler. When I thought about it, I realized we'd been wasting our time. But now we could finally settle everything.

"By the way, Kyon," said Sasaki, her tone full of concern for me. *"Fujiwara's serious this time. There's not going to be a curtain call after this is over. He means to finish things. He tried to keep it from me again, as usual, but misdirection doesn't work on me. I'm pretty good at seeing through people, if I do say so myself."*

She was. I'd never met anyone, man or woman, young or old, who could get the drop on Sasaki. Maybe Tsuruya, who so rapidly embodied her own sincerity. She had the swiftness to act before someone read her intentions.

"Still, Kyon, whether they're going to try to eliminate me or use me is an unknown factor. At the moment, I'm an uncertain element. The one certain thing is you, Kyon. You and your decisions are the key to everything." Sasaki's trademark chuckle came over the phone. *"But you don't have to worry about it too much. I can be certain that neither you nor I can affect the world as it is. What will change is the future. This is probably a very important moment for Fujiwara and Asahina, but we here in the present don't have anything to worry about."*

I didn't know what Asahina the Elder's intentions were. But I didn't want to have to see *this* Asahina cry.

"I think the future can be anything, Kyon." Sasaki spoke like a sparrow perched on a power line, talking about the weather. *"From their perspective, we're people from the past. But to us, they're nothing more than people from a future adjacent to our present. So the most important thing for us is the fact that this world is the present. That's our biggest advantage against them. You've got to remember that, Kyon. I'm sure you'll figure something out. After all—"*

Sasaki let slip a little chuckle.

"—You're the sole ordinary person Suzumiya chose."

I didn't feel like anything close to the chosen one. Sasaki sounded full of confidence, but her words only baffled me. I wanted to ask what all this nonsense about "choosing" or "being chosen" meant. I wanted to scream it. I knew that Nagato, Koizumi, and Asahina all saw me as special, and I'd done my best to be ready. I'd prepared myself for the worst last Christmas Eve. Even now it had sunk into my mind like fresh-made tofu. But while it pained me to do so, I couldn't help acknowledging that my current predicament was the result of Haruhi's subconscious—and still, Sasaki, you had to choose me too?

Haruhi was entirely unaware of this, but Sasaki wasn't. She was entirely aware that she was a godlike being. So if she understood, she should tell me, I said.

Tell me, why me?

"Heh. Heehee, Kyon. Your thickheadedness has always given me fits, but I'm shocked you'd take it this far." She wasn't mocking me; she was genuinely taken aback. *"Let's speak hypothetically. It could be anything, but let's say you've bought a lottery ticket."*

I never had before, but sure.

"The winning lottery number is drawn at random, then presented. The odds that your number matches the winning one are significantly worse than one in many tens of thousands."

Which meant you shouldn't count on it bringing in all the money you need to buy your dreams, I said.

"Speaking probabilistically, no. Only the house makes money with

gambling, and nearly all gamblers end up with a loss. But someone has to win. The odds of your purchased ticket matching the selected number are not zero. Do you understand? In this case, Suzumiya and I are the house, and you're someone holding a ticket."

Sasaki stopped talking for a moment, and I got the feeling that on the other end of the phone, she was taking a deep breath.

"And surprisingly, the numbers Suzumiya and I chose at random are the same, save for the last two digits. And your ticket matches too. Except you don't yet know what the last two digits you're holding are. No, indeed—they're being hidden from you. You can't see them yet."

What the hell kind of lottery was this, anyway?

"The digits are always changing. For now. But don't worry. I'm sure they'll settle soon. But the only reason you'll know what those digits are is because they'll be fixed. And to fix them, you have to observe them. If you just leave it unaltered in the back of your desk, the redemption date will pass, and the ticket will be no more than an ordinary scrap of paper. And then it won't even be a question of who you'll choose. It will all have been for naught."

Even I wasn't that stupid, I said. There was a lot of money on the line, after all.

"That's right, Kyon. That's why. You've got to fix the last digits. Will they be mine, or Suzumiya's? You're the only one who can decide. Not Fujiwara or Kuyoh. This is something they can't do. It's not possible for anyone in this world, nor anyone from the future, nor any extraterrestrial life form. That's why they're so fixated on you. Everything depends on you."

" . . . "

"Heehee. That's a very annoyed silence I'm hearing. You're so honest, Kyon."

If she knew that much, why wouldn't she switch places with me, and take on the task I'd been left?

"I don't want it either. But I . . . huh, how to put it? Ah, yes—I trust you; that's what I wanted to to say. The path you're on is the correct one. And that, Kyon, is something you've long-since realized, isn't it?"

Sasaki's tone was pleasant, as though she was just making small talk, and it had the effect of calming me down. She wasn't trying to lecture me. She wasn't trying to influence or instruct me either. My so-called close friend from middle school, whom Kunikida had labeled a "strange girl," had simply called to convey to me her true thoughts.

"All right, Sasaki. I get it," I said, gripping the receiver tightly. "Leave it to me. I'll see you tomorrow."

After a moment of silence, Sasaki chuckled. *"Right. I'll look forward to it. My trust in you is deeper than the crushing depth of a newly launched submarine. Go ahead and push the down-trim as much as you want. I don't mind a bit. See you, old friend."*

I remember hanging up the phone at exactly the same time as her, with no lag whatsoever.

CHAPTER 8

α — 11

It was already Friday.

I felt as though the past week had been unrelentingly busy. With Haruhi's brigade entrance examinations, and the establishment of Yasumi as the club's sole new member, it somehow felt as if I'd lived two weeks' worth of life. But after coincidentally running into that time-traveler guy, Kyoko Tachibana, that Heavenly Canopy Dominion terminal named Kuyoh Suoh, and to top it all off, Sasaki, no wonder I was feeling restless.

But it was strange. Given our storybook encounter, it seemed odd that I hadn't heard from them again at all. Normally you'd think the usual scurrying around would ensue, but there'd been no contact at all, which baffled me.

Perhaps unbeknownst to me, they were struggling with Nagato, Koizumi, or Asahina. It wouldn't be strange if the three of them had decided to cooperate in the service of preserving Haruhi's peaceful life, but why wouldn't they mention it to me? After all this, was I still an unconcerned party? Although I supposed if I got involved, not only would I not be of much use, I could easily be taken hostage.

Such thoughts occupied me as I arrived at the entrance to North High, and mechanically proceeded to the shoe lockers, opening mine.

"Bwuh?"

On top of my school slippers lay an object I hadn't seen in some time.

It was a colorful envelope printed with some licensed character or another. It was addressed to me. And on the back was written the sender's unmistakable name.

Yasumi Watahashi.

I read.

A flood of memories washed over me. How many times had something like this happened to me? First with Asakura—and her goal had been my murder. Next had been Asahina, but the adult version of Asahina, who'd given me an important hint, then disappeared. After that it was Asahina the Elder again, and in the course of following her incomprehensible directions, I'd encountered another time traveler, who'd hurled some bitter invective at me before things were over.

Given my experiences, I was well aware that an analog message waiting for me in my shoe locker was not a ticket to paradise.

And yet it felt as if circumstances were different this time. After all, it was from our brigade's new freshman member, who was a harmless-seeming, cheerfully active girl, whose height and build made it hard to believe she was even an innocent freshman. Given her house call yesterday, she was quite assertive.

"Did she…"

Was my dream of so many years about to come true? Was this truly a love letter? Had the spring of my youth finally arrived?

—I fell in love with you the moment we met, and I knew that I had to get into the SOS Brigade no matter what.—

"What am I, stupid?" I murmured to myself, unable to think of a single reason why such a cheerful, energetic freshman would make a pass at me.

Plus, every time I got a message like this, it was always the beginning of some crazy, unprecedented development. Two faces came to mind. So which would it be this time? Encroaching danger, or that perfect smile?

"All right—"

There was no telling who might spot me if I just kept standing stupidly in front of my shoe locker. If Haruhi or Taniguchi saw me, explaining the letter would be annoying.

I quickly hid myself away in a bathroom, and opened the envelope. A playing card–like slip of paper was contained therein, on which the following had been hurriedly scribbled:

"I'll meet you in the clubroom at 6 PM. Please come, okay?"

It was hard to know how to react. If I had to sum up my feelings in a single word, that word would be "suspicious."

I couldn't help recalling the incident with Asakura almost nostalgically. But my danger sense wasn't tingling at all, and no alarms were going off. My senses had not been particularly sharpened by the morning hike, but from what I could tell this was closer to the invitation I'd received from Asahina the Elder. I didn't fundamentally trust my own instincts, but maybe it wouldn't kill me to heed my intuition once in a while.

That said, there wasn't any danger in being careful.

It was just before homeroom started.

"By the way, Haruhi."

"What?"

"Say you've got a problem that you're not sure how to approach."

"Is this about study?"

"You could say that."

"Looks like you've kindled a bit of inclination toward academics. As brigade chief, I'm pleased that one of my members is upping their motivation. I assume you've given whatever your problem is a certain amount of thought on your own, yes?"

"Of course."

"If it's something you can solve by looking up, you should look it up."

"It's not a question of content."

"Huh? So what is it, then, math? In that case, you've gotta know how to solve the problem. What's the formula?"

"No, it's not math. And incidentally, I don't care about how to solve it; I just want to know the answer."

"You're not some grade schooler copying over the answers to your summer homework, and anyway, that's no way to learn something."

"Who cares? I thought as long as you could understand the thinking of the test-maker, that was good enough."

"Oh, so it's modern lit. You should've just said so. So the question's something like 'What was the writer thinking when they wrote this sentence,' right?"

"I guess that's closest, yeah."

"What a stupid question. This is true for novels and essays too, but when it comes to the question of what's written in a sentence, how would the test-maker know what the original writer was thinking? Even if you get the 'right' answer, that's just because whoever's grading the test happens to agree with you. So here's how I think problems like that should go: What was *I* thinking when I read this sentence? That'd be a lot easier for me to accept."

"I don't really need to go that far. In this case, the person who wrote it and the person asking the question are the same."

"Oh, that's easy, then."

"By all means, tell me."

"All you have to do," said Haruhi, leaning in and getting right up in my face, her overwhelming smile making me think of some kind of radiation, "is just ask whoever wrote it!"

And so come lunchtime, I left my bento box with Taniguchi and Kunikida and took action.

It was just as Haruhi said. If I didn't understand, going and asking

someone who *did* understand was a lot better than flailing around in ignorance. Especially when that someone was the only person who knew her own intentions. All I had to do was ask her, and everything would be cleared up. I'd have to get her to talk, but so long as I didn't get into a scuffle with her, I expected it wouldn't be too much trouble. I mean, she was just a nice little freshman.

So it was that I wandered around the building that contained the freshman classrooms, in search of Yasumi.

It might've been bad manners to ignore the note's order to come at six o'clock, but I would just have to make her understand that I was too curious to help myself. And so long as there was even the remote possibility of my getting knifed again, I had every intention of flushing as much of my intuition down the toilet as I wanted to.

Thus resolved, despite my high spirits, I stopped dead in my tracks.

"Wait, which class was she in, again?"

She'd written it on her answer sheet for the brigade entrance examination, but I couldn't remember it. My attention had been focused on her name and her strange answers at the time.

"Guess I shouldn't have come during lunch."

The halls that I had become so accustomed to the previous year were now filled with new students, and felt like another world. Even though the color of my school slippers was the only thing that was different, I couldn't help feeling nervous when I peered into the classroom of a different year. On top of that, the freshmen didn't seem to particularly enjoy an unfamiliar junior looking into each of their rooms as though they were some rare animal species.

As soon as I found Yasumi, I was going to call her over and take her someplace without any other people. That would probably seem a little suspicious, but I figured it would be all right since we were both in the same club. Still—

"...Where *is* she?"

The girl in question was nowhere to be found. I was hoping that her small frame would make her easy to pick out, but if anything it seemed to make her harder to spot. Wondering if she bought her lunch at school, I headed over to the cafeteria, but no dice. With all the wandering around I was reaching the limits of my own hunger. I'd made a good show of proving my endurance by wandering all over the school, but it had been wasted effort, and I cast my gaze upward. I was in the courtyard, and my eye just happened to land on the window of the literature club's room.

Surely not.

I headed straight for the room. I found it hard to believe anyone would go all the way over there just to eat their lunch, but there was always the possibility. Honestly, I should've brought my own lunch with me.

I opened the door that Haruhi and I would doubtless open again after school, and there was Nagato. And only Nagato. Taking in this all-too-ordinary sight, I waved briefly to her before considering turning around and getting my lunch—but I soon thought better of it.

Right here in front of me was the best person in the world for answering questions I couldn't answer myself.

". . ."

Sitting in her usual corner with a book on her lap, Nagato didn't so much as twitch an eyebrow at my intrusion, which told me definitively that things were as they ever were, here in this room. If I hadn't known she was an extraterrestrial life-form, the peaceful mood set by the girl silently reading her book here would've struck me as completely normal.

But I knew things weren't normal, and forgetting about the contents of my lunch box momentarily, I spoke to Nagato.

"Nagato."

"What?"

First things first. "What is she?"

"She is nothing."

Good old Nagato, she'd known instantly who my question referred to. But that said—

"That's going too far. Isn't the girl known as Yasumi Watahashi just a normal student?"

"No student with such a name exists in this school."

That answer made me take a step back—not physically, but mentally. About half a step.

She didn't exist? Which meant... My brain started multitasking. Oh right.

"So it's an alias. Someone's posing as a North High student and sneaking in just for after-school activities."

"That recognition computes."

Good grief. So Yasumi Watahashi's background *was* going to make her hard to deal with. I supposed I'd always known as much. She was obviously weird, after all. Her convenient appearance was an obvious plot twist from a silly novel.

So, who was controlling her? If I had to take a guess, it'd be—

An alien? I asked.

"No."

Time traveler?

"No."

Not an esper. She didn't seem like the type.

"Indeed. She is not. Nor is she from another world."

It wasn't like Nagato to offer information unasked for. Before I could get hung up on that, my ignorance-born curiosity got the better of me, and I opened my mouth.

"So Yasumi's just a strange girl with a slightly odd approach, then? And she's just posing as a North High student?"

Nagato looked up from the printed page, and returned my gaze for the first time. I couldn't help feeling sucked into her eyes, which were like toffee sprinkled with gold.

Her faint voice seemed only distantly related to the movement of her diaphragm. "I cannot say anything. Not right now."

Why not? Wasn't this the first time that Nagato had ever expressed reservations?

Then she added, "The determination is that this is the best course of action."

"What?" I shot back, despite myself. It was a lousy comeback, I know. But I was fully capable of understanding things like context and nuance, and I hadn't come here to chat with Nagato just for the fun of it. What surprised me was only one thing.

Nagato was refusing. She was refusing *me*.

This—surely this foretold calamity.

"So, you not being able to tell me something right now—who decided this? Was it the Data Overmind?"

"The reasoning that it will result in a higher probability of a favorable outcome is mine. Depending on time and circumstances, operating in restricted space, the possibility exists that acting in ignorance can be more effective."

For some reason I didn't feel as if I was being complimented. Just as my discomfort level was nearing its limit as I wondered whether this was payback for something I'd done before, salvation came in the form of something I'd left in my pocket.

That, of course, was nothing less than the non-love letter from Yasumi Watahashi.

"So, about this letter…"

I felt a little bad showing it to someone else without asking Yasumi, but I didn't owe her that much obligation quite yet.

Nagato glanced at the paper without much interest. "You may go," she said vaguely.

Really? Well, then.

"She means you no harm. On the contrary—it can be inferred that she wishes to be of use to you."

I couldn't help groaning. Now that she'd said it, I realized I'd sort of guessed as much.

This was the spirited, light-stepping freshman who'd passed Haruhi's unreasonable entrance examinations as though they were nothing. Clad in her oversized uniform, she happily did everything from menial chores in the clubroom to redesigning the brigade's web page, always running around with her unruly hair and her childish features—such charm she had that it was impossible to feel any other way about her. She was like the platonic ideal of the junior member. Any suspicion my brain conjured up had to be mistaken.

Save one condition—the fact that she'd left a note in my shoe locker.

After that, I could get nothing out of Nagato except for "yes" and "no," so I took my leave and returned to my classroom. Immediately thereafter, the bell signaling the end of lunch rang, and with that I'd lost my chance to eat. I'd have to take my lunch in the clubroom after school.

Fortunately, the post-homeroom Haruhi-led study session was canceled on account of our new member. Side by side, Haruhi and I made for the ex-literature club room like flies sticking themselves to flypaper. Our routine was almost getting boring, but thanks to the new participant, my mind was starting to waver a bit.

But when Haruhi slammed the door open the way she always did, beyond it were only the old standbys of Asahina in her maid outfit and Nagato, who hadn't moved so much as a millimeter from where she was earlier that day. I wasn't much worried about the two girls, nor the sole other male brigade member, Koizumi—he'd probably been made class rep of his class or something and was enjoying some pillow talk with whoever the female class rep was. He was a good-looking boy, and if it hadn't been for the SOS Brigade probably would've been a lot more popular, and even if he were managing to conduct some kind of high-school-dating-sim-style life behind our backs, he was probably smart enough not to get caught—the guy was so canny he was probably the sharpest one out of the whole brigade.

I realized I was distracting myself.

"Is the new member not here yet?"

Yasumi's petite form was nowhere to be seen. She might have been on her way here from her real school, but Her Excellency Brigade Chief Haruhi was very strict when it came to delaying marches.

"Ah…" Asahina clasped her hands together as though apologizing for her own failings. "She's not coming today. She came right after class, said she had to take care of something that was desperately important for her life, and went home."

I'm not sure how she took the twitch of my eyebrow, but Asahina continued, speaking with an awful lot of emotion in her voice for a defense attorney.

"She seemed like she was in a terrible hurry. She bowed over and over, and seemed very, very sorry, talking about how missing two days in a row made her a failure as a person, and I just watched her with my eyes full of tears…ah…it's just…"

A flushed Asahina started to hug herself yet again. Evidently Yasumi had just been too cute to bear.

"She looked at me with those eyes, like a little baby animal…She was so…cute…"

As I watched Asahina deliver her pathos-filled monologue, I thought about what was happening.

I was positive that Yasumi's "something important" was her meeting with me here, at six o'clock. What did she want with me? And where did she plan to stay until then? Was she hiding somewhere on school grounds? Could she not even participate in the most perfunctory of club activities? The actions of Yasumi the mystery girl were indeed mysterious.

Just as I was hoping that it wouldn't invite Haruhi's displeasure—

"I heard over lunch. On my way to the cafeteria." Haruhi plopped down in her brigade chief's chair and lazily dropped her bag on the floor.

So what did she hear? I asked.

"That she was going to skip club activities today. 'I'm so sorry, you made me a full brigade member and I go and do something silly like this,' she was saying, bowing like a little flower, on the verge of tears."

I imagined the cheerful girl's form as she apparently humbled herself, wondering to myself that despite my long walkabout in search of her, there was a route that would have led me right here.

"Did you ask her why?"

"Look, Kyon. I'm not that much of a busybody—I'm not some Peeping Tom that's going to pry into every detail. And it didn't seem like she was regretting joining the SOS Brigade and trying to sneak out or something. I'm sure she really did just happen to have something unavoidable come up. You might be surprised to know that it's my policy to show my subordinates tolerance and forgiveness."

And yet somehow I doubted she'd apply that motto to me at all.

Realizing that further conversation was going to be fruitless, I put my bag on the table and went to sit in my usual chair, whereupon I noticed for the first time a sense of unease in the clubroom's atmosphere.

It was because there was something left by the window behind the brigade chief's desk.

When Asahina noticed my gaze, she spoke up with a voice as soft as fresh-made mochi rice cake. "Yasumi brought it over earlier, as an apology for missing the meeting."

Earlier? I was surprised we hadn't run into her on the way over, then. Oh well, whatever.

It was a small-mouthed ceramic vase, holding a single elegant flower.

Haruhi turned around and gave the flower a long, hard look. "I haven't seen that kind of flower before. Yasumi brought this?"

"Yes, yes." Asahina nodded. "She said she thought it was interesting, so she brought it over. She said she found it yesterday in the mountains nearby, and that it had to be pretty rare, so she thought it would make a nice decoration for the room. She gave it to me like it was some kind of treasure…"

Yesterday, huh? By the time I got home, Yasumi was already there. If she went to the mountains after that, it would've been getting pretty dark. And if by "mountains" she meant the Tsuruya family mountain (which was really the only one in the immediate area), then she'd been wandering around alone in a place unlit by artificial light. That seemed rather dangerous for a girl who'd only just started high school.

"...Mmm—" Haruhi folded her arms and regarded the flower. "Well, fine. I'm the one who asked her to bring something interesting; who knows, maybe for Yasumi this flower's really interesting. Indeed! Such decisive follow-up means that she's got the heart of a true brigade member. My brigade entrance exam didn't lie! Looks like it definitely identified her attributes, anyway. It's no overstatement to say that if we preserve that format, we won't have to worry about the brigade finding good personnel even after we graduate!"

I wondered about that. Would the Haruhi-style SOS Brigade test really be applied once we graduated? At the moment, club admission was determined by being able to endure Haruhi's demerit system, and it seemed as though Haruhi didn't actually want many rookie members. If the real truth of her heart were laid bare, I really didn't think Haruhi was welcoming Yasumi with open arms. I'd been through quite a lot with Haruhi. I'd gotten so I could see where she was looking just by the angle of her eyebrows. And she was the kind of person who wore her heart on her sleeve, which made her easy to read, so my Haruhi observational skills yielded a single answer, which was that she was confused.

Essentially, Haruhi's evaluation of Yasumi was a complicated one, and she had not yet come up with a satisfactory answer. I imagined she felt something from the younger girl; Yasumi wasn't straightforward the way Asahina was.

The truth was I felt the same way. With the note she'd written me in my pocket, I wondered what her intentions toward the SOS Brigade were—it was a sort of mystery.

On the other hand, Asahina was in rare high spirits, her footsteps seeming lighter than normal as she went about making tea. I guess she just couldn't help how much happier having a new female junior member made her.

When I thought about it, I couldn't really say that Haruhi and I—to say nothing of Nagato and Koizumi—were exactly great underclassmen for Asahina. No way could I say that. Surrounded as she was by Haruhi the tyrant, the silent, stone-faced Nagato, and the stiflingly polite Koizumi, she probably didn't feel like anyone's senior. And I was not better—I was constantly forgetting that Asahina was now in the highest year of school. Given that her charm made her seem like a middle schooler, Yasumi seemed even younger, so it was no wonder she felt so fondly toward the girl two years her junior. As I watched Asahina excitedly fuss over which tea-brewing method to teach Yasumi tomorrow, I felt the heaviness that had settled in my heart lighten, but unfortunately there was a reason why I couldn't just keep staring at the SOS Brigade's mascot girl.

I sipped whatever herbal tea Asahina'd made that day, and glanced at my watch.

I still had time until six o'clock. Just as I was trying to figure out how I was going to get back to the clubroom after the day's activities were over—

"Hello, everyone—sorry I'm late." And there, smiling pleasantly like someone out of an acne medication commercial, appeared Koizumi. "There's just so much to do at the beginning of spring. The student council president is quite motivated this year, and negotiations with faculty are not what I'd call rare. I wish I could ignore them, but given that they concern consolidation and elimination of various clubs, I can't very well fail to attend."

As he entered the room, Koizumi casually explained his troubles, though no one had asked him to. He set his bag down on the desk, and paying the Chinese shogi set on the table no mind, walked over to the windowsill.

"Ah, what do we have here?" He peered in interest at the flower Yasumi had left behind. "Who is this flower a present from?"

"From Yasumi, I guess," answered Haruhi, poking at her empty teacup. Asahina noticed this and hurried to prepare more tea. I hoped it would be regular green tea this time.

Koizumi stroked his chin and regarded the slim vase as though he were looking at a triffid.

"If you'll excuse me," he said, taking his cell phone out of his blazer pocket and positioning it to take a picture of the flower. He snapped several pictures, and once he was satisfied, fiddled with his phone for a few moments, as though he were sending the pictures somewhere.

"What're you doing, Koizumi?" I asked. "Don't tell me that's wolfsbane or foxglove."

"Not at all." Koizumi slid his phone back into his pocket and flashed a reassuring smile. "It's not poisonous. I just thought it might be an orchid I'd seen somewhere else, that's all. I'm probably off the mark, but I thought I'd check to be sure, that's all."

After that, Nagato continued reading the lengthy nonfiction book she was reading, proceeding from the first volume to the second, while Asahina served us yet more mysterious-tasting tea that she'd obtained somewhere, as Haruhi fiddled with the SOS Brigade website. Incidentally, Haruhi's first Internet task was clicking through every spam URL on every forum she could find, which constantly crashed the browser.

Around the time I'd managed to install some free anti-malware software, that good old easy-listening music started to play over the school PA system.

Which meant it was about five thirty.

With excellent timing, Nagato snapped her book shut, and taking that as a sign, we all started getting ready to leave—although in my case, it was mostly fake, in service of my alibi. But if I didn't get everybody out of the clubroom, I couldn't start my meeting with Yasumi.

We had all passed through the school gate and started along the road that led alongside the school and down the hill. I prepared myself for the biggest role of my acting career, and while I was well aware it would seem pretty forced, I hadn't been able to think of a better line.

"Oh! Damn!" I said.

Haruhi and Asahina were a bit ahead, and stopped to turn around, wondering what the problem was. Nagato and Koizumi stopped at exactly the same time as each other, which I guess didn't surprise me.

"I left something in the classroom. I've got to go get it!"

I can't deny that my line-read sounded a little forced.

"Huh?" said Haruhi nonetheless. "You never bring your text-books home with you anyway—what could you have possibly for-gotten in the room?"

Normally she would have been right, and in fact she *was* right, but I needed a reason that Haruhi would believe.

"Uh, actually," I said, repeating the line I'd memorized. "I just remembered I borrowed a dirty magazine from Taniguchi. And I left it in my desk."

"Huh?" said Haruhi, her eyebrows instantly contorting.

"It's probably fine, but if anybody finds it I'll be in trouble. So—I'm just gonna go get it. You guys go on ahead! This is, like, a super-valuable porno mag. It's already been banned and gone out of print, so it's really rare. If it gets confiscated, I'll have to prostrate myself in front of Tani-guchi. If I don't go get it now, he'll make me his errand boy forever!"

Next to Haruhi's astounded face, Koizumi's grin, and Asahina's stunned expression, I met Nagato's gaze. I got the feeling that she nodded ever so faintly at me, but insofar as she was agreeing with me, it was on the micron scale.

I felt bad. If only I'd been able to come up with a better excuse.

"So, I'm heading back to the classroom. It'll probably take me a while, so you guys don't have to wait up," I said, then turned to go. As I started to climb back up the hill, Haruhi's voice came at me from behind.

"Don't talk about dirty books in front of maidens! Stupid Kyon!"

Maidens? Yeah, right. Although I'd have to apologize to Asahina the next day. Yeah, definitely.

*   *   *

In the no-man's-land between sunset and early evening, there was no trace of anyone in the school or on the field, so I was able to return to the clubroom without passing a single person. I opened the door.

"Thank you so much for coming." There in the room, tinted orange by the setting sun, Yasumi was waiting for me.

The girl I'd looked so hard for during lunch, with no success—the girl Nagato claimed was not a student here. Her charm held Asahina captive, and yet Haruhi found our newest brigade member somehow difficult to handle.

Her mischievous face smiled a smile as warm and soft as a freshly roasted marshmallow as Yasumi happily continued. "I knew you'd come. I believed it—that things would turn out this way. And I want to believe in what's going to happen."

I decided the best policy was to ignore mysterious statements I didn't understand.

"What business do you have with me?" I said, for starters. She had remained all the way through to the end of Haruhi's brigade member selection procedure. Anyone who could do that was not someone to be trifled with, I was quite sure. "What's going to happen next?"

Yasumi's answer came in a softly laughing voice. "I don't know myself."

What?

"But we'll know soon."

Yasumi brushed aside her soft hair. The grin on her smiley-face barrette seemed larger than usual; it must have been a trick of the angle.

Yasumi continued to look at me, and I didn't take my eyes off her face.

How much time passed like that, I wonder?

I heard someone knock at the door.

β — 11

Friday.

My enthusiasm had fallen asleep; apparently that was all there was.

I wondered if my sister's flying body press method of awakening me was the result of her calculating the worst possible way to do so. Having been forcibly awakened from a dream wherein I knew what my goal was but no matter where I ran I couldn't reach it made my body feel already fatigued, despite having gotten plenty of sleep. It didn't feel as if I'd rested up at all. It just made me feel even more tired than when I'd started.

I wished that sister of mine could at least have waited until the dream was over.

"...Ah..."

My eyes still half-closed, I sat up, whereupon Shamisen, who had been lying next to me, put his head on my pillow and started purring. If he'd been either in or on the futon, he would've fallen prey to my sister as well. This was not a place where there was any cause for shame at humanity's failure to keep up with cats, so I got out of bed, still wearing my pajamas.

I was grateful for the weekend's approach, but what happened after school that day would decide not only my fate, but the entire SOS Brigade's. Despite having awoken so sleepy-headed, I could remember that much.

But to be fully serious, I would need to be more awake, both physically and mentally. As I wondered whether the uphill walk to school was as good as a morning aerobics workout, I thought about how I'd go and do the radio calisthenics routine over summer break in elementary school, getting my stamp for it and everything before coming home to take a nap, which I supposed was fairly healthy so long as I didn't take too long a break from it. Why had I applied to this high school? There was a decent municipal high school in the neighborhood, and it made me want to go back and interrogate my homeroom teacher for the last year of middle school. All that talk about college acceptance rates had totally fooled me.

"Kyon!"

My early-to-bed, early-to-rise sister was in fine form. She carried Shamisen's sleepy, slack, morning-hating form around. He somehow reminded me of someone.

"You said you've got something important to do today, right? You told me to wake you up early today. You said if I didn't you'd never play video games with me again! I don't want that!"

I had no memory of any of that, but it was true that today seemed as if it was going to be a very important day for me. Not for school, or for my activities with the SOS Brigade—after classes I would leave the school, and a rendezvous with Sasaki and her rotten friends awaited me.

"Yeah…"

I looked at the face of my little sister, who seemed impossibly young for a sixth grader, as she held Shamisen, who yawned. My consciousness gradually cleared. The outline of the previous night's phone conversation with Sasaki had gotten sorted out during my sleep, and it started to come back to me.

I had to settle things with Fujiwara.

Why had he come back to the past and teamed up with Kuyoh and Kyoko Tachibana?

I had to settle things with Kuyoh.

For what purpose had the extraterrestrial forced Nagato into bed rest?

I had to settle things with Kyoko Tachibana.

After trying to kidnap Asahina, did the harmless-seeming fake esper who respected Koizumi so much really want to install Sasaki as the true god?

My pathetic little brain was tormented by other questions too.

Was Kimidori really nothing more than an observer? Would she just neutrally watch if the Heavenly Canopy Dominion tried to take over the Data Overmind?

Was the temporarily revived Asakura going to sit back and do nothing in such a case?

After she'd invited me into the past so many times, would I ever see Asahina the Elder again?

What about Koizumi's power? What about the Tamaru brothers, Mori, and Arakawa?

"Beats me," I said pointlessly, in a hoarsely rattling voice.

Something would definitely happen today. There was no doubt that something huge was waiting for me after school. It would be nice if I got answers to most of those questions. I wanted to be able to take a bath tonight while singing some vaguely remembered western song. No, I had to.

If I didn't end things here, my worries would only persist, and I'd begin my life as a high school junior by continuing to wait in the club-room for visitors who would never come—that's the feeling I had.

I wouldn't stand by while the place where I belonged was taken from me.

Ever since that fateful day during my first year of high school when sitting behind me, Haruhi had chosen me, the resulting loose gear wound up matching hers perfectly. Fate? You might as well throw that word into a neutron star. Haruhi wished for it, and I wished for it. And this time, this here and now was the result.

I didn't know anything about the future or past, but what I knew I had to protect was the present, not the notions of hypothetical aliens or time travelers. If anybody had a problem with that, they could tell me directly, or send me a text message or a letter. If they had any better ideas, I'd gladly refer to them.

But this much I couldn't forget: Everything would come down to me. No matter how clever a thesis was put forth, no matter how bright the genius whose view I was given, if I said no, the answer was no.

The only people who could convince me would have to be as smooth-talking as Koizumi, as trustworthy as Nagato, and as charismatic as Haruhi.

If there was someone who believed themselves to be the world's greatest, then let them show themselves.

I just wanted to say this much. If you had that much confidence in yourself, you'd better think about your own story first. Because you never knew for sure whether or not there were actually aliens, time travelers, espers, or even sliders all around you.

Before you worry about other people, you better pay attention to your own surroundings first. This is just my own little piece of irresponsible advice; in the end, it's all up to you.

I went to school and took my seat in the classroom to wait for the bell, no differently from any other day. The entire day fit into the category of "ordinary."

All except for the owner of the seat behind me fidgeting nervously all day thanks to Nagato's absence.

Not even the preview for a rerun of some anime was cause for as much suspense for Haruhi as Nagato's illness, and she clicked her mechanical pencil noisily all throughout class, and when called on by the teacher to answer a question on the blackboard, wrote unintelligible questions and then seemed to expect someone to go get a Rosetta stone just to translate them. Her lack of concentration made it seem as though her mind was somewhere out on the astral plane, but that was more or less how Haruhi always was, so our classmates seemed happy to let it slide. Haruhi being her Haruhi-ish self did come in handy sometimes. For better or for worse, the results spoke for themselves.

After class, Haruhi gave me only the most perfunctory of remarks before flying out of the classroom. I imagined she was going to grab Asahina and make for Nagato's apartment as if she was training for the downhill section of a cross-country race.

Such was the effect her absence was having. So long as she wasn't sitting in her usual corner, her small form absorbed in quiet reading, it wasn't going to feel like the SOS Brigade. We weren't complete unless all of us were there. That's how it worked with us. All I had to do was look back over the past year. When Asahina and Nagato and I had gotten tangled up in strange happenings, it was all well and good. And even when it came to the only one for whom that wasn't true—Haruhi—it still strengthened her friendship. Why? That, I don't know.

Or then there was the baseball tournament. Or the trip to the lonely island, or the summer break when we did all kinds of things, or the game against the computer club, or the filming of that ridiculous movie when she'd felt a sense of togetherness, of connectedness—or maybe when she'd helped out the rock band, or when I'd been hospitalized before Christmas, or when we'd had that trouble on the snowy mountain, or when it had been the litera-ture club versus the student council—

Or it was all of that. Somewhere along the line, Haruhi had changed significantly from her self of a year earlier. I'm remaining adamantly silent on the subject of her physical development, but mentally she was leaving her attitude from earlier behind, and ever so gradually, step by step, she was progressing, although even I had enough observational ability to tell it was happening slower than a sprinting Galapagos tortoise.

She still had more than enough energy to drag me around by my hand or necktie, but that was a far cry from her previous undis-criminating assaults, which went off like a hedgehog launching its rocket-powered quills in every direction.

It made me feel a little sad.

But that was probably only going to last as long as Nagato was sick. In which case—.

I thought.

I wanted to finish this quickly, and release Nagato from this ridiculous burden. That was the best possible medicine I could formulate—for her, and for Haruhi.

"Hey."

Sasaki greeted me with a wave of her hand when I arrived at the square in front of the station after having illegally parked my bike. She smiled the same calm smile she'd had the other day, which made her look as though she'd overcome some kind of cynicism— a Sasaki-brand original expression that made you wish she'd just keep quiet and smile. There was definitely a whiff of something Haruhi-like about that.

There was a time when, as a guy, I would've wished both Haruhi and Sasaki were a little more approachable—but that was ancient history now, as both of them gave off a strangely inexplicable attraction that transcended gender, and it had pulled me in like a fly to a bug zapper.

Ever since Haruhi had dragged me off to the clubroom where only Nagato had been, I felt as if my eyes had seen different scenery than other people saw. I don't want to think that my tastes had changed, but I honestly just don't understand myself. I'd leave that kind of analysis to Koizumi or Kunikida. Later.

Now, the important thing was the fact that Sasaki was flanked by two people, one on each side.

The boy and girl were Kyoko Tachibana with her small, unassuming form, and Fujiwara, who despite his height kept his gaze low and his face blank. The self-proclaimed esper Kyoko Tachibana, and the time traveler Fujiwara. With Sasaki, that made three, and apparently I'd made them wait.

"Kuyoh's not here."

Given Nagato's condition, Kuyoh was the one I had the most pressing business with. Or was she merely invisible, and standing right there? Apparently suspicion was written all over my face, as Sasaki answered.

"We couldn't contact Kuyoh. Her whereabouts are unknown at the moment. Of course, that's normally how she is, so even if we keep waiting, there's no telling when she might show up. But in any case, when she's needed, she'll appear. I guarantee it."

"Is that so?" I prodded Fujiwara.

"…Yeah." His face was as scornful as always, but there was

something rigid in his expression. Almost serious—no, that wasn't it. As though he was nervous, or unsure, and trying to hide it by making little jabs at other people. "She'll come." Fujiwara spat the words out like they were solid objects. "When it's necessary, she'll appear. It doesn't matter who might wish it. Must be nice to be an alien and have that kind of freedom, honestly. It's enough to make me wish I never had to deal with her again. Earth doesn't belong to aliens, nor does it belong to the people of the past. For us, you all have about as much value as common fossils. We're running out of space to throw you away."

. . . It was nice that I could count on him to always try to piss me off more. I could hate him as much as I wanted to.

"Uh, er—" Kyoko Tachibana stuck her face in from one side, blocking the murderous gazes that Fujiwara and I were directing at each other. "I've prepared a taxi. Shall we depart? Oh, and thank you so much for coming today."

I gazed at her hair as it bobbed in a quick little bow, and I just couldn't find it in myself to resent her. Her organization just lacked any sort of PR discipline. Actually, from a certain perspective, wouldn't she have been perfect for the job?

Well, it would take two years for me to start to doubt her. And given that Sasaki was here too, I decided to mark only Fujiwara as an enemy. Kuyoh's absence was something of a relief, since it meant Asakura wouldn't make a surprise reappearance. Or would it be a re-reappearance?

"This way, please." Kyoko Tachibana made an awkward gesture like some kind of bus tour guide, and led us on.

She seemed to be pretty nervous herself, tapping clumsily on the door of a cab that was stopped at the taxi stand. Surprisingly, it really did seem to be a public taxi waiting for passengers, with the driver dozing off in front of the open sports section of a newspaper. After several knocks the old cab driver opened both his eyes and the back door, and Sasaki, Fujiwara, and I climbed in. Kyoko Tachibana took shotgun.

"Where to?" asked the cab driver, stifling a yawn.

"North Prefectural High School, please."

With Kyoko Tachibana's words, I finally knew the day's destination. "Geez, right back where I came from?" I muttered to myself as the taxi started moving, making the four of us into traveling companions as we headed for the end of the journey. If I'd been told ahead of time, I could've just waited at North High.

"That's what I thought too." Fujiwara's words. "We probably didn't need to go to such trouble in today's course of events. Still, hmph. This too was a fixed event. There's no need to turn such a triviality into an adventure."

"Mm," said Sasaki, stroking her chin. "A fixed event, eh? So the four of us getting in a taxi and going to North High is, from the perspective of the future, an unchangeable matter of historical fact?"

"Yes." Fujiwara's answer was brusque. His face made it clear he didn't want to be questioned further.

Just then, Kyoko Tachibana turned around from where she sat in the passenger's seat. "You want to end this, don't you? This is a fixed event, so it's only logical to go along with it." She looked at me. "Heh, you've been rather abused by the 'fixed events' of various time travelers, haven't you? Well, this is just one more of those."

I opened my mouth to talk back, but surprisingly it was Fujiwara who took the initiative.

"Shut up," he said in a low, quiet voice that strangely resonated in my gut. It seemed to have an immediate effect on Kyoko Tachibana, whose face went pale as she sat back down in her seat.

Despite the suddenly leaden atmosphere within it, the taxi kept moving, and evidently our driver wasn't particularly attuned to subtleties. "So, you guys in high school? Nice to be young!" he said, unprompted. "Yeah, my kid just started sixth grade this spring. He's so into studying it's hard for me to believe he's my boy!"

"Ah."

Evidently Kyoko Tachibana felt it was her responsibility to be the driver's conversation partner, and so the talkative driver continued, pleased at having found someone to talk to.

—My sixth-grade son is really into science and chemistry, and is always talking about these crazy things. We've tried sending him to cram school, but he stopped going, saying something about the level being too low. We just didn't know what to do with him. For now we've hired a neighborhood high schooler to come and tutor him, but his grades still aren't going up. Still, the boy himself can't get his fill of study, and if he's got a notebook he's always writing figures and equations in it, but I wonder if it ain't just scribbling. The tutor kinda takes a hands-off approach, and I just don't know what to do—

At the appropriate times, Kyoko Tachibana would respond with "Oh," or "Ah," or "I see." I couldn't help thinking that our having gotten such a chatty driver was either good or bad luck. Given that she had arranged for the car, I assumed she was paying for it herself, which I admit was surprising, though unlike Koizumi's Agency her financial situation might not be especially rosy. She'd gotten a receipt at the café, after all. Anyway, I felt as though I'd heard the cab driver's tone of voice somewhere, but trying to place it would have been a pain, so I busied myself concentrating on the individuals sitting on either side of me.

"Is this some kind of trap?" I asked Fujiwara, whose attention was focused straight ahead.

After a moment of hesitation, he replied. "It's not a trap. We just have to confirm something. I don't know what it means either. I just know what we have to do. This is both the plan and the result."

Why did we have to go to North High? And where in the school were we going? Even if we went straight to the literature club, there wasn't going to be anyone there, I said.

"I'll bet not."

Did Sasaki have to come too? I asked.

"She is here, so yes."

What about Kuyoh? I thought she'd been the guy's most useful companion.

"I'm sure she'll show. When the time comes."

After delivering his brief answers, Fujiwara fell as silent as a wooden statue. If he hadn't been drawing breath he would've looked like one too.

"Those are perfectly reasonable questions, Fujiwara. I'm starting to wonder if you just don't like riding in cars very much."

Fujiwara was silent.

"I can only guess at what your future world is like. But I'll bet you're not used to riding around in petroleum-based-internal-combustion-engine-powered vehicles like this one, are you?"

Fujiwara's cheek twitched.

"So, what of it?"

"There's nothing to say."

Sasaki brightened. "Scientific development is one of my very favorite things. Naturally there are things I hope will happen in the future. The world has all sorts of problems in this age. My hope is that in your future, you will have left behind the folly of the past. Humans are a species that should learn, and keep learning. I want to believe that a higher level of scientific understanding will eliminate the destructive ideas and technologies that still plague us. How about it, Fujiwara? Don't you think people in the past can be forgiven for embracing such hopes?"

"Hope what you like. Wish for what you like." Fujiwara stared daggers at Sasaki. "That hope of yours made the future. Along with your recklessly misplaced confidence. Beyond that...heh, I suppose it's classified. And even if it weren't, I'm not so generous as to explain it the likes of you."

"Classified information...I don't think so," replied Sasaki. "You said this was a fixed event, didn't you? But, Fujiwara, you don't know what that means. All you know is that it's been specified in advance that you have to go to North High at a certain time today. You don't know who you're going to meet there, or what's going to happen. All you've been given is the reasoning that it's established history. So how could you even answer?"

Fujiwara snickered. "Impressive. If you were otherwise, you wouldn't be qualified to act as our instrument. Sasaki, you've

259

proven yet again that you have that capacity. You're the only other key to this universe besides Suzumiya. I'm sure you'll realize it soon. Although—you may not have that luxury."

Sasaki furrowed her brows and glared at Fujiwara's profile, but the time traveler ignored her completely. I realized the atmosphere had turned bad.

"What do you mean, instrument? This is the first I've heard of that," I asked.

"You'll understand soon enough," Fujiwara said to me brusquely. "Originally you were totally useless. But it's not in our best interests to oppose fixed events. For my part, I'd like to keep that to an absolute minimum. So that's why we called you along too. I suggest you sit back and enjoy your role as the sole bystander from this era."

How dare he look down on me like that. I wasn't going to let that go unanswered.

"Hey, Fujiwara. Are you trying to change the future you're from?"

Silence.

"If so, that's impossible." I thought back to what I'd heard on my very first mysterious phenomenon–searching date with Asahina. "Time is like a flip-book animation. No matter whether someone from the future interferes, it only amounts to scribbling on a single page of recorded time. It won't change anything about the future, will it?"

Silence.

"Honestly, I don't know what you're trying to do, but since you're talking about fixed events all over the place, I know that much. So just what do you think messing with this era is going to—"

"Shut up." The harsh voice stabbed into my ears. His gaze came with concealed malice. "Just shut up, you relic. If you shoot off your mouth any more, 'classified information' won't be enough to protect you."

His cold voice made me shiver. Fujiwara wasn't kidding. Evidently I'd stepped on one of his land mines.

Pathetically, my frozen heart warned me of the danger.

Sasaki casually tugged at my sleeve, and if she hadn't given me that wordless sign I might've just let things go at Fujiwara's pace. Thanks for telling me, Sasaki.

If the driver heard the conversation of the trio in the cab's back-seat, it seemed that worries about whether troublesome questions from a third party were forthcoming were unfounded. The driver was fully engaged in talking about his son to Kyoko Tachibana, enjoying his one-sided conversation with the girl who had so read-ily agreed to listen to him.

I felt a pang of sympathy for her, but reminded myself that Kyoko Tachibana and the SOS Brigade were antagonists. She was feeling less and less like an enemy, but that wasn't because I was being convinced; it was just that spending time with her was helping me understand her personality. And above all, Sasaki didn't seem to think she was dangerous. Sasaki was smarter and more perceptive than I, and I reckoned she had a good eye for people. So long as Sasaki was next to me, it was unlikely that things would turn in an unfavorable direction.

I was sure that was true.

The taxi stopped at North High's front gate, and the back door opened. Kyoko Tachibana paid the driver.

"Ah, I'd like a receipt, please," she said in her reserved voice, while I stood in front of the school's always-open iron gate for the second time that day.

The sky was already darkening, but I could hear the faint voices of the athletic clubs, which were evidently still wrapping up the day's activities.

"C'mon, let's go." Fujiwara took the lead and entered the school's grounds. Timidly Kyoko Tachibana made herself set foot on what was to her a foreign school. I myself looked up at the all-too-familiar school buildings as I entered the grounds—but stopped after a few steps.

"What…what? What's this?!" My eyes and mouth were wide open as I groaned the words.

The sky—

The sky was dyed a faint, cream-colored sepia.

The twilight sky with Venus's faint twinkle of just a few seconds earlier had disappeared, and was now filled with a light that was no natural phenomenon. It was a soft, gentle glow, a plain illumination that lit everything.

I knew this light.

It was the world Kyoko Tachibana had invited me into, after Sasaki had called me out to the café.

This closed space was the precise opposite of Haruhi's, and no one, not a soul, existed here.

"!"

I whirled around instantly, my reaction time not to be underestimated. And yet.

It was pointless.

Sasaki had gotten out of the taxi behind me, but she was nowhere to be seen. Nor was the cab itself.

Separated by only a few dozen centimeters on either side of the school gate, we were now in separate worlds.

The world I stood in was a world without sound. The echoes of the athletics teams I'd heard only a moment ago were gone. As were the cries of the birds, the sound of the wind over the hills—and any other sound in this space.

The only thing I saw was the sight of the unchanged school, and the all-suffusing sepia light that came down from the sky.

I made a dash for the school gate, but was gently pushed back.

"What—"

Just as when Haruhi had closed us off on the school grounds, a soft wall stood in my way. That could mean only one thing—I wasn't going to be able to easily escape this place.

"Do you understand your position now?" A voice reached me from behind. "This is no longer your world. Your reality, your sense of how the world works—such things do not apply here."

I craned my neck around to look behind me, and there was

Fujiwara's glumly hostile face. If beside him hadn't been standing an anxious Kyoko Tachibana, I probably would've slugged him right in the face. He ought to thank me for having such immense self-control.

"If I thank you, would you be satisfied?" he said.

"...Is this a trap?" I complained mightily.

"I wonder," said Fujiwara, dodging the question as he turned his back to me. "We still haven't arrived at our final destination. Won't you come with me? To finally settle all of this? For the sake of our future?" I saw only his profile, which was twisted into a sneer. "I'll have to thank Sasaki. She's the reason we succeeded in bringing you all the way here. Although I doubt she knows she was being manipulated into doing that. Come, don't be so angry. We'll need her to work for us after this. Once that's taken care of, you'll be free to go. You can flirt with her all you want after that."

Just as I was deciding I really was going to hit him, he continued as though heading me off.

"Shall we go, then?"

Where? I asked. Where could we possibly go within this closed space?

Fujiwara looked up. "To that shabby little room you call your home base."

I didn't have to look to know that at the end of his gaze was the literature club room.

But why? What was in that room? I asked.

"I figured you would know." I heard his voice as though it were at point-blank range. "The source of everything is in that room. It's the key to the future, a place where each power has met, combined, and influenced each other. Or perhaps you could call it a wedge. Within it exists every possibility, as well as the ability to end every possibility. The processes of both progress and stagnation are simultaneously extant there. I suppose it might be hard for an archaic human like you to understand."

Yeah, I didn't understand it. I didn't even want to.

But why was everyone so fixated on our clubroom? Like Nagato, the sole member of the nearly extinct literature club. And then Haruhi. And it had been the final destination at which I'd arrived after the world had been changed just before Christmas. And where the bookmark had slipped out of the slightest gap. And the old computer. The found keys. The "enter" key.

And the words Koizumi had once said to me.

—*That room has long-since been transformed into another dimension. Any number of elements are battling to cancel each other out there, such that it seems almost normal. Perhaps one could say it's reached the saturation point—.*

So that had been true, had it?

"Tachibana." I finally remembered there was someone here other than Fujiwara.

"Ah... er, yes?"

"You knew this, and you brought me here?"

"... No, I—"

I knew better than to expect a proper answer from her. At this moment Kyoko Tachibana was just as mystified by the current situation as I was. I could tell that much from the way she held both hands up and waved them side to side.

Which meant this was Fujiwara's scenario. And in all likelihood, Kuyoh was backing him.

Fujiwara calmly continued walking, striding directly into the school grounds as though he was playing some kind of RPG as he made his way toward the main entrance. He opened the glass door without even bothering to check whether it was locked. I followed him as he proceed into the school without even bothering to take his shoes off, and found myself seized by an irrational rage.

It was true that I'd cursed this school's name many times before. In addition to the long hill leading from the station, the old classrooms were so shabby that I had to assume they were built on a tight budget. There was no air conditioning and the rooms were drafty, hot in the summer and cold in winter, and pretty much the only nice thing about the place was that it was surrounded by mountain greenery, and that come nightfall you could get a nice view of the city lights from up on the hill. And yet it was North High, my alma mater.

This was the space where, along with Haruhi, Asahina, Nagato, Koizumi, Taniguchi, and Kunikida, I spent the greater part of my waking time. Seeing this outsider trample all over my territory like this was not something I could peacefully abide.

Worse, Fujiwara was our enemy. Why did I have to let a guy like that lead me around? I knew it was the logical thing to do, but my irritation was spiking right off the charts.

The most pathetic part of this was having to do everything the guy said. At that moment, I didn't know what else to do. If unloading on him actually would have changed anything, I would've done it. But it seemed as if that time had passed.

Without knowing what Fujiwara was going to do, I had no choice but to go along with it, whether it was a trap or not.

This was Sasaki's closed space. Koizumi couldn't enter. Nagato was out of commission. The notion of Haruhi and Asahina abandoning their nursing of Nagato to burst onto the scene and help me was absurd. And worst of all, Sasaki wasn't with me. I knew full well from the earlier incident at the café that she couldn't touch the inside of her own closed space.

Fujiwara, Kyoko Tachibana, and I were the only three people that existed within Sasaki's closed space. Kuyoh Suoh's absence did not come as any solace to me either. I might not have been able to see her, but I was sure she was around. The intuition I'd gained after so much time spent dealing with crazy supernatural phenomena was telling me so. I was sure she was somewhere on the palely lit school grounds, waiting for the worst possible moment to appear.

—In other words.

I was beset by enemies on all sides, and could see no way to fight back.

With a gaze as though he were looking at a vanquished opponent,

Fujiwara looked over his shoulder at me. "Shall we go, then? Or would you rather just crouch down with your hands over your ears? If so, I'll carry you in on my back. Free of charge."

"Shut your mouth."

I'd go. And I'd teach him to underestimate the literature club room, the SOS Brigade room. That was our spot. If I could just get there, I could do something about this.

Nagato wasn't there, but maybe there was a key hidden there anyway, or maybe I'd notice something I overlooked before—.

Fujiwara and Kyoko Tachibana had already started walking toward the school. They didn't seem to care whether I followed or not. The hell with them. I wouldn't be ignored. That room was ours. It was where Haruhi, Nagato, Asahina, Koizumi, and I all belonged. I wouldn't stand by while enemies invaded.

I smiled faintly as my willpower filled my legs with strength anew, and I followed after the two of them.

CHAPTER 9

α — 12

After a while, I heard someone knock at the door. It was slightly too forceful a knock to be considered reserved, which said something about the interpersonal skills of the person on the other side of the door.

Reflexively I looked toward Yasumi, and saw a strangely satisfied smile upon the face of the mysterious freshman girl, as though she were the foreman of a large construction project that she knew was in no danger of falling behind schedule.

...Just who *was* she, anyway?

Did she know someone was going to follow after me? Or had she summoned someone? Did she know who was there?

...But I didn't have time for such questions.

As no reply was forthcoming from inside the room, the doorknob turned with a click. The door started to open, and soon the room's rectangular entrance was clear.

The light of the setting sun in the west streamed through the clubroom window and illuminated three figures in the doorway.

In a flash, the possibility that Haruhi had returned with Asahina and Koizumi vanished.

The three figures had faces I knew. You could say that's why I was so surprised. My astonishment at the three people was so profound that it brought about sudden-onset aphasia.

"Wha...?!" was all I could say before my mouth froze open. If I'd had a mirror, I could've seen that the face I was making would probably have ranked in the top three all-time dumbest faces.

But there was no need to go to the trouble of bringing a mirror. After all—.

β — 12

Led on by Fujiwara, we came to the door to the literature club room.

I didn't feel any kind of premonition. It didn't seem as though I was going to be able to do anything here in this Sasaki-less, Sasaki-brand closed space, and the only person around who possibly could do anything was Kyoko Tachibana, and she was on Fujiwara's side. Even if her weak-seeming self was more honest than I reckoned, I very much doubted she'd become my ally here and now.

I mean, if she had been on my side, I wouldn't have wound up completely trapped in this space.

Fujiwara didn't even bother looking at me as he roughly knocked on the door. The loud banging made it clear he didn't think of the people within the room as his superiors, or even his equals.

Without waiting for a response from inside the room, Fujiwara wrenched the doorknob and pushed the door open.

The light coming in through the clubroom's window was bright. I couldn't easily make out the features of the people in the room, backlit as they were.

But I could tell there were two people in there, and from their silhouettes I knew it was a boy and a girl, wearing North High uniforms.

…But…wait…

"Uh…?"

The shocked mumbles came in stereo, from both sides of the room.

"…What is this…?" Fujiwara said in a strangled voice.

"…What is going on here…?" Kyoko Tachibana expressed her astonishment more honestly.

Fujiwara continued, expressing emotion in a way I'd never heard him do before. "Where's Kuyoh Suoh? Both of you—no, *you*, who are you…?"

I was the one who wanted to know what this meant. What was happening here?

Why did he want to know where Kuyoh was? Wasn't this Fujiwara's and Kyoko Tachibana's plan?

Wait.

The setting sun?

This place was supposed to be suffused with the same faint light that permeated all closed space. So why was the sun putting on a grand display of a sunset as though seeing us off for the weekend? The light that streamed through the glass of the clubroom's window was a brilliant orange. Had this room alone changed?

But such questions went flying out of my head the instant I recognized the people in the room.

Because, there—.

α — 13

I wasn't the only one to turn speechless upon the entry of the trio.

The three visitors all stood there with three different expressions of shock on their faces.

"…What is this…?"

"…What is going on here…?"

One of the people whose voices I heard in a mismatched, crazy

271

stereo was that time-traveling bastard whose name I still didn't know.

Around this last February, he appeared in front of (Michiru) Asahina and me, and just when I thought all he was going to do was spout off a bunch of arrogant nonsense, he'd been the last one to climb out of the car that had carried the kidnapped (Michiru) Asahina, before disappearing like some kind of magic trip. I definitely wasn't senile enough yet to forget this delicate-featured bastard.

The other one was a small-framed girl whose face I knew; this was the third time I'd met her. I'm pretty sure she'd introduced herself as Kyoko Tachibana. She was the perpetrator behind the kidnapping of (Michiru) Asahina, and worked for an organization that opposed Koizumi's Agency. She seemed to be an acquaintance of my old friend Sasaki.

She'd been one of the ones we'd happened to run into at the SOS Brigade's usual meeting spot. The time traveler hadn't been there then, but in her place had been a strange-haired alien girl. But that alien didn't seem to be here. Naturally I didn't want that alien girl here any more than I wanted to see bedbug corpses being left behind when I was drying my futon. But anyway—none of that mattered.

What *did* matter was—.

"…Who are *you*?"

To be honest, I wasn't sure exactly who said that line. The moment I said it, I heard the words in my ears, and I was certain there wasn't any discrepancy.

"Who are you?" I said it again. And across from me, with exactly the same timing and pronunciation, the same intonation and words, the question was put to me. There was no mismatch, no lengthening or shortening, no difference at all. It was perfect unison, the single voice too closely matched to even be considered stereo, resonating through the space.

The last person to enter the room where Yasumi and I waited was—

—Me.

* * *

There was another me there, and he stared at me in total shock.

β — 13

It was me.

"Who are *you*?" was all I could manage to say before losing my words, and the first thing that occurred to me was to wonder if I'd done another time jump.

It was an obvious thing to wonder, since by that point I'd traveled back in time several times. As far as Fujiwara and Kyoko Tachibana went, they seemed to be very surprised, and hadn't yet recovered from their ill-posed statue states. Given that even Fujiwara was that way, this must have been a genuinely unexpected event.

But wait. Wasn't there something wrong with that?

I was quite certain that I didn't have so much as a scrap of memory in which I met my past self here in the clubroom. Which meant that if this was the result of time travel, I'd just met a version of myself from the future. So long as I hadn't conveniently blown away my memories of the past, then I hadn't yet experienced the reality of meeting myself face-to-face like this.

But if that were so, the other "me" was acting strangely.

If that "me" had really come from the future, there was no reason for him to appear so obviously, openly shocked upon meeting his past self. Because from his perspective, it was a fixed event. Back when Haruhi had disappeared, I'd traveled back in time with Nagato and Asahina, and saved the buggy Nagato myself. If that "me" was really my future self, he would have been ready for this. If he wasn't, then was he some kind of impostor?

"Ah…" said the other me.

Given this voice and expression, he'd just gone through the same thought process I had. Apparently he really, truly was me.

He hadn't come from the past, nor from the future. Which meant this wasn't time travel. This was something else, some other phenomenon.

Though I was speechless, my eyes went over to the girl beside "me." Who was she? She was small, wearing a uniform that was too big for her, and had a childish smiley-face barrette in her hair... wait. Where had I—?

In that moment, I felt something like electricity shoot down my back. The mysterious girl I'd encountered in my room the previous day and the image of the single flower she'd left behind thundered through my head like an express train.

When I looked, I saw that same flower on the windowsill behind Haruhi's brigade chief desk.

They were connected.

This world and the world I'd been in until now were not completely separate places. But if this wasn't time travel or space-time alteration, then what was it?

"Heehee."

Even in this moment, the girl smiled more softly and gently than the flower behind her ever could.

She was an anomaly, this girl... Who *was* she?

Did the other "me" know the answer?

α — 14

I didn't take my eyes off the other "me."

He was me. Myself. And he hadn't come from the past or the future. He didn't differ from my current self by a single second. He was exactly the same as me.

He seemed to have come to the same conclusion. I could see perfectly well that he'd fallen down the same double spiral of shock and doubt. Just as I had.

Which meant this was what he had to be thinking.

—*What the hell is going on here?*

And also this.

—*Who the hell is that Yasumi girl next to me?*

I could tell that much from a single glance at "me." After all, he was me.

The almost hilarious deadlock continued. Everyone was stunned. The still-unnamed time traveler, Kyoko Tachibana, me, and "me."

Everyone seemed to have lost sight of what they were trying to do. Except for one.

"Kyon!" Yasumi hopped forward. With that childish face of hers she looked back and forth between me and "me," then smiled again.

"Yasumi," I said in a hoarse voice. "Who...*are* you?"

Yasumi giggled in a childish voice, then stood up and took my hand as I stood there uselessly.

Next, she reached her other hand out to the other "me," who looked just as helpless as I did.

"I" raised "my" hand as though it was sucked up, and Yasumi continued to hold onto mine. As though it were the most natural thing in the world.

Yasumi pulled me and "me" close.

And then—

"I am Watahashi," she said, and gently forced my hand onto "my" hand.

And then I understood everything.

β — 14

It was as though everything had frozen, as though time itself had stopped, and the only one moving was the mysterious girl.

"Kyon!"

The girl hopped forward. With her childish features, she looked happily between me and "me," then laughed again.

"Yasumi," said my doppelgänger in a hoarse, strangled voice. "Who...*are* you?"

Evidently my other self only knew the name of this mysterious individual.

The girl named Yasumi giggled a childish giggle, and offered her hand to the other "me," who stood there uselessly.

Next she reached her other hand out to me, who was only able to muster about the same reaction as "me." *Come, now*—I almost heard those words, so natural was her welcoming gesture.

I raised my arm up as though it was pulled, and Yasumi the high school girl took it.

The soft, warm sensation of her fingers reminded me of something I knew.

Yasumi pulled me and "me" close.

And then—

"I am *me*," she said, and gently forced "my" hand onto my hand.

She was Watahashi. And then I understood everything.

FINAL CHAPTER

"Huh?!"

I wasn't even sure which version of myself those words came from. Probably both of us, simultaneously. But what reached my ears wasn't unison or a duet, but rather the voice of a single person.

Immediately thereafter, a terrible flood of memories rushed through my head. They were unfamiliar-tasting, memories that I can only describe as being completely foreign. I closed my eyes and spun on. I put my hands over my ears reflexively, as my instinct was screaming at me to refuse any more outside information.

"Unggh…"

This confusion was far worse than time travel with Asahina, and it churned my brain. Unfamiliar scenes, unfamiliar actions, unfamiliar situations, unfamiliar history…they attacked me, becoming scenes, actions, situations, and history that I *did* know. They swirled like a yin-yang symbol, and it felt as though I had been tossed into the middle of that whirling maelstrom.

A series of flashbacks played against the insides of my tightly closed eyelids, flowing by like a revolving lantern.

—The entire SOS Brigade going over to nurse the fallen Nagato— the rage I'd spat out when I ran into Kuyoh, the revived Asakura, and the mediating Kimidori—myself, meeting several times with Sasaki, Fujiwara, Kyoko Tachibana, and Kuyoh—being taken by Fujiwara to Sasaki's glowing closed space—myself, being tutored by Haruhi after class—the brigade candidates failing the entrance examination Haruhi was pushing on them—Yasumi Watahashi, the only one left behind—that same Yasumi learning how to brew tea from Asahina, then futzing with our website—the paper airplane saying she'd found the MIKURU folder—the mysterious flower—

Both of these were definitely me. All of these were my memories, without contradiction or incoherence.

What was going on here?

Haruhi's recruitment efforts, fueled by her spring fever upon the start of the new semester. Nobody coming to the clubroom. The room overflowing with applicants. The phone call I'd received in the bath. The person on the other end of the line—.

That was where things split.

I now know it was Yasumi Watahashi, but at the time it was a voice I hadn't recognized.

The phone call from Sasaki had been a serious matter for both me and the SOS Brigade.

That was the moment.

From that moment on, the world had been split in two.

Into the foolish brigade entrance examination and the serious lecture from Haruhi. I had seriously agonized over the time line of the latter. Sasaki's closed space and the cosmic horror of Kuyoh Suoh's reaction. And then Asakura's reappearance and Kimidori's serious-business mode...

The sole successful applicant, the new brigade member Yasumi Watahashi's mysteriously positive actions, with Nagato's total lack of reaction and Koizumi's vague statements.

Two versions of my memories of the past week now existed within me.

What was going on here? It wasn't a question of which was true and which was false. Both were true, real memories. The only thing I could conclude was that I myself had split and experienced the same time line twice.

Because neither set of memories felt at all strange. It wasn't like I had absolute confidence in my powers of recollection, but if we were talking about things I'd experienced, that was a different story. The only commonality in them was the phone call I'd received in the bath, where one was Sasaki and one was Yasumi—and from there, they were totally different.

From that moment until now, I'd been leading two lives. That was all I could imagine.

And then those two sets of memories were trying to fuse like elementary particles colliding at the speed of light. I could practically hear my synapses crackling; I held my head in my hands.

"Guh...rgh..."

My head didn't hurt, nor did I feel nauseated or drunk; it was just that the speed at which my memories were revolving was—this is no way to explain it, but—they were like a spinning yin-yang symbol moving so fast all I could see was gray. Does that help? The differing colors of the two sets were blending into a single color. The spinning didn't stop, and it just kept being gray...

"...Mmph...hngh...unh."

I stiffened my body like a hermit crab, but finally the typhoon in my head slowed. Though I still felt confused, I'd recovered enough to open my ears and eyes; enough to steady myself against the brigade chief's desk, and stand on slightly trembling legs.

I had barely enough energy left over to take a look around the inside of the room, however fuzzily.

And that's when I noticed.

I was one again. The other me who had been here just a moment ago had disappeared somewhere. But that didn't seem particularly strange to me. Why? The reasoning was quite simple. One plus one is indeed two. But I knew there were times when that wasn't so. For example, if you add one pile of sand to another pile of sand, all you get is one big pile of sand.

Instead of addition, a more appropriate form of arithmetic for the occasion was multiplication. And even an elementary school student knows what you get when you multiply one times two. You get two.

The other me had disappeared. In his place, I now had two sets of memories.

In one set, Nagato was perfectly fine, Haruhi had conducted her brigade entrance examinations, and Yasumi had made her appearance. In the other, Nagato was sick, I had spent a lot of time talking with Sasaki and company, Kuyoh had attacked me, and Asakura had been revived.

The two sets lined up perfectly in my head. It didn't even feel strange, somehow. I understood everything so well that that fact itself was mystifying. If you have two sets of memories in your mind at the same time, shouldn't that be confusing?

—*Not necessarily.*

Yasumi's voice answered. *Only* her voice.

—*They're both you, Kyon. It's not that one is true and one is counterfeit. You just have two slightly different histories. Of the same time, in the same world.*

I looked in the direction from which her voice was coming.

She wasn't there.

Yasumi Watahashi had disappeared. Along with the other "me," like smoke from a sparkler, as though she'd never been here in the first place, she had completely vanished.

Where had she gone?

In the case of "me," I understood immediately.

Fusion.

When Yasumi had placed my and "my" hands atop one another's, we had been unified within this time line. It was simple. We'd had the same personalities to begin with, because we were the same person. It was only because of someone's speculation, or some strange circumstances, that I'd been split.

And now I'd returned to normal.

Still, what about Yasumi? Why had she been able to do such a thing? And where had she gone? The window and door were both still closed. To disappear from the middle of a group of people— had she teleported, or had she been an illusion to begin with?

But what I couldn't explain was that Fujiwara and Kyoko Tachibana had apparently seen Yasumi. Their expressions of surprise were certainly not faked. And going by their reaction to me being in the room, they hadn't expected that either.

Thus it was with a rare show of emotion on his face that Fujiwara spoke. "Defying the chain of fixed events...? It can't be...Was there someone who released the prohibition ahead of me...? Who—who could possibly...?" he said in a voice that showed rage, bafflement, and irritation all at once. "What's that? A nonstandard abnormality that's not on the schedule? That's the first I've heard of it. Whose work is this? Who called her here?"

He stomped on the floor in irritation.

"Dammit, this wasn't part of my plan. Kuyoh, where are you? What's going on here?"

A peal of thunder rang out.

The dingy window of the clubroom flashed, throwing shadows on everyone in the room. The sudden lightning that fell from the sky had an indescribable color to it. I reflexively looked outside, and was greeted by a scene that was even harder to believe, and groaned.

"...What's happening with the sky...?"

The heavens swirled. The faintly glowing cream-colored sky was interrupted by an angry blue-gray swirl, colors intertwining like colliding galaxies in a bizarre display. Here and there, pale light and dark gray tendrils wriggled, as though fighting for control. The color was like india ink dropped into a container of light paint, stirred by the brush of some mad artist.

It wasn't just the sky—everything framed by the rectangular

shape of the window was being drowned by the two colors. The grass in the courtyard, the tall school building, the hallways, the leafed-out cherry trees—everything.

I could tell that this was still the palely colored world. I was still inside the closed space that Sasaki created.

But the other color that wriggled and squirmed as though fighting against those pale hues—I'd seen that before too.

It was Haruhi's closed space.

Haruhi and Sasaki were struggling with each other, right here, right now.

Why? I knew that there existed a world I'd occupied with Sasaki up until a moment ago. I wondered if the reason Kyoko Tachibana brought me all the way back to North High was to somehow extract its essence.

But why had Haruhi's closed space now appeared? Haruhi was supposed to be at Nagato's apartment…no, wait—she was just on her way home from school—ah, damn. I didn't know.

What were even less clear were the geometric patterns that flickered here and there throughout the world here as I saw it. I'd seen this before too. It was very similar to the data jurisdiction space that Asakura had created.

What was happening to this world I'd found myself in? It was like every weird phenomenon I'd ever seen was happening at once. Seriously, what the hell?

"—This is the beginning. The division point of every possible outcome…"

A gloomy voice reached my ears. I looked up and before my eyes was a figure with bizarrely ink-black hair down to her knees, dressed in a black blazer.

With less expression than a Roman statue, Kuyoh Suoh stood between Fujiwara and Kyoko Tachibana. There was no emotion in her eyes. Her pale lips moved minutely, vibrating the air.

"—Past and future, and even the present, do not exist here. Matter, particles, waves, and will. Consciousness of reality. The future becomes the past, and the past, the present…"

I didn't feel obligated to be surprised at Kuyoh Suoh's sudden appearance. But would it kill her to at least pretend to breathe?

But before I could complain at her—

"Did you betray me?" said Fujiwara, his eyes those of a predator staring at its natural enemy.

Kuyoh smiled. Nobody could keep up with the sudden emotional changes of these extraterrestrial-made agents anymore.

"No. I have come here. That is the answer."

"So what is this, then? It's like the world is—" Fujiwara's words cut off, and he went stiff, as though he were receiving some kind of divine revelation. Then, he continued in a strained voice. "—I see. I can't believe it. So it's already diverged, has it? Who in the hell...?"

And then, with timing as though not wanting to give Fujiwara a chance to finish his question—

Click.

The door abruptly opened.

"Hello, there." With that easygoing smile as if it was any other day, he waved casually to the room, giving me an extra little wink. Unsurprisingly, my reaction was immediate.

"Koizumi?!"

"Indeed, it is Itsuki Koizumi, just as you say. The one and only, in the flesh. I was actually hoping to make a slightly more dramatic entrance, but it couldn't be helped. You know, something like crashing in through the window. But there just wasn't time to consider it."

"Surprise" is the number-one word I don't want to nominate for describing how I felt in that moment. "Shock" is number two. So, how, then, should I express it? I honestly don't know myself.

Itsuki Koizumi strode grandly into the room, then glanced at me, Fujiwara, and Kuyoh, finally giving Kyoko Tachibana a look as though he were regarding a little sister.

Kyoko Tachibana looked even more stunned by Koizumi's sudden appearance than I felt. "It can't be," she said in a high, shaky voice. "This is Sasaki's closed space. Koizumi, you shouldn't be able to enter it!" She sounded like an honor student who'd gotten a big fat *X* on a test she'd been sure she aced.

"Unfortunately," said Koizumi, giving an exaggerated bow as though he were on stage, "As far as this school is concerned, it does not exist only within the world you and your comrades closed off. Feel free to look outside."

I didn't have to. I'd already seen the gray and sepia tones mixing together. This was a world where Haruhi's closed space intermingled with Sasaki's—I was forced to admit that was the only way I could describe the view that greeted me.

"That can't be. This isn't Suzumiya's—..." Kyoko Tachibana began, then gazed up at the void. Her body trembled like a doe sensing the footsteps of an approaching hunter. "So that girl from before...that's what she was...?"

She spoke as though having realized something, but—what? Why did they understand something I didn't? Why, when I was at my utmost limit just trying to resist the desire to hold my head in my hands from the total confusion of it all?

To make matters worse, I soon realized that the trials of my psychological limits were only beginning.

From behind the lanky form of the lieutenant brigade chief emerged another form, at whose appearance I felt the strength leave my body. I'm surprised I didn't collapse on the spot. Honestly I think the only thing that stopped me from falling backward was the strength I'd naturally gained from walking up the hellish hill to school every day. I'd like to say it was the first time since starting high school that I was thankful for my commute, but I'll reiterate that at that moment my mental capacity was maxed out with processing the visual data from my immediate surroundings, so my brain was stressed nearly to the point of explosion.

So it's no surprise that at the appearance of that particular individual, neither my mind nor my mouth was capable of any reaction.

"Hello, Kyon."

She wore a white blouse and tight skirt that did nothing to disguise her curvy figure. She was like the platonic ideal of the sexy teacher, and I was indebted to this beautiful woman many times over. She smiled that same tender smile I'd seen so many times before.

"...Asahina, what are you doing here...?"

It was all I could do to squeeze out that one strangled line.

The adult version of Asahina. Asahina the Elder, the grown-up version of my Asahina. The true-blue, dyed-in-the-wool time traveler emerged from behind Koizumi and stepped forward.

"I got Koizumi to bring me. Infiltrating closed space is one of his abilities, after all. You do know that, don't you?"

I thought back to the time when Koizumi had taken my hand and brought me into the closed space that existed in the city. When it came to the freezing enclosure that was closed space, I'd experienced it once with Koizumi, and once with Haruhi.

"I really wanted to have all the cleaning tools ready before I appeared, but...time travel wouldn't bring me here," Asahina the Elder pouted, sticking out her tongue a bit. She was just as seductive as ever, and it threatened to turn me into Jell-O. She was no different from when I'd seen her during the Tanabata incident four years earlier, her beautiful adult body bountiful in all the right places...

While my mind was occupied with such revolving-lantern illusions, the high school esper boy/lieutenant brigade chief addressed the person next to him in a deeply satisfied tone of voice.

"I'm honored to finally meet Asahina's true form. I'm glad you seem well. It doesn't seem as though you're operating under many restrictions here, so if possible I'd like to have a nice long chat."

"That's not necessarily true. This is the first I've heard of it. It was special, a top-level classified secret. As far as this operation goes, I'm just a single piece of it."

I only recognized a small part of her statement, and understanding it seemed likely to take an infinite amount of time. I had absolutely no idea what she was talking about.

Asahina the Elder was controlling Asahina the Younger, but was there someone above even her who was moving the pieces around on the board? What kind of person was that? Was there really a level above Asahina? An Asahina Deluxe? But no, this was no time to be thinking about that kind of thing.

"Hey, Koizumi," I said, finally. "Which Koizumi are you?"

Koizumi lifted his arms in a familiar shrug. Overacting no matter what the circumstances was the guy's specialty.

"I'm both. I too was fused a moment ago. If pressed, I suppose you could say I'm the α version."

α? What kind of code was that? I asked.

"Ah, pardon me. It's merely a convenient label. You're in the same situation. Both of us, as members of the SOS Brigade, now have two sets of memories. One is from the version of history where we were busy with the entrance examinations for new members, and the other is the version where Nagato fell ill, throwing the the SOS Brigade into dysfunction. It occurred to me that it would be useful to be able to differentiate between the two, so I started calling the first one α, and the second β. Any objections?"

No, none. He could call 'em *A*, *B*, or *N* for all I cared, since either way, they were unified now.

Koizumi looked at Fujiwara, Tachibana, and Kuyoh in turn, chuckling. "It seems that your expectations have been significantly disrupted. And indeed they have. We can't have you underestimating us. None of you yet understand Haruhi Suzumiya. Undoubtedly you've done your homework and prepared your countermeasures. Otherwise there's no way you could've implemented a bold battle plan. But Suzumiya, our awe-inspiring brigade chief, cannot be outsmarted by a half-baked time traveler, a shabby esper, or a barely competent alien. She may not be a god. But even as only a being who happens to possess godlike power, she's a human beyond your abilities to analyze."

Koizumi reached into his blazer pocket and produced a fancy slip of stationery.

"This morning, I found this in my shoe locker. Shall I read it?"

I acted as the representative for everyone in the room. Read it, I told him.

"Please come to the school gate at six o'clock this evening."
The sender name was—Yasumi Watahashi.

So Yasumi had left a letter for someone other than me. But why Koizumi?

"The β version of myself followed after you, when you headed here with Sasaki, Kyoko Tachibana, and that time traveler. Meanwhile, the α me came to the school gate as directed. There, the two versions of myself saw the same thing—good old closed space. But I hadn't felt any premonitions of its appearance, so it was rather surprising. Then, Asahina here called out to my β self. Then just before I entered closed space with her, I met my α self alone. You know the rest. The moment we touched we became one person, and I understood everything."

"That's your weakness, Koizumi," said Asahina the Elder. "Although it's certainly true that you were necessary."

"You must be joking!" Fujiwara's angrily shouted words echoed in the room.

I assumed he'd lost his temper with Koizumi's rambling explanation, but his keen, laser-scalpel gaze was aimed only at Asahina the Elder.

Fujiwara's body shook, and the rage within him distorted his features; compared with his usual state of looking down on everyone and mocking them constantly, he was like a different person. This was the first time I'd seen him express such raw emotion.

"You're…you're really going to go this far in interfering with me? Are you really trying to solidify that future, even if it means splitting the world in two?"

"Even if you edit an already-fixed time plane, our future will not change. No, it must not be changed," said Asahina, her expression pained, but resolved.

"It will change. Not because of you, or me, or anyone here. It's impossible for us. But with the power of Haruhi Suzumiya, it's possible. If I could use her power, I could remake everything about the space-time information I've lived in," said Fujiwara. "I could completely and perfectly rewrite everything from this point on into the future. Not by individually altering time planes little by little, but by correcting every plane on into infinity!"

Fujiwara stopped shouting, and looked down as though having just finished vomiting. He murmured.

"I just... I don't want to lose you, my sister."

It was an astonishing line. Huh? What did he say? Sister? Asahina was his sister? As in, Fujiwara's? Which meant Fujiwara was Asahina's younger brother... but the Asahina I knew had never given a single hint of that, or anything remotely like that. Was this some kind of once-in-a-lifetime joke from Fujiwara?

Asahina the Elder shook her head. Her chestnut hair swayed sadly. "... I don't have... a brother. And likewise, the me who is your sister does not exist. History that's lost... people that are lost... can never return."

Asahina the Elder's answer only spurred on further confusion. But Fujiwara's expression only turned more serious. "That's why I came here! To this time plane, where people wallow in the folly of their lives! Back to this foolish past, that we can never forget though we might wish to. I want to get you back—that's why I joined forces with that extraterrestrial intelligence. What other reason could there be for dealing with such a—"

"Please, forget about me. You mustn't use the TPDD for such things. We're not beings that should be here in the first place. You must understand how important Haruhi Suzumiya is for this time plane. If it weren't for her, our future would be..."

"I know. That's why I bet on a second possibility. What the future needs isn't Haruhi Suzumiya, but her power. If it could be transferred to someone else, other possibilities appear. And my ally, Kyoko Tachibana, found the perfect person."

Kyoko Tachibana's shoulder shook again. When I looked at her she was looking down, but then her slightly teary eyes met mine.

Little by little, I was starting to understand.

Of course. This "perfect person" was Sasaki.

"She can control it much more skillfully than Haruhi Suzumiya. It would be better for us. We'd be able to access infinite possibility. We wouldn't be trapped by fixed events. We'd be able to erase them—we could choose our future. That's what I want, my sister! I want to choose a future with you in it!"

He was just going on and on. I wanted to tell him he was an idiot. By now I knew perfectly well just how kind and decent Asahina the Younger was. She hadn't been told anything. Not about the intentions of the future, nor about the usefulness of Haruhi and Sasaki.

That was a rare virtue. Who cared whether she was skilled or useful? Asahina the Younger was the most lovable time traveler I knew. She was our time plane's only ally, because she wasn't trying to change the past, nor was she trying to control Haruhi.

That's right. Just think about it. If I could travel into the past and move around however I liked, I would certainly use my knowledge to interfere with history. Ten years ago, a century ago—the further back I went, the less likely it was that I would resist such a desire.

But Asahina hadn't done anything. She came from the future just to play with Haruhi. I was only then realizing just how incredible that was. No one other than Asahina could possibly have filled that role. If Fujiwara had been in her place, I doubted the SOS Brigade would ever have been founded at all.

"No," continued Fujiwara. "I don't care what happens to the world. I can't lose you."

"The person native to your time line is not me. I do not have a younger brother."

"It's the same thing. The fact that you were lost in my time line means that you will be lost at the intersection point in the future."

"The future can be changed. As you changing things can be changed."

I wanted to compliment my ears and brain for not missing that line. What did she say? What had Asahina said just then?

"It cannot! Your future is the past to someone beyond it. You yourself should know that fixed reality must remain unchanged—you know that perfectly well!"

"That's why we exist."

"But we cannot travel back past four years ago. There's no way to correct the time plane. A rupture always appears. So we should be able to do it *here*."

"That's something I can't allow. Do you understand what you're saying?"

"I understand better than anyone. You're not the only ones constantly adjusting the time plane in order to ensure the correct future. That's right, the TPDD."

Fujiwara kept going, as though he'd forgotten that Koizumi and I, to say nothing of Kyoko Tachibana and Kuyoh Suoh, existed.

"A double-edged sword can be useful. Time travel using the TPDD is necessary in order to maintain the normal state of the time plane. But that same travel damages the plane itself. It wasn't simple to repair the holes in time caused by the TPDD. But while I was pursuing this, I discovered other phenomena. We cannot change the past. Nor the future."

"So why are you here?"

"For the sake of now, this time. By accumulating instants, moments of time, we can construct time itself. We'll bring the material of the 'present' into the future and continue to change it. We'll need only to keep repairing dislocations in the time plane."

"That's impossible. Do you have any idea how much energy is required to destroy fixed events?"

"It can be done. I'll say it as many times as I have to. If we have Haruhi Suzumiya's power, it can be done."

Kyoko Tachibana did not seem to be able to keep up with the conversation. "Um...er...just what does this..." She couldn't erase the dazed look on her face.

Fujiwara ignored the poor girl entirely, and continued.

"I'll rewrite all of space-time from this time plane through to the future. I don't care about the history along the way. If we can fix space-time in our future, then we'll have the luxury of being able to worry about the past." His face slightly green, he gulped. "And Haruhi Suzumiya has been doing *that* for a long time now. Since long before we came here."

"That's an unforgivable act. You're...you're trying to commit what is a serious time crime in your time line."

Asahina the Elder's expression was full of sorrow, and no small measure of unmistakable desolation.

In the midst of the time travelers' dialogue, Koizumi suddenly spoke up in a somewhat jovial tone, as though he'd utterly failed to read the room. "Sorry to interrupt the argument, but I'm so pleased to finally meet you, Asahina. I suppose this isn't actually the first time we've met, but I thought I should reintroduce myself, just in case."

"Koizumi..." Asahina the Elder forced her downcast eyes up to regard Koizumi.

"Asahina, from your perspective, we haven't had an encounter in quite some time, correct?"

"That's probably true." Asahina the Elder's face bloomed in as beatific a smile as Koizumi could ever manage. Like a witness who'd noticed a prosecutor's leading question. "I can't tell you anything, Koizumi. You're a highly dangerous person, even among people of the past. There are things that even I am prohibited from doing. But no, even if it were something I could say, by my own judgment I wouldn't. You're simply too clever. A single careless word from me could become ten words' worth of information for you. I'd love to reminisce with you, though. That is the truth."

"I quite understand. Those words alone are enough for me. You've told me what I am, and how I'm viewed in the future. Even if that was fake, it amounts to the same thing. I'll do my own information analysis. Above all, I should thank you, Asahina. Thanks to you coming here, I've understood what it is I need to do. The fact that you appeared in front of me is quite extraordinary. Which means that I'm going to face that extraordinary thing myself too. You could not face what's going to happen alone; you must need my power. No, not only my power—Suzumiya's power too. Am I wrong?"

"Asking questions you already know the answers to is an interesting hobby. I felt this way before, but even so...Koizumi, out of all the STC data, you truly are an irreplaceable individual. That's why you were invited into the SOS Brigade. You were chosen by Suzumiya."

"I've become aware of that, yes. At first I only half believed it, and explained it away as the product of happenstance, but now I no longer doubt it. I am part of the SOS Brigade. As is Nagato, and your younger self. So what about you, the grown-up Asahina? What did you learn when you returned to the future? Why have you come back to this past, or are you merely here to interfere with your former self? Please, explain your position to me."

"What if I said it was...classified information."

"I would not be surprised. I'm sure if I went back into the past, and the inhabitants there asked me that question, I would tell them the same thing. However"—Koizumi's keen eyes regarded Fujiwara and Asahina the Elder equally piercingly—"I would ask you not to underestimate the humans of the past. We are not so very foolish, you see. I won't go so far as to say this applies to all humanity, but humans deeply concerned with the future certainly do exist."

I was struck by the sight of an aggressive edge to Koizumi's gaze that I'd never seen before.

"Little by little I've come to understand this, thanks to all the commotion that the various aliens have caused. Suzumiya's ability...the ability to change reality—it's not permanent, is it? It's not that it weakens with use, but it's not something that she will possess forever. Eventually it will disappear. Am I wrong?"

"Well..." Asahina said, obviously attempting to evade the question.

"It's not as though you're being pressed to choose. When they want to do something, they control you as they please, thereby controlling Suzumiya. The power she has can even be transferred to another. Nagato once managed to do something similar, so these aliens can surely do likewise."

Kuyoh was standing there like a wooden statue; Koizumi shot her a contemptuous look. "It may be presumptuous of me, but there's something I simply must say. So I shall." He took a deep breath, and once again revealed his true thoughts. "I'd like to ask you not to underestimate the people of Earth. We're not such stupid creatures as you might think. Regardless of what the Data Overmind or other alien intelligences might say, we're quite clever in our own way. At the very least, there are those among us who strive for that."

He regarded the enemy time traveler with a smile that had more than a hint of challenge in it, and continued. "Wouldn't you agree, Fujiwara?"

"Shut up. Your clever nonsense makes me want to vomit," spat Fujiwara, his eyes looking as though he'd already prepared himself for utter ruin.

A warning signal was blaring away in my head, flashing red and yellow lights. This was bad. He was getting ready to snap. Fujiwara had obviously lit the fuse on his own self-destruct mechanism. The premonition of it overwhelmed my psyche like a magnitude-nine tsunami.

Fujiwara's state of bitter self-recrimination was made clear by his dark muttering. "...I'm an idiot. I should've done this from the beginning. Heh. No matter how many words I waste on them, these ignorant fools will never understand. Kuyoh—do it."

Everyone put their guard up. Kuyoh did not so much as blink.

"What's wrong, Kuyoh? Carry out our agreement," came Fujiwara's overbearing order. "Go kill Haruhi Suzumiya!"

What to say in this situation, given this development? For my part, should I say that I was able to consider those shocking words calmly?

A container. Yes, Haruhi's powers could be stolen. Even Nagato had done it before.

A container. Which meant Haruhi's powers could be given to anyone. But it would all depend on the person.

A container. Who was closest to Haruhi now? It went without saying.

The quickest way to force Haruhi to lose her powers would be her death. A corpse had no will. And it would be a shame for that wonderful supernatural power of hers to go to waste...or so the alien, time traveler, and esper were all thinking.

And conveniently, there was a perfect container right at hand. One less capricious than Haruhi, less eccentric, one less incomprehensible, one who wasn't the chief of the SOS Brigade, one with more serenity and common sense. My former classmate.

Sasaki.

It was enough to make a strange thought flash through my head. What if Haruhi's godlike powers had blossomed in Sasaki from the beginning?

That was what Fujiwara was trying to do: kill Haruhi and turn Sasaki into the new god. She wouldn't rampage the way Haruhi did. Naturally Sasaki wouldn't easily go along with whatever Fujiwara and the others told her either. But Fujiwara and Kuyoh might have been confident that they could force her. Maybe they would brainwash her, or deprogram her, or...take someone hostage. That hostage could well be the entire world.

Or me. Would I be made a pawn in this game?

The hell with those idiotic ultramaroons.

If they gave Sasaki any trouble, I'd do everything I possibly could to resist them. And it wouldn't be just me. I was sure I could depend on Koizumi and Asahina the Elder. And if Nagato were here, she'd want to help too. She probably still couldn't move very much, though. Otherwise, I imagine she would've shown up right about when Kuyoh did. At this point, I'd take Asakura or Kimidori too.

So come, already. Hurry up. Actually—why hadn't they? Damned useless aliens. The next time I saw them I was going to give them an earful.

Fujiwara pressed Kuyoh again. "Bring Haruhi Suzumiya's life to an end! You said you could!"

"—"

Her unfathomable expression frozen, only Kuyoh's crimson lips moved.

"—Some phenomenon is hindering my movement. Or, the Haruhi Suzumiya present in this space-time continuum is surrounding me three levels deep. Also, I cannot escape from this closed space. Complying with your directive code is difficult."

Fujiwara clucked his tongue. "Damn you, we come all this way and you expect me to be satisfied with that?"

"I said it was difficult—" Kuyoh's long hair began to float up. Next, her eyes flashed red, her mouth pinched into an upside-down V. The words that came to my mind were "evil witch."

"—However...I can summon the subject...yes, like this—"

She raised her thin arm, and pointed out through the window with her index finger.

Everyone, including me, looked in the indicated direction.

"Augh...!" I couldn't help letting out a cry, and I didn't have time to hate myself for it.

Because—

Outside the third-story clubroom, floating in space a few meters past the window past the brigade chief's desk, was—

"Haruhi!"

It was none other than the school uniform–clad form of the person I'd spent the entire first year and change of high school with, the owner of the seat directly behind me in class, whose face I'd seen nearly every day, the master of the literature club room, and the chief of the SOS Brigade.

Immediately I rushed to the window and threw it open, and you can bet during that interval I didn't avert my gaze or close my eyes for an instant.

"Haruhi!"

There was no response. Haruhi was floating there in the air, eyes closed as though she were asleep, her face the picture of innocence. Her lips were slightly parted and her body moved as if she was breathing. I couldn't tell if she was genuinely sleeping or if she'd been rendered unconscious. With her arms and legs hanging loose, she looked like a broken doll, and she didn't open her eyes when I called to her.

"—I have forcibly transported this entity from outside closed space. The entity in question is recognized by all present as Haruhi Suzumiya. I have fulfilled my obligation."

"Not yet." Fujiwara turned back and glared at Kuyoh. "My requirement was the death of Haruhi Suzumiya. I didn't ask for her to be brought here alive."

"—Implementation forthcoming." Kuyoh's mechanical face reddened ever so slightly. "Given the gravitational acceleration of this planet, a human falling to the ground from this altitude will sustain fatal injuries—. Within this high-mass atmosphere, this is the most basic form of death. As a method of ending the function of an organic life-form, this has been determined to most closely match the available natural phenomena."

"I see," said Fujiwara maliciously. "That's a rather roundabout way of doing it. If that's how the Heavenly Canopy Dominion thinks, I'm impressed."

Having said so, he turned back to me.

"So this is how it is, you pathetic throwback. Killing this girl is trivial. So what will you do? I'd love to hear your decision. Will Haruhi Suzumiya's life be ended here and now, or will you make your dear Sasaki the new god? Come now—which will it be?"

What a cheap threat. And his acting was a total cliché.

Rage welled up within me. Time travelers and aliens were both idiots. Did they think I—or, uh, Haruhi—would be able to do something about this? Saying "die" or "I'm gonna kill you" only proved that he was an angry child. Honestly, if this is what people from the future were like, then I didn't have much hope for the fate of humanity. Were we really going to entrust the future to these jerks? Really?

They shouldn't have underestimated me. They shouldn't have underestimated Haruhi. More than anything, they shouldn't have underestimated Haruhi.

"Stop!" cried Asahina the Elder. "This is meaningless! Is it catastrophe you wish for? By the laws of time travel, this would be the worst crime imaginable!"

"I don't wish for this. But if it will ensure the existence of my time line, I'll wish for a new time. Even if it means I myself disappear, I'll bet on you. You'll remain, sister. I'll *make* you remain. That's all I want."

Fujiwara chuckled grimly, as though trying to sound as evil as possible. "Kuyoh, construct a symbol that's easier for this dense audience to understand."

Her body not moving at all, Kuyoh's faintly shining eyes swiveled toward Haruhi.

As Haruhi floated in the air outside the clubroom and three stories up, her body began to change position. Her torso was raised and her feet pointed down. Both arms extended straight out, and from behind her, a shadowlike mass oozed out of nowhere. As I watched and wondered how to express what I was seeing, it was obvious that no matter what world this was, the same word applied. This object was a cross.

That…bastard…what sort of farce was he making this?

Haruhi was now being crucified on a cross of darkness.

She was unconscious, her head slumped over to one side, and her eyes were still closed as though she were asleep. The sense that she was suffering might well have been my imagination, but in any case this was not a situation she would've wished for.

To say nothing of how Kuyoh and Fujiwara were declaring their murderous intent.

They really were idiots. Presiding over such an obviously villainous plot was incompetent even in a third-rate manga from the last century. And if acting satisfied at the crucifixion of a girl is third-rate, then this idiot sneering at me was even worse than that. It was all so obvious that it was like some kind of slapstick gag. *This is dumb. This is so dumb, Fujiwara.* He didn't have any talent as an actor. I understood all too well, now. Out of all the life-forms existing in this space-time, he was the lowest of the low. He was lower than algae.

But this absurd cliché did have an effect. Oh, it had an effect, all right.

"Dammit...!" I leaned bodily out of the open window and reached out with my hands. She was too far to reach, but I still wanted to grab Haruhi. Even if it meant embracing her in a hug, I had to pull her back into the clubroom. I wanted to slap her face and wake her up.

And more than anything else, I would never forgive Fujiwara and Kuyoh for what they had done to Haruhi. I wouldn't let them think they could get away with this. I was going to kill them both, I swore.

As though having seen my hate-crazed eyes and correctly guessing my thoughts, Fujiwara started to mock me. "So, how do you like having the most precious person in your life being used as a pawn? No matter what you've thought up until now, Haruhi Suzumiya is the most important phenomenon in the universe to us. There isn't a single other human with more value. No matter how you live the rest of your life, it's worthless and meaningless. Haruhi Suzumiya's power will determine everything from here on out. And if we transfer her will and consciousness into a different container, Haruhi Suzumiya herself will also become worthless."

I was grinding my teeth so violently I chipped one of them. There was no way in hell I was letting this bastard get away with this.

"Wait!" Asahina shouted plaintively. "There's no proof that that's the real Haruhi Suzumiya. It could be an illusion! Kyon, it might be some kind of trick to force you into making a decision."

"I'm afraid not," said Koizumi decisively. "No trick would deceive me, since I am, in a sense, a tool of Suzumiya's subconscious. Our sleeping beauty over there is not a clone nor an illusion. She's the genuine article, 100-percent-pure Suzumiya. My—no, *our*—beloved brigade chief."

That was the truth. Koizumi wouldn't lie to me. There would be no point to a bluff now. So what could I do...

"—"

Kuyoh was silent. She seemed to be waiting for someone's command.

"Ah...uhh...um..." Kyoko Tachibana seemed totally confused, as though she were completely unable to keep up with the rapidly developing situation.

"Looks like there isn't going to be any negotiating," Fujiwara muttered in a calm, darkly resolved voice. "I'm going to end Suzumiya's life. Don't worry, Sasaki will handle her remaining duties. For you in the past, nothing will change. You can just live out your full, happy lives all the way through to old age without Haruhi Suzumiya."

Was that true? Was there nothing we could do?

In desperation I looked to Asahina the Elder. With that lovely teacher style of hers, the adult Asahina gently covered her eyes. I didn't understand what the earlier exchange about brothers and sisters had meant. And I definitely didn't know which one of them was telling the truth. But I felt as though I could understand Fujiwara's goal. So did that mean Asahina the Elder's aims were blocking it? Was that all?

Engulfed by a maelstrom of doubt, what brought me back around to the present was the clear, refreshing voice of my comrade.

"If you think you can do it, by all means please try."

The counterattack I'd been hoping for came from an unexpected person. Koizumi stood in front of Fujiwara, blocking his way. It seemed as though he intended to object to the time traveler's murderous intention, but what was it that kept his face so calm?

Did Koizumi have some kind of plan? There was no way I could be that calm, looking at Haruhi, about to fall three stories to her death. We didn't have time to plan any tricks or set any traps, so ad-libbing seemed unlikely to work. Damn, damn, damn—it was so pathetic it made me want to cry.

If I lost my temper and flew into a rage here, all that would happen would be a mark on my permanent record showing that an idiotic high school boy had resorted to violence without actually accomplishing anything. If Sasaki were here, at least she could've managed her trademark smooth talk. If Nagato were in her normal mode, I wouldn't have had anything to fear from Kuyoh.

The advantage was overwhelmingly with our opponents. Even if I could ignore the faltering, terrified Kyoko Tachibana, even the Data Overmind's humanoid terminals Asakura and Kimidori didn't know how to deal with Kuyoh. This utterly foreign alien had joined forces with Fujiwara, and turned the clubroom into a danger zone.

I stood there, teeth clenched, when someone pushed me from behind. "It's always the prince's role to save the princess when she's imprisoned in thorns. Not just his role—his duty." Koizumi shrugged. "Of course, I don't have any idea about our captured princess up there. Am I wrong?"

He wasn't. But Koizumi, I told him, I still had important business with Fujiwara that involved socking him right in the face.

"I'll handle that." A volleyball-sized sphere of red light appeared above the palm of Koizumi's right hand. "I rather feel as though I've become the protagonist of an esper manga. I may not have this chance again, so I hope you'll let me seize this one. This is my last chance to make my dream come true, you see," he said happily, but I could tell he was well and truly angry.

Go right ahead, Koizumi. After all, if you didn't exercise your physical abilities every so often, your body would get weak.

After patting me on the shoulder, Koizumi pushed me forward, escorting me to the courtyard-facing side of the room, which was illuminated by the madly shining sky.

Several meters of space separated the edge the windowsill from the place where Haruhi hung in the air. It wasn't a distance I could bridge just by reaching out my arms. How was I going to pull her back in?

"Kuyoh!" Fujiwara's scream grated against my ears. "Do it!"

In that instant, Haruhi began to slip free from the cross. With her head hanging down as she slumped over, she looked like a saint being freed from the bonds of crucifixion. The stone floor of the courtyard was directly under her, and headfirst, she began to fall.

"Haruhi!"

I didn't think about anything. Not about consequences, memories, or any kind of duty or sense of righteousness. I didn't need to. I just kicked off the window frame and jumped out into thin air, like I expected wings to sprout from my back. As though pushed by someone's invisible lifting force, I caught Haruhi in my arms just as she fell. And then, naturally, pulled by gravity, we both fell. Headfirst.

Haruhi's body was more delicate than I'd imagined. I'd never seriously embraced her like that before, so I'd never noticed.

But the sense of warmth, of softness, made me realize that this really was Haruhi. She was just a second-year high school student, in the bloom of her girlhood—just an ordinary girl.

This was the true form of sleeping beauty. Even if I died the very next moment, her name would live on, carved in history. The girl softly breathing in my arms was, beyond any doubt, Haruhi Suzumiya.

She was the real Haruhi. She wasn't some illusion from Kuyoh, or a fake prepared in advance. To threaten me, Fujiwara was using the real Haruhi.

He really was serious. Fujiwara would really go that far. Was this what you wanted? You'd lay out your disturbing future, your desire not to lose Asahina, and you'd even go so far as to put Haruhi on your death list, just to bring the future you wanted to create into sight?

But all I could see was the form of the person right in front of me.

Koizumi, Asahina the Elder—I'm sorry. There's nothing else in my eyes.

Haruhi Suzumiya.

Our brigade chief and the ruler of the clubroom. That arrogant, confident optimist. Happy to manipulate anyone or overcome anything, surging forward toward her goals like a bowling ball shot from a linear catapult. My only boss. She was all I could see.

Ah.

The ground was getting closer. Owing to her unconsciousness, Haruhi's body was limp, and slightly feverish. It was just as Koizumi said. That delicate body with its curves right where you'd expect them, the surprisingly slender shoulders, the slight fragrance—I knew better than anyone else that this was Haruhi.

When humans fall from high places, they die. I didn't have to guess at what my skull would look like after falling at this rate of gravitational acceleration and slamming headfirst into the stone pavement.

Had I been a little too hasty? At the very least I could've set up a mat on the ground, or strapped on a parachute—.

Of course, I didn't have time for such introspection. The only thing I thought of was the faint notion of curling around Haruhi and putting myself between her and the ground to absorb some of the impact.

The sound of rushing air roared in my ears. I would be hitting the ground soon.

I closed my eyes. Tight.

I embraced Haruhi. As tightly and closely as I possibly could.

The distance of my suicidal free fall was short enough that there shouldn't have been even enough time for the turn of a revolving lantern. Not wanting to see the fast-approaching ground, I'd shut my eyes, praying to Mother Earth that she would awaken to her duty to cushion our impact.

I prayed.

But.

Then.

The instant I resigned myself, the backs of my eyelids were illuminated with a blue glow.

"?!"

A hairsbreadth from impact, I felt the sensation of sinking into some kind of soft object.

I opened my eyes.

Haruhi and I were surrounded by blue light. I hastily looked around in every direction and saw that we were floating just a few centimeters above the courtyard's stone floor. Somehow, this shining blue something had cushioned our fall.

When I looked up, it was like a vast wall that reached all the way up to the madly swirling sky.

"It's—!"

But no, it wasn't. It was a <Celestial>.

There was a <Celestial> standing in the courtyard—surrounded by a faintly glowing outline, whose arms could destroy any building, the lonely master of this gray space.

"It can't be!" I heard Fujiwara's distant voice. "How can that thing be..."

The <Celestial> had reached out with its great hand and caught Haruhi and me.

The dimly shining giant was taller than any of the school buildings. I would never forget I'd seen this terrible embodiment of Haruhi's frustration rampaging through closed space.

Haruhi and I were side-by-side in the palm of its hand.

The <Celestial's> intentions couldn't have been clearer—it had meant to save us from falling to our deaths.

But why had the <Celestial> been able to appear here? Its creator, Haruhi, was unconscious, and moreover, this was a world where Haruhi's and Sasaki's closed spaces were being mixed together. And even supposing that it could appear, this giant that even Haruhi couldn't control was now acting like her faithful servant and saving her—I just couldn't see how it was connected to this particular situation.

From the soft, almost fluffy palm of the <Celestial> I looked up to the clubroom, just as an orange-colored explosion blew through the window. I guess Koizumi had finally lost his temper. I didn't care about Fujiwara, but I hoped that Asahina the Elder and Kyoko Tachibana were safe.

"Nn..."

Haruhi stirred in my arms, and a small moan escaped from between her parted lips.

As though cooperating with her, the <Celestial> raised its other arm and made a fist. It then brought it down on the clubroom with a punch of tremendous force—

The same instant, I was assailed by a sensation of time compression. Everything seemed to move in slow motion.

I looked up into the sky and saw a small figure standing on the roof of the clubroom's building.

She was wearing a baggy uniform, and her permed-looking hair cut an unmistakable silhouette—Yasumi Watahashi.

New Brigade Member Number One, who'd vanished as soon as my two selves were reunited, now stood on the edge of the rail-less roof, looking down on me and Haruhi. In the dim, hazy light I couldn't make out her face, but I was suddenly sure that she was smiling.

She executed a clumsy bow, then raised her head and faced forward.

Drawn by where she was looking, I also directed my gaze to the side of the courtyard opposite the clubroom—but that seemed to be the limit.

My field of vision distorted, twisting. But just before it did, I saw three figures on the roof of the opposite school building. One had short hair, one had long hair, and the third's hair was in-between, and all of them were wearing North High uniforms...

So they'd come. I knew it. Kimidori, and Asakura, and—.

No longer confined to a sickbed, looking as quiet and keen as ever, it was Yuki Nagato. I couldn't imagine that these three would have failed to notice the distortions in the axis of time. Positioned outside the world, the Data Overmind would know...just like in that endlessly repeating August.

There was no doubt that they had been observing everything, including me...

"...!"

My vision went suddenly dark, and I was disoriented by a crazy floating sensation. The dizzy feeling I'd gotten so sick of during all my time traveling had returned.

Just as I was about to black out entirely, Yasumi's shadow waved at me. As a way of saying good-bye it was more than sufficient. Whether it was meant for me, or as a greeting to the three humanoid interfaces, I would probably never have a chance to ask. I just had that feeling...

But that was all right. However far we fell, we'd be together.

Darkness fell.

After a floating sensation, I felt free fall again. I put more strength into my arms, telling myself that Haruhi was the one thing I would never let go of.

From somewhere far in the distance, I thought I heard Asahina the Younger's voice.

Whump.

"Ow!"

The shock came from my tailbone. Feeling pretty stupid for landing on my butt, I opened my eyes, then quickly closed them again owing to the brightness.

Having become used to the dimness of closed space, my irises couldn't adjust immediately. And yet—where was I? Based on the nonvisual information available, my hand and rear end were touching something like grass, and my sense of hearing reported a bustling mix of several male and female voices.

Hesitantly, I opened my eyes a sliver, and saw that I was definitely sitting on the corner of a wide lawn, and around me were what had to be male and female students dressed in street clothes. Some were groups walking around, and here and there were couples cuddling together on the grass.

"What? Where am I? Where did I get sent now?"

Across the lawn I saw a building that appeared to be a clock tower.

Compared with North High, it was an absurdly modern structure. And the groups of students that were walking around seemed somehow more refined than high school students. This seemed as if it had to be a college somewhere. The breeze was warm. I wondered if it was spring…

My immediate impression of my surroundings was that they were very well-made. But, why? Why was I here?

Just as I was starting to get really worried—

"What's wrong, Kyon?" The all-too-familiar voice of a girl was directed at me from above.

Still sprawled on the ground, I looked up.

"Haru…" I managed to say before becoming totally speechless. I can't even remember if I rubbed my eyes or not.

There was Haruhi, looking somehow grown-up. Her hair was longer than I remember it being, and she wore a spring ensemble of soft, seasonally appropriate colors, perfectly matched to the cardigan over her shoulders. No, she couldn't be this grown-up yet. The Haruhi I knew had only just started her second year of high school.

And yet the Haruhi before me was clearly several years past that. I mean, how should I put it? I can't really say it right…but yes, she had clearly matured.

"What're you doing? Hey…" This Haruhi smiled jokingly at me. It made me dizzy. "What do you think you're doing, wearing that old uniform? Kyon…Wait—you seem kind of…young…?" she said, then turned around as though someone had called her.

"Huh?"

My vision started to dim again.

Someone was calling out to that Haruhi. Looking surprised, I heard her say "Huh? You're over there—?" before turning back to me again. "Wha?"

I think she had an expression of shock on her face.

But my consciousness was rapidly fading. The figure of Haruhi standing on the lawn began to grow distant, as though it were being filmed by some kind of special camera move. I didn't move, and neither did Haruhi—a distance merely opened up between us.

Darkness began to close in around me. This was the door. The will of time was trying to return me to my original place.

The moment the walls of darkness closed completely, I could only see the shape of Haruhi's mouth as she spoke.

—*See you again, Kyon*, her kind, beautiful smile said.

Again I was falling as though having lost my footing, floating such that I'd lost all sense of equilibrium, and had no idea which way was up or down.

Had that been a dream? Or an illusion? To be honest, I knew that I was suffering from time-sickness. During the events surrounding Tanabata, I traveled back and forth through time on multiple occasions, and my body had quite thoroughly learned the truth of the saying that one personal experience was worth hearing a hundred stories. I probably wouldn't get used to it no matter how many times I did it, and in the process had learned that the semicircular canals in my ears were quite weak. But anyone would feel this way if they had to ride in a car with bad suspension along a winding mountain road. The inside of my stomach was already about to flip.

Just how long was this plunge into darkness going to last?

But it didn't take very long before I reached the next transition. Just as I reached the end of my short fall, it felt as though I was carried by a gentle force that opposed gravity. I felt myself lean into a sensation of breaking, and then a strangely elastic object struck my body. At that, I opened my eyes.

"Nguh?!"

The truth was I opened my eyes both literally and figuratively. I still hadn't shaken the unreal feeling of being inside some incoherent dream; I was completely awake, feeling the unmistakable sensation of waking up after a moderate amount of sleep. I could even remember the dream I had just had. Not that it mattered.

It took my highly intelligent brain about three seconds to grasp the situation.

"...? Where is this?"

I was in a dark room, on a bed. I could immediately tell that it was not my own. The surroundings had the unfamiliar scent of someone else's home. It reminded me of the way my sister's room smelled, but wasn't quite the same. I was certain it wasn't a room I'd seen or been in my entire life.

So where was it? Where had I been dropped?

"What...are you doing?" I heard a muffled voice from directly below me. It sounded unnaturally quiet, and there was more than a hint of challenge in it. It was a voice I'd certainly heard before—in fact, it was a voice I hear almost every day.

As slowly as possible, I looked down.

Haruhi's face was directly in front of me. Despite the darkness, there was enough light coming in through the slightly open curtains that I could see upon her face an expression of shock unlike anything I'd ever seen before.

Beyond that, I seemed to be down on all fours on Haruhi's bed, looking down at her, where she lay faceup, pinned by the comforter that I was inadvertently holding down with my hands and legs. If an impartial jury had been present and witnessed this scene, they would've unanimously convicted me without a single hesitation. There wasn't any space in this situation for a single speck of an excuse.

"...Is this...?"

I finally realized it. Somehow I'd neglected to ever visit Haruhi's house, to say nothing of her room, which explained why this place was so unfamiliar. I probably couldn't have noticed any sooner, but this was without a doubt Haruhi's room. By process of elimination, that was the only possibly answer.

This was Haruhi's room, and Haruhi's bed. And it was the middle of the night. Haruhi was wearing pajamas, and looking up at me with eyes that were past astonishment.

"Kyon, just what do you think you're—"

I'll have you know, Miss Haruhi, that I'm the one who has no idea what's going on here. No, seriously—I would never, ever have guessed that the destination of all that falling would have been Haruhi's bed.

"Wait!" Haruhi said in a rising voice. "Just—close your eyes... and put the covers over your head!"

She slowly sat up and elbowed me aside, and my vision was soon blocked by the covers going over my head. I heard rustling.

I took the chance to peer through a gap in the covers and look around at the room's furnishings. No, this wasn't anything perverted. There was just something I needed to make sure of.

What I was looking for was on Haruhi's bedside table.

It was something you'll find in almost anyone's bedroom—a digital alarm clock. Haruhi didn't live in the Edo era, so I assumed she wouldn't have a rooster next to her bed.

Fortunately, Haruhi was considerate enough to have a model that displayed the day and month in addition to the time, which indicated that the sun would soon be peeking out from under the horizon.

And the day happened to be a day in May.

So... what did that mean? The day I'd fallen into the glowing blue hand of a <Celestial> was an evening in the middle of April, so assuming Haruhi's clock wasn't completely out of whack, then—crap—this was nearly a month in the future from that day.

I've had all sorts of experience with leaping into the past and then back to my own present, but this would be the first time I'd jumped into the future. Who'd forced me ahead in time? Asahina the Elder? Or was this a previously unknown ability the <Celestial> had?

Haruhi was still rummaging around. Given the sound of rustling cloth, I assumed she was changing, but my interest was elsewhere.

Hanging from Haruhi's wall was a simply designed calendar. The black numeral indicated today, this day, the day on which the sun was about to dawn, had been plainly circled with a red magic marker. The edge of the circle had been embellished with little flower petals, like a mark of praise from a teacher on a kindergarten student's drawing.

I knew perfectly well what today was the anniversary of.

After all, I'd done something similar for a day on my calendar's April page.

So she'd remembered. Well, *I* remembered, so I guess it's not surprising. One year ago today was a day that was as important to us as our school entrance ceremony.

This day was—.

Just then, I heard the sound of a small bump against the window.

Both Haruhi and I straightened at the sound. Haruhi had finished changing into regular clothes, so she didn't complain when I pulled the covers off of my head. She seemed more interested in whoever was making the noise outside of the window, and walked quickly over to it. I went and stood beside her.

It was here where I learned that Haruhi lived in a normal house and had a room on the second floor. I found it deeply mysterious that I didn't know this already.

When she pulled back the curtains and looked down, three figures were illuminated by the streetlight in front of the house.

There wasn't a single doubt about their identities. It was Asahina the Younger, Koizumi, and Nagato.

Seeing our response, Koizumi raised a tired hand, while Asahina put both hands on her chest. Nagato simply stood there stock-still as usual. I felt a deep sense of relief.

Haruhi quietly opened the window. Outside it was silent, not unlike the closed space I'd been in just a short while earlier. This was probably a residential area where the loudest noise they got was the paperboy making his rounds.

We hadn't coordinated anything ahead of time, but Haruhi and I still wound up holding our breath together, as Koizumi gave us a light wave.

I had just noticed that he seemed to be holding some kind of small package in his other hand when our lieutenant brigade chief made a wind-up motion and tossed the item toward us. The toss traced a lazy parabola—was that Nagato's doing?—before landing perfectly in my hands. *Strike!*

The neatly wrapped box had a card attached to it with a ribbon. Despite the low light, I was able to easily read the writing on the card.

*   *   *

In honor of the first anniversary of the founding of the SOS Brigade. From the brigade members to Her Excellency the brigade chief, with a year's worth of our deepest thanks.

The irregularity of the handwriting made it seem as if each brigade member had written one of the phrases. My handwriting was among them, though I had no recollection of putting it there.

...That's right. This date, this very day, marked exactly one year since Haruhi had declared the foundation of the SOS Brigade. Having received her divine inspiration, she'd slammed the back of my head into her desk, and as soon as our lunch break arrived, dashed up the stairs and made straight for the literature club room, then after school, declared she was taking it over, and the very next day, captured poor Asahina.

—*From now on, this room is our clubroom!*

—*The SOS Brigade! Saving the world by Overloading it with fun, Haruhi Suzumiya Brigade!*

That was the moment our mysterious club members came together and established a base from which we would spread trouble throughout North High.

Isn't that right, Koizumi, Nagato, Asahina?

That's the reason I'm here, is it not?

"Haruhi."

I held the present and turned my body to face Haruhi.

"Wh...what?" She acted as if she didn't know, but I could tell she understood what was going on. She glanced back and forth between looking at my face and the box, seeming like a treasure hunter's sidekick who knew she was about to receive a great treasure but didn't know what to do with it.

Times like this, you just gotta approach things head-on. I handed her the treasure box with card attached. "Thank you for your hard work as our brigade chief. I hope you'll favor us moving forward."

"Idiot," she said, but still politely took the box. After scanning the card, she closed her eyes and held the box tightly close. Somehow it felt like a sentimental breeze blew by, and then—

"Kyon, how did you get in my room?"

Ah...well, it sure as heck wasn't through the front door. "I climbed up the drainpipe and came in through the window. You've gotta be more careful with your locks. I was lucky your lock was tired of being closed."

I have to admit I was pretty impressed with myself for being able to spout such a pack of lies on demand.

"Isn't that kinda overdoing things? Someone could've reported you while you were climbing up." Haruhi's expression was somewhere between laughter and tears, but then she suddenly looked down at my feet. "And why are you wearing your school slippers? Take those things off this second—you're gonna get my floor all dirty."

I'd totally forgotten about that. Up until just a moment ago I had been at North High—and so had she. But unfortunately it looked as if I was the only victim of this particular time slip.

Haruhi watched me take my shoes off, then, going back over to the window and gazing down at the three who were still standing there in the driveway, she took a deep breath.

"If you were gonna do a surprise event, you could've picked a better time. I was sort of expecting it, but I have to admit I didn't think it would be this late at night."

"It wouldn't have been a surprise otherwise, would it? This is the only way we could surprise you," I said. My pretentious ad-libbing was pretty persuasive, I gotta say, thanks to all the crazy stuff Haruhi had put me through. It would've been nice if we didn't have to go to such lengths to get the drop on her.

Haruhi was still looking down, smiling with tears in her eyes. She obviously didn't care whether or not the window had actually been locked. The point was that I was there.

"Kyon"—Haruhi drew close to my face and whispered in my ear— "I'll show you to the front door, so follow me and try not to make any noise." Her breath tickled as she spoke, but I managed to deal with it.

Haruhi descended the steps on tiptoe so as not to alert the household, and with the skill of a veteran safecracker, opened her front door.

Now I was finally able to meet up with the brigade members waiting outside. Since it was a residential area in the wee hours, everyone was silent. But I could read their faces. Although I still didn't understand what happened, I could tell that everything had finally worked out well.

Nagato had brought with her my favorite pair of sneakers, which she held out to me. This was the usual Nagato. Not stricken with fever, this was her unchanging, ever-reading face, and it had no need for emotional expression.

Asahina—the Younger, of course—peered worriedly at me and Haruhi. I gave her a thumbs-up, and her sigh of relief quickly became a smile.

With all the friendly openness of someone who's just returned from an all-night convenience store, Koizumi spoke. "My apologies for coming so late at night, Suzumiya, but there was someone here who just had to express their deep feelings, you see."

Why did he look at me as he said that?

Well, I knew. I faced Haruhi and spoke in my most composed tone of voice. "We had to figure out how to surprise you. If we didn't strike while you were asleep, we couldn't have done it."

But whether Haruhi was listening to me or not, she looked at Asahina and the rest in turn. "Well...thank you."

She held her present close and smiled a smile that would've outshone the full moon. Normally her grin blazed like a vast star, but this was like a peaceful moon, and it made me kind of...how can I say it? No, I couldn't say anything. All I could do was gaze back at her.

Somewhere a crow cawed. Damn dark bird. I didn't remember ordering any sound effects.

As though taking that as her cue, Haruhi looked up from her package. "It's pretty late. Let's meet up later in the clubroom—also, what's inside?"

"I hope that you'll look forward to opening it and finding out. Incidentally, the person who chose it is your bedroom intruder here," said Koizumi. "He even wrapped it for you. He was rather insistent about doing it himself, so the rest of us merely acted as observers. Perhaps we should have just left everything to him."

I finally managed to shut Koizumi up by stepping on his foot.

Still, apparently my past self had been the one to pick out the present's contents. I could understand the reasoning.

Haruhi looked back, then looked back again as she returned to her front door. "Take care on your way home. Koizumi and Kyon, you better make sure Yuki and Mikuru get home safe, got that? That's an order from your brigade chief."

She left us with those words, spoken at a surprisingly reasonable volume, then went back inside her house. She really was being considerate of both her parents and neighbors. I suppose she does have a cuteness to her.

After we left Haruhi, the three other brigade members and I walked along the deserted night street.

I knew that it was the middle of May. I also knew that from my perspective, being summoned to the clubroom for a showdown with Fujiwara and Kuyoh, and my soft landing with Haruhi in the palm of a <Celestial>, were things that had happened just a short while ago, but I had now jumped nearly a month ahead—but given that I'd previously jumped through time amounting to years, this wasn't that much of a surprise to me, and just felt like a novel discovery.

In other words, for me this was the world of the future, and as such was unexplored territory, I said.

"Indeed it is." Koizumi's unconcerned tone as he spoke was frustrating. Maybe it was because he was in such high spirits.

"Which means I'm going to have to do another time jump."

"Yes. It will be rather inconvenient if you don't."

"Um, er—" Asahina raised her hand slightly. And as befit the time travel expert (apprentice) that she was, she stumblingly explained the situation to me.

And according to her, right after I was saved by the <Celestial>, I jumped ahead in the future—that would be now.

Which meant that I had to go back in time once more, to a month ago. Asahina would send me herself, very shortly.

I looked to Nagato. She looked back at me with the eyes of a nutcracker doll. I couldn't sense so much as a particle of the weakness that she'd suffered from back when Haruhi was nursing her.

"Can't I just sleep in a time-freeze until the right moment comes?"

"No," answered Nagato instantly. "That is not a suitable solution for the problem."

What did that mean? I asked Koizumi.

"Actually, there's another you that exists in this time. The one who returned from this time to a month ago."

I seem to have been fusing with other versions of myself quite a bit these days, I said.

"That was a different case. There, your original self had split into two versions, but in the case of time travel, there really is only one of you. So if you don't return, your double existence here remains unresolved."

Asahina looked up at me from one side. "And it would go against the fixed event, so . . . we really need you to go back. From our perspective, you returning to the past is part of reality."

So that was how it is. The proof that I did return to my proper time was in the fact that there was another me in this time. The "me" that returns to the past here becomes the other "me" that now exists here. Anyway, it was just a month. Compared with three years, that was hardly anything.

"We wanted to bring the you that exists in this time period along too, but you insisted that you really didn't want to meet yourself. So just the three of us came."

That's certainly what I would've done.

"Incidentally, I was told to keep the nature of Suzumiya's present a secret. Please give the matter some thought once you return to your proper time," Koizumi said mischievously. "And please don't forget to tell the us of next month about today. Although I'm sure you'll remember."

"..."

I was at least relieved to see that Nagato had returned to her normal silent, expressionless self.

"My past self will explain everything to you. Actually, I already have."

"Yeah, I'll ask you right away. Is the clubroom all right for that?"

"No, we'll actually be meeting in a different location. As for where—well, I suppose I'll leave that to you. You needn't overthink the matter."

I looked to Nagato.

"..."

The ever-silent girl said nothing. Back in the courtyard, the last thing I saw had been those three figures on the roof. There was no question that one of them had been Nagato. And Koizumi had said that the α-route Nagato hadn't suffered any changes. Far from it, he'd even mentioned something about Yasumi summoning her to go.

Did you know everything, Nagato? What Yasumi was, and the reason the <Celestial> appeared back there...

But Nagato silently turned her back to me, walking off with Koizumi, who gave me a wave before leaving.

I might as well believe Koizumi. According to him, he'd already given me an explanation. To the me of a month ago, that is.

I turned to Asahina, the other person that had been left behind. "Shall we go?"

"Yes!"

Asahina seemed pleased that there was something useful for her to do. And she probably was. After following orders she didn't understand from her superiors for so long, she was trying to take the initiative to use time travel on her own.

But first.

"Asahina."

"What is it?"

"Do you have a brother, Asahina? Particularly a younger brother—I'd like to know."

Asahina giggled and put a finger to her lips, winking a perfect wink. "Information about my family is top-level classified information."

I'll just bet.

Having experienced it several times, I was finally starting to get used to time travel, and the weightless, dizzying feeling soon passed. Maybe that was because a time span of one month was less than three years, so the time travel involved was shorter.

In any case, when I opened my eyes next, I was on my own bed, in my own room.

Perhaps startled by my sudden appearance, Shamisen, who had been curled up napping on my pillow, jumped to his feet and stumbled off the bed, then glared at me, his tail puffed up. I gave the room a quick look. Unsurprisingly, Asahina was nowhere to be seen.

First I checked the time.

On a day in early April, a Friday, eight PM, I had returned to my room.

Just two hours earlier, in the literature club room, I'd been involved in a desperate struggle for the fate of the world, or the future, and if I were to seriously tell anyone about it, the only person who would believe me outside of the people that had been there was probably Sasaki. Not that it was a story I particularly wanted to broadcast.

I stretched a big stretch, and murmured a few words to celebrate my return to normal life.

"Guess I'll take a bath and go to bed."

I decided to take one day out of the weekend to clear my head.

EPILOGUE

When the new week started, the world was again a peaceful one.

Nagato had recovered as though nothing had ever been wrong, and returned to school. I still had both sets of memories in my head— one of her felled by the fever, and another where she sat silently reading in the SOS Brigade clubroom while the entrance examinations took place. No matter how much I rethink them, there are no discrepancies between them, and the sensation of those overlapping memories remains a strange one.

As for me, both histories are part of reality, so it's not the case that one of them is true and one is false. They cover the same time, and both actually happened.

When I actually think back over the week Koizumi calls the α version, I have no trouble seeing Yasumi and everyone else's faces, and in the β version, my exchanges with Sasaki and her group are perfectly clear in my mind. And the two layers of memory aren't confused at all. When I think of one, that's all I'm conscious of, and when I think of the other, the actions I took in the first don't come to mind at all.

If I calm myself down and really focus, I can manage to connect the two weeks as I recall them. It's something like the non-intersection of a double-helix staircase. I ascend two sets of stairs that feel as though they should cross each other, but they never do, despite having the same start and end points—that's how the experience feels.

A new Monday succeeded that busy, eventful week. Nothing about my pilgrimage up the hill to school had changed, and while time might have gone kind of crazy, spatially speaking it felt exactly the same, and as I cooled myself off in the spring breeze that blew through the open window next to my seat, and as the chime signaling the beginning of class sounded, the blissfully unaware source of all this commotion barely made it into the classroom.

With a strange half-smiling, half-disappointed look on her face, Haruhi adroitly kept her composure as she took her seat behind me.

As I looked at her face, the grammatically complex sentence "This Haruhi is not yet the Haruhi that I already have met a month from now" forced itself through my head. The tenses of the statement were quite confusing, but it was the truth nonetheless. At this point, Haruhi didn't have the slightest idea that I was going to appear in her bedroom in the middle of the night.

...So why did she have such a strange expression on her face? I asked.

"Yeah, about that." Haruhi put her elbows on her desk and rested her chin in the palms of her hands. "Yesterday Yasumi came by my house."

...Oh ho.

"And she said she was really sorry, but that she had to decline her brigade membership."

Oh?

"I was really surprised. Turns out she was still in middle school."

...Oh, so that explained it.

"She goes to a nearby middle school, and her sister graduated from North High, so Yasumi borrowed her uniform and snuck into the school, she said. She just had to join the SOS Brigade, so she was only sneaking in after class ended. She'll probably be able to get admitted to North High without any trouble, but she said she just couldn't stand to wait. Can you believe she was such a prankster?"

So that's why she hadn't been in the classrooms when I'd gone all over the school looking for her during lunch. She hadn't even been a North High student, so no wonder I couldn't find her.

Haruhi laid her head down on her desk and stared vaguely out the window. "But Yuki's better now, and the brigade entrance examinations were fun, and the weather's nice today, so I guess I can't complain. She was such a promising girl, but there's no way she could keep posing as a high school student."

I didn't know if Yasumi had actually gone to meet Haruhi. It was entirely possible that had never happened. But Haruhi said so, so that's how it was.

"Won't she be properly entering high school next year, though? Just readmit her to the brigade without another exam, then."

"I forgot to ask what year she is in middle school. It might take two or three years, honestly." Haruhi sounded a little lonely, but then she suddenly looked up, and got right up in my face. "Hey, by the way—you're not hiding anything from me, are you? Did you meet with anyone this Saturday? Or, like, make some kind of strange plan behind my back…"

She was getting more and more perceptive with age. The truth was she was exactly right, but—

"I didn't do anything. I slept for half of Saturday and took Shamisen in for immunizations on Sunday, that's all."

Haruhi fixed me in her gorgon-like stare, and it took several seconds before she released me. "I see. Well, fine, then."

"Hey, Haruhi." I wonder if I spoke up because as she turned sideways and looked out the window, her face was illuminated by the rays of sun in a way that made her look much more grown-up.

"What?"

"Suppose someone invents a time machine not too far in the future. If the you from a few years in the future met your current self, what do you think your future self would say?"

"Huh?" Haruhi scowled dubiously. "I guess in a few years I'll be a college student. So if that person met me now…hmm. I think I'd probably look at my future self and tell her she hasn't changed at all. Because, I mean, I'm pretty confident that my values aren't going to change in just two, three, or even five years. But what makes you ask?"

"I was just wondering. I got to thinking about what kind of person my future self is going to grow up into."

"Well, don't worry. You'll probably be the same as you are now. Or, what, do you want to think you psychologically matured enough to be able to lecture your middle school self?"

There wasn't room for even a vague grumble in objection to that.

But, Haruhi—when my just-barely second-year high school student self travels through time and meets the future you, I hope you'll be nice to me. I hope you'll give me the gentle smile I remember seeing.

That goes for *my* future self too.

Haruhi opened her mouth as though to further talk at me, but with perfect timing I was saved by the bell, which rang just as Mr. Okabe strode jauntily into the room. Thanks, bell. Ditto to our hot-blooded instructor.

So, then.

My memories of each person in the split world had been fused such that there weren't any inconsistencies. Both existed in my mind, and having two sets of memories meant that they'd been unconsciously arranged in a system such that when I was accessing one, the other one didn't come to mind.

So I had the memories of Haruhi nursing the downed Nagato, but also the memories of Yasumi.

Of course, most parts of each world, which Koizumi had termed α and β, were the same, so the only places where significant differences arose between them, not counting things related to the SOS Brigade, involved Taniguchi, Kunikida, Sasaki, Kyoko Tachibana, and so on.

We ended up with zero new club members, which settled things nicely.

Incidentally, just as the ever-perceptive Haruhi had guessed, I had hosted Koizumi and Nagato on Sunday.

Or rather, I called them over. Unsurprisingly I had no energy whatsoever to leave my house, so I had them come to me. And at the time I had a pile of questions I wanted to ask them—for example, about what happened after I'd fallen holding Haruhi into the palm of the <Celestial's> hand and gotten sent into the future.

What had happened in the clubroom after that? How had the two worlds been reconnected? What happened to Fujiwara and Kuyoh and Tachibana? And just who was Yasumi Watahashi?

Not counting Haruhi, the month-later versions of everyone else in the SOS Brigade had had distinctly knowing looks on their faces, which meant their counterparts here and now had to know.

When the intercom buzzer rang right on schedule, I went to greet them, accompanied, for some reason, by my sister and Shamisen. Koizumi was dressed in street clothes as if he was about to go on a date or something, and he gave a chagrined smile. Nagato returned my look as though she were a marble statue, her dark eyes clear as ever.

Koizumi notwithstanding, I was deeply relieved to see Nagato standing there, her usual expressionless self.

The pair removed their shoes in the entryway, and Shamisen came over and rubbed his face on both of them. This seemed less as though he was trying to be a good host and greet his guests, and more like feline instinct, reacting to the scent of people to whom he was connected. He seemed especially eager to rub against Nagato's ankles, purring loudly as he did so, perhaps because of the something-or-other life form that had been sealed within him.

Meanwhile, my sister greeted our guests.

"Yuki! Koizumi! Welcome!" She followed them around with a smile like a blast furnace, and I had to send her to the kitchen so I could bring them to my room.

Somewhere along the line Nagato had picked Shamisen up, so I wound up temporarily housing two people and one cat in my room. Well, it wasn't as if it mattered if the cat overheard our conversation.

"So, where shall I begin?" Koizumi sat cross-legged on my bed. "But first, I'd like to hear your side of the story. You and Suzumiya both disappeared right in front of us. I knew instantly where Suzumiya had gone, but…"

What conclusion was he leaping to now? I asked.

"She was in her house. Both α and β returned there like normal. Just like that. She might have remembered feeling faintly uneasy, but that's not a problem."

Nagato sat on the floor and silently put Shamisen in her lap, and began to rub his belly. Shamisen purred loudly. He seemed to have taken quite a shine to her.

When it came to what had happened in that crazy, mixed-up closed space, there was something I wanted to know more than anything else.

"Nagato."

"…" Nagato ceased her gentle massaging of Shamisen and looked at me.

"Has your fever gone down?"

Nagato only nodded as she poked at Shamisen's paw-pads.

"Did you manage to complete any, uh…high-level communication or whatever, with the Heavenly Canopy Dominion?"

"That has been temporarily aborted." Shamisen rolled over on his back, and Nagato stroked his throat. "Both the Data Overmind and the Heavenly Canopy Dominion determined that each had received the minimum necessary amount of information. My ability to relay information has been recognized as insufficiently accurate for the task. Thus I have been relieved of that duty, and given new orders— to passively observe and report on Haruhi Suzumiya and Kuyoh Suoh."

So Nagato's restoration was because the Heavenly Canopy Dominion had temporarily ceased interfering with her. I was just happy she was back to normal, I said.

"Not necessarily," said Nagato without any trace of disappointment. "We have moved on to phase two of a plan to achieve mutual understanding. I was merely judged insufficient for the task of conducting communication for phase one. I have not been informed which individual will be succeeding me, but they will undoubtedly perform better than I did."

They should've just let Kimidori handle it from the beginning.

"Wait a second." Did that mean Kuyoh was still in this world? I asked.

Nagato tugged on Shamisen's whiskers. "She had not disappeared. She is currently attending Koyoen Academy, where she will remain as a student. Her primary goal is to achieve autonomy, which will take some time."

"And Fujiwara?" I addressed this question to Koizumi.

"I doubt we'll see him again. Or maybe it would be more accurate to say that he'll never be able to travel back to our present again. It seems that his future time line was severed. Just as that which prevents Asahina and her comrades from traveling further back than four years ago, Suzumiya created a new time fault—or so Asahina the Elder explained to me."

So she'd had time to explain things, then? I asked.

"Immediately after you and Suzumiya disappeared, the <Celestial> started to disintegrate. It was a rather familiar scene, for me. After that, the closed space completely collapsed. Not only Suzumiya's, but Sasaki's too. The world returned to a peaceful state. In that moment, it was just the adult Asahina and myself—and Kyoko Tachibana, I suppose. Fujiwara and Kuyoh Suoh were nowhere to be seen."

And neither was Yasumi Watahashi, I guessed.

"Did you talk with Asahina the Elder at all?"

"A bit. She seemed very sad about what happened with Fujiwara, but that's just a guess based on how she looked. But she did say that his actions were half-impulsive, and that he had probably been used to protect the time line he was attached to. There isn't enough information to understand all the details, so that's about all I can say."

I wondered what had changed from when Fujiwara planned to

kill Haruhi and install Sasaki as the new god. Was that somehow a problem for Asahina the Elder's future?

"Still," said Koizumi, gazing at Shamisen's twitching tail, "Asahina did let slip that even if the space-time continuum were completely overwritten from this time plane onto her own future, it would all end up converging anyway. And she sounded sincere."

Huh. And then?

"She gave me a sad smile and left the room. I followed right after her, but she was gone. I assume she returned to the future."

I wondered how much of this I should believe. Both of Koizumi's statements, and Asahina the Elder's words. "What about Kyoko Tachibana?"

"Once the two worlds were fused, she was stunned. She stayed there for a while, holding her head and moaning, but eventually calmed down and just slumped there. She seemed deeply disappointed."

I'll bet she was, I said.

"She returned home, totally depressed. I suppose her burden was quite heavy." Koizumi then took out his cell phone. "But before we parted ways, I exchanged numbers and addresses with her."

After all that confusion, he was always so clever. Koizumi the ladies' man.

"She sent me a text right away. In it..."

Apparently for a variety of reasons, Kyoko Tachibana had decided to withdraw from all of this. She saw all too keenly that she couldn't keep up with these aliens and time travelers. Though apparently she was still holding on to the hope that she would be able find something she could do.

Koizumi snapped his phone shut. "Don't worry. If she appears again we'll take the necessary measures."

He didn't have to sound so happy about it.

"Based on her postscript, she plans to be reclusive for a while. Her comrades have all gone underground, and she's simply going to try to remain Sasaki's friend. I wonder how that will go."

I was quite confident that Sasaki would not be sweet-talked by Kyoko Tachibana any time soon.

As Koizumi and I talked, it seemed as though Nagato had become Shamisen's personal masseuse, and was focused entirely on petting his fur. Perhaps she had no interest in our conversation, or perhaps the entity that had been transferred into Shamisen was simply more interesting.

"Kyon! Yuki!" My sister opened the door and bounced her way into the room. "Yuki! Let's play! C'mon, with Shami too! We've got all sorts of kitty toys downstairs, so let's play!"

" . . . "

Nagato took Shamisen and quietly stood, allowing herself to be pulled out of the room by my excited sister. Perhaps she'd read the situation, or perhaps playing with a cat and a girl was more interesting than hearing a recap of events she'd already experienced.

In any case, thanks to her Koizumi and I could now speak one-on-one, so I was grateful to her.

"So I know that that was Sasaki's closed space back there. Hers was extremely stable, after all. But why did Haruhi's closed space also appear?" I got confused just thinking about the swirling jumble of dark and light back there.

"There's no room for doubt there. Suzumiya intentionally made that happen, such that I could be allowed in, and such that a <Celestial> could be created."

That was weird. At the time, Haruhi had been outside the school, and she hadn't been conscious of what was happening with us, I pointed out.

"What if I told you that she was fully aware?" Koizumi smiled like a nasty cram school teacher, looking at me as if I was giving myself fits trying to answer a question even though the solution was right in front of me. "Have you forgotten that there was someone else besides us in that space? She just suddenly appeared, and she wasn't an alien, time traveler, or esper. Despite us never really understanding her true nature, at some point she stabilized her position there, and summoned both you and me to the clubroom. Yes—our α versions."

Yasumi Watahashi, huh?

What *was* she? I asked.

Koizumi answered immediately. "Her true form is Haruhi Suzumiya. She is an alternate self created by Suzumiya."

By this point I had sort of gotten that feeling, but I wanted to hear the details. When had Koizumi figured that out? I asked.

"It was explained to us from the very beginning. Quite simply, actually. Can I borrow a notebook and pen?"

I handed them over as asked, and looked on as in a graceful hand he first wrote the words "Yasumizu Watahashi" on the paper.

"It's a very simple anagram. It can be solved without any hints at all, so none were given to us. Reading this as it is should make the solution quite obvious."

I told him to cut the chatter and get on with it.

"The reading of the kanji for 'Yasumizu' as 'Yasumi' was misdirection. This should be pronounced as 'Yasumizu.' If we write it out phonetically in the alphabet, it turns out like so—"

—*ya-su-mi-zu wa-ta-ha-shi*

"Then, if we rearrange the letters—"

—*wa-ta-shi-ha su-zu-mi-ya*

Watashi ha, Suzumiya.

I am Suzumiya.

Koizumi dropped the pencil on the notebook as though having proved his point.

"Suzumiya unconsciously used her abilities. As a precaution, you see. That's why the world was split. One was the world as it originally was. The other was a world that didn't exist. Despite being unaware of it, she sensed the danger, and protected the world. If she hadn't split reality, our enemies would've been able to do with you as they pleased. Essentially, she saved both you and Nagato."

So this was what it felt like to be at a loss for words.

"As for when it began, I can only speculate. The last day of spring vacation and the first day of the semester both seem likely. At that point Suzumiya guessed what was going to happen. Subconsciously, of course. This was some kind of miracle. I suppose you could call it an unconscious prediction."

So far as I could remember, the world had been continuous until, still in the bath, I put the phone receiver my sister brought me to my ear.

And then the world split—into one where Sasaki spoke to me, and one where Yasumi did.

"Suzumiya was aware that a future awaited in which both you and Nagato were in danger. So that's where she made her move. That's what I'm calling the α route, where her other self appeared. Not only does she not know about her own power, she may not even *want* to know, to say nothing of whether the knowledge is accessible to her in the first place."

Koizumi's face looked somehow terrified.

"Yasumi Watahashi was Suzumiya's unconscious instantiation. I say 'unconscious' because she represents actions taken literally outside the realm of her own awareness. Furthermore, even if Yasumi Watahashi did not disappear but instead was reintegrated into Suzumiya, Suzumiya herself has no knowledge of that. She is no more than a dream that disappears upon awakening. And who knows, she may well have been an actual dream. We may have been in an illusory world created by Suzumiya. It's possible that we came perilously close to non-being becoming reality."

Don't make me remember that again. Could Haruhi do *anything*?

"It's a mind-boggling thought. I've always taken a skeptical approach to the Haruhi-as-god theory, but I may have to revise my opinion."

I doubted she particularly wanted his worship, though.

"When I said that Suzumiya was gradually losing her power, that may well have been a wrong guess. She is evolving. The possibility has emerged that she will be able to consciously control the manifestation of her emotional power. The deliberate actions of the <Celestial> speak of that possibility. Although she does still remain unaware. That's precisely why it's so awe-inspiring. If you sit down at a keyboard and randomly mash on the keys, the odds of you writing a sentence with meaning are so faint they're near zero. But if you press them consciously, it's trivial, is it not? She can do this without even being aware of it. She can completely ignore probabilities. She's transcended godhood."

So there's nothing more we can do, then, I said.

"It's just a guess. Psychoanalysis of Suzumiya is beyond my abilities—all the more so if she's undergone some kind of apotheosis. Go read up on your mythology. The will and words of the gods are always mysterious and capricious. Sometimes even unreasonable. But it's not the case that they have no affection for humanity. If there's one thing we can learn from the strangely human faults they sometimes show, it's that myths were written by humans. So what would be a god, to a god?"

I had no idea either, I said, but it didn't much matter either way.

I asked about the relationship between Asahina the Elder and Fujiwara—or more to the point, about the time travelers' theory of time.

"We know from personal experience that it's possible to split the time line. So long as it overwrote space-time, neither you nor I could notice it. Just like that last somewhere that we repeated how many tens of thousands of times. The fact that we have memories of two separate routes is paradoxical proof."

And?

"The bifurcation that we experienced was thanks to Suzumiya's manual alteration of space-time. However, we don't know how that affected Asahina and Fujiwara's future. They could have been from the same future, or individuals from different realities, or one of them could have been lying, or the possibility even exists that both of them were presenting false testimony. There's no way to know for sure."

It didn't seem like "classified information" was the only reason why time travelers didn't talk about their true feelings, I said.

"Indeed. This is only my intuition, but I feel that be it thanks to either natural phenomena or deliberate action, the future is split into many different paths. But the diverging routes to those destinations are limited, and they will eventually reconverge to a single path. And we've become conscious of one such divergence, then reconvergence—that is my guess. If I were to draw a diagram—"

Koizumi picked the pencil back up, and started doodling lines in my notebook.

"As I just mentioned, the path we were originally supposed to take was the β route. But then Suzumiya forcibly intervened and created the α route, which is what led us to where we are now. Who's to say what would've happened without the α version of you and me, along with Yasumi Watahashi."

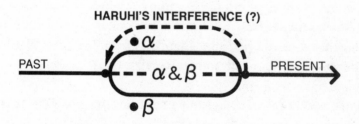

"On the other hand, if Asahina and Fujiwara's futures are separate, then we can postulate it would look something like this, diverging thanks to some event, then converging again."

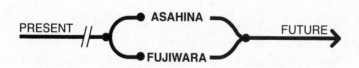

"There is also the possibility that there are futures that do not converge, remaining fragmented and unchanging. Asahina may have come back in order to prevent her own world from tapering off—to guide the flow of time such that it leads to her future."

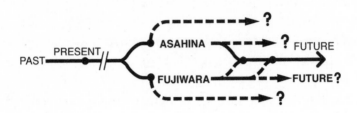

Good grief. I couldn't keep up with this. I wondered if Nagato could offer an alternate explanation...and as I was thinking about it, something totally different occurred to me.

"This is changing the subject, but you and Mori...and Arakawa too, come to think of it—what's your relationship? I just assumed that Mori was your boss."

Koizumi peered at me, an intrigued look on his face. "Now, why would you have thought something like that? Do you have any problem with the Agency?"

"Mori always calls you by your name, but I was wondering what she calls you when we're not around."

He seemed momentarily taken aback, but Koizumi soon recovered his amused smile. "We're all colleagues with the same goal. As such, we don't have the kind of hierarchy that exists in a corporation. There are no superiors—everyone is the same. There's no hierarchy among comrades. Mori is simply Mori. And she's free to call me whatever she wishes."

Huh.

Well, I'd leave it at that for now, I decided. I didn't particularly want to know, and it was rude to pry.

"Ah, there is one other thing. This is a trivial matter, but I thought

I would let you know. It's about the flower that Yasumi brought to decorate the room. I sent a photo of it to be analyzed, and it turns out that it's a completely new variety—we could even assign fresh Latin taxonomy to it. She kept her promise—she was told to bring something interesting to the brigade, and she faithfully did exactly that. Despite being Haruhi's alter ego, she might just be a little more charming than the original...though I suppose that's a bit rude to say. In any case, I hope we can meet her again some-how."

Koizumi stood with a slightly bashful smile, and thus did my weekend meeting conclude.

Incidentally, when I escorted him back downstairs, I should add that we encountered Nagato and my sister ignoring Shamisen in favor of a game of animal shogi. According to what I heard later, my sister had beaten her alien opponent several games in a row. I wonder about that.

I still think about it sometimes.

—What if.

What if I had chosen Sasaki? What if I had switched sides from Haruhi to Sasaki, and joined up with that fake SOS Brigade? What if I had traded Koizumi for Kyoko Tachibana, gotten Kuyoh Suoh in exchange for Nagato, and discarded Asahina in favor of Fujiwara, finally siding with Sasaki?

I might have been killed. Probably by none other than Ryoko Asakura. Third time's the charm. Kimidori probably wouldn't have stopped her. And there was no telling what Nagato would do in response. It was probably overestimating my own importance to imagine that Nagato would've really rebelled against the Overmind.

Anyway, I hadn't done it. I couldn't have.

I was far too deeply involved with the SOS Brigade. I could no more extricate myself than I could swim out of the deepest part of a swamp without scuba gear.

That's why I stayed in the shallows. Here at the edge of a long, shallow beach, where I could stay with my friends, never growing tired of gazing at the far-off horizon.

I didn't feel like asking some other unspecified person. I wanted to stay like this. I didn't need anyone's opinion. Haruhi and Asahina and Koizumi and Nagato. Their view was my view, and there was no doubt that my thoughts were in concert with theirs.

So I just wanted to go on like this. As far as we wanted to. We could jump over as many bent rails as we had to, building our own tracks as we went.

On until the end of time.

On Monday, after class ended, some sudden caprice compelled our brigade chief to declare club activities for the day canceled and leave school immediately, and feeling fortunate, several of us brigade members—including Asahina and Koizumi—went our separate ways home.

I felt as though I wanted a little bit more time on my own to think things through, and I was grateful for the opportunity to do so.

Only Nagato remained in the clubroom, absorbed in reading, perhaps out of some sense of obligation as the president of the literature club. I could only pray no hopeful literature club members-to-be dared to set foot in that cursed location. I wondered if Nagato would do some kind of sneaky data manipulation to prevent that from happening.

After school ended I got my bike out from the bike parking lot in front of the station, and passing by the road home, pedaled on down a different route.

My goal was the SOS Brigade's "usual spot," the square in front of a certain train station. Although come to think of it, lately I'd been running into Sasaki, Kuyoh, and Kyoko Tachibana there quite a bit.

Of course I didn't have any arrangements to meet up with anyone. I just had the idea that if I went there, I might be able to anyway. Just like flipping a coin, I figured the odds were about fifty-fifty, but it seemed that my guess had been anticipated.

"Hey."

Sasaki stood in front of the square and waved.

"I thought you might come here," she said. "It's not very scientific, but sometimes it's not a bad idea to trust your instincts. Although betting everything on gut feelings or prophetic dreams is just bad reasoning."

I illegally parked my bike and walked over to Sasaki.

She was calmly watching the people come and go, and as I approached she invited me to sit on a nearby wooden bench.

For a while we were silent, watching the students heading home after being spit out by their schools, and the many other people coming and going like so many freshwater fish in a river.

It was Sasaki who finally spoke up.

"Good work the other day. I mean, I suppose in the end it didn't wind up being involved at all, and getting ditched in front of the school like that totally threw me for a loop. So that was the closed space I've been hearing so much about?"

What had happened to her back then? I asked.

"I didn't have anything to do, and it seemed like if I hung around the area I'd only get in the way, so I just retreated. You go up and down that steep hill every day, huh? To be honest, I'm impressed."

It wasn't that big of a deal. Once you got used to it, it was easier than walking around underground shopping districts in the city.

"I heard most of the details from Tachibana." Sasaki kept her gaze fixed on her dangling loafers. "I feel bad for Fujiwara, but it sounds like things worked out all right. For me too. I've been released from god duty, apparently."

I could tell from her tone that Sasaki was being sincere. Not for nothing had I spent so much time with her in middle school. There was just one thing—

"There's something I want to ask you," I said.

"What might that be? What could there possibly be for you to ask me, apart from academics? I seem to recall you doing that all the time in middle school."

"When you came to my house, you said there was another reason for it, besides the stuff going on with Fujiwara and the rest. What was it?"

Sasaki's eyes widened considerably. "Oh that? I'm surprised you remember. I'd meant to say it casually enough that you'd forget it right away. I suppose I shouldn't have underestimated your memory."

Sasaki chuckled under her breath and looked up at the sky.

"It happened about two weeks ago. Someone confessed his feelings to me."

In that moment, every comment that came to mind was sealed away, and I found myself forced into total silence. It was as if every word of Japanese had gone flying out of my head, and I couldn't say anything.

"It's a boy from my school. At the time I couldn't help but feel like, wow, there's no accounting for taste, and I wasn't quick enough to be able to reply right away. It felt like such a sneak attack. So I've kept putting it off."

When I thought about it, Haruhi and Sasaki were alike in some ways. So long as they didn't open their mouths, their looks would draw an above-average amount of attention from the opposite sex, but if they just stood there silently, their eyes would chase those same guys away.

"In other words, I came for advice on my love life. Did you ever imagine I would come over with less than a single strand of messenger RNA's worth of business? But at least I had the good fortune to be able to meet your sister."

Well... I felt bad that I hadn't been useful, I said.

"Don't worry about it. It would've been better for you if I'd come for advice like that, given the circumstances. I thought about it and decided that it really was the sort of problem I needed to solve myself. It wouldn't have been very considerate of me to just add noise to your life."

We fell silent again. I thought about making some kind of stupid joke, but nothing came to mind. Pathetically, it seemed as though I needed to brush up on my vocabulary. I'd have to ask Librarian Nagato if she had any recommendations.

The stagnation surrounded us like a jelly, and it was Sasaki again who finally broke it, with yet another shocking revelation.

"Suzumiya and I went to the same elementary school. We were always in different classes, but even I could tell how much she stood out. She was like the sun. Even in a different class, I could feel the light she gave off."

That had to be some kind of joke. There was no way Haruhi had met Sasaki before I did.

"I was always thinking how nice it would be to be in the same class with her, but it never happened. So when it turned out we were going to different middle schools, I felt kind of complicated about it. I was sort of lonely, but also relieved... It's true, if you stare at the sun too long you'll injure your eyes. But if the sun disappears, we lose the warmth of its light... or so I guess you could say. Does this make any sense, Kyon?"

Yeah, more or less, I said.

"Thanks to some family issues, my last name changed when I started middle school. That's why Suzumiya didn't recognize me when you introduced me as Sasaki. My appearance has changed quite a bit too. I'd grown my hair out to try to look more like her, but then I cut it. It's for the best, though. If she noticed me now, I feel like it would just make me self-conscious. So keep it a secret, would you? This particular confession is pretty embarrassing for me."

I'm pretty sure I exhaled.

I felt a renewed sense of just how many human connections happened without my knowledge. It felt obvious in retrospect. There are billions of people in the world, and each one of them encounters many others—there are meetings, partings, and reunions. Countless little dramas playing out, all the time.

And in the end I could only be aware of the relationships in my immediate surroundings. No matter what incidents, what romances might happen, there was no way for me to ever recognize such unknowable things as real, I said.

"That's not true, Kyon," said Sasaki, having regained her bright smile. "Are you saying the only reality is that which is reported on? It's true that as humans, our knowledge is finite. What exists at the edge of the universe, what is there beyond the universe, and what *is* the universe, anyway—for me, these truths are still out of reach. But just because you can't recognize something doesn't mean the answer doesn't exist. This is what I think—even if humanity as a species heads for extinction, so long as there's some life form somewhere ready to observe things we can't understand, then we could call that being a god."

I definitely didn't understand anymore, now that she'd brought things out to the cosmic scale, I said.

"We humans have been given the power of imagination. That's the one thing humans can brag about to the natural world. We can compete with godlike beings. It's our one weapon, our single arrow." Sasaki chuckled, and continued. "If you like, Kyon, I'll stand in for Suzumiya whenever you want—or so I'd say, but I know you'd never wish for even a tiny bit of that. And I'm sure you know what my wish is. In any case, that possibility is now too tiny to be expressed in digits. It would be presumptuous to describe it even as 'zero.' It does not exist."

She really was always right, I said.

"And in the end, I didn't do anything. I'm really not built for this god stuff."

Given this world full of people doing all sorts of things that were better off left undone, Sasaki herself should have been well aware just how beautiful it was to hear someone say they weren't going to do something that they shouldn't have been doing, I said.

"Yeah. I didn't want to just become a simple bad guy. I didn't want that kind of price on my head. My plan is to avoid being close enough to ruin that I have to take on that kind of work. It's like an actor playing a cheap trickster even though they have an order of magnitude more talent than that—but that's where the nuance comes from. But I'm not an actress, and I don't belong onstage. For good or ill, I can't act."

The only person I know who seemed as if they'd make a decent actor was Koizumi. Definitely not me. I was pretty confident I'd have a lot of complaints for the screenwriter who wrote the script too.

"It just means that I can't be anyone besides me, and you can't be anyone besides you. No one can pretend to be Suzumiya. She probably couldn't even consciously do it herself. There's no room for conscious intervention there. No matter how wise or capable you are."

These riddles are serving their purpose, I told Sasaki. Just how long was she planning to continue this pseudo-philosophical conversation?

"How rude. Well, I'm done." Sasaki's face turned suddenly serious. "You seem to have steadily increased the number of lovely friends to whom you're connected and discovered quite a bit of pleasure there, but I've been thinking. I want to focus on my studies. I really don't have the luxury of slacking through my classes and enjoying myself the way we did in middle school. I'm not even paying much attention to how I talk. My school was boys-only until a few years ago, and girls are still a minority, so it's not an environment I find particularly enjoyable. But I suppose being so lazy before means it's about all I can expect to come slamming into a wall. That's why, Kyon—it's only ever been you. Those times we put our desks together and ate lunch are more precious to me than anything now. I wanted to say something but after thinking about it, I won't. Yet there's only one boy in the world who both kept his distance but also paid attention to me, and afterward treated me totally normally, and that's you."

She giggled again.

"Gosh, it really sounds like I'm confessing to you, doesn't it? It really wasn't my intention to be misunderstood, though."

Nobody's misunderstood anything. There's something screwy in the head with anyone who got the wrong idea, I said. Kunikida's brain specialized in academics, so he had a strange ability to remember stuff like this.

"That's true. The things you don't really want to remember get forgotten the instant you don't need them anymore. I've already forgotten all the knowledge and techniques I memorized to pass my high school entrance exams. I'm sure the memories I have now will be gone after three years," said Sasaki sunnily. "But that's fine. I'll remember other things—the things I *want* to remember."

Sasaki hopped to her feet as though freed from something.

"Well, I've got to get to cram school. I'm glad we could talk, Kyon."

Sasaki started walking, heading for the station's turnstile without looking back.

I called out to her slender form with as much energy as I could muster. "Good-bye, old friend! I'll see you at the next reunion!"

I don't know whether she heard me or not, but she didn't raise her hand. No matter how many years it would be until our next meeting, something about the way she walked away made me think she'd already decided upon the words she'd say. "Hey, friend."

Thus did Sasaki and I begin our walk down opposite paths. I wasn't sure if I should hurry, or if I should take my time—I felt sort of ambivalent about it, but the question was whether a month was enough time in which to come to a conclusion about something. I suppose it depends on the something.

In any case, the direction I was walking in would lead me toward days during which I would have to decide what present to get Haruhi.

If anyone had any ideas, I would've loved to get a text message or

letter about them. I had the feeling it would make a good reference for me to make the best possible choice I could.

The next day, Tuesday.

Despite having trudged up this hill for an entire year, its irritation never seemed to abate, so yet again I found myself climbing it in silence.

"Heya there, Kyon ol' buddy!" I felt a whack on my back as if someone was trying to kill a cockroach there, and stumbled forward without any intention of exaggerating the impact.

I turned around and there in front of my face, gleaming like a laminated rare card, was none other than the great Tsuruya.

"Ah, Tsuruya. Good morning."

"Hey, Kyon! Lookin' nice and clear today, eh?"

I looked up at the sky to confirm that it was indeed cloudy, then back at Tsuruya, who cackled.

"I'm not talking about the weather! I'm talking about you, boy, you! You've got a nice pleasant look on your face, like something that's been bothering you for a whole week has finally cleared up— that's what your face looks like!" she said, as though having seen the entire sequence of events herself.

In a way, Tsuruya had even sharper instincts than Haruhi herself. I didn't even find it strange that she'd been able to read so much from my face, although I was surprised at how normal that felt.

"There's something I've been meaning to ask you, Tsuruya."

"What might that be?" she said, falling in step with me.

"What kind of guy do you think I am? I mean from your perspective."

"Huh? Did something happen? My impression's not gonna do you any good!"

"I want to hear your honest opinion on the matter. Not only can I not get a straight answer out of Koizumi or Nagato, but they just spout off intellectual nonsense that I can't understand."

Tsuruya laughed. "I guess you can't really ask Mikuru either.

She'd pretty much only flatter you." Then Tsuruya suddenly peered at my face. "Hmm, well, Kyon…you're…like a well-liked minor character. You're not particularly easy to talk to, but when someone does say something, you always come back with just the right response. You don't really laugh when someone says something funny, but you also don't get irritated when someone's being boring. There really aren't very many people who will just give you a straight answer like that. That's you, Kyon!"

I asked if she didn't have anything a little more, well, flattering.

"I guess you're a decently cute guy."

Unsurprisingly, Tsuruya's visual acuity was about as good as a military Landsat bird. Go on, I said.

"But not *that* cute."

The nice feeling I'd been experiencing popped like a balloon.

Tsuruya cackled again. "But I don't think you're on the wrong track! You just gotta trust in that. You don't seem like you tease Mikuru too much, after all! You're just living out your high school life here, normal as can be!"

Nothing about life in the SOS Brigade was normal, I said.

"I wonder," said Tsuruya, light shining in her eyes. "It seems like it's kinda become normal to you! You've got Haru-nyan, and Mikuru, and Nagatocchi, and Koizumi. Who else do you need?"

Nothing, I could immediately say. I'd had more than enough of new brigade recruits.

"Nyahaha, I'll bet!" Tsuruya skipped a step and pulled ahead of me. But then, turning around, she continued. "Don't forget the blossom-viewing party at the end of the month! I've got all kinds of stuff planned, so if you don't come we'll bring the cherry blossoms to you!" Then, finally: "Just let me know when you need that weird toy you left at my house! Bye!"

With a light tone and a wink, she left me behind and tripped her way up the hill. In her receding figure, I saw someone who was going to take life by the horns and wring every bit of fun out of it.

I was no match for Tsuruya. I probably never would be, not in my whole life. But that sense of inferiority only kindled a strangely warm sensation in my heart.

Just as Tsuruya's form was shrinking in the distance, a different acquaintance of mine slapped my back. When I turned, I saw lined up there the two people with whom I mysteriously always ended up in the same class—Taniguchi and Kunikida.

"Yo!" said Taniguchi, who from what I could tell of his complexion, had finally recovered from his encounter with Kuyoh Suoh. Ever since that random encounter, I'd had a strangely hard time looking at him, but Taniguchi the Ladies' Man seemed to have bounced back quickly.

"Hey, Kyon. For starters, you gotta introduce me to a girl."

And now he was an idiot again.

"From what Kunikida told me, this Sasaki girl's quite the cutie, right? And you're not gonna do anything with her, are you? It's not like you're some jerk that's gonna ditch Suzumiya and go playing around with other chicks. So c'mon, man!"

I told Taniguchi to shut up. If he wanted something, he could go get it himself. Especially if it was the only thing he'd thought about from the big bang up until this moment. Anyway, I said, Sasaki wasn't his type. Did I need to remind him how terribly he'd been dumped by Kuyoh? Where should I write it—his forehead, maybe?

Taniguchi made a clumsy gesture of dissatisfaction. "Hey. Not only do I not have any worthwhile girls around me, there aren't even any decent guys. If I ever make nice-nice with an idol pop band, I ain't gonna introduce 'em to you, Kyon. Remember that. And you'll think back on what you said and cry."

Oh, I'd cry, all right. I'd be laughing so hard tears would come out of my eyes, I said.

"Sure, go on. If you spend all of high school babysitting Suzumiya, you're gonna get to graduation day and wonder, 'Why, oh why, did I waste my youth so?' But then it's gonna be too late for regrets!"

I thanked Taniguchi ever so much for his kind warning. I'd be sure to take care. But at the moment I was too busy enjoying the height of my high school life. He could do whatever he wanted, so long as he didn't date any more aliens. That could cause problems.

Perhaps sick of hearing Taniguchi's idiocy, Kunikida cut into the conversation. His expression was comparatively serious.

"Hey, Kyon. It's pretty common for people with similar characteristics to repel each other. It's actually true that opposites attract. The proof is in nature, right? For example, a magnet's north and south pole, or a positive or negative charge."

This was a little more serious of a lecture than I wanted when I was walking around. It seemed like a review of a physics lesson, I said.

"But—and this is going to get into some physics—if we go even lower, to the world of molecules and atoms and even smaller things, we see the existence of a force even closer than electromagnetism. Aside from hydrogen, every atom's nucleus has protons and neutrons in it. Since neutrons have no charge, by the electromagnetic charges of the protons, they should repel each other. So why is it that these protons actually wind up sticking together and getting along inside the nucleus of an atom?"

I don't know.

"If your name was Hideki Yukawa, you'd understand. He was Japan's first Nobel Prize winner. He predicted that there was an even smaller particle mutually binding one proton to another. His hypothesis stated that the force was far stronger than electromagnetism or gravitation, and in the following years, his theory was proven true. This won Professor Yukawa the Nobel Prize, and set physics on the road toward the discovery of the quark and hadron."

So how did this biography of Hideki Yukawa have anything to do with the current situation? I asked.

"Kyon, from my perspective you and Suzumiya are very similar. You both have a positive charge. Normally that would mean that you would mutually repel, and I assumed that your relationship would collapse. Because you're too similar, you see. That's still the impression I get, really. You're too like each other, so it's obvious that you'll repel. But far from it, you and Suzumiya have become inseparable. This is where the nuclear force Professor Yukawa discovered comes in. The strong force that keeps protons that should go flying apart from doing just that is the same thing keeping you and her together. That's all I can figure. Of course, it's not any of the four elementary forces we've discovered so far—not the strong nuclear force, weak nuclear force, electromagnetism, or gravity. It has nothing to do with the natural forces we know of."

So what was he saying it was? I asked.

"How am I supposed to know? Maybe it's something new, some fifth element. But that's just wishful scientific thinking. Considering it from the standpoint of human relationships, I think the people around you are very important for the bond between you and Suzumiya. Koizumi, Asahina, and Nagato are definitely fulfilling some kind of role, but it would be irresponsible of me to speculate about its nature. I get the feeling the SOS Brigade is structured like an atom. On the large scale it moves around, sticking to some things and bouncing off others, but internally it's very cohesive and stable, and nearly impossible to split. In order to disrupt the balance, all you can do is impact each mutually reinforcing element, but I don't think there are very many people in the world capable of that. Tsuruya could probably do it, but even if she knows that, she's probably chosen not to."

Even I knew that much, I said.

"Tsuruya's actually really perceptive and smart. Her being a North High student is actually the only reason I came here."

...Really? I was getting a lot of shocking revelations today.

"It's a little embarrassing. You're the only person I've told." Kunikida glanced at Taniguchi; our excitable classmate was ogling a group of freshman girls on their way to school. Having confirmed Taniguchi's attention was elsewhere, Kunikida continued in a low voice.

"Don't tell Taniguchi, okay? As far as I can tell, Tsuruya's an honest-to-goodness genius. I just wanted to be close to her, but thanks to you and Suzumiya, I've actually been able to be friends with her, for which I'm really grateful. I've gotten to know just how unfathomably smart she is. But it's a little depressing—knowing a genius has made me realize I'm not a genius myself. That much I'm sure of."

The fact that he understood all that stuff was impressive enough, I told him.

"Not at all. I'm far from being a genius, and well within the realms of the very smart. To reach such heights the only thing I can do is study as hard as I can, but when I think about how much further I have to go before I reach her level, it makes me dizzy. But it's not like I'm going to give up. I'm going to where she is, no matter how many years it takes. Of course, by that time she will have gone even higher. And then I'll just have to aim for that place. It's like Achilles and the tortoise. Yeah, I feel pretty good right now. The person I've set as my goal is charging on ahead, and I'm gonna have to work hard to keep up. I get excited just thinking about it. This probably sounds pretty weird to you."

It didn't sound strange at all. He had a wonderful aspiration, I said. And incidentally, I'd never known he was so talkative. I guess you can never tell about some people.

Even Koizumi had decided Tsuruya wasn't worth trying to keep up with, which meant she didn't just look down on all of North High; she gazed out over all humanity. I bet Kunikida could get to a pretty good place. Tsuruya being Tsuruya, she'd probably like someone who'd forced himself to be smart. The best I could probably hope for was being treated like a much younger brother. Or maybe a nephew.

When I got to the classroom, Haruhi had already taken her seat, and she glared up at me.

"We're back to normal operation today. Come straight to the clubroom after class."

Sure, sure.

After putting my bag on my desk, I turned around. "Hey, Haruhi."

"What?"

"Why'd you come to North High?"

Perhaps suspicious of the sudden question, Haruhi glared at me as though she were a crocodile in an oasis eyeing an approaching group of water buffalo. "I just felt like it. I could've gone to a private school, but I got the feeling this place would have at least one interesting club."

Huh.

"What's with that grin? I know what you want to say. You're gonna tell me that my intuition was bad, because there weren't any good clubs after all."

Not at all, I said. But her idea of an interesting club wasn't anything that existed yet. And anyway, would a club that hung up a huge sign saying something like COOL CLUB ACTIVITIES HERE have passed her test? I asked.

"I guess not. I just hoped there would be a club that didn't seem like it did much, but actually did all kinds of stuff in secret. But there wasn't at all. And when I say 'secret' I mean it spelled out in hiragana, otherwise it's not a s-e-c-r-e-t."

Watching Haruhi's lips as she pronounced the words in that childish way, I nodded.

Your wish really did come true, Haruhi. The secret organization you founded was rooted in this school and didn't seem likely to be shaken anytime soon. At least not given how silly it had made certain time travelers and extraterrestrial life-forms look.

Haruhi continued to glare at me, but finally folded her arms on her desk, laid her head down, exhaled a sigh, and for some reason, she recited a poem by Sugawara no Michizane.

"In this moment, with no offering to bring, see, O Tamuke Mountain! Here are brocades of red maple, as a tribute to the gods."

Its meaning aside, I knew at least that it wasn't a poem for spring.

After school.

"Yo," I said as I opened the clubroom door and was greeted by the sight of all the usual suspects save Haruhi, who had remained in the classroom on cleaning duty.

Asahina had already changed into her maid outfit, Nagato was sitting in the corner reading, and Koizumi was staring at the Chinese shogi board he'd set up.

Nagato did not look up, while Koizumi greeted me only with a glance, and surprisingly, even Asahina did not turn around, remaining with her back to me by the windowsill.

I looked more closely.

"Ahh..." Asahina sighed as she changed the water in the vase Yasumi had brought.

She finally turned around to face me. "She was just so, so cute! It's really such a shame...I just wanted her to look up to me..."

As soon as she said it, I realized I'd never really treated Asahina like a senior. She just looked younger than me, so it was hard to treat her as if she was older. But that was all right. Asahina was Asahina, and I couldn't even be sure of her true age.

"I guess she was really a middle schooler all along...no wonder I kept thinking she seemed like a younger sister."

It looked as though, as far as Asahina was concerned, Yasumi's situation was exactly as Haruhi had explained it.

"I wish I could've gotten to talk with her more."

I realized something as I gazed at the maid-clad Asahina, she in turn staring out the window with eyes misty.

This Asahina right here would somehow eventually become the adult version of herself. At the moment, Asahina the Younger hardly knew anything. If I were to tell her everything I knew thanks to my repeated encounters with Asahina the Elder and Fujiwara, there was a real possibility it could affect the future. At the very least, it would probably cause some change in Asahina the Elder's actions, wouldn't it...?

As I busied myself with estimations, Asahina came tottering over. "This got left in the clubroom."

I took the item she offered me, and it was a barrette I had seen before. No close inspection was necessary to tell that it was the smiley face that Yasumi had worn in her hair.

Had she left it here on purpose, or had it been an accident?

Asahina touched a petal of the orchid Yasumi had left in the room. "I wonder if we'll ever see her again. Next year I'll be…"

By all rights, as a senior, Asahina would be graduating in a year. Which meant she wouldn't be able to stay here anymore. Would her last year be cut short by some time traveler–related incident? I wondered if that was why Asahina was a year ahead of us, instead of being in the same school year.

How was I supposed to know?

I didn't really care, though. The time travelers could take care of the future however they liked. I was a person of this time; the past and the future had nothing to do with me. There were any number of things I could do, but as far as ten or twenty years in the future went, that depended on my future self. If they had something to say to me, they could tell it to him. I doubt I will have changed very much, if I do say so myself. My future self will probably still be doing what has to be done and not bothering with stuff that doesn't seem important. As to whether that was the right thing to do, I'd let my future self worry about that. That was life, after all. And it's probably not just high school students that think so.

Just as I was starting to sink complacently into uncharacteristic philosophizing—

"Sorry I'm late!"

Haruhi came bursting through the door, with that smiling face of hers that always gives me a bad feeling.

I had to assume she'd gotten some crazy idea into her head during cleaning duty, as she beamed like a sunflower at the height of summer.

She ignored my immediately guarded posture and headed straight for the brigade chief's desk, but stopped halfway there and peered at the contents of my hand.

"Huh?" She snatched the hair accessory away, and gave it a good hard look for several seconds. "Oh this. I used to have one just like it. Now I remember. I knew I'd seen it somewhere before. I used it in elementary school, but I lost it when I started middle school. So she used one too, huh?"

Haruhi's voice sounded quite affected, and she held on to the item in her hand as she passed by me.

Seeing her from behind, I immediately thought of the future Haruhi I'd seen in my vision.

Who had that Haruhi called out to, I wonder.

Was the person she'd turned around to face someone I knew? Or was it some third party I'd never met in my life?

If so, that hadn't been a very nice vision—but when I realized what I was thinking, I forgot to feign shock, and simply accepted it. I couldn't pretend otherwise, now.

But the future was not set. I hadn't forgotten the new information, however vague, that I'd gleaned from Fujiwara and Asahina the Elder's conversation. I didn't know anything about changing history or diverging world-paths, but I knew that the future was something that split up, stuck back together, and changed.

I'd seen myself—if only for a moment, I'd been able to catch a glimpse of the future. I planned to remember it, and I would aim to be in that place.

To do that, I still had a lot of things to accomplish. Like taking advantage of Haruhi's tutoring services. My high school life still had two years left in it. During that time, I doubted that Nagato, Asakura, and Kimidori's boss would stay quiet, to say nothing of Kuyoh and the Heavenly Canopy Dominion. Or maybe some other mysterious organization besides Tachibana's would show up to play the part of the mid-boss before the final boss.

Oh well. I'd figure something out.

Fortunately, I wasn't alone. I had Nagato and Koizumi and my Asahina as well. I even had that idiot Taniguchi, the always-calm Kunikida, and the flawless Tsuruya. Thanks to all the running around we'd done, I'd gained the not-insignificant knowledge that my friends were the key. And Sasaki too. She'd waved good-bye, but I didn't buy it. Her sentimental little parting gesture didn't fool me for a second. She'd show up again. After all, I really wanted her to.

But right then, I couldn't worry about whether or not stuff was going to happen in the future—I had something right in front of me I had to take care of. The SOS Brigade's First Anniversary and the attendant surprise for its brigade chief, for example. It was a few weeks away, so I didn't have to start panicking yet, but before then I had Tsuruya's cherry blossom–viewing party, and it was by no means certain that Haruhi had given up on recruiting new members yet, so it was going to be a busy month.

With the five of us all working together, we could do anything.

No matter who we faced.

But that was not my biggest problem.

The greatest matter of concern currently facing me was what in blazes to get the brigade chief as a present—or rather, what *had* I gotten her? I didn't have the faintest idea of what to do. I wished I could consult an expert of some kind.

As I'd been standing there monologuing to myself, Haruhi had put the barrette away in one of the brigade chief's desk drawers, then whirled around and approached the whiteboard.

Wordlessly she took out a pen and wrote out a phrase, then turned back around. As I looked at her, her smile was so bright I thought I could feel my retinas burning.

"Kyon, read it!"

She was the brigade chief, and orders were orders, so I did as I was told.

" 'Second Annual New Year's SOS Brigade Meeting' . . . wait. We're having a meeting today? First I've heard of it."

"I told everyone and nobody had any problems. Didn't I tell you? Well, sorry. I guess I forgot. But now you know, so it's fine!"

I started to look around for a stinkbug—if I could find one I'd put it in my mouth and bite down good and hard so I could taste its rotten juices, which would just about match my rotten expression. But for better or for worse, no stinkbug was forthcoming, and I avoided eating such a nasty morsel.

"So, just what is this supposed meeting about, huh?"

Haruhi rapped the whiteboard with the back of her fist. "Isn't it obvious? We've been invited to Tsuruya's blossom-viewing party. But it would be a shame to just eat and drink—the SOS Brigade's spirit of service and my sense of pride won't allow that! So, Kyon, Koizumi, Mikuru, Yuki—"

Koizumi grinned, Nagato remained blank, and Asahina covered her mouth with both hands—and each of them looked right at me.

A very bad premonition closed in on me as if it was falling down a descending escalator.

"We're gonna put on a sideshow! A show that'll get everybody there applauding like crazy!"

"Now, wait just a minute. The Tsuruya family blossom party is a big deal, you know? All kinds of local celebrities and important people come to this thing."

"The quality of the audience will be—what, you say? High? Laughter knows no bounds! What kind of show would it be if it can't make a few politicians and captains of industry laugh? We're going to entertain young and old, men and women, regardless of race or nationality! Such is the very heart of the stage!"

It was all very well and good for her to be excited, but exactly where in the neologism section of the thesaurus can I find the joke I assume she was making? I was willing to bet it wasn't in the *Britannica*. Cracks were already starting to appear in my heart of glass.

"We're gonna do this sideshow! No—maybe we should just call it the main event. The SOS Brigade presents The Greatest Laughs on Earth, a fresh new entertainment experience that will bring peace to the entire planet!"

Haruhi's smile could've compressed the entire Taurus open star cluster—.

Her mouth opened so wide she could've swallowed the entire Red Sea—.

And in a high, clear voice, she proclaimed, "I now declare this strategy-planning meeting *open!*"

AFTERWORD

My apologies for having caused all this trouble. I'm Nagaru Tanigawa.

I should first extend my deepest regrets for the lengthy interval between the last volume and this one.

Although this book is a direct continuation of the story from *The Dissociation*, as regards the reality of the extreme delay in its delivery, I find I can offer absolutely no excuse.

To the many individuals involved in its production, and in particular to illustrator Noizi Ito, along with the many bookstore employees I've no doubt caused unspeakable inconvenience, I feel especially obliged to shout the following.

I am so sorry!

And above all, to the readers who have doubtless been waiting for the pathetic conclusion to this ridiculous work, I send ten billion apologies and a hundred billion thanks via neuro-telepathic transmission, broadcast at full power in all directions. They will bring good luck to anyone who receives them—thus is my completely baseless assertion.

In place of the author, Haruhi is also groveling. Hopefully you'll let her off the hook with a mere body blow.

So this work, *The Surprise of Haruhi Suzumiya*, represents a direct continuation from the previous volume, *Dissociation*. My apologies if this is the case, but for those readers who have long since forgotten the events of *Dissociation*, I humbly suggest that a re-read of that volume may help you understand this one. I mean, it's a bit of a pain, so you don't have to, but if you did—if you would do me the honor—I personally would be happy enough to shed tears of joy, though I feel obligated to point out that it is absolutely not compulsory.

Now, if you're wondering why this book is so late, to be completely honest, there's no particular reason. There really isn't, and that's the problem. All I can say is that all of a sudden, I couldn't do anything, and it even started to interfere with my regular life. People would ask me what the problem was, and since I didn't know, trying to explain my inexplicable self to other people was the hardest thing of all.

No matter what I say, it will sound like an excuse. For example, my until-then-beloved computer started throwing up blue screens of death without any warning, and I would lose whole sentences right as I was in the middle of writing them, or I'd have strange nightmares that made it incredibly hard to wake up, or I'd realize I'd been watching analog TV all along without having been notified about the switch to digital—

See? Nothing but excuses. We humans certainly are full of excuses. If they were a little more interesting at least they'd be fodder for my writing.

The obvious deduction may well be that the sloth that has provided the underpinning for my life thus far finally caught up with me.

When I think about it, I really haven't done anything worthy of praise in my entire life. All I seem to have are memories so humiliating they make me want to collapse in agony. I mean, I have to admit I'm a bit impressed that I resisted the temptation to smash my head to bits against a concrete wall, but let's be honest—I just didn't have the guts.

If you'll excuse my insufferable rambling, I'd like to reminisce a little bit. It was some years ago now that I was fortunate enough to enjoy my debut as a novelist. Exactly which month it was has become a little vague by now, but it seems emotionally accurate to guess that it was around June 10, 2003. Even now I worry that I was more than a little trouble to the fine people of the editorial departments of Kadokawa Sneaker Bunko and Dengeki Bunko, which I'm sure I'll never forget. As I think uncertainly back on it, I find myself again tempted to go charging into that concrete wall.

It's thanks to them that the reality that my stories were being published felt exceedingly faint; and right about the time that *The Melancholy of Haruhi Suzumiya* and *Gakko wo Deyo! 1* were going out into the world, I was already feeling boxed in by other things, which was fun in its own way. It was probably the most educational period in my life.

It seems likely that after having gotten my fill of having my capacity pushed right to its gasping limit, I immediately came up with the idea for *The Disappearance of Haruhi Suzumiya* and wrote the series of stories that came bubbling up in its wake, which makes me think that my stance of "when in doubt about whether or not I can actually do this, just write everything" was mostly correct.

Speaking of *Disappearance*, did you go see the theatrical version?

It's difficult to find the appropriate words to offer the production staff at Kyoto Animation for the amazing work they did. My head is bowed as though it has a one-ton weight on top of it. Words of thanks feel inadequate in response to my silly follow-up to *Melancholy* being made into a motion picture. Thank you all so very much. Surely no film could capture my delight. Please accept my humble apologies for being such a useless creator.

I may well be totally useless and weak-willed, but if my readers have enjoyed my works even a bit, I am fortunate indeed.

I plan to continue being a weirdo who writes weird things, so even as I hope you'll not abandon me, and even as I will labor to fix the more troublesome aspects of my personality, I think it is time to bring this afterword to an end.

I hope we will meet again, someday, sometime, somewhere, somehow.

Until then!